RHODE

Weddings

RHODE ISLAND
Weddings

Heartache Matures into Lasting Love
within Three Romantic Stories

JOYCE LIVINGSTON

BARBOUR
PUBLISHING

Down from the Cross © 2005 by Joyce Livingston
Mother's Day © 2005 by Joyce Livingston
The Fourth of July © 2005 by Joyce Livingston

ISBN 978-1-59789-842-3

Cover image © Fraser Hall/Getty Images

Published by Barbour Publishing, Inc., P.O. Box 719, Uhrichsville, Ohio 44683, www.barbourbooks.com

Our mission is to publish and distribute inspirational products offering exceptional value and biblical encouragement to the masses.

 Member of the
Evangelical Christian
Publishers Association

Printed in the United States of America.

Dear Reader,

I love Rhode Island! It is always a joy when I get a chance to visit there. It's a beautiful state filled with some of the nicest people you'll ever meet. If you haven't been there, I hope these three stories will whet your appetite and make you want to go. On our first trip to Rhode Island, we toured four of Newport's famous mansions.

I remember walking and gawking through those lovely homes with my mouth gaping open. What luxury! What opulence! Yet when you hear the stories of those who lived in some of those museum-like houses, their beauty fades. So much misery, strife, deceit, and family bickering took place, it makes you wonder if some of those people ever truly had a happy day. I'd much prefer to live in the mansion our heavenly Father is preparing for us. How about you?

How I wish you and I could sit down together, sip glasses of iced tea, and just visit. I would love to know all about you—your joys, your sorrows, your ups and downs, what inspires you, and how God is working in your life. I remember how my grandmother and grandfather used to spend every evening sitting on their front porch visiting with neighbors, waving at the passersby, and enjoying their time with one another. No pressures, no TV to distract them, no cell phone. Sounds good, doesn't it? It seems we're so busy these days, the average family has trouble just scheduling one night a week when they all can have dinner together. I'm so thankful for those wonderful unrushed family times Don and I had with our children when they were growing up. Nothing can replace the time we spend together. So many people don't find that out until it is too late.

As many who read my books know, my precious husband went home to be with the Lord several years ago. Don was (and is) my inspiration for the hero of every book I write. I dedicate this book to him, the love of my life.

Joyce Livingston

DOWN FROM THE CROSS

Dedication

To my dear husband, Don Livingston, who went to be with our Lord in 2004. Of all the books I have written, this one—*Down from the Cross*—was his favorite. Don died of a brain tumor five months after he was diagnosed. On his way to the hospital, he turned and with tears in his eyes said he wanted the Lord to allow him to live long enough to hold the published book in his hands. You see, he was in this writing ministry with me. Each time one of my books was released, Don would purchase a number of copies and mail them to family, friends, and those he wanted to see accept Christ as their Savior. He believed so strongly in the message of *Down from the Cross*, he wanted to live long enough to share it with a long list of people, many who were in the public eye.

True love never dies. I love Don even more today than I did when he was with me. Love like ours only comes around once in a lifetime.

Chapter 1

Keene Moray loved Providence, Rhode Island. If he could choose one place in the lower forty-eight to live on a permanent basis, it would be Providence, right in the heart of the New England area. Unfortunately, his profession required him to live elsewhere—in New York City—but not by choice. It wasn't that he didn't love the Big Apple. He did. But it had become too crowded, too demanding, and far too busy for his liking.

"This is the city for me," he said aloud, flipping on his turn signal as he drove his new BMW convertible down Francis Street toward the convention center. "With its relaxed, laid-back atmosphere. Someday I'm going to have myself a house in this city. Maybe a lovely old brick mansion."

He sped up and then reached to insert a new CD into the player in the dash. It slipped from his fingers and fell onto the thickly carpeted floor. With a quick glance to check the traffic ahead of him, he bent to retrieve the elusive CD.

Suddenly his body lunged forward, only to be yanked back by the seat belt, the noise of crashing metal deafening his ears. The car's air bag pinned him against the seat back, and his head slammed into the headrest. The BMW filled with a misty gray haze from the air bag's powdery substance. Although the bag deflated instantly, Keene found it difficult to breathe. He instinctively yanked the buckle open on his seat belt, found the car door handle, and pushed open the door, staggering out in search of fresh air to fill his lungs.

That's when he fully realized what had happened.

∽∾

"Uggh!" Jane Delaney leaned her forehead against the steering wheel, her heart pounding erratically. *What happened? Why is that horn honking?* With trembling fingers, she reached for the knot forming on her forehead. "My car!" She pushed away and struggled to open the door, but the handle wouldn't budge. "Oh, dear Lord, I've been in an accident. Please, God, don't let my car be ruined!"

Though it hurt to move, she forced herself over the console and passenger seat, wincing at the stabbing pain in her left leg. She pushed her way out the door, nearly falling when she tried to stand to her feet. With the bright morning sun blinding her, she hobbled around the front of her car, placing her palms on the hood for support. She felt faint, light-headed, and woozy, and it scared her. She'd never felt this way before. However, her fright didn't compare with the feelings of helplessness and exasperation she experienced when she caught sight of the driver's side of her car. She stood staring, gaping at the damage, everything going in and out of focus.

A hand gripped her arm. "Are you all right? I am so sorry! I must've run a red light!" The man let his hold on her relax long enough to pull his cell phone from his belt. "I've got to call 911! You need an ambulance!"

∽৩৵

Keene grabbed for the woman, nearly dropping his phone, but despite his efforts she fell into a heap at his feet. "What have I done?" he shouted, quickly kneeing beside her and punching 911 into his phone. The dispatcher answered immediately.

"Help, someone, help! I've just run into a woman's car, and I think she's unconscious!"

"Give me your location, sir, and we'll have someone right there," the dispatcher answered calmly with an authority that did nothing to calm Keene's frazzled nerves.

He looked around quickly, hoping to find a street sign or some other indication of his location. "I'm. . .I'm on Francis Street."

"Where on Francis Street, sir? Can you give me the name of a nearby cross street, maybe a familiar landmark?"

His mind raced. "I—I don't know. . .I was on Francis Street heading toward the convention center. . ." He paused, trying to remember what happened.

Several people were gathering now, one man bending over the young woman with great concern. Keene leaned toward him, his own breath coming in short gasps. "Where am I?"

Apparently familiar with the area, the man looked up and said, "Francis Street and Sabin."

"Francis Street and Sabin," Keene barked into the phone, relieved to be able to relay accurate information.

"Thank you, sir. They'll find you."

"Tell them to hurry, please. I don't know how badly she is hurt, but her head is bleeding. How could I have done this?"

"Ugghh."

Keene turned quickly at the sound. At least the woman was alive. He pulled a freshly ironed handkerchief from his pocket and pressed it to her forehead. If only he could stop the bleeding. "Hang on, lady. Help is coming. Someone should be here any minute." Blinking hard, he covered his face with his free hand. *How could this have happened? One minute I was driving along, putting a CD—the CD! It dropped onto the floor, and I reached for it! I didn't even see the woman's car!*

He scanned Francis Street in both directions for any sign of the emergency vehicle, his frantic gaze locking on the stoplight. *A stoplight! I ran a stoplight! I could have killed that woman!*

The wail of a siren brought him to his feet. Keene moved quickly out of the way yet stayed close enough to see and hear the things going on as an ambulance pulled up beside him, followed by a police car, then a fire engine.

"Can you tell me what happened, sir?" Clipboard in hand, the police officer hurriedly exited his car and began making notations.

"It was my fault!" Keene gestured toward the stoplight. "I—I didn't see the stoplight."

Poising his ballpoint pen over the clipboard, the officer took on a dubious expression. "I'll need your full name and address."

"My. . .my name is Keene Moray. M-O-R-A-Y. I'm staying at. . .at. . ." His mind went blank. "I'm staying at. . .at—oh, what is the name of that place?"

He described the complex where the condominium he had rented for the next few months was located, and fortunately, the officer recognized it by its description and came up with the name, Kennewick Place.

Keene nodded. "Do you think she's going to be all right?" He craned his neck over the crowd that had assembled, trying to get a glimpse of the woman when the EMTs lifted her onto the gurney.

The officer turned, looked briefly in her direction, and then continued writing. "Don't know. Sometimes these intersection collisions can do more serious damage to the drivers than to the cars." The officer stopped writing, his slight frown converting to one of understanding. "Hang on a minute, and I'll see what I can find out."

Keene watched as the man strode over to one of the EMTs, conversed with him for a second, jotted down a few notes, then walked back. The two stood watching the men loading the gurney into the waiting ambulance. Then the doors closed, and it headed back down the street, lights flashing.

"He said it didn't look like her injuries were life-threatening," the officer told him. "She probably fainted from the trauma of the accident and the loss of blood. That happens sometimes, especially if it's the person's first accident. However, they were concerned about her left ankle. They're taking her to the hospital to make sure she's all right and there are no internal injuries. Standard procedure for this type of thing." He let loose a slight chuckle. "Guess she gave them quite a battle. She didn't want to go to the hospital, kept saying she didn't have insurance and couldn't afford it."

Keene stared at the twisted wreckage of the woman's little economy car, then at his solid BMW. While her car looked to be a total loss, his had sustained only minor damage to the hood, bumper, and lights, and he felt terrible. "I'll pay for her hospital bill, and of course, I'll have her car repaired or replaced. It was my fault."

The officer peered over his sunglasses with a hint of a cautioning smile. "Don't think your lawyer would be happy hearing you say that. I'm going to have to give you a citation for running that red light, you know."

"Did you get her name?" The least of Keene's worries right now was the cost of the ticket he would have to pay. Without a doubt, he was the one who had caused the accident, and he would be more than willing to answer for his carelessness and irresponsibility. That poor woman! He could have killed her.

"Oh, yeah," the officer said, looking up from his book. "I got it. It's Jane Delaney."

Jane winced and sighed in frustration. She had been in a hospital a number of times, but she had never been a patient.

"Well, how are we feeling?" A big-boned woman in a heavily starched nurse's uniform came bustling into the cubicle. "You were pretty upset when they brought you in. You're looking a little better now."

How are we feeling? Jane wanted to smile at the woman's question, but her sore face would not allow it. Even the slightest movement hurt. Besides, she had more important things on her mind. Like how would she ever pay for all of this? She had not been able to make a car or insurance payment in over three months. A letter from the insurance company was sitting on her dresser right now, saying they had already canceled her. And what could she use for transportation now that one whole side of her car had caved in?

The nurse bent over her, tugging the cover up beneath her chin. "Are you hungry? It's nearly noon. I think I can get you a lunch tray. Yummy, yummy! Chicken noodle soup, celery sticks, cherry Jell-O, and chocolate pudding!"

"No, thank you. My. . .my stomach doesn't feel like food right now." Jane struggled to get comfortable on the narrow bed but winced when a sharp pain in her injured leg prevented it. "Ouch!"

"Oh, are we hurting?" The woman bustled around the bed, filling the water glass and straightening the side table.

I don't know about you, but I am! "A little, I guess. I've got to get out of here."

The woman gave her a pleasant smile. "You're not going anywhere until the doctor says you can. How's the head doing?" She bent to look more closely at the wound. "Umm, they did a good job putting those sutures in. Shouldn't leave too much of a scar. You're lucky that cut is in your hairline."

Jane's free hand went to her head. "I'm. . .I'm kind of light-headed. Dizzy. You know what I mean?"

The woman nodded. "I'm not surprised with a knot like that. I'm amazed you don't have an unbearable headache." She quit her fussing and gave Jane a sudden frown. "You don't, do you?"

"Not really. It's not too bad. It's my leg that hurts." She scooted to the edge of the bed and slowly hung her legs over the side. "I—I have to go to the restroom."

"I brought you a walker. Do you think you can hobble to the bathroom by holding on to it?" The nurse took a firm grasp on her arm and tugged her forward. "By the way, my name's Mildred."

Warily, Jane slid one foot to the floor, placing a hand on the mattress to brace herself.

"Whoa, take your time, and let me keep a hold on you. I don't want you falling." The nurse grabbed on to the walker's handle grips. "Steady there. Get your bearings before you try to take any steps."

"Are you sure she should be out of bed?" an anxious-sounding male voice asked from the doorway.

Jane spun around, realizing too late she had moved more quickly than she should. She all but fell back into Mildred's arms.

The man rushed toward them, but Mildred shooed him off. "I've got her. She's fine." She helped Jane lower herself back onto the bed.

Jane clutched at the front of her hospital gown and scooted her hips back onto the mattress.

The man turned his head away, apparently realizing for the first time that he had invaded her privacy. "I'm. . .I'm so sorry," he stammered, looking every direction but at the two women. "It's just that I've been so worried about you. It seemed no one would tell me anything about your condition."

Jane eyed him inquisitively as she lay back down. He was a handsome man, maybe ten years older than she, with dark, closely cropped hair, big brown eyes, and dark lashes. "Are. . . are you sure you're in the right place?"

"Oh, I'd recognize you anywhere."

His quick answer mystified her, yet after taking a second glance at him, she realized he did look vaguely familiar. Her mind raced to pull up his identity from the depths of her brain's database.

He hurried to the side of the bed, hovering over her like an overattentive mother. "I'm. . .I'm the one who put you here."

She instinctively pushed back into the pillow. "You work for the hospital? I'm sorry. I don't have insurance and I—"

He shook his head vehemently. "Oh, no. You have it all wrong. I—I ran the stoplight. I didn't mean to, really I didn't. I didn't see it. The sun. . .my car. . .the CD on the floor. . ."

What is he saying? Her muddled mind registered a big fat zero. His words made no sense at all.

"I didn't see you," he said, peeking around the nurse, "then suddenly I hit your car! I was so afraid. I mean. . .you were bleeding. . .I called 911. . .the officer wanted my address and I couldn't remember it."

Mildred took over. "Slow down, Mister. I don't even have a knot on my head, and I have no idea what you're talking about. From the confused look on my patient's face, I'm sure she doesn't either." She sent a quick glance toward Jane.

He reached forward and grabbed on to Jane's arm. "Please, hear me out. I'm sorry for being so incoherent, but. . .but I've never injured anyone before."

Jane felt herself staring at the man as jagged pieces of her memory processed his words. "You're the one who hit me?"

He lowered his head and gnawed on his lower lip. "Yes, but I intend to make things right with you. After all, it was my fault! I'd. . .I'd like to talk to you, if you feel up to it."

Mildred rolled her eyes and shook her head as she drew a chair up close to the bed and motioned him toward it. Then, wagging her finger in his face, she said, "I don't want you upsetting her, you hear? I'll be right here watching you."

He seemed relieved and moved into the chair. "Let me start at the beginning."

Jane looked from the stranger to Mildred and back to the stranger again. "I'm listening."

"I don't live in Providence," he began. "I live in New York City, but I'm making my residence here for the next few months." Seeming to weigh his words before saying them, he sucked in a deep breath and exhaled slowly. "I was driving on Francis Street near the convention center and was nearing the intersection when I decided to change CDs. But when I went to insert the new one in the CD player, it slipped from my fingers onto the floor. I checked the oncoming traffic then reached for it and. . ."

"That's when you hit me?" Jane shuddered, remembering the dreadful sound of the collision and the instant pain it had caused.

He nodded. "Yes. With the sun shining in my eyes when I looked up, I guess I didn't see the stoplight. All of a sudden, I felt myself being thrown forward and my air bag inflated. I never even saw your car before I hit you."

"I had the right of way! The light was green!" she nearly screamed at him. "Do you have any idea what you did to my car?"

The man closed his eyes tightly shut and shuddered. "Yes, I did see what I did to your car, and I'm so sorry. I can't begin to tell you how sorry."

Normally Jane was easygoing, but she felt her temper rising. A temper she did not even realize she had until a vision of her battered little car surfaced in her mind. "You wrecked my car! It's not even six months old. The first new car I've ever owned, and now I'll have to make payments on a car that probably won't even run!" Tears burst from her eyes.

"I'm sure your insurance would cover it, but don't worry about that." He leaned toward her, both hands gripping the edge of the mattress. "I plan to make amends. My insurance company will pay to have your car fixed, and if it can't be fixed, they'll replace it for you."

"And what about this?" She held out her battered leg, cringing with pain as she extended it. "I don't have a nickel's worth of insurance to cover the hospital costs."

"I'm sure my insurance will cover that, too, but if it doesn't, I will," he assured her once again. "Please don't be concerned about it. Things will work out."

She looked away from him and stared at the wall. "Don't be concerned about it? That's easy for you to say. You're not the one going through this!"

"I—I know, and I'm so sorry you have to go through this unexpected ordeal. I wish I could undo what happened, but I can't."

Her fingers rubbing at her temples, she let out a deep sigh. "You don't know the half of it, Mister."

"I'm sure you're going to be greatly inconvenienced until your injuries heal, and I will be happy to do anything I can to help you. Anything."

He seemed sincere, but there was no way he could help her. Her injuries and the loss of her car were only the beginning. "Nothing you can do. Not really." She felt her chest heave up and down, the memory and magnitude of her problems nearly overwhelming her. "Only a miracle from God can help me now."

"I wouldn't expect anything like that if I were you," he said matter-of-factly, shrugging with a hopeless gesture.

Upset by his words, she gave him a cold stare. "Why? Why would you say such a thing? God can perform miracles. He's done it in my life many times."

His look was patronizing, and she resented both it and his implication that God could not answer prayer.

"I don't mean to upset you, Mrs. Delaney, but—"

"Miss. It's Miss Delaney."

"Like I said, I don't mean to upset you, Miss Delaney, but there is no scientific proof that there is a God."

Her dander rose at his words. "What a ridiculous thing to say, when there's so much evidence to the contrary!"

"As an educated man, I have no choice. I must bow to the scientific scholars."

"What do they know? How do they explain the miraculous birth of a baby, or the sun rising and setting at exact times, or like my father used to say—a black cow eating green grass and giving white milk and yellow butter?"

He sent a quick glance toward Mildred. "Look, Miss Delaney, I'm sorry. The last thing I want to do is upset you." His voice was soft and kind and seemed to bear no malice. "I should never have started our conversation this way. I merely meant you do not have to rely on some unknown God for a miracle. I ran the stoplight, I hit your car, and I'll gladly face up to my responsibilities and take care of all of it—your car, your hospital and doctor bills, and anything else you might need."

Balling her fists, she glared at him. "That's all well and good, but do you realize your carelessness has ruined my life?"

"Yes, I realize that, and all I can do is say I'm sorry and do the best I can to make up for it. I am a man of honor." He shifted nervously, rattling the change in his pocket. "I'm sorry about what I said. About your God. I didn't mean to offend you in any way."

His words about God *had* angered her, but his softened voice and apology helped soothe both her anger and frustration. However, she had to let this man, who appeared to have no financial problems at all, know what this accident had done to her already messed-up life. Stressed to the limit, she sucked in a deep breath and counted to ten before speaking through gritted teeth, enumerating her problems by counting them on her fingers. "I don't expect you to be interested, but my car and hospital bills are just the beginning of my problems. Two days ago, the company I have worked for the past twelve years told me they were going to cut back and lay off a number of their employees. I happened to be one of them. I am the caregiver to my aged, ailing mother, which keeps me from getting a second job even if I could find one. She needs medicine I can't afford to buy for her, the landlord just raised our rent five percent, and my beautiful cocker spaniel died last week of pneumonia. Now do you see why I am upset? Tell me what you're going to do about *those* things?"

He gave her an incredulous look. "Even if there is a God, I'm not sure even *He* could take care of all those things to your satisfaction. That's a pretty tall order."

On the verge of tears, she pressed herself into the propped-up pillow, squeezed her lips tightly together, and crossed her arms, locking her hands into her armpits. "Well, for your information, nothing is too hard for my God. I'm trusting Him to take care of everything, and I know He will!"

"If you are counting on God to provide you with a job, you may be out of work for a long time," the man countered with a smile that held no hostility. "You'd be much better off going to an employment agency. At least they'd know where the jobs are."

"God will provide. He always does," she responded with a positive air, willing herself to remain calm and trying to maintain her dignity. Mildred moved up close to the bed, carefully eyeing her patient. "I'm not sure this conversation is good for you."

Keene leaped to his feet. "I–I'm so sorry. I never meant to upset her. I'll come back tomorrow when she's feeling better. I know this day has been hard on her, and she needs rest."

"I won't be here tomorrow. I'm going home as soon as the doctor releases me." Jane stared at the man, amazed he had taken the time and effort to come to the hospital so soon after their accident. He didn't need to check on her, yet he had. He could have simply let his insurance company take care of the details and not been bothered. From the look of his beautifully tailored suit, starched white shirt, and designer tie, he was probably some highly paid executive. However, unfortunately, he lacked the best thing in life. A relationship with the Lord Jesus Christ. Some things money simply could not buy. "Besides, I'm sure you have better things to do with your time than check up on me."

He leaned against the bed, took her hand, and cradled it in his. "Oh, but I wanted to check on you. I'm afraid you're going to be hearing from me a lot for the next few weeks, until you're fully recovered."

"That's not—"

He gave her hand a gentle squeeze. "Oh, but it is necessary. I may not believe in God, but I believe in doing the right thing. Making sure you are all right, your hospital and doctor bills are paid, and your car is either repaired or replaced are going to be the number one priority on my agenda until things are back to normal for you." He gave her a smile that resonated with warmth and concern. "Now, tell me, is there anything I can do to help you?"

Jane stared at him. *Is this guy for real?*

"Just tell me, and I'll do it gladly."

She continued to eye him suspiciously. Although it appeared money was not a problem for him, it was nonetheless a generous offer.

"I don't want you worrying about anything but getting your head and that leg well," he said, and from the sympathy she could read in his eyes, he surely meant what he said. "You must let me do something to help you. Just name it."

She forced a small smile. "Well, if you hear about any job openings, you might let me know."

He paused thoughtfully. "What sort of skills do you have?"

She gave a slight shrug, wincing at the pain in her leg. "I—I really don't have any skills. The only place I've ever worked is Big Bob's Discount House. I started there my senior year of high school, stocking new merchandise, and I've been there ever since, nearly twelve years now."

He gave her a slight frown. "Did you take typing or any business courses in high school?"

"I'm not sure if I took typing or it took me." She chuckled. "I made terrible grades. That typing teacher was cranky and so demanding I cringed every time she looked at me. Even now, all these years later, just the thought of that pretentious woman makes me shudder. I've often thought maybe if I'd had a different teacher, I might have been a better typist. Who knows?"

Keene rubbed his chin as if in deep thought then strode to the window. Jane watched, waiting for him to make some comment, like her dad had done so many times, telling her she should have knuckled down, learned to type, and forgotten about the arrogant teacher. But he didn't. After a few minutes, he turned slowly and, keeping his piercing brown-eyed gaze on her, stepped forward. "I think I may have an answer for you."

Chapter 2

Jane stared at him, trying to shake the cobwebs loose from her fuzzy brain. *What answer can he possibly provide to my employment dilemma, other than suggest filing for unemployment benefits? As if I haven't already thought of that!*

He moved closer to the bed, so near that without any effort at all she could reach out and touch him if she had a mind to. "When you feel like it, I'd like you to come work for me. Until you can find another job," he added hastily.

If she had felt like laughing, she would have. "Doing what?"

He studied her face, looking at her as if he were seeing her for the first time and perhaps already regretting his blurted job offer. "It's kind of hard to explain."

I thought it was too good to be true.

"I guess you don't know who I am."

She leveled a serious gaze at his handsome face. "You said your name was. . ." *Did he tell me? I can't remember.*

"I'd say that's about enough. I don't want you tiring my patient." Mildred nodded toward him in drill sergeant fashion, moving from her place by the door to stand at the foot of the bed, her arms crossed firmly over her ample chest. She gave the man a stern-nurse look.

"I'm okay, Mildred," Jane answered, curiosity about his answer to her question getting the better of her clouded judgment.

He hesitated, but when the woman continued to stand her ground, he continued. "I need someone to stuff envelopes for mailings, do some filing—general office stuff, answer the phone, run errands, and take things to the post office, that sort of thing. Nothing complicated. I'm sure you could do it, and I wouldn't pressure you. You should be able to drive soon, since it's your left leg."

"I'm not the world's best typist."

He laughed out loud. "I gathered that. I don't need you to break any speed records on the keyboard." He hesitated, and she wondered if he was afraid to ask his next question for fear of her answer. "You do know how to work a computer, don't you?"

She gave him a smile. "Yes, I'm pretty good on the computer, just not a good typist. One of the men at our church gave me his old computer when he bought a new one, and it has become my hobby. I'm on it, surfing the Net, whenever I can find a spare moment."

He appeared relieved. "Good, because I just bought a new one with all the bells and whistles. I'm a novice myself, so I'll be absolutely no help to you."

Now that his offer had finally sunk in, she could hardly believe it. "You're actually serious? About me coming to work for you?"

"Absolutely. You need a job and I need an assistant." His warm and friendly smile was welcome. "I'll pay you whatever your former job paid you, and once that leg of yours heals, you can take off whatever time you need to apply for a more suitable occupation."

Aha! The caveat! "I may not find a job right away. Jobs in Providence are pretty scarce right now. You do understand that, don't you?"

His smile continued to be friendly. "Look," he said, taking her hand in his, "I don't expect you to find a job right away. In fact, I hope you don't." He chuckled mischievously. "You don't know how far behind I am in my filing and myriad other things. But once you have worked for me—if you do a decent job—I'll be able to give you a good recommendation. That should help you find another job."

His offer sounded like God's answer to the prayer she had been sending up to Him since the moment she was placed on layoff status. But what did she know about this man?

"Jane, I just heard about your accident!"

Jane glanced past her guest and Nurse Mildred, smiling as she caught sight of Karen Doyle, her best friend and prayer partner, bounding into the cubicle clutching a small bouquet of baby roses.

"Oh, sweetie! This is just awful!" The pretty blond-haired woman dressed in a pale blue jogging suit hurried to Jane's side. "I've been so worried about you since Pastor Congdon called and told me some man had run his BMW into your little Chevy Aveo. Are you all right? Does your leg hurt very much?"

"I'm going to be fine. The accident broke my ankle," Jane said, gesturing toward it, "and I got this nasty bump on my head, but other than that, I think I'm doing okay."

Karen's eyes widened. "Oh, honey, are they sure you don't have other injuries? I mean, you could have—"

"No, no other injuries," Jane assured her, gesturing toward Keene. "This is the man who caused the accident. He's just offered me a job."

Karen gave him a snarling stare. "You caused the accident?"

He nodded then looked back to Jane and raised his brows. "Do we have a deal?"

She hesitated. How could she resist such an offer? But what if she couldn't perform the work to his satisfaction? Or he turned out to be difficult to work for?

"You're Keene Moray!" Karen's face filled with a pleased look of surprise.

Jane's gaze immediately shifted to the man's face.

"Jane and I have all your CDs!" Karen went on, moving quickly to stand by him. "What are you doing in Providence, of all places?"

Awestruck herself, Jane pulled up to a seated position and stared at the man, her jaw dropping. "You're Keene Moray!" Her hand went to her chest, and her heart pounded wildly. "I can't believe I didn't recognize you."

He brushed past Mildred, nodding. "Yep. Guilty. That's me."

Nurse Mildred tapped him on the shoulder. "I don't care if you're Elvis Presley come back to haunt us. This girl needs her rest, and you two are keeping her from getting it."

Keene gave the nurse an agreeing smile. "You're absolutely right. She's had enough excitement for one day." Then, turning to Jane, he said. "We'll talk later. Just do what the doctor tells you so you can get well."

Karen patted Jane's hand. "I'd better go, too, honey. I'm due at work in half an hour, but I wanted to see how you were doing and bring the flowers by. I know you like baby roses. Call me when you get home." She turned to Keene with a grin, sticking out her hand. "It was so nice to meet you, Mr. Moray. I can't wait to tell the girls at my office I've actually met a star!"

He took her hand and smiled back at her. "It's always nice to meet a fan."

Both he and Jane watched Karen, and then he turned to her, his smile fading. "I'm sorry, Miss Delaney. I truly am. I never meant for this to happen. I meant what I said. I'll do anything to make this up to you."

Although she was furious with him for his carelessness, his sincerity touched her heart, and she found herself mellowing. Especially now that she knew who he was. "I'm sorry for my outburst, Mr. Moray, but you have no idea how. . ." She paused, gulping at the enormity of the problems she was facing. "Thanks for coming."

"My offer of a job still stands," he said kindly. "But I really need your answer as quickly as possible. Good-bye, Miss Delaney."

Jane nodded and then watched until the curtain closed behind him. Turning to Mildred she asked, "How soon do you think I can leave?"

Before the nurse could answer, the doctor entered, wearing a warm smile. "I've already signed your release papers. You can leave as soon as you're ready."

⁓

Keene sat in the hospital lobby, waiting, unable to think of anything except Jane Delaney. Even with that nasty bump on her head and her dark hair pulled back in one of those ponytail things, he could tell she was beautiful. One look at those wounded blue eyes, and he knew he had to do whatever he could to right the wrongs he had caused. She looked so vulnerable lying there on that bed, her head bandaged, her leg broken. He had wanted to sweep her up in his arms and take care of her, tell her everything was going to be okay. Good thing he'd had a chance to speak to that doctor as he'd left her room. Otherwise, he wouldn't have known she was being released right away.

What a day this had been. He had left the state capitol area, fully intending to drive past the convention center and then return to his condominium to get a little work done. Instead, he had spent the last hour in the hospital emergency room. Not that he minded, because he didn't. The accident *had* been his fault. The least he could do was try to make things up to the poor, unfortunate woman who had been driving the other car.

He snickered audibly as their conversation about her God filtered through his mind. *Too bad she is willing to put her faith in a myth. How can she possibly believe there is a God?* Although his years of training had centered on his voice and his music, he had taken a few scientific courses in college that totally disproved God's existence. Surely, no one with any sense at all could believe in such a fairy tale.

Well, her beliefs were her own. As long as she did not try to force them on him, they would get along fine. Drumming his fingers idly on his knee, he glanced at the big wall clock. How long could it take to check out of the hospital? He had already told the accounting department he would take care of all her bills.

"Could you call a taxi for me, please?"

He turned quickly toward the voice coming from near the reception desk, and there she was, sitting helplessly in a wheelchair, her foot propped up on the footrest. Jane Delaney. The woman whose life he had ruined in one careless second. He rose and hurried to her side. "You don't need a taxi. I'll take you home."

The look she gave him told him that his plans were not her plans. "Thank you, Mr. Moray, but that won't be necessary. I—I know you're a busy man. You've already done enough by paying my bill." Her voice was gentle but firm, leaving him unsure of what to say next.

"But I insist. I'm the one who upset your life."

With a sigh that could only mean exasperation, she gave him a disparaging look. "I've already asked this nice lady to call for a taxi. I don't mean to be rude, and I *am* a great fan of yours, but—"

"You're afraid to ride with a stranger, is that it?"

"I—I guess so."

"I'm completely harmless, I can assure you." He moved a step closer. "Taking you home is the least I can do."

She turned to the woman at the desk, who sat waiting for further direction, the phone still in her hand. "Go ahead, please. Call a taxi. I can't impose on this nice man."

Keene had never taken rejection kindly, in any form. "You're sure you won't change your mind?"

Jane fiddled with her purse's shoulder strap, and he knew she was avoiding his eyes. "I—I'd better take the taxi home."

He stood staring at her, thinking how people crowded around him at the end of his concerts, begging for his autograph. And how he couldn't go anywhere without someone literally hanging on to his coat sleeve, trying to strike up a conversation about one of the arias he'd sung or their favorite CD he'd recorded. However, this woman was different. She was actually trying to avoid being with him, and somehow he found it almost refreshing—challenging. He raised his brows in question. "You are going to accept my offer, aren't you?"

She lifted her big blue eyes to meet his, and once again he noticed how pretty her delicate features were, despite the huge knot on her forehead. Her complexion was flawless, giving those blue eyes a China doll quality.

"Do you really want me to work for you, or are you just being kind?"

"Of course I want you to work for me. I made the offer, didn't I?" He hoped his smile was convincing.

She returned his smile, although it seemed somewhat guarded. "Then, yes, I accept, but only until I'm able to get out of my cast and find another job."

He decided to push once more. "You'll come to work for me, but you won't accept my offer of a ride home?"

∽

Jane felt a flush of warmth rush to her cheeks, and she couldn't do a thing to stop it. Keene Moray, the man whose voice echoed through her apartment nearly every night, was standing in front of her. The man she'd admired since she had been old enough to buy her own CDs. Most of her friends had laughed at her when she told them her favorite artist was an opera singer instead of a country music vocalist. Even Karen had laughed, but once she had visited Jane's apartment, ridden in her car, and listened to his rich voice and elegant phrasing, she, too, had become hooked on the music of Keene Moray. When he'd recorded his *Love* album, featuring the most romantic songs of all time, both she and Karen bought two copies—one to play and one to save. She had dreamed about attending one of his operas or concerts someday, when she could afford it, seated in the front row, close enough to see his handsome face and watch his expressions. Now here he was—offering her not only a ride home but also a job! A real job! Though only a temporary one.

"I'd like to, but—"

"But you never accept rides from strangers, is that it? Even if they've demolished your car and put you in the hospital with a broken leg and a banged-up head?"

"I—I have to admit I do feel a bit strange about it." She felt her blush intensify. What a fool he must think her. And she certainly didn't want him, the famous Keene Moray, to see the dingy, low-income apartment she lived in. "I—I hope you understand. I don't mean to offend you."

He gave her a compassionate grin that made her feel a bit better. "Okay. Let's strike a deal. If you refuse to let me take you home, at least let me pay for your taxi. Remember, it's because of me and my carelessness that you're not able to drive your car."

He was right about that. His carelessness had put her in this quandary. She was glad he acknowledged that fact. "Okay. I guess."

"Your taxi is here," the receptionist said, gesturing toward the double glass doors.

Jane allowed Mr. Moray and the orderly to help her through the doors, out of the wheelchair, and into the waiting taxi. She watched from the backseat as he spoke a few words to the driver and paid the man with a bill that would do far more than cover her trip across town. Waving at him through the window, she mouthed the words *Thank you* and then settled back for her ride home, resting her injured leg on the cab's leather seat. Good thing she'd worn a dress that day, instead of her good slacks or jeans; otherwise, they would have had to split them up the sides, and she certainly couldn't afford to buy a new pair.

When the car moved forward, she suddenly realized she had not even given him her phone number, and she had no idea how to call him. How could she go to work for him if neither one knew how to reach the other? Then she remembered he had taken care of her hospital bill. Perhaps he had written down the information from that.

When they reached the exit from the parking lot, the driver pulled to one side and waited, holding his microphone and relaying the address she had given him to the dispatcher. Assuming he was waiting for a response, she was not surprised when he continued to wait before pulling out onto the street. After a few minutes, he nodded into the rearview mirror and pulled out into the line of traffic. Curious, she turned and glanced out the rear window.

There, not more than twenty feet behind them, sat a dark blue BMW convertible, bearing a dent in its fender and hood, a broken headlamp, and a few scratches to its bumper, with Keene Moray at the wheel. He was following them! Surely, he would be turning off soon. He wouldn't follow them all the way to her home, would he? *Please, Lord. No! Even though I am thankful to have a roof over my head, I do not want him seeing where I live!*

Stealing a glance every so often, she kept close watch on the BMW, hoping the next time she looked it would be gone. It didn't happen. Each time the taxi changed lanes or made a turn, the BMW did, too.

"This it?" The driver pulled the taxi up in front of one of Providence's low-cost housing development apartment buildings.

With a final backward glance, she pointed to the group of apartments at the far end of the development. "There, just beyond the playground equipment, where the lady is standing beside the wheelchair."

He pulled up to the curb and waited while the friend Karen had called from the hospital helped her into the chair. After making sure the door was closed, the driver nodded and drove off, leaving her sitting at the curb with her friend when the BMW pulled up beside her.

She watched, her heart pounding, as the handsome singer flashed her a smile that set her head reeling. He was even better looking in person than he was on the TV shows she had seen. "I—I didn't know you were going to follow us," she stammered, feeling utterly ridiculous.

"Of course I followed you. That man was a stranger. You'd never ridden with him before." The glint in his eye made her blush again. "I wanted to make sure you arrived home safely."

"This is my friend and neighbor, Ethel Cawkins," she told him, gesturing toward the frail, white-haired woman standing beside her. "My friend called her before I left the hospital. She was kind enough to loan me her wheelchair now that she no longer needs it."

He gave the woman a pleasant nod. "How nice of you, Mrs. Cawkins." Then, turning back to Jane and grasping the chair's handles, he said, "I'll help you to your door."

Panic set in. If he left that BMW convertible parked there with its top down for even five minutes, someone would no doubt remove the CD player and strip off the hubcaps, maybe even take more items. She had seen it happen before. "No, you can't!"

However, he was already pushing her toward the door with Mrs. Cawkins trailing behind. "Oh, but I must. A true gentleman always sees a lady to her door. I'm afraid you're stuck with me."

"But. . ."

Ignoring her protest, he rolled her right up to the door. "Through here?"

She stood her ground. "Wait! You don't know what happens to fancy cars like yours. The hoodlums who live here can trash a car quicker than you can imagine. I can't let that happen to you."

"But we have things to talk about." He grabbed the door handle. "I need to know when you can come to work for me, a phone number where I can reach you, that sort of thing. And I want to make sure your car is taken care of properly and in a timely fashion. Until you have it back, or one to replace it, I am going to be your chauffeur! Take you wherever you want to go."

The Keene Moray? *Her* chauffeur? The thought actually made her want to giggle. Moving quickly, she yanked the handle on the right wheel, spinning the chair around so it blocked the doorway. "You can't do that!"

"Oh, but I want to. Or, if you prefer, I'll rent you a car."

The latter offer had more appeal. She would not allow him to be her chauffeur, no matter how much he insisted.

"My, but you're a stubborn little thing. I can see by your expression you would rather be independent. Well, I cannot say that I blame you, although I would be happy to chauffeur you anywhere, at any time. Since you will not accept my offer of being your chauffeur, I will phone my car dealer and have him deliver a nice rental car to you. Is that acceptable?"

This had to be the most thoughtful man she had ever met or ever hoped to meet. She did need a car to get around, and what he said was true. Through his carelessness, he had taken away her only means of transportation. "Yes, a rental car would be very nice, but you really don't—"

"I want to. I cannot bear the idea of you being without transportation. Besides, you'll need a car to get to my office." That grin again, and she nearly wilted.

"This is far enough, Mr. Moray. Mrs. Cawkins will help me get into my apartment. Thank you for making sure I got home okay."

He raised a brow. "Are you sure? I'll be happy to see you safely inside."

She shook her head. "No, this is fine."

With a slight shrug, he reached into his pocket and pulled out a small notepad. "If you insist." He scribbled something on it and handed it to her. "This is my address and phone number. I don't want to pressure you, but I could really use your help. Give me a call when you feel up to going to work."

"I'm sure I'll feel up to it by next Monday. The doctor said I can begin walking on this leg in a few days, though I may need crutches or a walker for a while. Would Monday work for you?"

"Monday will be fine."

He eyed the wheelchair.

She nodded toward her neighbor. "Mrs. Cawkins has been kind enough to loan me her walker, too. I'm sure I'll be able to manage without help."

"Good." He seemed satisfied with her answer and backed away a step. "If you have any trouble, you give me a call. Why don't you report for work about nine?"

Work. How good that word sounds. God works in mysterious ways. If it hadn't been for the accident, with the scarcity of jobs for unskilled workers, I might have been without a job for weeks. What would Mom and I have done then? The few hundred dollars I've managed to save for a rainy day sure wouldn't have gone far.

She gave him a broad smile. "Nine on Monday."

"I can count on that?"

She laughed. "Yes."

They bid one another a friendly good-bye, and then Jane and Mrs. Cawkins moved into the dimly lit hallway. Instead of heading toward her apartment, which happened to be on the ground floor, she positioned her chair in a shadowy area off to one side of the door. A chill ran through her when the BMW moved out of sight. *I am actually going to be working for Keene Moray!* Quickly, she bowed her head, promising God she would do her best to be a testimony for Him to this man who didn't believe in Him.

❧

The following Monday, with fear and trepidation and Karen at her side, Jane parked the rental car in the visitor parking lot of prestigious Kennewick Place and pulled out the walker Mrs. Cawkins had loaned her. She had tried to use a set of crutches another tenant offered, but they made her feel wobbly and hurt her armpits. She felt much more secure using the walker. She hobbled her way to the elegant entryway, questioning her sanity. *Whatever made me accept his generous offer?*

Despite its beautiful exterior, the elaborate building gave her the creeps. She had no business being in a place like this—for any reason—and she felt like an intruder. Kennewick Place reeked of opulence and wealth. With Karen's help, she opened the door and moved inside. A brass-framed roster on the wall listed the names of the occupants, and she began to scan it for the name *Keene Moray*.

"Wow, this is some place," Karen said, surveying their beautiful surroundings. "I know you were afraid to come here alone your first time, before you had a chance to check things out, but are you sure he won't be mad that I came with you?"

"I hope not." Finally locating his name, she pressed the button beside it and they waited. After what seemed an eternity, his magnificent baritone voice boomed out at her from the speaker.

She identified herself, waited until the buzzer sounded, allowing the door's lock to be released, then manipulated the walker carefully down the hallway and headed for his condo. She'd been leery about coming to a near stranger's condo, but after he explained he was using it not only for a home but also as an office while he was in Providence, she'd felt much better about it.

"Look, Karen. It's plain and simple," she said, hoping to convince herself even more than her friend. "I need a job and he needs an assistant. This is nothing more than a business arrangement. One of my friends, a secretary, has worked for an attorney who has his business office in his home for a long time, and it's worked out very well for both of them."

Karen gave her hand an assuring pat. "I'm sure things will be just fine."

Jane's heart raced at the idea of facing Keene Moray again. She had been so out of it the last time she saw him. Probably even giddy since the doctor had given her something to mask the pain in both her leg and head. Now it was even hard to remember the conversation they'd had. Had she made sense? She doubted it. Having never taken pain medication before, there was no telling how it had affected her. She didn't even want to think about it.

She closed her eyes and held her breath as each step took her closer to his condominium. What was she doing here anyway? She hoped this wasn't a mistake.

"Well, you made it! Come in."

Sucking in her fear, she looked up into Keene's smiling face when he met her in the hallway. "Good. . .good morning, Mr. Moray," she managed to mumble, nearly losing her balance manipulating the walker through the wide opening. "I asked Karen to come with me. I hope you don't mind."

"Not at all. Hello again, Karen." Turning his attention back to Jane, he said, "I hope that leg hasn't caused you too much pain." He gently took her arm and walked slowly beside her a few yards down the hall to an open door.

Causing me much pain? It has been nearly impossible to get comfortable. "It hasn't been too bad."

"How's the head doing?"

It's really been hurting. "Not too bad. The doctor is going to take the stitches out Wednesday."

"And the rental car they brought you? Did it meet with your approval?"

There was no reason for her to avoid the truth here. "My approval? Oh, yes! It's the nicest car I've ever driven. Much nicer than my Aveo, and way bigger."

He laughed good-naturedly, stepping out of her way once they were inside. "Good, I'm glad you like it."

Karen grabbed a magazine from a stack on the coffee table and seated herself on the sofa. "I'll sit here while you two talk."

Jane nodded. She was greatful her friend had come with her.

Keene's condominium astounded her. The living room was large and filled with sunlight from the long stretch of sliding glass doors that opened onto a huge balcony overflowing with potted flowers and palms. Both the walls and the sculptured carpets were off-white, with the furniture upholstered in shades of green and burgundy, and highlighted with touches of royal blue and rose. A grand piano stood in the far corner, an oversized vase on it filled with fresh flowers. It reminded her of a room from a movie set or an architectural magazine. Far more impressive than any she had ever been in before.

"My place in New York City is a bit nicer, but this one will do. I'll only be here for a few months. A friend of mine owns this condo, but he's spending a year in Europe, so he's been kind enough to loan it to me." He clasped his hands together and raised his brows. "May I get you something to drink? Water, soft drink?"

Jane shook her head, feeling like a country bumpkin for the way she allowed herself to stare at both him and the room. She couldn't help it. It was all so grand. "Nothing, thank you."

He motioned toward a wide hallway. "Do you need to rest before I show you where you'll be working? I'm sure it's not easy getting around in that walker with your leg in a cast."

"Oh, no. I'm fine, but. . ." Although she was eager to see her working quarters, she paused, wanting to give him another chance to change his mind. The idea of her, a nobody, working for a famous opera star was ludicrous. "You were very kind to offer me this job, Mr. Moray, but if you'd like to back out—I'll understand. I'm sure in time I can find another job."

He carefully nudged her on, his touch nearly melting her. "I won't hear of it! You need a job, and I need an assistant. I'm sure we'll have a pleasant working relationship."

"It's okay. You don't have to help me. I can make it on my own. In fact, in a few days I hope to completely rid myself of this walker." She tried to escape his grasp, but he wouldn't allow it.

"Just take your time. We're in no hurry."

"Remember, I don't have any office experience," she reminded him.

He stopped and stared at her, his demeanor light and teasing. "Office experience? How much office experience does it require to file things in alphabetical order?" He gave her a mischievous grin. "Didn't you learn that little song when you were in kindergarten? You know the one I mean. A, B, C, D, E, F, G, and so on? The one that ends, 'Now I've sung my ABCs. Tell me what you think of me.'"

Even though it was a silly children's song, Keene Moray had just sung those few words for her—personally, an audience of one! The idea made her head swim.

"Well, did you?"

"Yes," she finally admitted, "only I have another version I like better."

"Oh? Sing it for me." He moved to stand in front of her and waited.

She nearly fainted at the thought. *Me sing? For the great Keene Moray? Unthinkable!* "No! No, I couldn't do that."

He gave her arm a slight squeeze, sending icy chills through her body.

"Come on. I insist. You do sing, don't you?"

"Yes, a little."

He tipped his head, eyeing her. "I'll bet you sing at church."

"Yes."

"In the choir?"

She nodded.

"Then you must sing for me."

He waited expectantly, and she knew he was not going to give up until she had sung the little alphabet song for him. She swallowed a lump that had suddenly arisen in her throat and sent up a quick prayer. *I promised You, God, I would be a testimony to this man. Make me brave enough to sing it for him.*

"Jane. Sing. I'm waiting. Come on. I sang mine for you."

"Promise you won't laugh at me?"

"I promise," he said, sobering and crossing his heart with his index finger.

She began, hoping she had started in the right key. "A, B, C, D, E, F, G. Jesus died for you and me. H, I, J, K, L, M, N. Jesus died for sinful men, a-men! O, P, Q, R, S, T, U. I believe God's Word is true. U, V, W. God has promised you. X, Y, Z. A home e–ter–nal–ly."

The ridiculing look she expected to see on his face did not happen. Instead, the faintest of smiles appeared as Keene seemed to be assessing her words. "That's pretty cute. Great way to learn the alphabet. Did you make it up?"

She could not help but smile back. Every child who had ever attended her church had learned that little song. And they had sung it at every youth camp she ever attended. "No, I didn't, but I wish I could take credit for it. Everything it says is true."

"You have a nice voice," he said, leading the way down the hall and pushing open the door that led to his office.

She couldn't be sure if his compliment was sincere or merely polite, but she was grateful for it anyway. *Thank You, Lord!*

"How long have you been singing in your church choir?"

She followed him into the room, trying to keep her mind on his question instead of the magnificent office that surrounded her. She had nearly forgotten about Karen waiting in the living room. "Since my first year of high school, but I've belonged to the junior choir since fifth grade."

He motioned her toward an upholstered chair in front of a wide cherrywood desk and then seated himself in a chair next to it. "Ever done any solos?"

She sat down in the comfortable chair and swiveled it to face him, lifting her foot and resting it on the edge of a heavy metal wastebasket. "Yes, a number of them, although I'm not that good. They only call on me when they're desperate or someone is out sick."

He gave her an accusing grin. "I doubt that. I think you are just being modest. From the little bit I just heard, I'll bet you're very good."

"Is. . .is this where I'll be working?" she asked. This time it was she who wanted to change the subject. Discussing singing with Keene Moray was like racing a rowboat against a cruise ship, and it made her ill at ease.

"Yes." He turned and pointed to a pile of boxes lined up along the wall. "Those are what I need filed. Most of it is sheet music. Some are contracts. The rest is a conglomeration of letters, clippings, research, and I can't even remember what else. I had all that stuff shipped here to Providence, hoping to find someone like you who could go through it, sort it all out, and set up a filing system for me." His finger pointed toward a row of boxes piled on top of one another. "Those boxes are all empty filing boxes. I figure once they are filled, it will be easy to ship them to my office in New York. And those boxes are filled with office supplies," he said, pointing to a few boxes at the far end. "Mostly file folders, labels, envelopes, staplers, that sort of thing. If I missed anything you need, we'll get it."

He pointed to a big box on the credenza behind the desk. "That's fan mail that needs to be sorted and answered. I guess I could write out a simple letter, have it duplicated, and send it to everyone, like many of my artist friends do, but I like to respond to my fan mail with a personal note to each person who has taken the time to write me. From the looks of things piled around here, you can tell I have gotten way behind. I'll need you to take care of those for me, too." He gestured again toward the stack of mail. "Maybe you could start with those fan letters. That way you wouldn't have to walk around very much. I don't want you overdoing it."

She stared at the boxes, taking them in one by one. "What if I have questions? Will you be here to answer them?"

He threw back his head with a raucous laugh. "Oh, yes. I will be here, but you'll probably wish I wasn't! I'll be learning and practicing a new opera for next year's season, and I'm afraid at times I get very loud." He sent her a toothy grin. "Perhaps I should provide earplugs for you."

Earplugs? To block out that fabulous baritone voice? Never! "I won't need earplugs, Mr. Moray. I'll love hearing you practice."

A deep frown creased his brow, and she feared she had said something wrong.

"Look, if you and I are going to be working together, you'll have to quit calling me Mr. Moray. Call me Keene. That is my name, you know. My real name, I might add. Not a stage name."

Her flattened palm went to her chest and her eyes widened in awe. "I can't—"

"Oh, yes, you can. You must call me Keene. I insist." His smile returned. "And I can assure you I get pretty testy when I don't get my way." He pointed to her walking cast again. "By the way, when did the doctor say you could get rid of that thing?"

"Hopefully in five to six weeks. I'm ready to start work if you'll show me what to do. But first I'd better tell Karen she can go on home."

He rose, rubbing his hands together briskly. "Fine! Let's get at it."

"You're sure you don't need me to stay?" Karen asked when Jane hobbled into the living room. "Can you really trust that guy?"

Jane smiled. "Yes, I'm sure I can. Go on now, and I'll call you tonight."

"Good thing we each drove our own car," Karen added with a nod toward the hallway. "Call if you need me."

Jane assured her she would. Once the door closed behind her friend, she headed back down the hall, confident she was perfectly safe with her new boss.

For the next three hours, they worked side by side with Keene opening the boxes containing all the items he had mentioned, going over the contents in detail, and telling her how he wanted them sorted. At noon, he called for sandwiches to be delivered by a nearby deli. Although the sandwiches were delicious, Jane found it hard to swallow. Just being in the presence of this famous man made her stomach quiver and her hands shake with delight. His kindness toward her was amazing. He stopped her from doing anything that would hurt her leg or cause her discomfort.

They worked until three when Keene suggested they call it a day. When the door closed behind her, Jane leaned against the foyer wall and breathed a deep sigh. She had gotten through her first day of working for Keene Moray, and it hadn't been half bad. It fact, it had been extremely pleasant. Now if she could just come down off cloud nine and get home without tripping over something.

❧

As soon as Keene heard the door close, he moved into his office and phoned the garage where they had towed Jane's car. "You are going to repair it as good as new, aren't you?" he asked Biff Hogan, the job manager.

"Depends on how much your insurance company wants us to do," the man said. "That's a pretty light little car. That BMW of yours banged it up real good."

"Perhaps it'd be better to replace it. From what the owner said, I assume it's around six months old, and I doubt she's put very many miles on it."

"You're right about that. She's chalked up less than four thousand miles." There was a pause on the other end. "I doubt your insurance company will replace it. They rarely do, but the costs to repair it back to its original state are going to be pretty hefty."

Keene pondered his words carefully. Somehow it didn't seem right to repair something that had been nearly new before he damaged it. "I'll be right over. I want to take a look at it myself before you do anything, okay?"

"Sure. You're the boss."

All the way to the garage, Keene's thoughts were on Jane and the misery and inconvenience he had caused her, and how sweet she had been about the whole thing. He thought about the time the two of them had spent together that day, going through the boxes, setting up the filing system, and eating lunch together. Although he regretted meeting her by running into her car and causing her injuries, it seemed fate had brought her to him. She was exactly the kind of person he'd hoped to find to fill the temporary assistant position during the time he would be in Providence. Even with that cast on her leg slowing her down, he knew she'd do the job efficiently, and it would be nice to have someone with her pleasant disposition around the condo, not to mention the strain it would remove by having someone to field his incoming calls.

He smiled to himself. Especially the calls from the many women he had dated while in New York and even those who often called from Paris—beautiful, well-educated women who knew and appreciated good music. He loved having a beautiful woman on his arm when he attended the many social functions required of him as a performer, but there wasn't one among them he would ever want to marry. No. When, and if, he ever married, it would not be to some debutante who had more interest in maintaining her figure and keeping her artificial nails in perfect condition than in being a loving mate to her husband and bearing his children. It would be to a real woman. One who would put him first, and if God allowed—

If God allowed? He laughed out loud. *God? There is no God. I merely quoted a figure of speech! Like talking about the tooth fairy or Mother Nature.*

He pulled into a parking stall in front of the automotive shop and turned off the ignition, for the first time realizing he had been humming to himself. A tune he couldn't place at first. Then it hit him, and he began to sing aloud. "A, B, C, D, E, F, G. Jesus died for you and me." An audible huff escaped his lips. *Jesus? Jesus never actually lived. He was a fable—a myth, just like God! Nothing but a silly myth!*

Biff walked toward him and stuck out his hand as Keene entered the building. "Looks like you're gonna have to have that little Chevy Aveo repaired instead of replacing it. Your insurance company won't go for the whole ball of wax," the man shouted over the loud noise of grinders and sanders. "Come on into my office!"

Keene shook the man's hand and followed him into the office, seating himself across from Biff's beat-up old desk. He looked the man directly in the eye. "Tell me, Biff. . . If this were your daughter's car and you could either fix it or replace it, without any insurance company being involved, and you were the one responsible for wrecking it, what would you do?"

The man remained silent for a minute, then grinned. "Well, as the owner of this body shop, I'd say I'd fix it up."

"And as a father?"

Biff Hogan rubbed his fingers across his cheek, roughing up the small amount of stubble that had grown there since his morning shave. "If I were the father, I guess I'd have to say replace it. Wouldn't seem fair to pawn off a repaired car to replace one that had been nearly new and without a scratch before I banged it up."

"I agree wholeheartedly. Haul that Aveo over to the General Motors dealer and tell him to get in touch with me with a price for a new one—exactly like it, using this one as a trade-in. Okay? It's the only fair thing to do."

Two days later, at the end of their workday, Keene led Jane through the Kennewick Place lobby to the parking lot, where a red Aveo was parked.

"My car!" She rushed over to it and then realized something was different. Peering in the window, she noted that both the dashboard and the upholstery were a different color than hers. Backing away quickly, she felt a flush of embarrassment rush to her cheeks. "I—I guess I made a mistake, but it looked like my car."

Without a word but smiling broadly, Keene reached into his pocket and pulled out a key. "It is your car, Jane. A brand-new one. Here, try this key in the lock."

Puzzled, she stared at him. "But your insurance agent said my old car could be fixed up to look like new."

"*Look* like new—that's the operative word, but your car would always bear signs of being wrecked. If not on the surface, at least underneath. If you ever tried to sell it or trade it in, it would depreciate the value. I couldn't let that happen. I caused the wreck. I had to replace it with one that had not been wrecked. I—I hope you like it. I told the dealer I wanted it to be as close in appearance as possible." He stepped forward and rested a hand on the car's top. "If it isn't right, or you'd rather have another color, I told—"

"No! It's perfect just as it is, but I never expected you to buy me a new car!"

"I only paid the difference between what my insurance paid and the selling price of a new one. I'm just glad you like it. Now," he said, still holding on to the key, "go on and enjoy your evening. I'll see you in the morning. Don't worry about the rental car. They'll be picking it up this evening."

After taking the key and opening the door, Jane smiled at him with tears in her eyes. "I've never met anyone like you, Keene."

He chuckled. "Let's just say you bring out the best in me." He rested his palms on the top of the car after she climbed inside and rolled down the window. "I've never met anyone like you either."

His words made her tingle all over. She hoped they were a compliment. At least, she was going to take them that way. She handed him the key to the rental car, said another sincere thank-you, then a quick good-bye, rolled up the window, and turned the key in the ignition. Taking in the fresh smell of her new car, she backed out of the parking space and headed for the exit. If she could have her pick of men, it would be a man like Keene Moray.

The next few weeks flew by as Jane worked at a whirlwind pace, trying to put things in order the way Keene wanted them. At times she felt frustrated when her walking cast kept her from moving as quickly as she would like, making certain projects tedious and laborious, but he never seemed to mind the delay and was more than patient with her.

That patience was tested the day before the doctor was to remove her cast. In her excitement, she accidentally knocked a file box off a chair. It contained the sheet music Keene was using to rehearse for the next season, and every piece ended in a heap in the middle of the floor, mixed up and scattered. Knowing how important the order of his music was to Keene, she began to cry as she knelt and tried to gather them up, barely able to read the titles and page numbers through her tears.

When he entered the room and realized what had happened, he waved his arms and spouted a few profanities, which only made her feel worse. Unable to deal with her self-recrimination, much less his fury, she collapsed into a heap beside the mess she'd made, weeping her heart out, her cast sticking out awkwardly in front of her. She had wanted so badly to please him.

He crossed the room slowly, coming to stand beside her, wringing his hands as if he had no idea what to do or say. Finally, he knelt on one knee and wrapped his arm about her shoulders. "I'm. . .I'm sorry, Jane. For a moment there, I lost my head. I'm not mad at you. Seeing everything on the floor like this upset me because I knew how much work you'd put into filing that box full of sheet music."

She lifted her eyes to his, tears cascading down her face. "I—I thought you cursed because you. . .you were mad at me! Maybe now that I'm getting rid of this cast, it's time for me to get out of your way and look for another job."

"No! Like I said, I'm not mad at you! Things happen. I have done far worse than spilling a box of mere paper, and I wasn't even wearing a cast. Look what I did to you and your car. I know how hard you've worked to get everything in that box in order!" He stroked her hair gently then wiped a thumb across her damp cheek, clearing away a tear. Tilting her face up to his, he gazed at her, his deep brown eyes filled with regret. "I apologize for my language. I am sure you are not used to hearing words like those. And don't you even talk about finding another job. I would like you to stay on right here until I am ready to leave Rhode Island. I—I don't know what I'd do without you."

She had a hard time finding her voice with him so close she could feel his breath on her cheek. She wanted to say something profound, something that would convince him of his lack of reverence for God, but the words wouldn't come. *Lord, help me! I promised to tell Keene about You and Your saving grace, and I'm making such a mess of things!*

Her boss gave her a gentle smile. "For your sake, I'll try to have better control over my mouth in the future, but old habits are hard to break. You may have to remind me occasionally. Give me a swift kick. But I really want you to stay. Promise me you will?"

"I—I'd like to stay, if you're sure you want me," she murmured, dazzled by his touch and enjoying being near him.

"I said I did, didn't I?" He gave her a warm smile. After searching the room for a larger empty box, he helped her put the fallen items into it. "You can refile these when you have time. Why don't you quit and go on home? This will wait until tomorrow," he said once everything had been picked up from the floor. "Besides, I have a dinner engagement, so I'll be leaving early myself."

Her heart sank. Even though she was nothing more than a temporary employee, it hurt to think of another woman sitting beside him, smiling at him over some exotic candlelight dinner at a swanky restaurant. She had never considered the fact that he may have a girlfriend in Providence. Of course he would! This was Keene Moray, the singing idol of thousands of women throughout the world. Somehow, the thought filled her with jealousy, a feeling completely foreign to her. Realizing the fallacy of her thoughts, she snickered.

"What?" He pulled away from her and rose. "What's so funny?"

Embarrassed and unable to think of one reasonable excuse to explain her silly actions, she simply gave him a blank stare. "Ah. . .it was nothing. Your. . .your statement about having dinner reminded me of something, that's all."

He tilted his head and lifted a brow. "Oh, you have a hot dinner date, too?"

His choice of the word *hot* distressed her almost as much as the word *too*. Her face probably showed it. She had never used the word *hot* in that context, let alone had a *hot* dinner date of her own. "No, Mr. Mor—Keene, I don't have a dinner date. I'm planning on reading a book tonight."

"Hey, I'm sorry." He placed a placating hand on her wrist. "I never meant to offend you, Jane. *Hot* was just a figure of speech. You know—like exciting—no, not exciting. Interesting. Special."

Keene Moray actually looked—embarrassed? If she hadn't been offended by his use of words, she would have enjoyed it.

"I think I know what you mean," she offered, amused to see someone so famous put on the defensive for something he had said, and to her, of all people. A nobody.

"Hey, since you're from around here, maybe you can help me decide where to take Camellia for dinner tonight. It's her birthday, and I want it to be a surprise."

"I—I really don't know much about Providence's fancy restaurants, but I have driven past The Green Goddess a number of times. It looks pretty fancy."

Knotting his hands into fists, he pressed them into his lower back and arched, stretching first one way and then the other. "I guess I should get more exercise. I sit at the piano far more than I should." He gave her a lopsided grin. "I'm going to be an old man before my time if I don't change my ways."

"You could join the YMCA." The words slipped out before she realized what a ridiculous suggestion she had made. Why would he join the Y when he could afford to belong to the fanciest health club in town?

She watched a slow smile creep across his mouth. "Not a bad idea, except for

36

ne thing. There are great workout facilities right here in this building, and I don't even take advantage of those."

She felt just plain dumb. "I—I hadn't realized."

"I didn't know it either until two days ago." He grinned again. "Too bad you have that cast on your leg, or I'd invite you to try out one of their treadmills."

"I–I've never used a treadmill," she admitted dolefully.

"I hate them. My idea of exercise is a fast game of tennis. Now that's a real workout."

"I've never played tennis either." She had worked weekends one summer at the local country club, waiting tables for those who did know how to play tennis or at least walked around the clubhouse carrying their expensive rackets and wearing cute little tennis outfits.

"I was kidding about the fast part. I'm not very good myself. Always too busy to take the time to improve my game." He tossed an imaginary ball into the air, swinging at it with an imaginary tennis racket, and then chuckled. "See, I didn't even get it across the net."

She loved his sense of humor. Surprisingly, nothing about him seemed pretentious or conceited. She giggled, covering her mouth. "Maybe your racket has a hole in it."

He pretended to be lifting it up, observing it carefully as his hands twisted back and forth. "You know, you may be right. Maybe I'm a better server than I thought."

"You. . .you don't look like you need to exercise. You look, umm, fit to me." *More stupid words. I'll bet his Camellia wouldn't say something that stupid. She would probably ooh and ahh over him, stroking his biceps and saying how strong he looks.*

He smiled again. "Aw, thanks."

"Well, I'd better get out of here so you can get ready for your date." She stood and picked up her walker, setting it directly in front of her before swinging the strap of her bag over her shoulder. "I'll see myself out."

She started for the door, but the phone rang. Out of habit from answering it the past few weeks, she reached for it without even looking his way. "Keene Moray's residence. This is Jane. How may I help you?"

There was a pause on the other end of the line, then a sneeze. "I need to speak with Keene." Another sneeze. "Tell him this is Camellia."

He took the phone, and after a few "uh-huhs" and an "I'm sorry," he said, "Perhaps another time, when you're feeling better." Before hanging up, he stared at the phone for a few moments then turned to Jane.

Chapter 3

Camellia had to cancel our plans for this evening. How about having dinner with me at that swanky restaurant you told me about? The one with all the cars in the parking lot. To celebrate the official removal of your cast tomorrow."

Jane's knees threatened to bend of their own accord. If she had not been hanging on to the desk, they probably would have. "No. . .no, I'm sorry. I—I can't."

"Why not? You have to eat supper. We can order a take-out dinner for your mother, if that's what's stopping you."

"It's not that! Mom is able to get herself something to eat when I can't make it home."

"Then why?"

Her gaze immediately went to her simple tank dress and chiffon cover-up blouse. "I'm. . .I'm not. . ."

He must have caught her concern. "Okay, we'll go somewhere else. Maybe have a steak at one of Providence's famous steak houses. Would that be better?"

Seeing that he wasn't going to give up easily, she glanced at her watch. "I have choir practice at seven thirty."

His smile was devastating. "No problem. It's nearly five. If we head out now you should have time to do both." He stepped toward her and placed his hand on her shoulder.

Ripples of joy coursed through her at his touch. To think that he—Keene Moray—would invite her—Jane Delaney—to have dinner with him was nothing short of incredible.

"Come on, Jane. Say yes. I get tired of eating alone. You'll be doing me a big favor."

"Well. . .I guess. . ."

"Is that a yes?"

She nodded. "I—I guess. If you're sure. . ."

His hand went from her shoulder to cup her chin as he lifted her face to his. "I'm sure. Now put that walker in gear, and let's go have a steak."

❧

A few minutes past seven thirty, when Jane arrived at the church, choir practice had already begun. She slipped into the seat next to Karen as quietly as she could.

opened the folder lying on her chair, and pulled out a piece of sheet music, frantically searching for a word or phrase that would give her a hint as to which page they were on.

Karen leaned toward her and whispered with a grin, "You're late. Page four, at the bottom."

"Thanks." Although Jane loved singing in the choir and learning new music with which to praise her Lord, she found her mind wandering back to the wonderful time she'd had at the restaurant with Keene. He was gorgeous, with such a striking presence it had seemed all eyes turned toward him when they entered. Something about him and his appearance commanded attention. He exuded confidence and an assurance about himself that few men did. She found herself still in awe of him. Apparently, others did, too. Several people came to their table seeking his autograph.

When the last note had been sung, choir director Ben Kennard smiled and held up a folder. "Okay, folks, you've got that one down pat. We'll be doing it a week from Sunday. We'll go over it one more time next week."

Karen slipped the music back into her folder and leaned toward Jane. "You're never late. What happened?"

"You'll never believe it. I'll tell you later."

"Take out the music for *Down from the Cross*," Ben told them, holding up a fairly good-sized book. "We're coming along quite nicely with this. I am proud of all of you, but remember, we not only have to know *how* to sing the music, we have to sing it with feeling. Why?" He paused for effect, his eyes scanning the faces of the 150 members of Randlewood Community Choir. "Because we're singing it for our Lord. Yes, there will be those in the audience each of the eight nights we perform *Down from the Cross* as a citywide Easter pageant whom we hope and pray will be touched by what we sing, but touching those hearts is God's job. If we give Him the best we can, He will do the rest."

"I—I have a hard time singing this cantata without crying," Emily Stokes, one of the altos, said as she opened her folder. "The words really speak to my heart."

"Me, too," Gene Reynolds, the lead bass singer, boomed out. "God had to have inspired the man who wrote this music."

Winnie Martin touched her handkerchief to her eyes. "Just thinking how Jesus suffered and died for us—well, I praise Him for. . .for. . ." Halting, she began to weep.

"It's okay, Winnie. I think this cantata touches each of us in a special way." Ben bowed his head and said softly, "Lord, each of us comes to You this night with our own special load of baggage. We ask You to take it from us, lift it from our backs. Cleanse our minds of all thoughts except those of You. May we praise

You with each word we sing, that Your name may be glorified. We ask these things in Jesus' name."

"Amen," the entire group said in unison.

Ben motioned toward an empty seat in the baritone section. "As most of you know, Jim Carter has been having some physical problems lately, and he's asked for our prayers. I'm. . .I'm sorry to have to tell you, but they have determined he has throat cancer. He has an appointment with a specialist tomorrow to see how best to proceed. We need to continue to pray for him. The prognosis does not look good."

Winnie stood to her feet, her eyes round with concern. "But he always sings the part of Jesus! What if—"

"If he can't sing," Sarah Miles interrupted, tears evident through her thick glasses, "will. . .will we have to cancel the cantata?"

Everyone waited for Ben's answer.

Ben frowned, gripping the edges of his music stand. "At this point, Sarah, I would have to say yes, that's a distinct possibility, but it's in God's hands. Easter is only eight weeks away. It would be very difficult for someone else to step in and learn the music at this late date. I know you are all disappointed to hear it, but *Down from the Cross* may have to be canceled. The church board will be making the final decision within the next day or so. Until then, I guess we'll carry on as usual."

"But—" Sarah began.

"Let's not discuss this any further tonight. We need to get on with our practice. The best thing we can do at this point is pray for a miracle for Jim when he goes to the specialist tomorrow. We all know God is able to perform miracles."

Karen leaned toward Jane. "We simply can't do the cantata without Jim."

Jane gave her a weak smile. The news had upset her as much as everyone else. Jim Carter, a professional performer who traveled most of the year with a Southern gospel quartet, had sung the lead baritone part in their cantatas for as long as she could remember. Although she had heard him many times over the years, his rich voice still sent chills down her spine, even in rehearsals. "I know. We'd better pray hard."

After another hour of practice, Ben dismissed the group.

"Jane, can you stay?" he asked as she moved out of the choir loft. "I'd like to go over your solos again."

"Sure, Ben. I've been working on them at home, and I could really use your help. But if *Down from the Cross* has to be canceled—"

"It hasn't been canceled—yet." He motioned her toward the microphone. "I'm wondering about the part on page fifty, Jane. Even if we have to cancel the cantata, I still want you to sing this part on Easter Sunday at all three morning services."

"You do?"

"Yes, I do." He adjusted the microphone for her and then stepped aside. "Remember, you're playing the part of Jesus' mother. Before you begin to sing, think how Mary would feel. Put yourself in her place. Try to experience the same emotions she would have felt. Elation when she witnessed the miracles He performed. Sorrow when He was mistreated and falsely accused. An overwhelming grief as He was led to the cross."

Ben's words tore at Jane's heart, and she found herself unable to speak.

"For these few minutes, you *are* Mary, the mother of Jesus. Be her. Respond the way she would respond. Weep as she would weep. Cry out the way she cried out. Forget about the audience. Do this for Him, Jane. Your Lord. Your God. The One who took your sins upon Himself and died on the cross for you. Think of His pain, His agony as He hung there on the cross, as Mary would have thought of it. Take on her personality. Her demeanor. And yes—her burden. If you cry—so be it! If you have to stop and compose yourself before you can go on—so be it! Become Mary, Jane! Forget who you are, and be who God wants you to be at that moment: Mary—the mother of Jesus—and sing it from the depths of your heart."

Without picking up her book, Jane lifted the walker and moved one step closer to the microphone. She knew her part by heart. She had memorized it weeks ago. With a quick prayer to God, she nodded toward the pianist and began to sing. It was as if it were not her voice she heard but the voice of Mary, singing the way Mary would have sung it, and her heart rejoiced. *This is for You, God; I'm singing it for You!*

"That's it!" Ben rushed to her side when she finished. "That's exactly what I wanted. Oh, Jane, that is the best you have ever done it. Surely God has touched both your voice and your heart."

Tears of joy flowed down Jane's cheeks later when she thought over the evening's events while hobbling her way across the nearly empty parking lot to her car. "Thank You, Lord, for giving us Ben Kennard as a choir director. Surely, You sent him to us. Help me to sing the part of Mary as I did tonight, so souls in the audience may see their need of a Savior and turn to You. And please, God, be with Jim Carter. He needs your touch."

⁂

"Well, did you make it to choir practice on time last night?" Keene asked when Jane entered his office at ten the next morning, fresh from a trip to the doctor's office.

Jane smiled at him, holding out her leg, minus the cast. "Not exactly on time, but close."

"You finally got that thing off. Congratulations!" He knelt and wrapped his hand around her slim ankle. "How does it feel?"

"Nude!" She laughed, shocked at the word she had used to describe the weird sensation of having her ankle exposed to air once again. Hoping to make him forget her ridiculous remark, she hurriedly added, "It seems a bit strange to walk on it, but it feels marvelous—absolutely marvelous—to finally be rid of that cast."

"I'm sure it does. I'm amazed you've done so well with it."

He followed her down the hall to his office. "So how did choir practice go?"

"Wonderfully well." She wanted to tell him all about the things Ben had said to her, about becoming Mary when she sang the part, and how, because of his words and guidance, she had sung better than she'd ever sung before, but she knew he wouldn't understand and kept it to herself. "We've been working on our Easter cantata for weeks now. It's beautiful."

"Easter cantata, eh?"

"Yes, it's called *Down from the Cross*. The writer had to have been truly inspired by God."

He waited until she was settled in the desk chair where she planned to work on his fan mail and then seated himself in the chair opposite her, resting his elbows on the desktop. "I don't know about that. Think of all the wonderful works of music that haven't been inspired by God. Many of them have survived the test of time quite nicely."

She could not hold back a grin. Chalk one up for God! Keene trapped himself by that admittance and did not even realize it. "Haven't been inspired by God? Does that mean you acknowledge His existence?"

He reared back in the chair with a hearty laugh. "Oh, you thought you caught me, didn't you? That is not what I meant at all. I meant, *you* thought they had been inspired by God. Not me!"

Somehow, singing the part of Mary in the strong way she had the night before gave her a new boldness. "What about Handel's *Messiah*? Was it not inspired by God? Do you think that man came up with it all by himself? We've all heard the story of how that miraculous piece of music came to be written. Handel himself declared it had been inspired by God."

"I think you and I could argue this point until doomsday and never come to a resolution." He stretched his arms first one way and then the other. "Too heavy a topic for this early in the morning. Besides, I've got practicing to do, and you've got mail to work on." With that, he stood and headed for the door. "I'll call for pizza for lunch. That okay with you?"

She nodded, forcing a smile, fully aware he was dodging the issue. How could he be so blind?

Thursday and Friday went along routinely, with Keene practicing in his room and Jane working in the office. Occasionally, she would open the door a crack, listening to the voice she loved to hear, amazed at the way the two of them had been brought together. However, in her heart she felt like she was failing God. She had promised to be a witness to Keene. Now, all these weeks later, he'd come no closer to believing in God's reality than the day they first met. "Lord," she prayed in a whisper, "this is the most wonderful man I've ever met. He has been kind, considerate, and gentle with me, yet each time Your name is mentioned, it's like a wall goes up between us. I don't know how to reach him. I need Your help, Your guidance. I don't know what to do. Help me, please."

Everyone sat in the chairs, waiting. The choir director was late to choir practice.

"Maybe we'd better go on without him," one of the men suggested impatiently.

"Maybe he's had an accident," one of the female choir members said with concern.

All eyes turned as Ben entered the side door and moved up to his place in front of them. From the downcast look on his face, everyone could see something was troubling him. A hush fell over the choir, creating an awkward silence in the big sanctuary.

"I'm—" He stopped and cleared his throat noisily. "I'm afraid I have bad news. After a number of tests and a biopsy, the doctor has determined Jim does indeed have throat cancer and cannot sing with us. He'll be seeing another specialist tomorrow to decide how best to proceed."

Jane and the others turned toward one another, audibly voicing their sorrow and concern that something this terrible could happen to such a wonderful, dedicated man. One who used all his talents for his Lord.

Ben raised a hand to silence them. "The church board called an emergency meeting. They've asked me to tell you we are definitely canceling the Easter pageant."

Women began to cry, and men shook their heads, many of them blinking back tears as well.

"Without Jim Carter to play the part of Jesus—" He didn't have to finish his sentence. Everyone knew, without Jim, the pageant would not happen.

"We're all disappointed, Ben," one of the tenors volunteered, standing to his feet. "I'm sure we'll all be holding Jim up in prayer."

Everyone nodded in agreement.

"I'll tell him. I know he's counting on your prayers." Ben swallowed hard and then continued. "I honestly thought this year would be our best year yet, with more souls saved than ever. *Down from the Cross* has such a message to it. Like all of you, I'm. . .I'm sorry and disappointed, but without Jim, we have no alternative. Believe me, Jim is more disappointed than any of us. He'd really looked forward to this year's Easter pageant."

Josh Steward rose slowly. "I really praise the Lord for Jim. Some of you who have been here as long as I have will remember the first time we talked about doing an Easter pageant here at Randlewood Community Church. A number of us—including me—were very much opposed to even having an Easter pageant, especially with an earthly man playing and singing the part of Jesus. Somehow it seemed irreverent. A group of us on the church board attended the pageant another church was performing, just to get a firsthand look at the performance and the audience reaction. I sure wasn't prepared for what we saw that night, and I don't think most of the other board members were either."

J. T. Fortner rose, nodding. "I went that night, and like Josh, I was one of those who did not want our church to do an Easter pageant. Although I knew the man hanging on the cross was only another man, a sinner just like me, I can't tell you the emotions that rushed through me as I sat in that audience. I'd never attended anything like it, and for the first time—seeing an actual scene of what it must have been like for my Jesus to suffer and bleed. . ." He paused, covering his face with his hands. "I—I think that's when, for the first time, I really came to grips with what He has done for me. I remember turning to the chairman of our board and telling him I'd changed my mind. I wanted our church to do an Easter pageant."

Wiping his eyes with his handkerchief, Elmer Bones stood, too. "That night will be embedded in my memory forever. Oh, I know some folks think it's wrong to portray Christ's life and death in a dramatic way, with mere mortals acting out the scenes, but since our church started having annual Easter and Christmas pageants, I daresay we've seen hundreds of lost souls flock to the front when our pastor gave an altar call. My. . .my. . ." He stopped, weeping openly, and gestured toward a lovely white-haired lady in the alto section. "My. . .my dear wife was one of them, praise God." He sniffled and rubbed a tear from his cheek with his thumb before going on.

"I have to wonder how many of those people would have accepted Christ as their Savior if they hadn't been in that audience that particular night. I, for one, am glad our church board had the foresight to vote unanimously to do these pageants. I have seen God's hand at work not only on those who attend the pageants, but in the lives of us choir members. I say—if there is any way possible—we keep doing them."

A rousing "Amen" sounded from all persons sitting in the choir loft.

"Isn't there someone else who could sing Jim's part?" one of the sopranos asked, blotting her eyes with her hanky.

"The board thought of that, but we only have about eight weeks left before Easter. For someone to step in at this late date, even if we could find a suitable substitute, would be nearly impossible. They'd not only have to learn the singing part but the stage part, too, with all its movements and locations. No, with the little amount of time we have left, that would never work, and we cannot risk doing a shoddy performance. Not for our Lord. He deserves only our best."

"You're right. I'm sorry I mentioned it." The soprano lowered her head and sat down.

Ben brightened and smiled. "We still have this Sunday's specials to practice." He turned to the group of six sitting on a long pew in front of the choir. "On your feet, gang." The six immediately moved into position, picking up their guitars and strapping them on while the pianist took her place.

Karen leaned toward Jane and whispered, "How could God allow something like this to happen?"

Though she had not voiced it, Jane wondered the same thing. The news about Jim's illness hit her hard. For the fourth year in a row, she had been asked to sing the part of Mary. Though she had nearly turned Ben down the first year he asked her, the other members of the choir had encouraged her to do it, many saying her lovely alto voice would be perfect for the part. Even now, she could remember how terrified she had been at the idea of singing the solos before the many thousands of people who came to hear their Easter cantata each year. Nearly every one of the tickets for the eight performances were given out weeks ahead of Easter. Their church never charged those who attended, but you had to have an advance ticket to get in. Many nights, people were waiting in line as early as six o'clock, hoping folks wouldn't show up and they'd be given their seats at the last minute.

There had been talk of moving the performance to another place, like the city's convention center, but the board had always voted it down. They feared moving it to a location outside the church would make the cantata lose some of its warmth and atmosphere. Besides, over the years, the behind-the-scenes production committee had learned to handle things quite well in their familiar surroundings.

As their practice ended, Ben clapped his hands loudly. "Attention, everyone. Since we won't be needing the music for *Down from the Cross* any longer, leave your books on your chair, and I'll gather them up and take them to my office later." He offered a sympathetic smile. "Maybe next year Jim will be back, and we'll be able to sing it."

Jane rose slowly, giving the precious book one last look. Though she had bought her own personal copy so she could practice at home, she never brought it with her for fear she would leave it at the church. She had also bought the accompaniment tape. She allowed her fingers to trail lovingly across its cover of deep royal blue. Below the title was an empty wooden cross with a long diagonal blast of sunlight reflecting from behind it, shedding light on the otherwise dark cover. The symbolism touched her heart deeply. *Christ came to a dark world to take on my sin and die a tragic death for me! But His life didn't end there. He arose. Praise You, Father.*

"I'm just sick about this." Karen Doyle placed her book on the seat with a shake of her head.

"So am I, Karen, but God is sovereign and promises to work all things for good to those who are called according to His purpose." Jane carefully placed her book on the seat, slung her purse strap over her shoulder, and moved toward the aisle.

Karen followed. "A lot of people are going to be disappointed. I've really been talking it up at the office where I work. I'd planned to get at least twenty tickets to pass out to my coworkers, and I think most of them would've come. I've been trying to tell them about their need of God in their lives, but it's so hard. I'd so hoped *Down from the Cross* would touch their hearts and make them want to accept God."

Jane allowed a sigh to escape as she trudged toward the door, her heart heavy with disappointment. "I was hoping my boss would come, too."

Karen's face brightened. "You really think he would have?"

Pausing, Jane turned to her friend. "Maybe. I haven't asked him yet, but I'd planned to."

Karen harrumphed. "You needn't worry about that now."

"Yeah, I know."

The two friends hugged and went their separate ways, promising to have lunch together soon.

～◦～

"What's wrong, Jane? You have been quiet all morning. Aren't you feeling well?"

Jane had not been able to get the church's Easter pageant off her mind since choir practice the night before. She almost hated to tell Keene about it, sure he would gloat and remind her that God wasn't real, that if He had been real, He never would have let their main soloist become ill.

"Jane? I asked if you weren't feeling well. Did you hear me?"

She looked up at him, blinking back tears. She hated getting emotional on him, but that's the way she was, and she couldn't do anything about it. This had really upset her. Jim Carter was a Christian brother, and she felt for him and his family in this time of crisis. She felt bad for all the choir members who had worked so hard learning *Down from the Cross*, and all those who were helping with costumes, makeup, scenery, tickets, and the hundreds of other things that supported a production of this size and magnitude.

Keene circled his arm about her shoulders and looked down into her face. "What is it? You can tell me, you know that, don't you?"

"It. . .it's nothing you'd be interested in."

Using his free hand, he pulled a pristine white handkerchief from his pocket and blotted her tears. "I've never seen you so upset." A tiny smile turned up the corners of his mouth. "Except when I crashed my BMW into your little car."

"I'm just disappointed, that's all."

He frowned, and in his eyes she could see a genuine concern. "Oh? At someone or something?"

She gave him a wistful look. "The man who always sings the part of Jesus in our Easter pageant has throat cancer, and his prognosis doesn't look good. Without him, we've had to call it off, and I was so looking forward to singing the part of Mary. We're all praying for him, but even if he has surgery, there's no way he'll be able to sing by Easter. Maybe never!"

Keene pondered her comment for a moment then asked, "Isn't there someone else who could sing his part?"

Jane checked the coffeemaker and, finding Keene had already made their morning coffee, poured each of them a cup. "No, not the way he sings it. He has sung the lead part in our cantatas for as long as I can remember. Besides having a great voice, he really puts his heart into it."

"Thanks." He took the cup from her hand and stared into the rich brown liquid. "Well, learning an entirely new score in such a short time would be quite difficult, but learning the stage moves and timing that quickly, too, would be nearly impossible. It'd be difficult for me to do it, and I'm a pro."

"Enough of this kind of talk." She picked up her own cup, forcing a smile. "I've got work that needs to be done today, and you've got practicing to do. See you at noon."

He gave her a mock salute with his free hand. "Yes, ma'am."

The phone was ringing when she entered the office. Another one of Keene's many girlfriends, this one calling from London, wanting to know why he had not returned her calls.

"I'm sorry. I've given him all your messages," she explained to the impatient woman. "However, I can tell you he is in the midst of learning new music for his next season and is quite busy." She took the woman's name and number again. *How many times has that woman called?*

At noon, she gave him the call slip, along with several others—most of them from women who had called before. "You're a popular man," she said, smiling at him over a carton of sweet and sour chicken. "It seems most of the calls I take for you are from women."

He grinned. "What can I say? I admit I enjoy the company of beautiful women."

She eyed him with a frown. "But you've never married?"

"With my schedule and all my traveling?"

It is none of my business, but I am going to ask you anyway. "Don't you want a wife and children?"

He stared off into space thoughtfully, and she knew he was weighing his answer before stating it. "Sure, I'd like to have a wife and family. However, with my lifestyle, it just would not work. Besides, there's an even greater problem than my schedule and traveling that keeps me from getting married."

"Oh? Dare I ask what it is?" She looked at him cautiously, wishing she could retract her words. He may have a physical problem he would prefer not to discuss with her. She would never want to embarrass him—or herself! And what business was it of hers anyway?

Quickly turning his attention toward her with a mischievous smile, he confessed, "I haven't found the right woman."

Her mouth gaped. That was not the answer she had expected. "You've got to be kidding! With all the women who call you? Keene! Surely you're not serious!"

His expression sobered. "Oh, but I am serious. As much as I value the many female friendships I've made over the years, and the times I've enjoyed the pleasure of a beautiful woman's company for an evening, I can honestly say I haven't found a single one I'd want to marry and call my wife." He dipped his head shyly. "That sounds a bit pompous, doesn't it?"

She considered his remark. "No, I don't think it makes you sound pompous. If you haven't found that one perfect love—the one God. . ." She stopped short and bit her lip.

"The one God intended for me?" He gave her a playful wink.

"Yes, that's what I was going to say," she answered demurely.

He set his carton of lemon chicken on the table and reached across, cupping her hand in his. "Is that what you're waiting for, Jane? A perfect man?"

She felt her eyes widen. "I'm not looking for a perfect man. I'm looking for the man God has intended for me. No earthly man is perfect." She took a deep breath. *I have to say this right, so he'll understand.* "Keene, God has a plan for each of us. His perfect plan. If we love Him and want to serve Him, He'll guide us to the one with whom He would have us spend our life."

He gave her hand a slight squeeze. "Does that mean—out there somewhere—the man of your dreams is looking for you?"

She offered a nervous snicker. "I hope so, but only if God intends that I marry. Maybe, in His perfect plan, I'll remain single all my life."

Keene reared his head back with a hearty laugh. "No way! You are beautiful, intelligent, and one of the most caring, considerate women I have ever met. Some man is going to come along and snatch you up. Take my word for it."

His complimentary words caught her off guard, and she found herself speechless.

"Actually," he said slowly, sizing her up, "those qualities are exactly what I'd like to have in a wife."

Although she couldn't see her own face, she knew it must be as red as a radish.

"Tell me, Jane. What qualities would you like your husband to have?"

As his thumb stroked her hand, she actually felt goose bumps rise on her arms. She hoped that he wouldn't notice. "Ah. . .I. . ."

"Surely, you've thought about that. Don't be shy. Tell me."

Oh, Lord—give me the words. "First and foremost, he'd have to love God as much as I do."

Keene leaned toward her with a tender smile. "Knowing you, I expected that to be your first priority."

Thank You, God. "Well. . .he'd have to be kind, caring, and considerate."

"You haven't said handsome or rich," he prodded with a teasing smile.

"Neither of those things is important to me," she confessed honestly. "I want him to be beautiful on the inside, of course. I don't care about handsome. Nor do I care about rich. I know the man God would have me marry would want to provide adequately for his family. We'd be a team."

"What about children?"

That subject always made her smile. She longed to be a mother someday. "Oh, yes. He'd want children. I cannot imagine God ever pairing me with a man who didn't. Not with the love for children He's placed in my heart. I'd like to have at least four or five."

Keene blinked hard then stared at her. "Four or five children? Really?"

She nodded. "At least. Don't you want children?"

He released her hand and leaned back in the chair, locking his fingers over his chest. "If I didn't have to travel. I could not bear the idea of going off and leaving a family behind. Kids need their dad around."

"It would be difficult. I know I couldn't do it."

He rose quickly. "I've got an appointment in half an hour. I'd better be heading out." He reached for his empty cartons, but she got to them first.

"You go on. I'll take care of this."

He wadded up his paper napkin and stuffed it into one of the empty cartons before making sure his wallet was in his back pocket and heading toward the door. "Been good visiting with you. I enjoy our little talks."

She gave him a sheepish smile. He'd never know how much she enjoyed them. "Me, too."

Jane worked at the desk, taking care of routine things like making out checks for Keene's bills, answering the many phone calls that came in from all over the world, getting out the mailings he'd prepared for those on his select fan list, and dozens of other chores. But something niggled at her mind all afternoon.

At four o'clock, she called her pastor.

Jane glanced nervously at the clock on the wall in Pastor Congdon's office. Nearly eight o'clock. Without warning, a side door opened and Kevin Blair, a longtime member of Randlewood Community Church, crooked his finger at her. "You can come in, Jane. We're ready for you now."

As Jane followed Kevin into the large room adjoining the pastor's office, she glanced around the big table at the many familiar faces of those who served on the church board.

"Gentlemen, I received an interesting phone call from Jane this afternoon. I have invited her here this evening to tell you, in person, what she told me. I think you'll be interested."

Jane's heart sank into her shoes. She rarely spoke to a group, other than to the women of her Bible study, and even then she shook while she talked. She waited until Pastor Congdon had seated himself before drawing a deep breath and asking the Lord to help her state her purpose clearly and concisely.

"I—I. . ." *Please, God. Calm me down.* "I'm as upset as anyone about our Easter pageant being canceled. Those of us who sing in the choir and have had the opportunity to practice *Down from the Cross* were excited about its message and how both the words and music could touch hearts. It's. . .it's the most powerful testimony to God's mercy and grace that we've ever heard."

She paused, glancing around the table at each person. *God, give them open minds, please.* "I have an idea—a way that will allow us to go ahead with our plans to present the Easter program."

"Without Jim Carter?" one of the older men interjected quickly, his beady eyes staring at her over funny little half-glasses perched low on his nose.

"Hear her out," Pastor Congdon said quickly.

Jane gave him a grateful smile then continued. "I won't go into detail, other than to say that through a series of circumstances that I feel came from the hand of God, I now work for Keene Moray. Some of you may recognize that name."

Some nodded their heads, acknowledging that they did indeed know who he was, while others gave her a blank stare or turned to the person seated next to them in bewilderment.

"Isn't he that famous opera singer?" one of them finally asked.

She nodded. *Don't let them close their minds before they hear me out, God.* "Yes, Keene is quite famous, highly respected in the music world, and very much in demand."

"What's that got to do with our problem?" The man with the little glasses leaned back in his chair, crossing his arms over his chest.

"Like I said, I work for Keene. He is making his home in Providence for the next few months, learning and rehearsing the new opera he will be performing next year. We've. . .we've become good friends."

Pastor Congdon cleared his throat. "Go on. Tell them your idea, Jane."

Her heart raced. If she didn't feel God's guidance in this, she would run out of the room and never look back. "I—I don't know if Mr. Moray would have any interest in what I am about to propose, or if it's even possible with his contract, but I'd like the board's permission to ask Keene to sing Jim Carter's part—the part of Jesus—in *Down from the Cross*."

One of the younger men leaped to his feet and glared at her. "Do you have any idea what it would cost to hire someone like him? I know the church wouldn't be able to afford it!"

"I'm sure he has a contract of some sort that requires union fees. We sure couldn't afford to pay him that kind of money," another added.

Jane chose her words carefully. "I—I was hoping he'd figure out a way to do it for a minimal fee, maybe even gratis."

"Why would he do that? He's never even been to our church, has he?" another asked.

Pastor Congdon stood and leaned forward. "Gentlemen, if I may, I'd like to add something to what Jane has said."

All eyes turned his way.

"When Jane called me, I was skeptical about this idea just like you are. But the more she talked, and the more I listened, I realized this could be the answer to all our prayers—prayers that, in some way, God would make it possible to provide this community with the truth of His Word through our Easter presentation."

He paused and rested his palms on the conference table. "This man may not even consider Jane's idea, but then again, maybe he will. She feels it is worth a try to ask him. I agree with her."

"But is he saved? Does he know the Lord?" a man seated next to the pastor asked.

Jane felt she should answer his question since she was the only one personally acquainted with Keene. "No, he is not saved, though I have been witnessing to him nearly every day. At times he seems open, and I'm praying he'll confess his sins and ask God's forgiveness before he leaves Rhode Island. He's a wonderful man and a gentleman. You'd all like him."

"I've always questioned anyone playing the part of Jesus, even Jim Carter, but an unsaved man? I'm not sure that would be wise," another man offered, concern written on his face.

"I understand what you're saying, Milton," Pastor Congdon said kindly. "But let's think about this carefully. What is our goal here? Is it not to reach the people in our community with the message of God's Word? Through music and the spoken word? Isn't that the reason we always have an altar call at the end of each performance?"

"But an unsaved man singing the part of our Lord?"

Pastor Congdon rubbed his chin. "Tell me, Milton, do you know for sure that each member of our choir is saved? We have a big choir, some 150 people on any given Sunday. Some folks just like to sing and want an outlet for their talent."

Milton stared at him for a moment before answering. "I hate to admit it, but you may be right."

Pastor Congdon gave the man an appreciative smile. "Let me bring up another point here. We have a fairly large orchestra to back up our choir on Sunday mornings, right?"

Everyone present nodded.

"Have you forgotten we hire about half of those people? They are not even members of our church, but we hire them because they are professionals and we need them. The other half are our own dedicated church members who do it for free because they want to serve God with their talents. Should we fire those whom we hire or think any less of the musicians and their capabilities because they may not claim to be Christians?"

Milton spoke up again. "But hire a man to play the part of Jesus? Shouldn't the man who plays that part be a Christian?"

"That's what we're here to decide," the chairman of the board said, scanning each face. "At this point, we don't even know if Mr. Moray would consider such an invitation should we decide to offer it. He may give us a flat no, and that'll be the end of it." His face took on a gentle smile. "But I personally think Jane's idea has great merit. Think about it. Each year, though we fill our sanctuary for eight straight nights, and we've done everything but get down on our knees and beg the newspapers, radio, and television stations for coverage, we've had very little publicity. And," he went on, "I'm sorry to say, but although many people come forward for salvation or rededication, most of those in our audience are Christians."

Pastor Congdon nodded his head. "He's right. All you have to do is look at the attendance cards we ask everyone to sign."

"What if—" The man's eyes sparkled as he continued. "What if Keene Moray, a famous opera singer, were to sing the lead part in our Easter production? Think of the possibilities to reach people with the gospel, gentlemen. People from all over the state would come to hear him! What would it cost them to attend a performance at the opera? Maybe $60 or $70 a seat? And they would be attending our performance for free! I am not sure we would be able to contain the crowds! Do you think we'd have to beg the media for coverage with him singing the part of Jesus?"

Milton shook his head. "I know you're right—Mr. Moray singing in our church's Easter pageant would be a real drawing card—but could he do it? I mean portraying Christ would be extremely difficult. Not many men could do it without offending those in our audience. We sure don't want that to happen. I remember the first year we did a cantata that required someone to play the part of Jesus, we had a real uproar from a number of church members."

"That we did," Pastor Congdon said with a slight chuckle. "But after that first night, everyone agreed it worked out well, especially when so many people responded to the invitation. Jim Carter did a masterful job singing, and I don't really remember anyone complaining after that first night."

"But Jim was saved," a member who had been silent up to that point said meekly. "He sang it from his heart."

Jane could no longer keep her silence. "Keene Moray is a professional, just as those musicians we hire for the Sunday morning services are professionals. Granted, he doesn't know Jesus as his Savior, but that man is able to take simple words from a music score and put feelings and emotions into them that would amaze you. I know. I hear him every day. He's not only a singer, he's an actor. A marvelous actor. If he were willing to do it, he could take the music to *Down from the Cross* and make it come alive." *God, help me to make them understand!* "I—I have an audiotape at home of Elvis Presley singing 'Amazing Grace.' I've heard some say he was a Christian, but from his lifestyle, I have my doubts. Yet every time I hear him sing it, it touches my heart. Could not Keene's voice singing the part of Jesus in *Down from the Cross* touch hearts in our audience?"

Pastor Congdon gave Jane a smile of agreement, and she felt herself relax.

"Thank you, Jane," he said, motioning toward the door. "You've given us much to think about. The board and I will discuss this, pray about it, and get back to you. Thank you for coming."

Jane stood to leave and felt compelled to make one last plea. "I—I want to thank you for letting me come here tonight. Please. . .I'd like to leave you with one final thought. Keene is a gentleman with a fine personal reputation, one of which he is very proud. If you decide to allow me to ask him to do this for our church, and if he should accept the invitation, I can assure you he will give the performance of his life. Keene never does anything halfway. He would never do anything to embarrass the church, the board, or me, and especially not himself. Please pray about this and consider it carefully before making your final decision."

She walked out the door with a feeling of euphoria, knowing she had done the best she could. God had answered her prayers and steadied her heart and mind. She had to smile to herself. Getting the church to approve was only the first step. If they agreed, convincing Keene to do it—even if his contract and agent would allow it—might be more difficult. "But," she said aloud with a renewed confidence, "God can do anything!"

❧

The next morning, right at nine o'clock, the phone rang in Keene's office.

Chapter 4

The caller didn't need to identify himself. Jane recognized Pastor Congdon's cheery "Hello" immediately, and her heart soared.

"We did it, Jane. It took the board another two hours of discussion but finally they voted unanimously to ask Keene Moray if he would take over Jim's part in *Down from the Cross*. It's up to you now, but I want you to know each man on the board will be praying for you."

She gripped the phone tightly, her heart racing. "Oh, Pastor Congdon, don't think I slept a wink last night. I just kept praying over and over that God would have His will in this."

"Well, we're only halfway there. He hasn't said yes yet. You can be sure our prayers will be with you while you approach Mr. Moray."

She thanked him for his call then slowly returned the phone to its cradle, all the while smiling and already considering the possibilities if Keene agreed to accept their invitation.

"You're chipper this morning," Keene said, pushing open the door to the office and entering, carrying two glasses of orange juice from the kitchen. He placed her glass on the desk then glanced at the phone. "Who called? I heard the phone ring."

I can't ask him yet. I have to pray about this first. The time has to be just right. "My. . .my pastor."

He shrugged. "Oh, I was hoping Brian, my agent, would call. I need to talk to him today." Pointing toward her glass, he said, "Drink up. You need your vitamin C."

"Thanks, Keene."

She watched him move through the door, amazed at his thoughtfulness. *Lord, even now begin preparing Keene's heart for what I'm about to ask him.*

Fortunately, the work she had planned for the morning was busywork, requiring only repetitive hand motion and very little brainpower or concentration, giving her time to pray for the task she believed God had given her.

For lunch, Keene sent her to a nearby carryout to buy fried chicken dinners. By the time she returned, he had set plates and silverware on the little kitchen table and added ice to their glasses. She quickly fixed a pitcher of iced tea then sat down opposite him, noting he had been unusually quiet most of the morning.

"Something wrong?" she asked, hoping she wasn't prying. She lifted her head after sending up another quick prayer.

He spread a napkin across his lap with a deep sigh. "Not really. Just one of those down days. Nothing you need concern yourself about."

She reached across the table and cupped his hand with hers. Despite the warmth of his skin, cold chills crept up her spine. "Anything I can do?"

He scooted the bucket of chicken toward her. "No, I'm just a bit down. My mom died three years ago today. I wasn't even with her when she died. I was in Japan, singing at some meaningless concert. I've. . .I've never forgiven myself for not coming home when she asked me to."

In all the weeks they'd been together, she'd never seen him like this, and she wanted to do something—anything—to take his pain away. What could she do?

"The doctor had said she wouldn't make it a year. I knew that, yet. . .yet I only made it home to see her twice during all that time. Some son, huh?"

"I'm sure she knew you had obligations," Jane assured him, wanting to free him of some of his guilt.

"Although she was happy for me and my success, she never wanted to be in the limelight," he went on, cupping his free hand over hers and giving it a squeeze.

She watched him blink back tears. Sadness for him filled her heart. "She had every right to be proud of you."

"I remember one time I introduced her and made her stand up, and she nearly fainted." A tender smile played at his lips while he spoke of his mother. "She. . . she left me a letter. I found it in her things when I went home for the funeral."

"I'm sure you'll cherish that letter for the rest of your life."

He removed his hand long enough to wipe at his eyes, then placed it back on hers. "In some ways, she reminded me of you."

She gave him a quizzical stare. "Me? How?"

"She. . .she. . ."

His pause gave her cause for alarm. What could there be about his mother that could have been anything like her?

"She claimed to be a Christian, too."

Awestruck by his words, Jane sat staring at him. "You never told me!"

"Although I loved her with all my heart, those last couple of years I found her to be a little weird. You know, always reading the Bible, attending church, listening to Christian programs on the radio and TV. She used to bug me about going to church with her."

He pulled a handkerchief from his pocket and wiped at his nose. "It happened after she moved into an assisted-living home. Most of the times when I visited her, she'd be her usual old self, bragging about winning at Bingo, planning a trip to Las Vegas to gamble with some of the ladies in the home. But all of a sudden, not long before she died, all she could talk about was God and His love. I could not believe the change. I figured some preacher had come to the home and gotten her all stirred up. However, when I asked her what had happened, she explained that some woman from a nearby church started a weekly Bible study there at the home, and she had been attending. The change in her amazed me. She preached at me like you wouldn't believe. Even on her deathbed when she could barely talk for the pain, all she seemed to have on her mind was God. In that letter she left for me, she kept saying she hoped I'd settle things with God so she would see me in heaven."

"I'm sure it's a great comfort to you to know that she's in heaven with her Savior."

He drew back slightly, his dark eyes locking with hers. "It would be, Jane, if I believed in God. But I don't."

"Your mother believed in Him. Keene, why is it so hard for you to believe He's real?"

He stood, towering over her, his hands on his hips. "You really want to know?"

His aggressive tone frightened her. "Yes, I'd like to know what could make you so bitter toward God."

"My dad walked out on my mom and me when I turned twelve, without so much as telling me good-bye, and I begged God to make him come back home." He dropped to one knee, his eyes level with hers. "You'll never convince me God is real, Jane. I sort of remember a scripture my mom tried to teach me once. Something about an earthly father who wouldn't give his son a stone if he'd asked him for bread. Then it went on to say how much more the heavenly Father wants to give good things to His children if they ask Him. I decided, right then and there, if there really was a God, He would answer my prayers. But nothing happened. I never saw my father again."

"That doesn't mean He isn't real, Keene," she said softly, hoping her words would soothe him. "We can't tell God what to do. We can only ask Him for what we'd like Him to do. I can't pretend to tell you why your father left you or why he stayed away, but I do know God has promised to be a Father to the fatherless."

Keene closed his eyes and blinked hard. "But He let my father walk away from me at a time in my life when I really needed him."

"God would like to be your Father, if you'd let Him."

"Isn't God supposed to be a God of goodness? If He is, why did He let my mother work night and day at a hotel maid's job to keep a roof over our heads? That woman literally worked herself to death!"

She shook her head sadly. If only she had answers. "I don't know."

"If God is real, why did He let that man at your church get throat cancer? And why now? When your church needed him? Answer me that!"

Now, Jane, now. Ask him now, a still small voice seemed to say from within her.

Now, Lord? When he is so angry with You?

Trust Me, child. Trust Me. Now is the time, the voice said.

Jane swallowed the lump that had suddenly risen in her throat and sent up a silent prayer. *If You say so, God.*

"Well, do you have an answer for me? Why would God do such a thing? You've already told me there is no one to sing in that man's place."

Jane rose, her eyes never leaving Keene's. "Because He had a better plan." His stare made her wonder if she had sprouted wings.

"A better plan? Like what?"

Help me, Lord! "He wants you to take Jim Carter's place."

Chapter 5

W hat? Surely you're kidding!" Keene sputtered, nearly choking on his words.

She looked him square in the eye, once again feeling that new confidence she deemed a gift from God just when she needed it. "I've never been more serious."

Keene threw back his head with a laugh that echoed through the condominium. "You want me," he said, ramming one thumb into his chest, "to play the part of Jesus?"

"That's exactly what I'm saying. I've already discussed it with our church board, and they've given me permission to ask you." Though her heart thundered, she was amazed at how calm her voice sounded. "I know you're busy practicing next season's opera, but you're a quick learner. You could do both of them if you set your mind to it. And I'll be here to help you in any way I can."

"Impossible." He turned and strode across the room, leaning his hands on the windowsill and gazing into the blue sky. "Absolutely impossible."

She followed him. "Why? Why is it impossible?"

With a shake of his head, he swung around to face her. "For starters, my agent would never let me do it."

She lifted her chin defiantly. "Oh? I thought your agent worked for you. I didn't realize you worked for him!"

"He does work for me."

"Then tell him you want to do it."

He stared down at her. "I never said I wanted to do it."

She gave him a challenging smile. "But you do, don't you? Or do you think you're incapable of singing the part?" There, she'd done it. She'd waved her red flag in front of a bull, fully expecting him to charge, but she was prepared for him. After all, God was on her side.

"Of course I could do it. I—"

"It's a pretty difficult role."

He frowned at her, but the smile teasing the corners of his lips told her he was enjoying their repartee. "I've done more difficult, I can assure you."

She put her hands on her hips and took a step closer, jutting out her chin. "Prove it!"

"I'm up to your little game, missy." His hands moved quickly to cup her shoulders. "Look, Jane. Even if I wanted to do it, which I'm not saying I do, I'd have trouble getting this past the union."

"But. . .if you did really want to do it, you could figure out a way, couldn't you?"

He appeared thoughtful. "Maybe. I'd have to work on it."

A chill of excitement rushed through her, and she brightened. "Does that mean you'll try?"

"You realize, if anyone other than you asked me to do this, I'd laugh in their face." He let out a long sigh. "You're not giving me much time. What is it? Seven or eight weeks until Easter?"

"Actually, you'd have seven to prepare. We usually start performing it a week before Easter."

He rested the back of his hand against his forehead. "I hesitate to ask. Is there more than one performance?"

She nodded, beginning to feel quite confident. Hadn't God laid it upon her heart to ask him? "Eight, actually. One each night, including Easter night."

Keene frowned, placing his palms together and templing his fingers as his gaze returned to the window. "That's a pretty demanding schedule."

"I know."

"And you're singing the part of Mary?"

"Yes."

He stood silently for a long time, his vacant stare fixed on the billowy clouds floating aimlessly in the Providence sky. "I owe you, you know," he finally said without looking at her. "Not only for what I did to your car, but for the pain and suffering you went through with your leg."

"I know. I'm counting on that."

"It would be a challenge. I've never sung a part quite like it."

"I have no doubt you could do it."

"I'd have to put my practicing aside and work nearly full-time on learning something totally new."

"You've already told me you're weeks ahead on your new opera." She waited. Hoping. Praying.

"I'd have to work this out with the union."

"I'm sure you'll figure out a way."

He turned to her slowly, his gaze zeroing in on her face. "You think you're pretty smart, don't you?"

His question puzzled her. "Smart? Me? No."

"You just talked me into doing something I wasn't convinced I wanted to do, didn't you?"

His broad smile sent her skyward. She felt like she was floating on one of those billowy clouds. "I talked you into it? Does that mean you'll do it?"

"Only because you asked me. How could I refuse?"

Without thinking, Jane leaped into his arms and kissed his cheek. To her surprise, he held her there, their faces so close she could feel the warmth of his rapid breathing on her cheek.

"Somehow, some way, I'll work it out. You can tell your church board I will be happy to fill in for—what's his name? Jim?"

"Jim Carter," Jane said hurriedly as he continued to hold her in his arms, her feet dangling inches above the thick carpeting.

"Do you realize, Jane, this is the first time I've been asked to fill in for someone? I'm usually the star!"

His voice was teasing, and she knew it.

"This is a pretty humbling experience."

"In my book, you'll always be the star. Thank you, Keene. I know this is going to put a real strain on your time."

"Knowing you, I suppose you prayed about this, right?"

She grinned up at him as he lowered her feet to the floor. "Yes, I did."

He rolled his eyes and shook his head. "And I also suppose you just happen to have a copy of the cantata with you."

"Right here in my backpack."

"You're incorrigible, but you're sweet."

She reached up and touched his cheek with the tip of her fingers. "So are you." *Thank You, God.*

All smiles, he stuck out his hand, palm up. "You might as well give it to me so I can at least see what I've committed myself to."

She grabbed the backpack and quickly located the copy of the cantata and handed it to him. Reaching back in the bag, she pulled out an audiotape. "We'll be using a live orchestra, but this is the practice tape that came with the cantata."

His hand brushed hers as he took the tape from her, and he held on fast, locking his fingers over hers. She thought she was going to explode with joy.

"This should really help. I will start listening to it this afternoon. Right after I clear things up with my agent and the Musician's Union."

"Our next rehearsal is tomorrow night."

He screwed up his face. "That doesn't give me much time, does it?"

"No, but I'm sure you can handle it," she said, meaning it, thrilled that the wonderful voice of Keene Moray would be singing the part of her Lord. "Oh, Keene, I can't thank you enough."

His finger tapped the tip of her nose, and he smiled into her face. "You're right. You can't thank me enough. Now get to work before I fire you."

She watched him leave the office, closing the door behind him, and then sank into a nearby chair, exhausted but with a prayer of thanks on her lips. "You truly are an awesome God. You've answered my prayer above and beyond anything I could ever imagine, but I have one more request, Lord." She felt a tear slide down her cheek. "Speak to Keene's heart and make him realize his need for You and bring him to Yourself."

⌘

Keene closed the door then leaned against its frame. *Whatever possessed me to say yes? I must have been out of my mind to agree to such a thing. The people I will be working with are amateurs. If this Easter thing is not top-notch, it could hurt my career. Not only that, but it will certainly complicate something else going on in my life. Something else important enough to ruin my career.*

His thoughts turned to Jane. *She is the reason I said yes. How could I deny that woman anything when she has asked so little of me? She is the first woman I have met in a long time who did not fall all over herself in my presence. I can be myself with her, totally at ease. I like that. She is the bright spot in my day. I could almost fall for her, if she wasn't so. . .religious!*

Moving slowly to the phone, he dialed his agent's number. "Hello, Brian. You won't believe what I'm about to tell you."

Ten minutes later, after much explaining and arguing with his agent, the two of them reached an agreement. Next, he called the Musician's Union.

⌘

Jane waited impatiently for Pastor Congdon to pick up the phone. Finally, on the fourth ring, he answered.

"God answered our prayer!" she shouted into the receiver. "Keene is going to do it! He's actually going to do it!"

"Jane? This is you, I hope."

She could not contain the joyful laughter bubbling inside her. "Yes, it's me. Sorry I didn't identify myself, but I'm so excited!"

He laughed. "I noticed that."

"He's already called his agent to let him know, and now he's working things out with the Musician's Union. I've given him the music to *Down from the Cross*, and he'll be at our rehearsal tomorrow night!" She finally stopped talking long enough to suck in a deep breath.

"Wow, you work fast! How did you manage to pull it off so quickly?"

"I—I didn't do anything. God did! I just turned it all over to Him and watched things happen. He did it all!"

"Well, I must say, this is good news. I can hardly wait to tell the board and Ben Kennard. I know the entire choir has been praying about this. I'm eager to meet your Mr. Moray."

Jane settled herself into her desk chair and tilted it back, resting her feet on the heavy metal wastebasket. "You'll like him. He's. . .he's. . .oh, I can't think of words to describe him, but he's fantastic!"

"If you say so, I'm sure he is. I had better start calling everyone with the good news. Thanks, Jane, for coming up with this idea and making it work."

"But I—"

He interrupted her. "I know—you didn't do it—God did. But He used you to accomplish it. You were a willing vessel. I'll see you tomorrow night at rehearsal."

Keene didn't come out of his bedroom the rest of the day, but while Jane worked, off in the distance she could hear the faint sounds of *Down from the Cross* as the audiotape played. Keene was already at work on the cantata.

The same thing happened the next day. At noon, she had trouble coaxing him to come out long enough to eat a bowl of the broccoli-cheese soup she had prepared especially for him. After drawing a crude map showing the way to the church, she left his office at five with plans for them to meet in the church parking lot at 7:15.

He had already parked his BMW by the time she arrived. A light evening snow had blanketed Providence, causing everything to be slick underfoot. Keene rushed to open her door when she pulled into the empty stall beside him, taking her arm in his as they moved to the church's side entrance. Once inside, they brushed the snow from their clothing and headed for the sanctuary.

While they walked, he scanned the hallways. "This is a beautiful building."

Jane nodded in agreement then took his hand and tugged him along, moving down the long hallway with its many classroom doors on either side.

He stopped long enough to peek into an open classroom. "I wasn't expecting anything like this."

She gave him a grin. "We have indoor plumbing, too." She yelped when she felt a slight pinch on her arm. "And electricity!"

Keene pushed open one of the big double doors when they reached the sanctuary, holding it so they could pass through.

Ben Kennard quickly left his place on the platform and rushed toward them, his hand extended. "Mr. Moray. What a pleasure to meet you. Jane has told us all about you."

Keene gave the man's hand a hearty shake. "Knowing Jane like I do, I'm not sure I want to hear that. We have worked together closely the past few weeks. I'm afraid she knows all my bad habits."

Ben continued to shake his hand. "Believe me, it was all good. You have a real fan in Jane."

"I know."

They walked toward the front of the church with Keene tightly latching on to Jane, cupping her elbow with his hand and sending her a smile that made her toes curl.

She felt a flush rise to her cheeks. "I—I thought maybe it would be best if Keene just listened to our practice tonight, to kind of get a feel for what we've been rehearsing."

"Good idea." Ben reached into his attaché case, pulling out a copy of *Down from the Cross* and handing it to Keene. "You'll want a copy—"

Keene held up the one he had brought with him. "Already have one. Jane gave me hers—the accompaniment tape, too." He motioned to an area off the platform, in the center of a front pew. "Why don't I sit there? That way I can see the faces of the people in the choir as they sing. I want to get to know everyone."

After Ben introduced Keene and explained he had graciously consented to take on the lead part and the pageant would go on as planned, everyone took his or her place. They bowed their heads, and Ben thanked God for sending Keene to them by way of Jane, then practice began. Though Jane tried to focus on the choir director, her gaze kept inching off toward her boss. To her surprise, he was mouthing the words without even looking at the book. Then she remembered the many hours, both yesterday and today, she had heard the faint sounds of the audiotape being played while she worked. He had already begun to memorize the music.

At the conclusion of one of the best practices they had ever had, Ben smiled at his group of happy singers. "Okay, gang, listen up! This Saturday is the first of our all-day practices. Again this year, the Women's Ministries group has offered to provide our lunch, so all you will have to bring is yourself. I know it's going to be tough to give up all your Saturdays between now and the time we actually begin our performances, but those of you who have sung in past years know how important these all-day practices are if we are to do our best for the Lord. This is your service to Him. Hopefully, your number one priority. Plan on arriving at nine, and we'll try to have you out of here by four, no later than five." He turned and gestured toward Keene. "It won't be necessary for you to be here all day, Mr. Moray. I'll work with you on a schedule so you'll only need to be here for the time in which you'll be involved."

Keene rose and stepped up onto the platform, facing the choir. "May I say a few words?"

Ben nodded. "Of course."

"First of all, it's nice to be a part of this dedicated group, and I have to say I'm impressed with your singing. I will admit, when Jane first approached me, I thought she was crazy. But"—he smiled in her direction—"when she began to tell me how *Down from the Cross* had been canceled due to Jim's illness, and I saw the look of disappointment in her eyes, I actually found myself wishing I could do something to make her feel better, never realizing the very next day she'd ask me to sing Jim's part." He chuckled. "At first I thought her request might be nothing more than a joke, and I laughed, but then I realized she was dead serious. If anyone other than Jane had asked me to do this, I would have given them a definite no, instantly, without any consideration whatsoever. But Jane? I could never refuse her anything. Not after I turned her life upside down the day I ran a red light and—" He gave her a quick wink. "I'm sure you've all heard the story by now."

Karen gave Jane a playful jab with her elbow.

Keene lowered his head, gazing at the floor for a few seconds before going on. When he looked up at them again, his face was somber. "Jane is a Christian. I am sure most of you are, too. I will not make any pretenses. I am not, but I want you to know I respect your beliefs. I have played many parts in my life as a vocalist, but I have never played the part of Jesus. And although I do not believe in God, I can tell you being asked to play this role is quite humbling, and I am sure it will be the hardest role I have ever taken on. I will give it my very best. That's a promise."

Ben placed his hand on Keene's shoulder. "I'm sure I speak for everyone here, Mr. Moray, when I say we'll all be praying for you. Thank you for your honesty. It's much appreciated."

Turning back to the choir, Keene said, "I'll see all of you at nine on Saturday. Tell those ladies from that women's group to count me in for lunch. I plan to be here all day."

Ben grinned at him. "Jane told us you never do anything halfway. We'll see you Saturday, and welcome aboard!"

It seemed Keene shook hands with each of the choir members before he and Jane were ready to leave, greeting each one cordially and asking their names, telling them how nice it was to meet them. She watched, amazed at his sincere attitude. Then she remembered that this man was not only her friend, her employer, but he was Keene Moray and well used to meeting and greeting fans. She wondered if that smile was really sincere or merely a promotional tool. Either way, the choir members were enjoying it.

"You really didn't have to stay until the last person left, you know." Jane slipped her hand into the crook of Keene's arm and held on tightly as they walked onto the slick parking lot.

"I know, but they're a great bunch of people. I really enjoyed watching them this evening. I think we're going to get along just fine."

The night air felt cold, and a slight breeze had come up, whirling the snow about their feet, giving her an excuse to press in close to him as they walked. "Were you really serious about being there all day Saturday?"

He cupped his warm hand over hers and smiled down at her. "I have to learn an entire cantata. What better way than to follow the book and sing it along with the choir?"

"But you don't have to learn the entire thing, just your part."

"Sorry, but that would never work for me. To do my best I have to know everyone's part, feel the emotion, and see the drama. I cannot just step in and sing. It has to come from here." He took his hand away from hers long enough to point to his heart. "If I'm going to do this, Jane, which I promised you I would, I'll put as much effort into it as I do any of the operas I sing or any of the concerts I perform."

She realized his words should have made her happy, but a thread of disappointment surged through her instead. "Oh, I forgot about your reputation. Who knows? There may be someone from the newspaper or a television station in the audience. You wouldn't want to let them see anything less than a stellar performance."

He stopped walking, grabbed her by the shoulders, and with a deep frown, spun her around to face him. "Look, let's get something straight right now. Yes, you are right about me wanting to give a stellar performance, as you called it. That has been my creed and my goal since the first concert I ever gave—to give my audiences my very best, and I have always done that. Even on nights when I was so sick I could barely hold up my head. If I were singing *Down from the Cross* for an audience of one, I would still give it my very best. That is me, Jane. That is what I do. The performance I give for your church will be the best performance I am capable of giving—regardless of who may be in the audience."

She felt awful. How dare she question his motives, especially after he'd been concerned about her and her church's problems enough to step in and help, taking away from the valuable time he'd set aside to come to Rhode Island and learn a new opera? She lifted her tear-filled gaze to his. "I'm. . .I'm so sorry, Keene. My stupid comment was way out of line. I had no business questioning your motives. Can you forgive me?"

Hoping he understood, she felt a great sense of relief when his intense grasp on her shoulders began to relax. Even in the dimly lit parking lot, she could see her words had hurt him. *God, why do I barge ahead like that? Speak without thinking? I only hope Keene can forgive me. I hope You can forgive me!*

"It's okay," he said softly, still peering into her eyes. "I think I deserved that. I have made some pretty crummy remarks about your God and Christianity. No wonder you doubted me."

"Regardless, I had no right to question your dedication to your profession. I knew—"

He raised his hand to silence her. Then without a word, he gently traced her lips with his fingertip. "Forget about it, okay?"

"But, Keene, you've—"

Suddenly she felt his lips on hers, and she froze, not sure how she should react. Keene Moray was holding her in his arms, kissing her. What should she do?

He backed away slightly then rested his forehead against hers. "I—I couldn't help myself," he murmured as he continued to hold her in his arms. "You looked so kissable."

Jane stood motionless, afraid to breathe or even bat her eyelids.

"You're not mad at me for kissing you, are you?" he asked in a whisper.

"N—no," she finally managed to whimper.

"Would you get mad if I kissed you again?"

Her heart banged against her chest so fiercely she felt sure he would notice. "No."

His lips touched hers again, and she thought she would die of happiness right there in the church parking lot. The moment was wonderful. Spectacular! And she never wanted it to end. Without meaning for them to, her arms wrapped themselves about his neck, and her fingers twined themselves through the slight curls at his nape. Though the pleasant smell of his aftershave made her woozy, she reveled in it.

"Whew," he said, finally releasing her. "I'd better let you get home. It's later than I realized." He reached out his hand.

Confused, Jane stared at it, caught up in the moment, his kisses still fresh on her lips.

"Your keys," he said with an impish grin.

"Oh!" She yanked them from her pocket and watched while he opened her door.

"I've really enjoyed this evening," he told her after she climbed in and rolled her window down.

She struggled to find her voice. "Me, too."

"I'm glad you talked me into this." He gave her a teasing smile. "See you in the morning."

Still having trouble finding words, she simply nodded. Keene gave her a slight wave and headed toward his car.

Jane's fingers rose to her lips as she watched him crawl into the BMW and start its engine. "I think I'm in love!" she nearly shouted, remembering the sweet touch of his lips on hers.

"Be careful, My child. Be very careful," a still small voice whispered from deep within her heart.

～∽◆∾～

Again, on Friday, Keene spent most of the day in his bedroom, the faint sounds of *Down from the Cross* filtering out from the crack beneath his door. Though neither mentioned their impromptu kisses, their relationship had changed. Jane couldn't exactly put her finger on it, but Keene's smile radiated tenderness, and his voice sounded a little softer. Several times during the day when they would pass in the hall or at lunch, he would slip an arm about her waist and pull her to him.

She even noticed her own response to him had changed. She no longer thought of him as her boss or the famous opera singer, but as. . . What was he to her? She was not quite sure. However, she knew her feelings toward him had changed drastically in the past twenty-four hours. Her every thought now centered on him. Her actions centered on him, too. She wanted to please him in every way. She also noted how much more protective she had become of him. No more did she pass phone calls to him that she thought he might not want. She screened them closely as if she were the FBI. No one could get to him without satisfying her that the call was important. *I am being ridiculous,* she told herself when she hung up from a very heated discussion with a fan who insisted on speaking with Keene. *Who do I think I am anyway? I am certain he got along just fine before I came along!*

The next call came from his agent, Brian Totten. She put the call through immediately and went back to work filing some of the new music he had ordered. But suddenly, even with the door closed to Keene's room, she could hear him shouting at Brian. She couldn't make out the words, but obviously Keene was upset about something.

Five minutes later, he stormed into the office. "I can't believe the gall of that man!"

Jane spun her chair around to face him. "Is. . .is there a problem?"

He towered over her, his hands on his hips, his eyes blazing. "Yes, there's a problem. He is having a fit because I agreed to do this for your church. Not because he's afraid of me taking the time away from my preparation for next year's season, but because he's worried about getting his commission! Can you believe that? With all the money I've paid him over the years!"

She rose and placed a hand on his arm. "I'm sorry, Keene. I never meant to cause trouble between you and Brian."

He shook his head as if trying to shake off his negative feelings, then wrapped his arms about her and pulled her close, nestling his chin in her hair. "You haven't caused any problems, Jane. Brian and I have a round like this a couple of times every year. But what really ticks me off is the trouble the union is giving me."

Her jaw dropped. "Is there a chance you won't be—"

"No, don't even think it. I will work things out with them. One way or another, I'll handle it." He tilted her face up to his, his frown replaced by a smile. "You've changed my life, Jane. I cannot tell you how much I enjoy being around you. You are a breath of fresh air. My life was pretty routine before I met you."

"And I've messed up that routine?"

"Oh, yeah! Big-time, and I'm loving every minute of it."

He gazed into her face, and the tenderness she saw there touched her in a way no man had ever touched her before, sparking an entirely new set of feelings.

"I—I think I could fall in love with you." His words were just a feathery whisper, and she wasn't even sure she had heard them correctly. Surely Keene Moray could not be saying these words to her. Plain little Jane? That is what her father used to call her, and she had felt like plain little Jane all her life.

"Be careful, My child." The words coming from the deep recesses of her heart frightened her and made her pull away from him, though she wanted so much to declare her love for him, too. A love she could no longer deny. She took another step backward, pasting on a conciliatory smile. "I—I think I'd better go. I promised Mom I'd be home early, and. . .and. . .I—I have laundry to do."

He reached for her, but she sidestepped him, picking up her purse and car keys from the desk. "See you at nine?"

He let out a deep sigh and pulled his hand away. "Yes, I'll be at the church at nine. I could pick you up."

Shaking her head, she backed out the office door. "Thank you, but I'll drive myself."

∼≈∽

Keene waited until the door closed behind her then rammed a fist into the palm of his other hand. *You bonehead! What did you think you were doing? You just told that woman you thought you could fall in love with her! Whatever possessed you to do such a stupid thing? Jane is not like the other women you have known. Any other woman would have been bowing at your feet if you had mentioned the "L" word to them. Now you have probably scared her off.*

After plopping himself down in her desk chair, he tilted it back and linked his fingers behind his head. *What is the matter with me? The* love *word? Since I met Jane, I have even considered the "M" word!*

The phone rang, and he gazed at it for a long time before finally picking up the receiver.

"Hey, buddy, what do you mean, hanging up on me?" the voice asked.

Keene sat up straight, angrily anchoring his elbows on the desktop. "Look, Brian, get this straight! I am only going to tell you one more time. I *am* going to sing in that church's Easter program, and nothing you or the union can say or do is going to stop me."

"But you know the rules. I hope you've made that church aware of what it's going to cost them to hire you."

Keene narrowed his eyes, wishing Brian were there so the man could see the dead seriousness on his face. "Don't worry about it. I've got that covered. They already know the amount, and they've agreed to pay it."

"Hey, you're smarter than I thought you were."

"But I also told them if the offerings they take every night don't measure up to the agreed-upon amount—"

"Not measure up? What about my—"

"Cool it, Brian. Let me finish. I told them they could go ahead and write out a check for the full amount and I would, in turn, make out a check to them for the difference and give it back to them, and they could consider it my gift to the church."

Brian laughed into the phone. "Wahoo! Good thinking, Keene. They get their little Easter pageant, I get my full commission, and you get a nice write-off! Good job, old buddy."

"Yeah, that should make everybody happy, and my tax man will love the idea."

"But what's with you, man? You don't go to church. I've heard you tell people you don't even believe in God. Why this sudden change and devotion to some church?"

Jane's adorable image immediately popped into Keene's mind. "You wouldn't believe it if I told you."

The next morning at exactly 8:45, the BMW moved into a parking space in the Randlewood Church parking lot.

❧

Jane was standing by the piano going over one of her solos when Keene entered the sanctuary. She stopped cold when she saw him, not yet feeling comfortable about singing in front of him. Not only that, her head was still spinning, almost as much as her heart, from the kisses in the parking lot Thursday night.

"Places, everyone." Ben tapped his pen against the microphone. "Let's get started." He turned to Keene, who was standing in the middle of the platform as if unsure where he should sit. "For now, why don't you have a seat there at the end of the fourth row, in the baritone section?"

Keene nodded and moved into the chair, shaking hands with those seated around him and giving them a friendly smile.

"Let's start on page thirty-nine," Ben told them, flipping the pages in his book. He motioned to Jane. "Your first solo is on the next page, Jane. Why don't you come on up to the microphone so you'll be ready?"

She cast a quick glance Keene's way as she moved into the aisle. Although she was still nervous about singing in front of him, her thoughts were on the kisses they'd shared, and her knees began to wobble. Finally, she moved into position, and the music started. She tried to concentrate, to become Mary as Ben had suggested, but with Keene so near she found it hard to do. *Lord, please settle my mind. I want to sing for You. Keep my mind focused on You alone, and may the words Keene hears as we sing* Down from the Cross *cause him to be aware of his sins and make him realize his need for You in his life.*

A calmness washed over her as she gazed at the words in the book in front of her, and suddenly she was Mary. The emotions Mary must have felt became her emotions. All thoughts of Keene disappeared, and the only face before her became the face of Jesus. When it came her time to sing, she opened her mouth and sang for her Lord.

◆

Keene stared at her, amazed at the quality of her lovely alto voice and the way in which she sang. Each note was crystal clear, her phrasing perfect. He listened carefully, knowing each word was coming from her heart. How many times had he tried to do the same thing? Sing an opera or a concert from the depths of his heart? And failed? Oh, perhaps the audience had not known it, but he had. It had been hard to muster up feelings for some of the roles he had sung. Meaningless stories and plots. Some of them silly and amazingly dull. Yet he had given them his all, but it had been with great effort. With Jane, there seemed to be no effort at all. Her singing came out that way because her emotions were sincere, pure, and he envied her. She was singing to God. The God she knew—and he didn't.

At noon, the entire group enjoyed the light lunch the women had provided, took a fifteen-minute break, and then went back to work. By four o'clock, they reached the place in the book that called for Keene's first solo.

"We'll skip this part until later," Ben said, motioning toward Keene.

Keene rose quickly. "I'm ready. There's no need to wait."

Ben motioned toward the microphone. "Great. Let's do it."

The pianist began, the choir did a short lead-in, and everyone waited breathlessly to hear the magnificent voice of Keene Moray.

Chapter 6

Keene took a deep breath and, with a smile he couldn't contain, began to sing in a high-pitched, falsetto soprano voice.

Every choir member's eyes bugged out, and they stopped singing and stared at him. Even the pianist stopped playing. Other than Keene's ridiculously funny voice still singing, the sanctuary was engulfed in silence.

When it became apparent he could stand it no longer, he gave a booming laugh that echoed throughout the big room. "It's a joke, folks!" he said, a giant grin plastered across his face. "I wanted to break some of the tenseness I felt. Look"—he held out his arm and pinched it—"I'm human. Please don't treat me like some freak. I am one of you now. We're in this together."

Somewhere in the top row, someone began to applaud, and soon the entire choir broke out with laughter and applause.

"He's really funny!" Karen said to Jane. "You must have a blast working for him."

Jane gazed at Keene, her heart filled with admiration and pangs of love. "Yeah, a blast," she said, grinning, once again remembering how wonderful it felt to be held in his arms. "You can't imagine what a blast."

Ben gave the pianist her cue to start again, and this time the magnificent voice of Keene Moray sang the words with feeling and emotion. By the time he finished his part, tears flowed from the eyes of almost everyone in the choir loft, including Ben Kennard.

Karen dabbed at her eyes with her sleeve. "How can he sing those words that way, with so much feeling—words right from the scripture—and not believe in God?"

"That's what I want to know." *Speak to his heart, God. As he memorizes each song, may his mind be filled with Your Word. I pray, through hearing and singing this music, Keene will turn to You. And, Lord Jesus, keep my witness pure. You know the temptations that face me every day I work with him. I—I love this man.*

"Got any plans for this evening?" Keene asked Jane as they walked to their cars. "I'd like to take you to dinner."

She couldn't help but smile. "I'd love to go to dinner with you—on one condition."

He tilted his head with a slight frown. "Oh, and what might that be?"

"That you'll go to church with me in the morning."

He tapped his finger on his lips thoughtfully. "I was planning to spend all day working on *Down from the Cross*."

"We can go to the early service at 8:30."

He locked his arm in hers. "You drive a hard bargain."

She smiled up at him, trying desperately to keep from looking at his lips. "Take it or leave it."

He pulled her toward her car. "I'll take it. Wear something nice. I am taking you to Capriccio's on Pine Street. The food is exceptional, the service is unparalleled, and the atmosphere is very romantic. You will go crazy over their seafood. I'll pick you up at seven."

She gave him a coy smile. "Seven will be fine. That way you can get a good night's sleep and make it to the early service."

<hr>

Keene had not prepared himself for the lovely creature who greeted him at the door when he arrived at seven. Wearing a simple black sleeveless dress, a string of pearls about her slender neck, and a pair of high-heeled black strappy sandals that made her legs look fantastic, the woman standing before him, with her shoulder-length dark hair swept up into an elegant French roll, bore very little resemblance to the woman he'd left only a few hours ago. That woman had been wearing a ponytail, jeans, and a sweatshirt. This woman was a real knockout, and she smelled nice, too.

"I hope I look all right." She did a graceful pirouette.

Words failed him. He responded with a low, drawn-out whistle. "All right? You're gorgeous!"

"I—I could change. I have a blue suit—"

He latched on to her arm. "No! You're perfect the way you are. I just wish I'd brought a can of mace."

"Mace? Why would you need that?"

He tugged her close to him, wrapped his arm about her waist, and whispered in a low, husky voice, "To keep all the men at the restaurant away from you."

Her nervous laugh made him smile. Actually, just being with her made him smile. Until he came to Providence, he had smiled very little. Or at least honest smiles. He had put on more false, on-demand smiles than he cared to remember. It was part of his job. But an honest, all-out smile from his heart? There had not been many. Until Jane came into his life and into his heart.

When they arrived, the maître d' took them to their table, calling Keene by name. Jane, who said she rarely had seafood, asked Keene to order for her, then oohed and aahed over the lobster as she dipped each bite into the drawn butter. They laughed their way through a pleasant meal, and to Keene's mind the evening ended all too soon. As they walked through the dingy, dimly lit hall with its torn carpet and burned-out lightbulbs toward the apartment she shared with her ailing mother, Keene had a sudden urge to take her away from all of this. Show her the world he lived in. Give her the fine things of life she had apparently never had. But why? She deserved so much more, yet he could not remember a single time since he had met her that she complained about her living conditions. How different she was from the many other women he knew. Each day, his appreciation for Jane and her values increased, and he found her more alluring than ever.

"I will see you at church in the morning, won't I?" she asked him while they lingered in the hallway.

"You'll see me before that. I'll pick you up at eight. You surely don't expect me to attend my first church service by myself, do you?" He slipped his arm around her waist and hugged her to him as emotions he had never experienced before took hold of him.

She smiled up at him. "Then you'd better make that 7:30 if you want to go with me. I have to be there early. The choir always goes over its special a time or two before we go into the service."

He frowned. "I forgot about you singing in the choir. Does that mean I'll have to sit by myself?"

She looped her arms about his neck and gave him a lighthearted smile. "Just during the first part. After the offertory, we go sit with the congregation. I usually sit on the front pew. Since I sing in the choir, I'll have to stay until nearly noon. I'm sure you won't want to sit through all three services. I can catch a ride home with Karen."

"Front pew it is. I'll save you a seat." He gazed into her eyes, amazed at her simple beauty. There was no pretense in Jane's life. No facade. No cover-up. She was who she was, and he loved that about her. With Jane, he could relax—be himself. Be the real Keene Moray, not Keene Moray the performer, and it felt good.

"I—I guess we'd better call it a night. I'm sure Mom is waiting up for me. I'd like to introduce her to you, but she hasn't been feeling well lately. Maybe another time."

"I'm looking forward to. . ." He could no longer resist her cherry pink lips, and his mouth claimed hers in a sweet, gentle kiss. When she did not pull away, he allowed his kiss to deepen. The feelings that flooded over him were a total surprise. He had never felt quite like this before. These were not the kind of feelings the guys at the gym talked about when they discussed the women in their lives. These were weird and wonderful feelings. Feelings of love and passion and, yes, even protectiveness. He wanted to scoop her up in his arms and carry her off to some faraway island where she could be his alone, without the pressures of everyday life and the demands of the world. *What am I doing, holding her and kissing her like this?* He backed away slightly and tried to shake such foolish thoughts from his brain. Other than the job she performed each day for him and singing in the cantata, they had practically nothing in common. Not only that, but she was a devout Christian. Her whole life centered on God. He did not even believe in God!

"Keene, is something wrong?"

Her words brought him back to reality. "Wrong? No. I—I'd better be going." He pulled his arms from about her waist after planting a brotherly kiss on her forehead. "See you in the morning."

Looking confused and a little embarrassed, she unlocked the door and moved quickly into her apartment.

Keene watched the door close behind her, his mind in a muddle. Jane Delaney had really messed up his life.

All night he lay sleepless in his bed, staring at the ceiling. He promised himself there would be no more kissing. From now on, things were going to be strictly business between them. Well, not exactly business, but he could not, and would not, allow their relationship to go beyond friendly. For both their sakes. It was not fair to lead her into thinking there could be any future for them. Future for them? What a ludicrous idea. He was a well-known performer with a brilliant career. A star in the field of music. He had only begun to tap the possibilities that lay ahead of him. He did not need a wife, and certainly not children—not with his busy schedule and his lifestyle of travel and glamour.

Jane, on the other hand, seemed to have no further ambitions than to marry someday and have children. She had no interest in social status, beautiful clothing, fine homes, or the other things money could buy. Obviously, the biggest problem separating them was this crazy, all-consuming love and devotion she had toward the God he did not believe existed! Even if they were attracted to one another in a way neither of them would admit, how would they ever get around such an obstacle?

Very little was said between them on the way to church the next morning. Despite his original intention to stay and take her home, he let Jane insist on riding with Karen and left alone after the first service.

༒

With so much to learn in such a limited amount of time, Keene kept mostly to himself the next few weeks, closing up in his room all day, taking only minutes out for a quick bite of lunch at noon. Though they often laughed and joked with each other, Jane could feel the strain in their relationship. She loved this man, no doubt about it. "Why," she asked God every day, "would You bring Keene into my life? Didn't You know I'd fall in love with him?"

To glorify My name, child.

"How, Lord?"

Trust Me, Jane. Trust Me.

∼❧∼

Checking the calendar on her desk, Jane shook her head. Only one week before the first public performance of *Down from the Cross*. So far, things were going quite well. Keene had his parts down pat, their first full dress rehearsal was scheduled for the next day, and every single ticket had been given out with hundreds of calls coming in from people who desperately wanted to attend but hadn't gotten their tickets earlier or who had just heard about it.

The church board was overjoyed with the response. Nearly every day since the word had gone out that Keene Moray would be performing the lead in *Down from the Cross*, there had been either an article in the newspapers or a blurb on TV or radio. Instead of having to call and ask for coverage, the reporters were calling them, clamoring for interviews and any interesting tidbits they were willing to give them. Every one of them expressed interest in doing a feature story about Keene.

She whirled her chair around at the sound of the office door opening.

"Jane, explain this to me."

She rose quickly.

He handed her his music book. "How could any man walk on water? I find it hard enough to believe that Jesus did, but it says here that Peter did, too."

She took the book from his hands, knowing full well the line to which he was referring. "Peter could only do it because Jesus told him to come to Him. When Peter took his eyes off Jesus, his faith wavered, and he began to sink."

Keene eyed her suspiciously, his brow creased. "You don't really believe all that, do you? Or that Jesus raised people from the dead?"

"Yes, Keene, I do believe it, and I believe all the other miracles we read about in God's Word."

"Then you're way more gullible than I am!" He shook his head while closing the book and stuffing it under one arm.

"It's not being gullible, Keene. I believe because I have faith that what God says is true."

He gave her a puzzled stare.

"God's Word says, 'Faith is the substance of things hoped for, the evidence of things not seen.' The entire eleventh chapter of Hebrews is filled with stories of faith."

"Taking things by faith seems kind of stupid. Like believing in fairy tales."

"Do you ever fly in a commercial airplane?"

"Of course. Who doesn't?"

"Do you personally meet the pilot before your plane takes off?"

"No."

"Do you ever board a plane without meeting the people who made that plane or those who serviced it at the airport?"

"You know I do."

"And you tell me you don't take things by faith?" A smile crossed her face as she gave his arm a playful pinch. "I rest my case, Mr. Moray."

He appeared thoughtful, his eyes locked with hers. "You really believe all this Bible stuff, don't you?"

She couldn't help but laugh. "Of course I believe it. I'm so *gullible* I even believe the part on the inside cover of my Bible where it says 'genuine leather'!"

He held the book out again. "How about the part where it says Jesus rose from the dead?"

Her expression sobered. "Yes, Keene, I do believe Jesus rose from the dead, and that He's sitting in heaven right now, at God the Father's right hand. And I also know He's preparing a place for me."

"A mansion? Like the words in one of the parts I sing describes?"

"Absolutely." *God, help Keene to continue to dwell on Your Word.*

"Remember that Bible you gave me? I've been reading it some. When I have a chance," he quickly inserted. "Some of it actually makes sense." He headed for the door but stopped and turned to her. "You know, it amazes me the way the people at your church work so hard. I mean, I have watched men building sets, some painting backgrounds. Women working tirelessly creating costumes. The choir members rehearsing hour after hour each week and never complaining. None of these people is being paid a penny, yet they work harder and with more dedication than any of the professionals I have worked with over the years. And to top it all off, they're nice! I like them."

The ringing of the doorbell brought a halt to their conversation. She rushed to answer it.

"Well, who are you?" the attractive woman dressed in a tight-fitting red suit asked, eyeing Jane from head to toe.

"I—I'm Mr. Moray's assistant."

Without being invited, the woman stepped into the living room and looked around. "Nice place, but certainly not as nice as his New York apartment, or the one he stays at when he's in London."

"May I tell him who is calling?" Jane asked, in awe of the woman's audacity, the way she waltzed in without even announcing who she was.

"Tell him his little Babs is here. Come to see him all the way from New York City," she drawled out in a Southern voice. Jane recognized both the name and the drawl instantly. Babs was one of the women who kept calling Keene.

He rushed into the room and took the woman by her hand. "Hey, Babs, what are you doing here? I wasn't expecting you."

Babs draped her arms about his neck and pressed her skinny frame against him. "I'm here to see you, sweetie. You haven't been returning my phone calls. I was afraid something had happened to you, so I just hopped on a plane and came here to see you."

Giving Jane a quick sideways glance, he grasped the woman's wrists and pulled her arms away from his neck. "You should have let me know you were coming. I don't have one free minute to spend with you. I'm. . .I'm in rehearsals."

Babs ran a manicured finger down his sleeve, lowering her lip in a pouting manner. "Babs needs to spend time with her Keene. She misses him."

Jane covered her grin with her hand. This woman was coming on so strong it was ridiculous. Surely, Keene could see through her. *Is this the kind of woman he is attracted to? Is this why our relationship has suddenly cooled off?* She swallowed the lump forming in her throat at the thought. *Relationship? What relationship? All there has ever been between Keene and me is a few kisses and an "I think I'm falling in love with you" comment during a weak moment, and even that I'm not sure I heard correctly. If there is any relationship between us, I'm afraid it's all one-sided.*

Babs, not to be discouraged, slid her arm into Keene's and pouted up at him again. "I'm hungry. Can't you take me to some nice place for lunch? You have to eat!"

He pulled free of her grasp and took a step away from her. "We're having lunch catered in. Pizza."

To Jane, the look on the woman's face was priceless. His answer seemed to take all the steam out of her unladylike advances.

"I'm sorry, Babs. I wish you'd called before coming to Providence." Keene sent another glance Jane's way, sucked in a deep breath, and let it out slowly, then focused his attention on Babs. "I hope you have shopping or other things to do while you're here, because I simply don't have a minute to spare for the next two weeks. My rehearsals are going to take all my time." He took hold of her arm and gently ushered her toward the door. "Please don't think I'm rude, but I must get back to work. Maybe we can get together next time I'm in New York."

Babs shot a glance over her shoulder and sent a frowning glare at Jane. "Does *she* have anything to do with your busyness?"

Opening the door for her, he gave Babs a stern frown. "I won't even dignify that question with an answer."

The woman huffed out the door without returning his good-bye, her stiletto heels clacking on the hallway's marble floor.

"I'm sorry you had to see that," Keene told Jane after he closed the door. "That woman has been driving me crazy for months. I have told her repeatedly to quit following me around! I had one arranged date with her when I was performing in London. That's it, but since then she has been calling constantly and turning up unexpectedly at almost all of my performances. She even turned up in Japan!"

"From the phone calls that come in every day, I'd say she's only one of your many admirers." Jane chuckled. "I hope they're not all like that."

He shrugged. "Sadly, most of them are. Spoiled little rich girls with time and money on their hands and overindulgent mommies and daddies to cater to their every whim. And to think I used to like that kind of woman."

With a grin, she tilted her head and raised a brow. "Used to?"

"Yeah, used to."

She wished she knew what that statement meant, but when he did not offer to elaborate, she decided to let it drop and get back to work.

༄

Keene stopped outside the closed office door on the way to his room, tempted to go inside and try to give Jane a better explanation about Babs's impromptu visit. But he decided against it and moved on down the hall. *What's with me?* he asked himself, settling down in a comfortable barrel-backed chair. *Not long ago, I considered Babs funny and charming, the life of the party. Now, with her pushy ways, she seems obnoxious. Her very presence repels me.*

He didn't have to ask himself that question a second time. He knew what was wrong with him. He was comparing all the women he had ever met with Jane, and all of them were coming up short. But why? What did Jane have going for her the others did not? Although he considered her beautiful, she was certainly no more attractive than most of the women who continually called him. Her wardrobe consisted of either jeans and a T-shirt or sweats. Those women were always beautifully coiffed and adorned in the latest Paris fashions. She mentioned she had taken a few college classes. Most of the others had graduated from prestigious women's colleges. If Jane outshone them, there was only one reason that made any sense. She was who she was, 24/7. No dishonesty. No put-on. No trying to impress people by pretending she was something she was not. Her life was pure, sweet, and innocent. And what made her this way? He hated to admit it, but her faith in God and her gentle ways were what made her beautiful.

༄

The dress rehearsal went even better than Keene expected it would. Though he had not said anything to Jane or anyone else from the church, he had been quite concerned about working with a group of nonprofessionals. The idea of the cast showing up onstage wearing chenille bathrobes and Roman soldiers carrying cardboard swords covered with foil had terrified him. In some ways, he was putting his career on the line, particularly now that *Down from the Cross* was garnering so much media coverage and promised to get even more once the performances started. However, the costumes were nothing like he had expected.

Whoever created them had done their research. Everything rang true to the times and the traditions, and anyone could tell by looking that no labor or expense had been spared. The costumes rivaled the most expensive, elaborately designed costumes in any of New York City's finest productions.

It was nearly five o'clock before Keene walked Jane to her car. "Long day, huh?"

She stretched her arms above her head and brought them down, letting her breath out slowly. "Um, yes, but a good one. I'm really excited about *Down from the Cross*. Not just because you are singing the part of Jesus, but also because I think the entire cantata has a wonderful message. It's my prayer that many in our audience will hear the plan of salvation through it and accept Christ as their Savior."

"You really do believe all of this, don't you?" The hurt look on her face told him his words had offended her.

"Keene," she began, her pale blue eyes filled with an unexpected intensity, "could you have been around me all these weeks and doubt my sincerity? You keep asking me that question. Yes, I do believe it. All of it! And I wish you did, too!"

He stepped in front of her and grabbed both her wrists. "Why does this always have to come back around to me? Has your God made you my keeper?"

Anger flared in her eyes, and she blinked away her tears. "Yes, I think He has! At least, He put us together so I could share my faith with you!"

His laugh came out haughtier than he intended, and he instantly wished he could take it back. "Next you'll be telling me God made me run that stoplight and ram my car into yours, breaking your leg!"

She lifted her face to his, glaring at him as she jerked her hands free. "He might have. He can do anything He wants!"

"You are incorrigible!"

"You're stubborn!"

"You're gullible!"

"You're blind!"

Nose to nose, Keene thought about the ridiculousness of their argument and how childishly they were both behaving, and he broke out in laughter.

Jane stared at him for a moment then joined in.

"We're quite a pair, aren't we?" he asked, still laughing as he whipped an arm about her waist and lifted her up in his arms, her feet dangling above the pavement.

She giggled and nodded her head. "I wonder if God is up there laughing at us."

He chuckled, too. "I don't know, but if He is, I hope He's watching!" With that, he set her down and planted a kiss on her lips. When she didn't protest, he gazed into her eyes then kissed her again as her arms willingly slipped around his neck.

When he finally released her and set her back down on the pavement, she gave him a long, hard stare he was not able to interpret. "Got any more names you want to call me?" he asked sheepishly.

"Yes, as a matter of fact, I do," she said, putting her fists on her hips. "Thoughtful. Talented. Handsome. Generous. A great kisser." A smile touched her lips. "Want me to go on?"

"No, it's my turn." He let loose a boisterous laugh and once again snatched her close to him. "You're beautiful. Kind. Caring. Smart. Funny. Terrific to be around." He suddenly turned serious. "And the best example of Christianity I've ever seen."

Jane reached up and cupped his cheek with her palm, smiling the sweetest smile he had ever seen on a woman's face, causing his heart to do funny things in his chest. "Keene, nothing you could have said would have pleased me more, except that you, too, want to accept God's plan of salvation for your very own. My prayer, since the day I met you, was that God would use me and my love for Him to reach you." She stroked his cheek with her fingertips. "God loves you, Keene, and so do I."

He stood mesmerized by her words while she climbed into her little car and drove away.

Chapter 7

Coral Mills, a longtime member of the church who was approaching her nineties, glanced at her watch. In only ten minutes, the first performance of her church's annual Easter pageant would begin. She reached across her daughter-in-law and took her son's hand. "I'm so glad you two could make it tonight."

Ralph Mills patted his mother's hand with a smile. "Me, too, Mom. I'm not that interested in the pageant, or whatever they call it, but I am really excited about hearing Keene Moray sing. Amy and I have been fans of his for a long time, but we've never heard him in person."

Amy's eyes widened as she peered around the crowded sanctuary. "I've heard the tickets have been gone for weeks. I'm sure glad you were able to get tickets for us, Mother Mills."

"So am I." Coral breathed up a prayer of thanks. *Lord, You know how long I have been praying for my son and his wife. They need You. Please, speak to their hearts through the music tonight. I so long to see them saved before I pass on. I'm trusting in You, God!*

Ralph glanced at the program in his hand then leaned across Amy. "Mom, I'd like to ask you a question. I don't claim to be a Christian, but I don't understand how come your church will allow a man to play the part of Jesus. Jesus was supposed to be perfect. How can you let a mortal man who is not perfect portray His part? Isn't that a bit sacrilegious?"

Coral smiled, glad he was considering such things. To her, it proved he was open. "Oh, son, the first year we decided to do an Easter pageant, there were all sorts of questions like this from our regular members. We didn't want to do anything that would bring reproach upon our Savior's name or the church's name, so we considered every conceivable complaint we might encounter and discussed it at great length. Your dear father served on the board at that time."

Ralph squeezed her frail hand. "I guess they must have decided it would be okay."

"Oh, yes. They decided it would be okay, but only after hours and hours of discussion and prayer. In the end, the board voted unanimously to go ahead with their plans. The church's sole purpose is to spread the gospel of Jesus Christ to all who would hear, to nurture and train Christians young and old, and to provide support

81

and encouragement to one another. Our yearly pageants do that very thing. Thousands of people from our community attend these special events. Many of them have never even been in a church, except to attend weddings and funerals, and this is the only time they will sit and listen to God's Word. There is something about hearing it set to music and seeing it portrayed in costume with an appropriate setting that makes them see the reality of what actually happened two thousand years ago and how God's love and plan relate to them."

He gave her an adoring smile. "Thanks, Mom. I knew if anyone would know the answer, it would be you."

As the lights dimmed and the prelude began, the Mills family, together with twenty-five hundred others, settled back in their seats to enjoy *Down from the Cross*.

~◦~

Jane wanted to fade into the woodwork. She felt like this every time she sang before an audience. Ben Kennard always reminded his singers that being nervous before a performance helped them to sing even better. It meant they had to be dependent upon God to get them through it, rather than their own talents.

She had not seen Keene since two o'clock when he left his apartment, saying he had an appointment. Which seemed strange, since he had not written an appointment on his calendar. Well, no need to worry. If he hadn't made it to the church by now, Ben Kennard would be tearing his hair out.

She hurriedly took her place in the darkness onstage with the others, ready to sing *Down from the Cross* to their waiting audience. The orchestra finished the prelude and spotlights focused on a scene set high up in one corner where there appeared a group of Jewish leaders, donned in fine velvets and decorative hats, discussing what they were going to do about this man called Jesus who had caught the attention of the people.

When the upper lights dimmed, other spotlights flooded the stage, which was filled with people milling about the marketplace, shopping and visiting, with children running to and fro. Someone hollered, "Jesus is coming," and they all began cheering and waving palm branches high in the air. Jane, in her costume as one of them, waved her palm branch, too, straining for the first view of Keene as he entered, playing the part of Jesus. Though she'd been to all the dress rehearsals and sung *Down from the Cross* many times, she'd never experienced the sensations that overtook her when she and the others sang, "Hosanna, Hosanna, blessed be the Lord!"

He moved about the crowd in his long robe and sandals, smiling at people, lifting children and tousling their hair. The way he'd let his beard and his hair grow long over the past seven weeks, and the marvelous job the makeup people had done in bronzing his skin and applying touches of color around his eyes, had all changed Keene's appearance. In her eyes, he now looked more like the likeness she had envisioned of her Lord than like Keene. *Oh, Father,* she prayed, waving her palm branch with the others, *even though this man is not a Christian, use him to win souls. May everyone forget this is an earthly man and think about Christ.*

Though Keene never spoke a word in the first scene, he was a powerful presence onstage.

She hurried offstage with the others while the next scene shifted to the temple where people were exchanging their money. She watched from the wings while Jesus moved in quickly, asking them what they thought they were doing and reminding them they were making His Father's house into a den of thieves, ordering them to stop. When they did not, He overturned the moneychangers' tables. He did it with such passion, Jane found herself forgetting she had a costume change and had to hurry while the next scene, the one in which the Jewish leaders met with Judas to arrange Jesus' capture, played above the stage.

Moving onstage once more, she watched Jesus move about the happy crowd, smiling, healing the sick, making the lame to walk, the blind to see, casting out demons, even raising the dead to life again. It was clear Keene was no stranger to performing. His stage presence was flawless and every cue right on time.

By the time it came for Jane's first appearance as Mary, Jesus' mother, her heart was so full of God's love that she found herself eager to sing, with all the nervousness she'd expected gone. But as she stood on the stage waiting for her cue, Jesus entered, bleeding, battered, and beaten, limping and falling under the weight of the heavy cross He bore on His shoulder. The scene of her Lord suffering like that, the flesh on His back literally torn from His bones, was nearly too much to bear, and she found herself weeping, her chest heaving with each sob. When they led Jesus to the cross, Jane cried like she had never cried before, her heart breaking for the Savior who had bled and died for her. *Lord, I will never get through this without Your help!* But when she opened her mouth to sing, even though she could not stop crying, she felt God's presence, and she sang it to Him.

When she came to the last few lines of the song, Jane fell to her knees and, raising her face heavenward, sang, "How can this be happening? How can this be true? Can it be, dear Father God, that you are crying, too?"

Even though she had sung those words many times, they took on a whole new meaning. Through tears of sorrow, she fixed her gaze on the body of Jesus, sprawled out upon the cross while the soldiers began to hammer the nails into His hands and feet, one by one, the sound echoing across the great auditorium. Jane had to wonder how Keene felt, lying there with his hands and feet being anchored to the cross, the pounding of the hammer so close to his head.

When the soldiers finally finished their heinous deed, along with the other performers and the audience, she watched them raise the cross with its sign nailed above His head: *JESUS OF NAZARETH—KING OF THE JEWS.* There Jesus hung in agony and excruciating pain, stripped nearly naked, taking on the sins of the world. It touched her heart so deeply she had to close her eyes lest she faint.

Like a bolt of lightning, Keene's voice rang out, splitting the heavy silence. "Father, forgive them, for they know not what they do!"

Like the scriptures said, the soldiers began to mock Him and cast lots for what little clothing He had left. Jane moved instinctively toward the cross and fell at its foot, weeping as Mary would have wept, feeling many of the emotions Mary must have felt. The man singing the apostle John's part knelt beside her, wrapping an arm around her. Writhing in pain, Jesus lowered His head, His face nearly covered with blood from the crown of thorns pressed into His tender flesh, and asked him to take care of His mother.

"If Thou be the Christ, save Thyself and us!" one of the thieves hanging on the crosses on either side of Him called out sarcastically.

The other thief lifted his weary head and rebuked him, saying, "Dost thou not fear God? We receive the due reward of our deeds, but this man hath done nothing!" Then the man turned his face toward Jesus. "Lord, remember me when Thou comest into Thy kingdom."

With great effort and pain, Jesus turned to the second thief. "Today thou shalt be with Me in paradise."

Jane watched, and from her heart she whispered, "Oh, Keene, you are like the first thief, denying the existence and deity of God. Listen to what you are saying! Don't turn your back on Him, or like that thief you'll spend eternity in hell." But he was too far away to hear.

They moved through the other scenes, each one so special, so touching. When the last scene ended, showing Christ ascending into heaven, and the final song had been sung, Pastor Congdon moved to the center of the platform and extended an invitation to anyone who wanted to accept the risen Christ as their Savior. Hundreds of people moved into the aisles, crowding around the front, weeping and eager to commit their lives to God. Jane watched from the wings, breathing a prayer of thanks to her Savior for using this means to reach souls for Him and for letting her be a part of it.

❧

Coral Miller held her breath when, out of the corner of her eye, she caught sight of her son rising and extending his hand toward his wife, with tears rolling down his cheeks. Amy, too, was crying. But before the couple moved past her and headed for the altar of the huge sanctuary, Ralph bent and kissed Coral's cheek, whispering how much he loved her and appreciated the prayers he knew she'd been praying for both him and Amy.

She watched her precious son slip an arm around his wife's waist and the two of them move forward to accept Christ as their Savior, her heart throbbing with grateful thanks to her Lord. For over forty years, she had begged God to bring her son into the fold, but he had never expressed the slightest interest in the things of God. Now, just months before her ninetieth birthday, God was answering her prayers.

Leaning back against the seat, Coral bowed her trembling head and folded her arthritic hands in prayer, tears running down her wrinkled cheeks. *Father God, You have blessed me more abundantly than I have had any right to ask. Thank You for letting me live long enough to see the deepest desire of my heart fulfilled—Ralph and Amy accepting You as their Savior. Lord, You can take me home anytime now. I'm ready to go.*

∼∾∽

Keene was waiting for Jane when she finally made her way to her car. She had stayed late to help counsel some of the young people who had come forward. She was surprised to find him there. The last time she saw him, he had been signing autographs for the many people who crowded around him after Pastor Congdon dismissed the audience.

"Well, we did it! Everything went off like clockwork. The members of Randlewood Church can be very proud of what they've done." He took her hand in his and gave it a squeeze. "You were wonderful as Mary. I knew you would be."

She sent him a shy smile. "Thank you." Though she was grateful for all the hours of practice he had put into *Down from the Cross*, she had to admit she was a bit turned off by his boastful tone. She had been so sure once Keene performed the part of Jesus, he would be so touched by the message he would fall to his knees and accept her Lord. But apparently it had not happened.

Patience, My child. Patience.

"You were amazing tonight, Keene. The audience thought so, too."

He gave her chin a playful jab. "I'm supposed to be amazing. I've had many years of practice, remember?"

"I mean. . .you sang with such meaning, I thought—"

"That I believed what I was singing?"

"Yes, I'd. . .I'd hoped so."

With a finger, he lifted her face up to his and gazed into her eyes. "Sorry, kiddo. I hate to disappoint you, but all I was doing was portraying a part and doing it the best I could. I still don't believe in God."

She blinked furiously, trying to hold back tears. "I'm still going to pray for you."

"By all means do, if it'll make you feel better, but don't count on any miracles." He grabbed her hand with a slight chuckle, linking his fingers with hers. "I'd invite you out for a cup of coffee, but I'll bet you're tired." He took her car key and opened her door. "Don't worry about coming in early tomorrow. I probably won't be in the office myself until about noon."

She nodded. "Thanks, but I'll be there long before that, and you're right. I am tired. I'll hold you to a rain check on that coffee."

"You've got it!"

❧

"Did you see your picture on the front page of this morning's newspaper?" Jane asked excitedly, waving the paper at him when he came into the office the next day. "And there's a wonderful article saying how you graciously stepped in when the lead singer was unable to perform due to his illness. They were quite complimentary about *Down from the Cross*, even mentioned how many people responded to the invitation to accept Christ."

He gave the paper a casual glance and began to shuffle through the mail. "That's nice. When you're finished reading it, put it in my publicity file."

"That's all you've got to say? That's nice?" She sent him a look of exasperation, upset that he had focused his attention on the mail and not on her words. "I was thrilled with the article."

He placed the mail back on the desk with a guilty grin. "I'm sorry, Jane. I have something else on my mind. I'm glad the writer of the article did a good job. What else did it have to say?"

She frowned. "What it failed to say could cause the church a real problem!"

"Oh? What's that?"

"They never mentioned that people needed to get a ticket to attend, and all of those free tickets have been given out! I talked with Pastor Congdon a few minutes ago, and although he wants a good turnout from the community, he is afraid many folks will come to the church expecting to get in, and there won't be any seats for them. We sure don't want to turn them away."

"He's right. It would be a shame for them to drive to the church only to find they have wasted their time. But I'm sure your pastor will figure out a way to handle things."

"I hope so. It also says you gave an amazing performance, and those lucky enough to be in the audience were given a real treat, as the Randlewood Community Church portrayed the true meaning of the Easter season."

Shivers assailed her when he sauntered close and circled her waist with his arm.

"It. . .it also talks about the beautiful costumes and sets and how they were all made by volunteers from the church who. . ."

She could feel his warm breath on her cheek. "Who spent many hours. . ."

She sucked in a gasp of air when his lips brushed her eyelid. "Who spent many hours working in. . ."

His lips trailed to her cheek, and she thought surely her heart would stop beating. "Working in the church annex. . ."

"Yes, go on, I'm listening," he whispered, lifting her hair and feathering the words against her ear.

"In. . .in the church annex, using their own tools and—"

He pulled her into his arms, and his mouth claimed hers, the newspaper falling to the floor. All her resolve to keep their relationship on a friendly basis dissolved into nothingness. She leaned into the strength of his arms, enjoying his kiss more than she knew she had a right to enjoy it. Enjoying Keene's kisses and letting her love for him escalate would only mean trouble and disappointment. She tried to back away, but he held her fast, his lips once again melding with hers.

"Don't pull away from me, Jane, please."

The phone rang once.

Twice.

A third time.

His arms wrapped around her even more tightly. "Let the machine get it." His voice was husky.

Placing her palms on his chest, with a prayer to God for strength to resist this man's charms, she pushed away and hurried to the phone, her hand going to her throbbing heart. "Ke–Keene Moray's office. This. . .this is Jane. How may—"

"Let me talk to Keene," a man's voice said, cutting into her salutation.

She covered the phone with her hand. "I think it's Brian."

Keene stared at the phone then took his time crossing the room to take it from her. "Hello."

By the time he finished his conversation with Brian, Jane had already started working at the computer, bringing his fan database up-to-date, and the spell that had come over them both had been broken. It was back to business as usual.

She finished her work and hurried home to fix supper for her mother and tend to her needs before heading back to the church for the second night's performance.

To her amazement, when she arrived at the church at six o'clock, she saw a number of panel trucks parked around the side door, with uniformed men scurrying in and out. The logo on their uniforms and the trucks said "Superior Audio and Video Services." What were they doing there? This close to performance time?

"Can you believe what's happening?" one of the wardrobe women asked while she sewed a new button on a costume. "They've actually installed huge television screens in the church gymnasium and the fellowship hall to take care of the overflow crowds. Last night alone, Pastor Congdon said they had to turn away over eight hundred people, and that did not count all those who called begging for tickets. Isn't God good?"

Jane nodded, trying to take it all in. "Yes, He is." She walked hurriedly up the steps to the gymnasium, meeting Pastor Congdon on his way down. "Oh, Jane. Glad you're here. Guess you've heard about the big screens they're setting up. After last night's performance and that wonderful article on the front page this morning, plus all the television and radio coverage we've gotten, the chairman of our board called an emergency meeting, and they voted to have the screens installed to take care of the overflow crowds we're expecting all week. Isn't that great? Just think of all the additional people who will see our cantata and be touched by the Lord."

She frowned. The magnitude of what was happening was overpowering. "But can we take care of all those people? Do we have enough counselors?"

"It won't be easy. My secretary has been on the phone all day, calling those who are qualified to be counselors and asking them to be here every night. Plus, don't forget we have a counselors' class going on right now, and although those people haven't received their certificates yet, they're trained and ready to go. That should give us at least another fifty. In addition, of course, there are the people like you, who sing in the choir, who are also qualified to lead them to the Lord. Beyond that, we will just have to leave it all in God's hands. Good thing we just added that new parking lot. We've even had to call on our college-age group to help the other guys direct traffic!" He headed on down the stairs after once again thanking her for bringing Keene to them and asking him to sing Jim's part. She leaned against the banister and stared off into space. *Lord, when You do something, You really do it in a big way!*

Even though they had expected it, people filled the sanctuary long before curtain time, with both the gym and the fellowship hall holding capacity crowds, some folks even sitting on the floor. Jane kept an eye out for Keene, but knowing he was probably in makeup, she went ahead and dressed in her costume. Though she had hoped to be over her jitters by now, she still found her hands shaking at the thought of singing before such tremendous crowds. But hadn't God come through for her the first night? Calming her and giving her courage? Of course He would do it again. After all, she was doing it for Him, and she knew He would never let her down.

Like she had done the night before, Jane stayed in the wings whenever she was not required onstage, watching and listening to each scene. The scene in which the religious leaders brought the harlot to Jesus especially touched her this night, when they asked Jesus what should be done with the woman who had been caught in sin. Those men were trying to trap Jesus into answering and condemning Himself by His own words. He knelt and wrote in the imaginary sand, and

Jane's heart stirred. When Jesus stood and took the harlot's hand, giving her a tender and loving smile, and said, "Neither do I condemn thee. Go and sin no more," Jane was not able to hold back her tears. How could Keene go through this scene and still ignore the truth of God's Word? *Don't you see, Keene? Don't you get it? God loves you and is willing to forgive you of your sins. Why, oh, why don't you let Him?*

Once again, when the pastor gave the invitation, the front of the sanctuary filled with those seeking forgiveness. With so many to counsel, Jane and most of the other members of the choir moved in to help. The leader assigned her to those in the church gymnasium. But when she passed through the lobby on her way up the stairs, she caught sight of Keene, surrounded by his many fans, smiling and signing autographs, and she felt such a burden for this man. *Why couldn't he have been one of those kneeling at the altar?*

She barely saw him Tuesday and Wednesday. With the studying and memorizing for *Down from the Cross* behind him now, he was spending most of his time closed up in his room, working on the new opera. Friday afternoon, he appeared in the office doorway saying he had an appointment and volunteering to drive her to the church that evening. She accepted, hoping to get another chance to talk to him about God's Word. If he didn't accept Christ soon, he would be on his way from Rhode Island, headed back to New York, and she would never have an opportunity to witness to him again.

On the way to the church, he chattered endlessly about the positive publicity the media had been giving their production and how many churches had been contacting his New York agent about him doing the same type of thing for them.

"I told my agent to let them know I don't plan to make a habit of this sort of thing," he said with a chuckle, maneuvering the BMW into a parking stall. "This was a one-time deal, and I only did it because a friend asked me to."

"It must be very gratifying to know you're in such demand." Although her words were meant to be a compliment, with the inflection in her voice they did not come out that way.

He turned off the car and stared at her. "Was that a left-handed compliment?"

She forced a teasing smile. "I only meant. . .well. . .I have been answering your phone, you know. I am definitely aware of how many invitations you get. Brian keeps me well informed, too. He takes every opportunity to remind you did this against his advice."

He chucked her under the chin. "Brian works for me, remember?"

She laughed with an exaggerated, "Touché! How well I remember."

Leaning closer, he asked, "Aren't you going to wish me luck with tonight's performance?"

"No."

He tilted his head quizzically. "You're not?"

"No, I don't believe in such a thing as luck. Good or bad. Nothing with God is happenstance."

"Oh? Knowing you, I should have realized that's what you'd say."

Again, Keene delivered a flawless performance. So did the choir and the soloists. Not that Jane wasn't still nervous. She was. But by now she knew her faith in God would see her through, and it did.

While standing onstage, watching Jesus serve the disciples at the Last Supper, Jane nearly lost her composure. The scene took on a reality she never expected. Knowing Judas was going to betray her Lord, she wanted to shout out to Him, to tell Him Judas had negotiated His life for a few coins, barely the price of a slave. But while Jesus sang to those assembled, declaring His love for them, she kept her silence. It was only a pageant. There was nothing she could do to change history, and even if she could, she would not want to. It was necessary for God to send His only Son to earth to die for the sins of man in order to redeem them. Judas, though he was a betrayer, was part of that plan.

Later, when Jesus led His disciples to the Garden of Gethsemane to pray and they all fell asleep, she wondered how those who were a part of that closely knit group, the ones who should have loved Him most, could have slept so easily knowing He would soon be taken from them.

She watched Judas betray Christ with a kiss, identifying Him as the one the soldiers were after, and the way Peter cut off one of the soldier's ears. She could not help it. She sobbed openly. How it must have grieved God to see His Son treated this way. Peter denied his Lord three times. How many times had Keene denied Him? Did Keene even care how many times he had denied God's call on his life? Did he not realize God had sent him to this very place, at this very time, that he might learn about Him and accept Him before it was everlastingly too late?

Clothed as Mary, Jane stood in the dressing room and lowered her head, once again praying for Keene's salvation.

In My own time, child. In My own time.

Chapter 8

Although Keene stayed in his room all morning and Jane had very little contact with him, she knew something was wrong. She sensed it. She could feel it in her bones.

A little before noon, when she asked him what he'd like for lunch and he told her, "Nothing," she knew she'd been right. An avid eater, Keene never missed lunch or any other meals. With two more performances to go, she knew he needed his nourishment.

"But I don't want any lunch," he told her in a firm tone when she knocked on his door for the third time. "I told you, I'm not hungry."

She turned the knob and pushed it open a bit, unsure how he would react to her invading his privacy. "Please, Keene, would you at least let me fix you a bowl of soup? I noticed you had a can of chicken noodle soup in the cabinet when I was looking for the cinnamon."

He yanked open the door and glared at her. "How many times do I have to tell you? I don't want anything to eat!"

"Okay, okay! I get the message!" She backed away, holding her palm up between them. "I'm just concerned about you, that's all. But if you want to get cranky about it, I'll get out of your hair." Lifting her chin in the air, she turned on her heel and strode off down the hall. "Just don't say I didn't offer!"

He followed her, catching up with her when she reached the office. "Look, I'm sorry! Give me a little slack, will you?"

She spun around, knowing she had fire in her eyes. Sometimes the man drove her crazy! "Give *you* a little slack? How about you giving *me* a little slack? I only wanted to help you!"

He tried to place a hand on her shoulder, but she brushed it away.

"Okay!" He cupped his palm against his neck. "If you must know—I have a sore throat. I felt it coming on last night and gargled with some lemon juice before I went to bed, hoping it would be gone by this morning, but it wasn't. In fact, it's getting worse by the hour."

"A sore throat?" She frowned the way her mother used to do when Jane was ill. "You poor thing! What can I do to help? Did you call a doctor? Have you taken any antibiotics? What about throat lozenges?"

"I've tried all of those things already, and yes, I called my doctor. But my throat is tighter and sorer now than it was this morning when I got out of bed."

She began to wring her hands. "Oh, Keene, you should've told me instead of shutting me out."

"And have you worried about tonight's performance?"

She stepped up beside him and slipped her arms around his neck. "Of course I'm worried about tonight's performance, but it's you I'm worried about most of all. Do you think this may be from having to perform so many nights in succession?"

"I—I don't think so. My doctor—" He shrugged and paused midsentence. "Never mind."

Grabbing his hand, she tugged him toward the barrel-backed chair. "You sit right down here while I go fix you a lemon gargle. Fortunately, I bought some lemons at the store yesterday when you sent me to pick up some of those bagels you like so well."

"I know. I used one."

"I was planning on making a pitcher of fresh lemonade to surprise you." She pointed her finger at him. "Stay. I'll be back in a minute."

When she returned, she had a cup of warmed lemon juice slightly diluted with water. She handed it to him. "Gargle."

Tilting his head with a grin, he said, "Yes, Mother."

She watched him take sip after sip of the lemon juice, gargling after each one. "Does it hurt very much?"

He nodded, wrinkling up his face after the last swallow.

Taking the empty cup from his hand, she leaned over him. "Let me look."

Turning away and rearing back from her advance, he frowned. "At my throat?"

She laughed. "Of course, at your throat! What did you think I meant? The empty cup?"

He covered his face with his hand, his embarrassment showing. "You really don't want to look at it, do you?"

"Of course I do. Now open your mouth and let me see."

Leaning his head back, he opened his mouth slightly.

"More."

He opened it a little wider.

"Keene! Open your mouth!"

She peered in when he finally obliged and screwed up her face. "It's really red! Are you sure this only started last night?"

"Okay, maybe two days ago."

"And you didn't say a word about it to anyone? Not even your doctor?"

"I kept thinking it would go away."

She leaned forward, hovering over him again. "I'm going to pray for you."

He bowed his head and shut one eye, peering at her with the other. "I suppose I have to close my eyes, don't I?"

"Yes, you do," she said, giggling. Then her tone turned serious. "Lord God, it's me—Jane—Your servant. I love You, Father, and I come before You asking You to touch Keene's throat and make it well. There are two performances left. If he isn't able to sing, they'll have to be canceled, and the thousands of people who would have heard Your Word when *Down from the Cross* portrayed the last weeks of Jesus' life, His horrible death, and His resurrection will not hear it and acknowledge their need of You. I don't ask You so it will glorify our church, the choir, and all those who have worked so hard on the production, or for Keene. I ask it so Your name will be glorified. That through the words and the music many may come to know You. And if it be Your will, Lord, may Keene come to know You, too. He is such a fine man, and we praise You for sending him to us and for his willingness to step in and take Jim Carter's place. Touch him, God. Even now, heal His throat. Use the talents You have given him to magnify Yourself. I pray these things in Jesus' name, knowing You can answer prayer above and beyond what we ask or think. Amen."

❧

Keene listened to the prayers of the woman in front of him, her forehead resting against his, her words on his behalf touching his heart in a way he'd never known. *Can all this God stuff she keeps spouting at me be true? Is there really a God up in heaven with the power to heal His children if they ask Him to?*

No one had ever prayed for him like this before. Perhaps his mother had, but never in front of him. Never laid her hands on his shoulders and prayed so earnestly. And if he ever needed prayer for the healing of his throat, it was now. Now more than ever.

He opened his eyes when she said, "Amen," hoping she wouldn't see his tears. Rising slowly, he opened his arms wide, and she slipped into them, looping her arms about his waist and hugging him tight. "Thanks, Jane. I—I don't know if your prayers will help, but they sure can't hurt."

She raised misty eyes to his, and the concern he saw there melted his heart. "Oh, ye of little faith."

"I—I wish I had your faith."

She pressed herself against him, burying her head in his chest. "It's yours for the taking. All you have to do is believe."

"It. . .it can't be that simple," he murmured softly against her hair.

Again, she lifted misty eyes to his. "What's really keeping you from it, Keene? Pride?"

"Maybe. And I'm not even sure, if there is a God, that He'd want me."

"Wouldn't want you? Of course He wants you! He said, 'Whosoever will may come.' That is you, me, the guy down the street, the woman behind the counter

93

at the grocery store, the greeter at Wal-Mart. Everyone. He isn't willing that any should perish but that all would come to Him." She reached up and cradled his cheek with her hand. "Be a man and face up to the fact that you're lost, and turn your life over to God. None of us knows what a day may bring. Tomorrow may be too late."

He folded her hand in his, bringing it to his lips and kissing her palm. "You really are concerned about me, aren't you?"

A tear rolled down her cheek as she gazed into his eyes. "Yes, Keene. I am truly concerned about you. You're. . .you're very important to me."

He stared into the pale blue depths of her eyes. He wanted so much to hold her and kiss her, but the reality of his sore throat hit him when he tried to swallow. The last thing he wanted to do was give his illness to her, so he held back. Looking at her longingly, he wished he could tell her how he really felt at that moment. But he couldn't. He knew, even if he told her that he loved her, she could not and would not accept that love. But he couldn't bring himself to lie to her either. To let her believe he accepted her God when he had not. From the beginning, he had been truthful with her. He could not start lying to her now. It would not be fair. "Keep praying for me, Jane. Who knows, someday I just might begin to believe in your God."

"I have to go now," she said, backing away and pulling free of his grasp. "The UPS man is coming to pick up some packages, and I don't have them ready." She motioned toward his bed. "Why don't you take a nap? It'll be good for your throat. I'll come back in an hour or so with another cup of lemon juice."

He gave her a shy grin. "You think your God needs the help of the lemon juice to heal me?"

She wagged a finger at him as she backed through the door. "He did make the lemons, you know!"

Keene watched her close the door then crawled into his bed and pulled the quilt up over him. His throat still hurt. He smiled, remembering her sweet prayer and the way she had knelt in front of him. Maybe this God thing would not be so bad after all.

At three, and again at four thirty, Jane brought warm lemon juice in to Keene, standing beside him until he had gargled with each drop. He almost hated to admit it, but his throat actually seemed a bit better.

She rapped on the door at five, saying she would see him at the church—if he felt like singing.

"I'll make it. I think the lemon juice is helping."

"The lemon juice or the prayer?"

From his place beneath the quilt, he snickered. "Both!"

At five thirty, he showered and dressed. Then he nibbled on the soft oatmeal bars and the fresh peach Jane had placed on a plate beside his bed after she reminded him he needed to get some food into his stomach.

By six thirty, he was seated on a stool in front of a makeup mirror while Shirley Gordon, one of the beauticians who had volunteered her services each night, applied bronzer to his face.

"Shirley, you're a Christian, right?"

She stared at his image in the mirror and gave him a weird look. "Sure, why do you ask?"

"You do know I'm not, don't you? A Christian, that is?"

"Yeah, I heard that you told the folks in the choir you weren't." She went back to applying the bronzer.

"And you really believe Christ died for our sins?"

"Sure."

"So you admitted you were a sinner?"

She tilted his face toward her and appraised her work. "Had to. Everyone's a sinner."

He frowned. "What could you have done that was so bad?"

She screwed the lid on the makeup jar and stared at him. "Hey, it wasn't any one thing that I did that made me a sinner. It was everything I did that separated me from God. The biggest sin of all was rejecting Him. I can't believe I put off confessing my sins and accepting Christ as my personal Savior as long as I did." She picked up a pencil and began darkening his already dark brows. "Close your eyes."

"So you're telling me it made a real difference in your life?"

"Difference? I cannot tell you what a difference. Not that everything has been rosy since then. It hasn't. We live in a mixed-up world with all sorts of temptations. Accepting Christ does not make you perfect. Far from it. But it does make you a sinner saved by grace."

He swiveled his chair toward her and grabbed her wrist. "Then why, Shirley? Why would anyone want to be a Christian?"

She paused thoughtfully, the pencil still in her hand. "Do you remember when you were a little boy and fell down and skinned your knee? Who did you run to?"

"My mother, of course."

"How about when you needed something?"

He thought about it before answering. "My mother."

"Who did you run to for comfort when the kids teased you or you felt bad?"

"My mom."

"And what did she do?"

He gave her a scowl. "She comforted me, of course, and told me everything was going to be okay."

Shirley leaned over him and dabbed her finger at his brow, removing a smudge. "Those are just a few of the things God does for us. He is always there waiting to kiss our boo-boos, supply our needs, and comfort us when we need comforting. My dad died when I was fifteen, and you know what? God promised to be a Father to the fatherless, and He was. Whenever I needed my dad's advice, I would go to my heavenly Father in prayer, and He always came through for me. My mom, bless her heart, missed him, too. God also promised to be a husband to the widows. I'm not sure she would have made it without my dad if God hadn't been there for her."

She pulled a tissue from the box on the counter and dabbed at her nose. "I'm a single mom, Keene, and I've had some rough times, believe me. There were many days when I was attending cosmetology school that I did not have the money for next month's rent. But I turned to God and laid my needs at His feet, and somehow the money always came in just in time. He supplied my every need and still does. He tells us to cast all our cares on Him, and do I ever!"

Keene gave her a warm smile, appreciative of her willingness to open up her heart to him. "I guess you'd highly recommend Him, right?"

Her thumbs-up appeared in the mirror. "Oh, yes, I highly recommend Him." With a wink, she pulled the plastic covering from his shoulders. "And if you're as smart as I think you are, you'll accept Him, too."

He rose and leaned toward the mirror, turning his face first one way and then the other. "You do a good job."

"Thanks. Oh, by the way, someone told me some big wheel is in the audience tonight, all the way from New York City."

"Big wheel?"

"Yeah. I think he said he was an editor from the *New York Times*. Probably came all this way to hear you."

Trying to appear nonchalant, Keene shrugged. "Could be."

～

Jane elbowed her way through the many people backstage and headed for Keene's dressing room, a classroom that had been assigned to him, anxious to check on his throat.

"Jane!" The voice came from somewhere in the throng of people near the wardrobe racks.

"Oh, hi, Pastor," she said, turning with a smile. "Can you believe the crowds that've been coming every night?"

"Amazing, isn't it? Sure glad the board voted to add those big screens. We never would never have made it without them, and the free-will offerings every night have been amazing. Even with the additional expense we've acquired, we'll more than adequately meet our budget, even after we pay Mr. Moray the full amount."

"Have you seen Keene?" she asked, scanning the wardrobe racks.

"No, but have you heard the managing editor of the *New York Times* is in the audience tonight? He called me when he arrived in town, asking for a ticket."

"No, I hadn't heard. I wonder if Keene knows he's here." She moved on past him, motioning in the direction of the classroom where she hoped to find her boss. "I'll be sure and tell him."

"There you are!"

Jane smiled warmly when Keene approached her. "How's the sore throat?"

He tugged her away from the hubbub of the busy wardrobe area toward the hall. "Better! Not gone. But better. I think the lemon juice gargle did it."

She lifted a questioning brow, a smile playing at her lips.

"Maybe the prayer," he conceded. "Guess we'll never know which."

"You'd better make sure to use that lemon juice gargle again tonight before you go to bed, and it wouldn't hurt to use it several times tomorrow. Maybe you had better hold your singing back a bit tonight. We don't want you to strain your voice and not be able to sing for tomorrow night's final performance." She snapped her fingers. "Oh, that reminds me. Did you know some editor—"

"Is going to be in the audience tonight? Yes, I heard about it when I was in makeup. If it's the guy I think it is, he's a pretty tough critic. I had better pull out all the stops tonight. I sure want a good review."

"But your throat!"

"I'll be careful, Mommy. I promise."

"I'll be praying for you," she hollered after him, watching him disappear into the crowd. She glanced at her watch then checked her makeup and garment in the full-length mirror mounted on the wall near one of the long wardrobe racks. *It's time to get onstage. The performance will begin in five minutes.*

Jane took her place after breathing a quick prayer for Keene, asking God to continue to place His healing hand on Keene's throat. She also prayed for the audience members, that God would open their hearts and minds while they listened to the gospel set to music.

Later in the performance, when it came time for the ascension scene, Jane hurriedly found a place in the wings where she had a full view of the stage. On each of the other six nights, she had been so busy helping everyone remove their costumes and hang them on hangers after her last time onstage, she'd missed it. The big platform was still clothed in darkness.

Suddenly a blinding light flashed, and in the center of the stage, Jesus appeared on a mountaintop, adorned in a pristine white robe, His arms stretched out wide, His countenance radiant. As He stood there, His face lifted toward heaven, the narrator's voice recited John 5:24. "Verily, verily, I say unto you, He that heareth my word, and believeth on him that sent me, hath everlasting life, and shall not come into judgment; but is passed from death unto life." When he finished, Christ ascended up into heaven.

On a small platform suspended up near the high ceiling, a spotlight trained on three trumpeters who heralded Jesus' entrance into heaven. Then a deep male voice boomed out dramatically over the speakers, "This. . .is my beloved Son, in whom I am well pleased."

On each of the previous six nights, she had thought Keene's performance could not have been improved. But tonight, even with his sore throat, he had outdone himself. Surely, it was because God, the Great Physician, had answered prayer and touched him. Then she remembered the New York editor. Could Keene have done his best for that man? And not for God?

She changed out of her costume and hurried to the gymnasium to help the other counselors, trying to put her crazy suspicions out of her mind. But when she pushed her way through the huge foyer, there was Keene, all smiles, standing with the man in avid conversation, nearly ignoring the many thronged around him seeking his autograph. She wanted to run off to some private place and cry. One more night. Just one more night. *God! Please!*

By the time the last person had left the gymnasium and Jane and some of the other women had helped the men straighten the chairs for the Sunday evening performance, the sanctuary was deserted. She cut through the semidarkened auditorium on her way toward the side door, but when she passed by the altar, she felt led to fall to her knees and pray for Keene.

Assuming she was alone, she folded her hands and lifted her eyes to the beautiful stained-glass window that graced the front of the church. She stared at the image of Christ knocking at the door, her heart clenching within her, and she began to pray aloud. She thanked God for bringing them through the past seven performances, for all those who had come forward to accept Him, and for touching Keene's throat. She thanked Him that her mother had felt well enough to stay alone in the apartment each evening. She praised Him for the way He led the church board into asking Keene to sing in Jim's place.

"Keene." Just saying his name sent a tingling flood of emotions wafting through her. "Lord, I'm so in love with this man it hurts, and I'm confused," she added. "At first, I thought I was in awe of him and his beautiful voice, but now I know that's not the reason. While I love his voice, it's not what drew me to him. It's the man, Father. Keene himself. Why did You let him come into my life? Didn't You know I'd fall in love with him?"

She pulled a tissue from her purse and blotted her eyes. "I don't care that he's famous. I don't care that he has fashionable apartments in both New York and London or a fancy car. I—I just wish he could love me the way I love him. But,

Father, the thing I long for most is that he would yield himself to You. God, I only want what's best for Keene."

⤚∾⤙

Hearing a voice, Keene held his breath when he returned to the church to retrieve the briefcase he had forgotten. Someone was kneeling at the altar! He pressed himself into the shadows of the dimly lit sanctuary, remaining motionless, not wanting to interrupt. Not even intending to listen until he heard his name mentioned by the person who was kneeling in prayer just yards from where he stood. It was Jane!

What? What did she say? She loves me? He took a cautious step forward, cradling his hand to his ear. *And she wants only the best for me?*

He continued to listen, barely moving a muscle, until she finally rose and moved slowly across the floor's carpeted surface toward the side door, dabbing a tissue at her eyes. Thankfully, she hadn't seen him. He lingered a few more minutes, his gaze locking on the stained-glass window of Christ standing at the door knocking. She had explained its meaning to him that first Sunday he attended the morning service and how it symbolized Christ standing at the door of our hearts. She told him how we have to open that door ourselves, from the inside, since there is no handle or knob on the outside. Sometimes, since he had been singing the part of Jesus, he had even felt that knock on his heart's door. But how? How could that be? He didn't believe in Jesus!

Sleep eluded him that night, no matter how many sheep he counted. The words of *Down from the Cross* filtered through his mind, mingled with the conversation he'd had with the New York editor, Jane's lovely face, and the scripture verses he'd read in the Bible she placed on his nightstand the first week she came to work for him. Before he came to Providence, he'd never thought of himself as a sinner, much less felt the need to confess those sins to God. A God he did not believe in. But being around Jane and the people of Randlewood Community Church made him wonder. *What if they are right? What if there really is a God, and I am turning my back on Him? Maybe I should consider this confession thing. I might even talk to Pastor Congdon about it sometime.*

But why? His time in Providence was about to come to an end. In a few weeks, he would be going back to New York City. Back to his old life of exciting performances, extravagant parties, lavish social events, and. . .and. . .boredom. If he were honest with himself, he would have to admit he'd had more fun working with Jane, listening to her tinkling laughter and sharing deli sandwiches and pizza for lunch, than he ever had at one of those stuffy parties. It did not make sense! Jane had so little to offer compared to the wealthy, high-society women who frequented those parties. Why, when he was with her, did he feel like a teenager on his first date?

Maybe once this pageant is over, Jane and I can get better acquainted. So far, we have been on her turf. Maybe that is the reason I find her so alluring. Flipping onto his side, he pulled the covers about his neck with a smile of satisfaction. *If she were on my turf, perhaps I would not find her quite so attractive.*

Then he remembered something Jane had said. "I could never have a permanent relationship with a man who doesn't share my faith."

Chapter 9

At seven the next morning, Jane phoned Keene's apartment to check on his throat. When he answered on the fourth ring with a sleepy "Hello," she thought about hanging up.

"I'm concerned about you. How's the throat?" She could almost see him running his fingers through his hair, squinting at the clock to check the time.

"Still sore, but improved slightly."

"I. . .I take it you're not going to church this morning?"

A big yawn sounded on the other end of the line. "Naw, I thought I'd sleep in. It's been a pretty grueling week, and I had a hard time getting to sleep last night."

"I'll see you tonight then."

Another exaggerated yawn. "Why don't I pick you up? It's right on my way."

"I hate to impose."

"No imposition. You know better than that. I'll pick you up at six. Okay?"

"Sure. I'll see you at six. And, Keene. . ."

"Yeah?"

"Nothing."

She was already waiting by the curb when he arrived a few minutes before six. He gave her a pleasant smile as he leaned across the seat and pushed her door open. "Hey, you're looking nice tonight."

"Thanks." She glanced down at her new jacket. She rarely wore anything this flamboyant, but she liked it and hoped he would, too.

"Looks good on you."

She felt herself blushing.

On the way to the church, they talked about everything but what was uppermost on her mind.

By the time they reached the church parking lot, it was already full, and Keene had to park on the street. "Looks like we're going to have another capacity crowd tonight." He took her hand as they walked toward the church. "I've got to get into makeup. Shirley is expecting me."

"Yeah, I'd better hurry, too. I promised the wardrobe lady I'd help her again tonight. Maybe I'll stop by your dressing room after I change into my costume."

She watched him as they entered the doors, and he moved on down the hallway, whistling some unfamiliar tune while he walked.

Jane helped the busy woman by checking over the costumes and making sure they were in the proper order on the racks then changed into her own costume and waited her turn at the women's makeup table. After she finished there, she headed for Keene's dressing room. She had to talk to him. By the time she entered, he was in full makeup and wearing the soft beige robe and pair of sandals for his first scene, Jesus' triumphal entry.

He slipped his arm about her waist. "I'm about ready to begin my warm-up. Are you here to check on my throat or to wish me good luck?"

With a heavy heart and a sigh, she forced a smile. "Actually, neither. I figured if your throat was still bothering you, you would have said something about it by now. And remember? I don't believe in luck, good or bad."

"Oh, yes, I forgot about that." He gave her a grin and wiggled his brows. "So that means you came to hear me warm up?"

"I love hearing you warm up, but I had another purpose in coming, Keene." Her heart pounding furiously, she gazed up into his eyes, hoping he would see her love for him and not be offended by what she was about to say.

"What is it, Jane? You're trembling." His voice was kind and filled with concern.

"I—I hardly know where to begin."

With his free hand, he brushed a stray lock of hair from her forehead. "Just say it. You know you can tell me anything."

She gazed into the depths of his dark brown eyes, promising herself she would not get emotional on him. "First, I have to tell you how wonderful it's been working for you these past few months. You've treated me with a kindness and gentleness I never expected."

"You've been a terrific employee. No one could've done a better job or been more dedicated than you."

"Then you stepped in, at great personal sacrifice, to sing Jim's part when your life was already full, learning and preparing for a new opera."

He bent and gently kissed her forehead. "No one twisted my arm. I did it willingly. For you."

"And you'll never know how much I appreciate it."

"But that's not what you want to talk about, right?"

"No, not exactly, but I'm leading up to it." She ducked her head shyly. "Since the day I started working in your office and you told me you didn't believe in God's existence, I've been praying for you." She lifted her gaze to his once again, feeling the need to look him directly in the eye when she bared her heart. "You are a fine man, Keene. Honorable. Respectable. And certainly talented. We have all been in awe of your breathtaking performances. Because of you and the way you have sung the part of Jesus the past seven nights, all of us have been drawn closer to our Lord. You've made us see how He suffered and bled and died for us."

He planted a soft kiss on her cheek. "I've done my best. I've given it my all, Jane."

"I—I know you have, but. . ."

"But what?"

"But if you don't believe in God, that also means you don't believe in Jesus. And if you don't believe in Jesus, then you must not believe in Easter." When he did not respond, she twined her hand in his, glad he had not seen fit to argue the point with her.

"The message of Easter isn't simply a story filled with symbolism and interesting thoughts. Everything portrayed in our Easter presentation actually happened to real people. God *did* send His only Son to earth. Christ *did* die a cruel death on the cross, taking our sins upon Himself. He *did* rise again and ascend into heaven to take His rightful place at His Father's right hand, and right now He's preparing a place for His children as He said He would."

"I never—"

"Let me finish, please. There's so little time left, and I have to say these things to you."

Giving her a weak smile, he remained silent.

"Each night, hundreds of people go to the front of the auditorium, Keene, to repent of their sins and accept Christ as their Savior because of seeing their need of God in their lives through your performance. I—I can't understand how you can sing the words and portray the part of my Savior like you do without it affecting you." She paused and caressed his cheek with her hand. "Is your heart so jaded and hardened by the world you can't feel the emotions your singing evokes in others?"

"Is that what you think? That I'm jaded?"

"I honestly don't know, but I'm so concerned about your soul. Promise me, tonight, as you sing each note, you will listen to the words with your heart. God loves you, Keene. I love you. Our pastor and choir director love you. The members of this church have learned to love you, and we've all been praying for you. Not for Keene Moray, the famous man who graciously bailed us out when our soloist became ill, but for Keene Moray, the caring man who has become our friend."

"But you—"

"Shh." She put a finger to his lips. "When you're up there hanging on the cross tonight, I'll be kneeling at your feet portraying the mother of Jesus, and I'll be praying for you, Keene, as I've never prayed before. Begging God to make you come to the realization that you are a sinner and to melt your hardened heart. He wants you for His own. Remember the stained-glass window in the sanctuary?

And how, though Jesus is knocking, He is unable to open the door because it has to be opened from the inside?"

He nodded. "I remember."

"Only you can open that door, Keene. That decision is up to you alone. No one else can open it for you. Think hard before ignoring His knock." After standing on tiptoe and kissing his cheek, she withdrew her hand and backed away slowly, her eyes still fixed on his handsome face, now bronzed with makeup. "The Easter story isn't just a pretty story filled with symbolism, lovely white Easter lilies, and beautiful music. It goes much deeper than that. It is the truest love story of all time. God loves you, Keene. I love you, too, and I want the very best for you. That best is Christ."

Jane turned and moved out the door of his dressing room, knowing she had done all she could and God was the God of miracles. Surely, it would take a miracle to make Keene swallow his pride and admit he was a sinner.

Pastor Congdon caught hold of Jane's arm as she moved into the wide hallway. "Is Keene still in his dressing room?"

"Yes, he is." Blinking hard, she turned her head away and scurried on down the hall.

❧

Keene stood staring at the open door. He had never seen Jane this emotional.

"Keene. I'm glad you're still here." Pastor Congdon hurried into the little room. "I'd like to pray for you before tonight's performance."

"Ah. . .sure. That'd be fine." *What is this? Stack it on Keene night? First Jane. Now Pastor Congdon?*

"Good. Would you kneel, please?"

Without replying, Keene lowered himself to one knee and bowed his head, feeling like a marauder in front of this godly man, Jane's accusing words fresh in his mind.

"Lord," Pastor Congdon began, placing his hands on Keene's shoulders. "I come to You tonight asking that, through this man who is so willingly giving of his time and talents, You will perform a great and mighty work. Use his voice as an instrument to speak to hearts, make Yourself real to those in our audience who have never accepted You as their Lord and Savior, and bring them to Yourself. Bless Keene, I pray, and may he feel the power of the prayer that has gone up for him. And most of all, may He feel Your touch upon his own life. Amen."

His hand still on Keene's shoulders, Pastor Congdon said with great sincerity, "You're a fine man, Keene. I am sure God has a special plan just for you. Thank you for everything you've done for us."

Keene rose slowly, his eyes fixed on the man's hand as it was extended toward him with a smile. "Thanks, Pastor Congdon," he muttered nervously, the prayer nearly overwhelming him. These people really cared about him. He reached out and shook the pastor's hand. "Being here, working with you and the fine people of this church, has been a wonderful experience I won't soon forget."

Suddenly the overture sounded. Glancing at his watch, Pastor Congdon headed for the door. "Guess you'd better get onstage. Remember, I'll be praying for you!"

"I will, and thanks." *It seems everyone is praying for me.*

∽◦✐◦∽

Putting on her Mary costume for the final time, Jane couldn't believe how quickly the week of performances had passed. Soon this year's Easter presentation would be over, Keene would be going back to New York, and she would be looking for a job.

But in some ways things had been different tonight. In each scene in which Keene had appeared, she noticed a difference in him. He had seemed more intense, more involved than she remembered him being the past seven nights. Was this the way it always was for him on the closing night of a performance? Knowing it would be the last time he would sing the part, did he put more of himself into it than on the other nights?

She moved into an area at the edge of the set, waiting for her turn to enter. Suddenly, just a few feet from where she stood, Keene appeared as Jesus, His body bowed beneath the weight of the cross. She listened to the words of the narrator reading passages from Isaiah as Jesus moved onstage. "He is despised and rejected of men; a man of sorrows, and acquainted with grief. Surely He bears our sorrows, and with His stripes we are healed."

Jesus stumbled and fell, and it was as if a dagger were plunged into her heart. How could her Lord have been treated this way? When He had done nothing but come to save people from their sins?

Stepping forward, she followed Him up the hill to Calvary, aching for the deep wounds His body bore from the many beatings He had suffered, the thorn of crowns piercing His brow, the blood running down His forehead and into His eyes, watching while the soldiers spat upon Him and jeered Him, shoving Him and making a mockery of Him. The script called for her to pretend she was upset and crying, but there was no pretense in the emotions racking her when she beheld her Lord suffering so. She could not hold back the flood of tears that overcame her. As Mary, she screamed out for them to stop!

But. . .they didn't stop.

Someone, a man from the throng that had assembled, took the cross upon his own shoulders when Jesus fell and carried it for Him, placing it where the soldiers directed.

Then, shoving Jesus down, showing Him no mercy, they placed Him on the cross, pulling his arms open wide while they held him there.

As it neared time for Jane to sing, she felt sure she would not be able to utter a word. She watched, feeling pain for her Lord, her breath coming in short, quick gasps and her chest heaving with each sob. But knowing she must do it for God, she pled with Him for the strength and the voice to go on. Moving closer to Jesus and lifting her face heavenward, she began to sing. With tears flowing down her face, she raised her voice to God. By the time she reached the final lines, she was weeping so hard she could barely get the words out, and she had to pause to catch her breath. *Sing it as Mary would sing it, Jane.* Ben's words, the words he'd said to her that first night they'd practiced her solo, came back to her. *For these few minutes, you are Mary, the mother of Jesus. Be her. Respond the way she would respond. Weep as she would weep. Cry out the way she cried out. Forget about the audience. Do this for Him, Jane. Your Lord. Your God. The One who took your sins upon Himself and died on the cross for you. Think of His pain, His agony as He hung there on the cross as Mary would have thought of it. Take on her personality. Her demeanor. And yes—her burden. If you cry—so be it! If you have to stop and compose yourself before you can go on—so be it! Become Mary, Jane! Forget who you are, and be who God wants you to be at that moment. Mary, the mother of Jesus, and sing it from the depths of your heart.*

Without orchestral accompaniment and holding her hands up to God, she sang the final two lines with all the emotion she had tried so hard to keep tucked inside.

"How. . .can this be happening?

"How. . .can this be true?

"Can it be, dear Father God"—*Help me, Lord!*

"That You are crying, too?"

The sound of the first nail being driven through Jesus' hand echoed throughout the sanctuary, the entire room falling into a riveting silence. Jane cringed at the sound.

Then the second nail was driven into His other hand, and it was as if she herself could feel the pain.

The soldier with the hammer stepped over Christ's limp and bleeding body and moved to His feet, securing one foot to the upright beam with a third nail. An audible gasp swept over the audience, many people turning their heads away.

The hideous sight made Jane sick to her stomach as the fourth nail pierced His other foot, anchoring it, too, to the beam. The sound penetrated her very bones. She would never forget it.

She leaned forward on a trembling hand, trying to get a look at Jesus' face as the soldiers moved in and lifted the cross into an upright position with Jesus hanging there. The sight was nearly too much to bear, and she wanted to turn her head away, but instead she kept her eyes fastened on Jesus' face, the reality of what He had done for her overpowering. Were those actual tears trailing down his cheeks? There was something in the expression on Keene's face. Something she had never seen before. A tenderness. A longing she had never witnessed, and her heart nearly burst with both love and pity for this man. He had so much and yet so little. *Speak to him, Lord!* her heart cried out.

"All we like sheep have gone astray," the narrator's words came slowly over the microphone. "We have turned, every one, to his own way, and the Lord has laid on Him the iniquity of us all."

Just as he had done every other night, Jesus lowered His head and tenderly asked the apostle John to take care of His mother.

Then one of the thieves hanging on a cross beside Him called out sarcastically, "If Thou be the Christ, save Thyself and us!"

Like they had rehearsed it, the thief on the other cross lifted his weary head and rebuked him. "Dost thou not fear God? We receive the due reward of our deeds, but this man hath done nothing!" Then, with great effort, he lifted his face toward Jesus. "Lord, remember me when Thou comest into Thy kingdom."

Gasping for air and in terrible pain, Jesus turned to the second thief, His mournful gaze fixed on the man.

Jane stared at Keene, waiting for his response, but he simply continued to look intently at the man, his chest heaving up and down as if he could not catch his breath.

The soldiers looked at one another, their faces filled with question.

One of the soldiers whispered, "Today thou shalt be with Me in paradise." But the man's helpful cue was ignored as Keene continued to stare at the thief, his eyes almost glassy.

From offstage, the stage manager called out in a low voice, "Today thou shalt be with Me in paradise."

But he, too, was ignored.

A buzz circulated through the audience. Something was wrong!

What was happening?

Why wasn't Keene saying his line? Surely, Keene Moray, the man who had sung many difficult parts to thousands of people all over the world, had not forgotten his lines. And if he had, why wasn't he taking his cues when they were repeated for him?

"Keene," Jane called out to him in a guarded voice. "Say your line!"

But he continued to hang there, his deep guttural breaths the only sounds coming from him and echoing out over the sanctuary's powerful speakers.

Chapter 10

It was all Jane could do to keep from shouting out the line to him. Off to one side, she noticed Ben slip onto the stage, an old robe from the wardrobe rack slung over his back to cover his street clothes. Cupping his mouth with his hands, he said in a lowered voice, "Keene! 'Today thou shalt be with Me in paradise.' Say it!"

Still no response.

The orchestra stopped playing, and all eyes fixed on Keene, battered and bleeding, his arms sagging with his body weight as he hung on the cross.

Once again, Ben called out. But still Keene did nothing but stare blankly at the thief hanging beside him, his chest rising and lowering as he sucked in deep breaths of air.

For the first time, Jane realized his tears were not only real, but he was sobbing from the depths of his being. Staying low, she crawled to the foot of the cross and, looking up at him, said in a pleading voice, "Keene! Say your line, please; everyone is waiting!"

As if he had suddenly come back to reality, he turned his head slowly and gazed down at her.

"Please, Keene," she implored softly, brushing away the tears from her cheeks. "Please."

Next he turned his head from one side to the other, taking in each face on the stage. Then his attention went to the soldiers who were standing at his feet, looking up at him with widened eyes, their faces filled with confusion.

"Get me down," he said in a whisper.

The soldiers looked to one another with bewilderment.

"Get me down."

The lead soldier looked toward Ben for direction.

With a frown, Ben shook his head. "Don't listen to him."

"I said, get me down," Keene said a third time, tugging on the fetters that held his arms.

"I think we should take him down," one of the taller soldiers told the others. "Maybe he's having a heart attack."

"No, don't!" another said. "Not without Ben saying it's okay."

With beads of sweat now covering his tired face and his body perspiring visibly, Keene took several more deep breaths. "Take me down from this cross."

Ben hunched over and moved to the foot of the cross. "We can't, Keene. It will ruin the cantata. Say your line."

Keene lifted his eyes heavenward, and on his face was a look of sheer torment.

Apparently forgetting his plaid shirt and khakis, the stage manager hurried to stand beside Ben. "Keene, are you okay? Do you need a doctor?"

A murmur went through the audience. Some began to stand, their curiosity getting the better of them. Others fell on their knees by their chairs, praying, while others simply sat staring.

"Get—me—down—from—this—cross—now," Keene said in a firm voice, again struggling against the cords binding his wrists and feet. "I have to get down from this cross! Now!"

Ben and the stage manager looked at each other then motioned for the soldiers to take him down. Several of the men from the crowd stepped forward to help hold his weight while another man climbed up the crude ladder mounted on the back side of the cross, loosening first one arm and then the other. Someone on the floor unbound his feet. Wrapping the long length of fabric that had been prepared to secure him across his chest and under his arms, they carefully lowered him to the floor.

No one spoke. Every eye in the sanctuary focused on Keene. As soon as his feet touched the floor, he pulled free of the wrap and fell at the foot of the cross, his back hunched, weeping loudly and gasping for air.

Having no idea what had happened or why he asked to be taken down from the cross, Jane wanted to throw her arms around him and hold him. But instead, like everyone else on the stage, she remained motionless, confused by the scene playing out before her eyes.

≈≈

Finally composing himself, Keene pulled himself to his knees. Every line of dialogue and every song he'd memorized while preparing for *Down from the Cross* came rushing to his mind. All thoughts of the people in the audience, the two men hanging on their crosses, his agent, his career, his future, had been set aside. Nothing else mattered except his relationship with a jealous but loving God. He, Keene Moray, was a sinner, just like Jane had said he was. Just like the Bible said he was. Why hadn't he seen it before? How could he have been so closed-minded?

Using his last bit of strength and holding on to the cross, every ounce of pride he possessed gone, Keene slowly rose to his feet, lifting his eyes heavenward. He stood there a broken man, feeling lower than the lowest and gazing at the empty cross.

Then, raising his arms high above his head, he called out in a loud voice that boomed out over the microphone, "Father, I've sinned against You! I am not worthy to portray Jesus! I can go on with this farce no longer. I am begging for Your forgiveness! Take me, God!"

A sweet peace came over him as he stood there, and he knew God had heard his cry. He was forgiven. *Thank You, Lord. Thank You.*

Relieved and pulling himself together, he turned slowly to face the audience. He had to let those who had not yet asked God to forgive them know that God loved them and allowed Jesus to die on the cross for them, too. They had to know that they, like him, could have eternal life.

Finally, he moved away from the cross, those in front of him parting. When he reached the front of the big platform, he held out his hands to the stunned audience. "Earlier tonight, someone I love very much reminded me that the Easter story isn't just an interesting little story filled with symbolism. It is true. Every word of it. It really happened just like you have seen it portrayed here on this stage tonight. She called it the truest love story of all time. And now, thanks to God and His mercy, I know that's true."

He paused and wiped his eyes with the back of his hand. "God loved us so much He sent His only Son, Jesus, to suffer and die on the cross for sinners like me." Lifting his hand, he slowly gestured from one side of the audience to the other, pointing his finger. "And sinners like you. Don't turn your back on Him like I did. This night, I have confessed my sins to Him and asked His forgiveness. I am turning my life over to Him. From this day forth, I am His. I want Him to use me in any way He sees fit."

Turning and walking slowly back to the cross, he began to sing with great emotion a song he'd learned by listening to Jane sing it while she worked in his office.

> *"On a hill faraway stood an old rugged cross,*
> *The emblem of suffering and shame;*
> *And I love that old cross where the dearest and best*
> *For a world of lost sinners was slain."*

Kneeling at the cross and wrapping his arms around it, he continued to sing.

> *"So I'll cherish this old rugged cross,*
> *Till my trophies at last I lay down;*
> *I will cling to the old rugged cross,*
> *And exchange it someday for a crown."*

When he had sung the last word, Pastor Congdon stepped onto the stage and took the microphone offered to him by one of the soloists. "We've all seen a miracle here tonight. One of God's children has come into the fold. Like Keene, I am sure there are many of you who have never surrendered your heart to Christ. Do it now. Do not delay. The Savior is waiting." He bowed his head as a lone violinist stood and played "Just as I Am."

Hundreds of people thronged to the front to accept the invitation as Keene continued to hold on to the cross, weeping his heart out to his God.

Jane moved up close to him, wrapping her arm around his trembling shoulders.

Her prayers had been answered.

~⌇~

Later that night, after closing himself up with Pastor Congdon in his office, Keene drove Jane home. Neither of them could contain their excitement as they discussed the evening's happenings.

"How could I have been so blind?" Keene asked, turning his car toward her street. "And stupid?"

Jane scooted close, as close as the console would allow, and leaned her head on his shoulder. "I don't know when I've ever been this happy, Keene. You have no idea how hard I have prayed for you. I'm sure God got tired of hearing me plead with Him to touch your heart and make you know He's real."

"Your words kept haunting me last night, and I barely got any sleep at all. Then, this evening, when you came into my dressing room—well, your concern for me really got to me."

"I didn't want to upset you, this being your last night to sing, but I wanted so much to see you get right with God before you left Rhode Island."

"Jane."

"Yes."

"I heard you last night, after the performance. I—I didn't mean to listen while you were praying, but I came back to pick up my briefcase, and there you were."

"How. . .how much did you hear?"

"All of it."

He had to smile when he turned his face from the road long enough to gaze at the rosy blush on her cheeks. "I heard you say you loved me. Did you really mean it when you told that to God?"

"I—I guess, but I didn't want you to know."

"Why?"

She sighed. "For three reasons. One, you didn't believe in God."

"I do now."

"Two. You're going to be leaving Providence before long, and I may never see you again."

"I think we can work that out. What's the third reason?"

She fidgeted in the seat before answering.

"Jane. . ."

"I knew. . .I knew you could never love me back. Not really love me, like I love you."

Without taking his attention from his driving, he leaned over and kissed the top of her head. "I learned something else tonight."

She lifted her eyes to his. "Oh? What?"

"That I do love you. Really love you."

She sat up straight and stared at him, her eyes rounding in surprise.

"I think I've loved you from that first day, but I was too stubborn to see it. You were everything I wasn't, and you made me feel guilty every time you talked about your God. I knew I was a sinner. I just didn't want you to know it. You were so pure and godly it scared me to compare myself to you."

He pulled the BMW up in front of her apartment house and turned off the engine. "Let's get out of this car. I want to hold you in my arms, and I sure don't want to have to crawl over this console." He hurried around to her side, opened the door, and held out his open arms. Jane ran into them, wrapping her arms around his strong neck when he lifted her and whirled her around. "I love you, Jane Delaney."

❧

"I love—" Before she could finish her sentence, his lips sought hers, and he held her close. Feelings of love and adoration tugged at her heart. Keene loved her! He actually loved her!

"I've wanted to kiss you like this for so long," he murmured. "Oh, I know I've kissed you before, but it wasn't the same."

She melded herself to him, reveling in his closeness. "I know. I feel the same way."

He smiled down at her. "Remember what you said a couple of nights ago? That you could never have a permanent relationship with a man who didn't share your faith?"

She gazed up at him, her heart so full she could barely remember her name. "I—I think so."

His finger touching her lip, he gave her a coy smile. "You do realize that now that I've made my peace with God, your reason number three is no longer a problem."

"Does that mean. . ."

"It means I'd like a permanent relationship with you."

She eyed him quizzically. "How. . .how permanent?"

"Like for the rest of our lives! You know. The 'M' word. Marriage. I love you. I want you to be my wife."

"Oh, Keene, as much as I'd love to marry you, I can't. At least, not now. Not yet." His frown broke her heart. "I'm not sure we would fit into one another's world."

"Jane, my dear, my beloved one, you wouldn't have to fit into my world. Don't you see? You *are* my world."

"I love you for saying that, but as much as I love you, I love Christ more. *He* is *my* world, my life, my breath. My heart tells me you are the man for me, but my head tells me we have to wait. At least for a while. You've just accepted Christ. You know so little of what it means to live for Him. You need time to grow, and we need time together. Time to really get acquainted. I want us to read the Bible together, pray together, attend church together. But how would we ever do it? You're never in one place very long."

"I'll reschedule a number of this year's singing engagements, and I'll continue to keep my office in Providence. Then once we're married, you'll be able to travel with me. We'll see the world together."

She gave her head a sad shake. "We have another problem. What about my mother? I could never go off and leave her. She's much too frail to live alone."

He appeared thoughtful. "I wouldn't want you to leave her. Your dedication to those you love is one of the things that first attracted me to you. Not many people are as concerned about their elderly parents as you are. Don't worry about it, sweetheart. We will work something out when the time comes. After all, she's going to be my mother, too, when you decide to let me place a wedding ring on your finger."

"What about—"

Pulling her quickly to him, his lips pressed hers, making it impossible for her to finish her sentence. Finally, he moved away, just enough to peer into her eyes. The love she saw there took her breath away. She smiled and was reassured when he smiled back.

"Do you honestly think God would have brought us together and put this love in our hearts for each other, and for Him, if He hadn't wanted us to be together?" Cupping her face in his hands, he asked, "Where is your faith, Jane? Or is it that you don't love me enough to want to spend your life with me?"

"My faith is strong—stronger than ever now that he has become your Savior, too. Oh, Keene. You will never know how happy it makes me to know you and I share the same faith. God has truly answered my prayers. And love you? I love you so much it hurts. Of course I want to spend my life with you! Let's just take things slowly, okay?"

He kissed her again, a sweet, tender kiss that made her fingers tingle and her toes curl. "We'll do it any way you want it." His lips still lingering, he kissed her a third time. Finally, he pulled back, his hands going to cup her shoulders, his brow bearing a slight crease. "There's something I have to tell you. Something I probably should have told you weeks ago."

The seriousness in his voice frightened her. What could be that bad? Was he going to tell her he would be leaving for New York sooner than expected? Or that he had a wife in another city?

"What?"

"Remember all those appointments I've been having lately?"

She nodded. "Yes, but you never told me what they were."

He freed one hand and rubbed at the stubble on his chin. "There was a very definite reason I chose Providence as the place I wanted to spend the months it would take me to learn the new opera." He stared off into space. "I—I. . ."

"What, Keene? You can tell me anything. I promise I'll try not to be upset."

He walked away, standing with his back to her and gazing off into the night sky, one hand kneading the muscles of his neck. "By the end of last season, I was beginning to notice periods of hoarseness. I had never had them before. They usually occurred after an exceptionally demanding performance or an unusually heavy practice day. At first I thought it might be a viral infection, but it didn't stop. I went to several doctors, but even with all the testing they did, nothing showed up, and the only advice they gave me was to get more rest and make sure I ate properly."

"But what did that have to do with Providence?"

"I'm coming to that. My voice is my livelihood. I couldn't take any chances, so I did some intense research and located a doctor in Rhode Island whose specialty is voice disorders. He was trained at Wake Forest University Baptist Medical Center where the Center for Voice Disorders is located, so the guy really knows his stuff. I've been working with him since the first week I arrived in Providence."

"Has he been able to help you?"

He turned around, facing her, crossing his long arms over his chest. "At this point, I'm not sure. At least he ruled out throat cancer. He's already done some pretty extensive testing, but until I finished singing *Down from the Cross* and could completely rest my voice for several weeks, we couldn't go ahead with a full laryngoscopy."

She stared at him. "A laryngoscopy?"

"He said by performing a laryngoscopy he would be able to detect certain types of lesions if they were present. Like nodules, cysts, papilloma, leukoplakia, and neoplasm. Wow, that's a mouthful, isn't it?"

"Could that mean surgery?"

"Maybe, maybe not. Nodules are callouslike masses that form on the vocal folds. He thinks that might be my problem. Though all singers dread them, sometimes asymptomatic vocal nodules don't seem to cause any singing problems.

Usually with nodules, not only do you have hoarseness, but breathiness, loss of range, and vocal fatigue. Other than the little bit of hoarseness, I have had none of those symptoms. I have known many vocalists who had untreated vocal nodules for years and were never bothered by them. The doctor says sometimes, with vocal therapy, they will even shrink or disappear. But—"

He let out a heavy sigh, and she could tell he was trying to make the best of an extremely difficult situation.

She looped her arms about his neck. "God is able to perform miracles, Keene. We both know that."

"I know. I am counting on it, but I have to admit I was terrified when Dr. Coulter explained all this to me. Now, knowing how much God loves me, well, I can assure you I'm not nearly as frightened as I was."

"Was it wise of you to perform in our Easter presentation? And you spent so much time practicing each day, too," she said with concern now that the full extent of what he had told her had finally sunk in.

He grinned shyly. "Most of the practicing for the new opera you heard coming from my room wasn't me practicing at all, but tapes I had prerecorded of myself practicing before I got here. Since I wanted to ease up on my singing, I stayed in my room listening to the tapes and following along with the music score. I practiced my part in *Down from the Cross* the same way. I recorded it once and then mouthed it over and over until I'd learned the part."

"I never knew!"

"That's what I was counting on. I didn't want you to worry about me." Taking both her hands in his, he gave them a loving squeeze. "When you came to me, asking me to take Jim Carter's place, I didn't want to have to tell you no. And I certainly didn't want to tell you what I would be facing in the future. I knew if I did, you would never allow me to sing the part of Jesus, and I wanted to sing that part, not just for you, but also for myself. I had never done anything quite like it, and I thought the experience would be a good professional stretch for me. Dr. Coulter said that since I would only be singing several songs and my speaking parts would be limited, it would not hurt to put both the resting period and tests off until after Easter. So it looks like I'm going to be in Providence for a while after all."

"I was so afraid you'd leave right away."

"You do realize the laryngoscopy may show there are other problems, problems that could be even more serious than a simple node. I don't even want to talk about those, but I do want you to be prepared, sweetheart. There is always the possibility that Dr. Coulter will discover something that will require extensive surgery. If that happens, Jane—"

She held her breath.

"If that happens, I may never be able to sing again. The vocal cords and folds are easily damaged during surgery. There are no guarantees." He blinked and swallowed hard. "My career would be over, and I'd be washed up. Out of a job. I would have to start all over again. Learn a new trade." His finger idly traced her cheek, his expression one of sadness. "Never be able to sing to my wife."

Jane couldn't help but gasp. Never be able to sing again? *Oh, dear Father. No! Surely, You won't let this happen to Keene!*

"Other than my doctor, you're the only one I've told. My agent doesn't even know."

She had to do something, say something, to comfort him. Forcing a smile, she cradled his face in her hands and kissed his lips. "Oh, my darling, don't you know? It's not your voice I love. It's you! We'll see this thing through together, and no matter what the outcome, God will take care of us. You'll see."

"I know that's true, my sweet, sweet Jane. I am at peace about this whole thing now. I have put it in God's hands. I am trusting in Him and His promises. I want His perfect will for my life. Even. . .even if it means giving up singing."

"He's able to do above all we could ever ask. We have to trust Him."

"I know that now. With God in control of my life and you at my side, I can face anything. I know very little about the things of God. It's all new to me, but I want to learn everything about God and His Word. I am sure there will be times I will need your strength and encouragement to help me through, Jane, but I want to be strong for you—the husband you deserve. With God's help, I will be."

"I will be at your side, Keene, for as long as I live. God intended a wife to be a helpmeet to her husband. He will never leave you, and neither will I."

"Does that mean you love me enough to want to spend the rest of your life as my wife? That there'll be a wedding in our future?"

She gazed up into his eyes, her heart crowding her chest with love for this man. The man she would have dared not believe could one day love her as much as she loved him. "Oh, yes, my dearest. Loving you and knowing you love me is a dream come true."

"For me, too, Jane. I can't praise God enough for bringing you into my life."

"I've loved you since that first day I walked into your office." She cupped his head with her hands and drew his face close to hers, her lips brushing his. "But I've never loved you more than the moment you came down from the cross to accept my God!"

His forehead touched hers. "I want us to be married now, dearest, before my surgery."

At his words, a gasp escaped Jane's lips. "Now? You mean like right away?"

He gave a slight nod. "Yes, as soon as possible. I know it's selfish of me, but there's always a risk to any surgery, especially one as delicate as the one the surgeon is going to perform on me. I may never be able to sing again." His hand ovingly caressed her cheek. "I want to sing to you at our wedding, sweetheart, nd I want to be able to say, 'I do,' loud and clear, so everyone present can hear ne. Am I asking too much?"

Though Jane's heart was racing, she tried not to show it. She'd always dreamt f a fairytale wedding with all the trimmings, the kind that required months to lan. But as she gazed into his eyes, that dream no longer seemed important. What was important was that she'd found her Prince Charming and that he loved ier and wanted her to become his wife. Gently cupping his hand she pulled it to ier lips and kissed his palm. "No, my love, you're not asking too much. I, too, want is to be married as soon as possible."

His grin sent her heart singing.

"Maybe we could have a small wedding now, and then, after my surgery is ver and I've recovered. . ." He paused, momentarily closing his eyes, as if trying o block out the other alternative. "Maybe then, we can have a huge reception nd invite all our friends and business associates."

Jane leaned into him, enjoying his sanctity of his masculinity, yet his gentle-ess. "I love the idea. The sooner I become your wife, the happier I'll be."

❧

The next few days were a flurry of activity as Jane and Keene put their plan into ction to make their wedding a reality. Though at times, Jane doubted they could ull it off so soon, one week later, she found herself standing before the cheval iirror in the bride's room of Randlewood Community Church, staring at her mage.

"Is that really me, Mom?"

Her mother smiled at Jane's reflection. "It's really you, honey. I always hought my little girl was beautiful, but I have to admit, I've never seen you look ovelier or happier than you do at this moment. You're positively radiant."

Jane smiled back at her. "I am happy, Mom. Keene is not only a fine man, e loves the Lord and he loves me. What more could I ask?"

"You're not disappointed you're not having the wedding you'd always reamed of?"

She gave her head a vigorous shake. "No, not at all, but I have to admit I m glad I'm wearing a white wedding gown. It was Keene's idea. Since this is he first wedding for both of us, he felt I should wear white." She snickered. "I id, too."

After giving one final touch to her veil, then smoothing at her dress, Jane urned to face her mom. "During all the years I've gone to our church, I've at-ended a lot of weddings. If there's one thing I've learned, it's that a big, fancy redding doesn't always insure that there's going to be a happy marriage. I can iink of several that ended in divorce even before they'd paid off the wedding bills. The size or the extravagance of the wedding is no longer important to me. What is important is that I am marrying the man I love. The man I know God has prepared to be my husband."

The door to the bride's room opened and Karen's smiling face appeared. "Time to go. You ready?"

Jane nodded to her maid of honor, kissed her mother's cheek then reached out her hand. "Ready and eager."

Giggling like schoolgirls, the three made their way the short distance down the carpeted hallway to the chapel. A lone usher, one of the men from the choir, took Jane's mother's arm and led her to the front pew and waited until she was seated. As the church pianist began to play, Karen gave Jane's hand a squeeze, took a deep breath then slowly made her way to the altar where Keene, his best man Josh Stewart, and Pastor Congdon stood waiting.

For a brief moment Jane thought of her father. If only he were there to give her away, but that was not to be. Even though he was gone, what a blessing it was that though in poor health, her mother was still with her.

As the sounds of *Here Comes The Bride* filled the small chapel, closing her eyes Jane lifted her face heavenward and breathed a quick prayer of praise to God, thanking Him for bringing her and Keene to this sacred moment. When she opened them, began to move toward the altar, and beheld her beloved waiting for her, she thought she was going to faint out of sheer joy, especially when Keene reached out his hand to her.

"I'm glad you're wearing white," he whispered as she grabbed onto his hand and stepped up beside him. "You're gorgeous."

She gave him an appreciative grin. "And you're handsome," she whispered back before turning her attention to their pastor.

"Dearly beloved, we are gathered here today to witness the joining of Jane and Keene in holy matrimony," Pastor Congdon began.

A chill ran down Jane's spine. Holy matrimony. Yes, that's what their marriage was, and what she wanted it to be forever.

She tried to keep her mind on the pastor's words but her thoughts and her gaze kept going to Keene. He, too, must have been thinking of her as his gaze was fixed on her face and he was smiling.

Think, Jane. Listen to the pastor, she told herself. *The vows you are making her today are vows you will live with the rest of your life. Remember what God said in His Word. It is better to have not vowed than vowed and not kept them. Listen. Etch these words on your heart. Never forget the promises you and Keene are making to one another.*

Though she was sure she would forget the vows she had memorized, she didn't. Nor did Keene forget his vows. The sincerity in his eyes as his gaze locked with hers told her he meant every word he was saying.

"This marvelous couple has come a long way since their cars collided at that intersection," Pastor Congdon reminded the small group of guests they had invited. "They've come through a number of adversities and still have a monumental hurdle to face. But they both know God and are confident he will see them through."

Keene's grip on Jane's hand tightened. "He will, Pastor. I know He will."

Jane smiled up at him. "God hasn't failed us yet, and He never will."

Though their ceremony was simple one, to Jane, it was the most important, emotion-filled time of her life. Especially when Keene pulled her into his arms and with his rich baritone voice sang the song Whitney Houston made famous, "I Will Always Love You." Though she didn't sing it aloud with him, in her heart, she sang every word. She would always truly love Keene, no matter what God had in store for them.

It was all she could do to keep from leaping into Keene's arms and smothering his face with kisses when Pastor Congdon finally said the words she'd longed to hear. "I now pronounce you husband and wife. May God bless your union abundantly and may you always live for Him."

Beaming with love and a look of satisfaction, Keene wrapped his arms around her and kissed her as he'd never kissed her before.

She was now Mrs. Keene Moray.

Epilogue

Jane Moray sat twisting the lovely diamond wedding band on the ring finger of her left hand. "Mom, can you believe it's been almost a year since our wedding day?"

Mrs. Delaney smiled at her daughter. "It thrills my heart to see you and Keene so happy."

"Isn't he wonderful?" Jane asked as they sat on a front pew of Fort Worth's spacious Briarwood Community Church. "The Lord has really been able to use Keene in a mighty way since his horrendous throat problems. Only God could have guided Dr. Coulter's hand and protected Keene's vocal cords during that intense surgery."

Mrs. Delaney grasped her daughter's hand in hers. "Yes, Keene *is* wonderful. He is like the son I never had and always wanted, and he has taken such good care of me. Without him, I never would have been able to afford to have my knees replaced. Now look at me. I can walk without my walker, and I am able to take care of myself while you two go traipsing around the world to all the exotic places where Keene performs. I have a nice place to live only minutes away from your lovely house in Providence, friends to keep me company, and a daughter and son-in-law whom I adore. God has blessed me more abundantly than I ever could have imagined."

Jane patted her mother's frail hand. "You know, Mom, the day Keene ran that red light and plowed into me with that heavy car of his, I thought God had forsaken me. The whole side of my little car was caved in, I had a broken leg and a massive bump on my head, was three months behind in my car and insurance payments, out of a job, and I had no idea where the next month's rent money was coming from or if we'd have food on our table. Now we have a beautiful home, and I'm able to travel with my dear husband as he performs in the opera and gives concerts." She gave her mother's small hand another loving pat. "God is good, isn't He? He has certainly provided well for our needs."

Mrs. Delaney leaned into her daughter, her face twisted into a mischievous grin. "Maybe someday you'll fill up that beautiful house with my grandchildren."

Jane could not contain her smile as her palm flattened against her belly. "Maybe."

"Don't wait too long, honey. I want to be around to enjoy them."

"I won't, I promise. Keene loves performing as a Christian artist, and he's already contracted to produce several albums over the next few years."

"Oh, my, how can he take on so many projects? Won't that mean he'll be away from home even more?"

Jane smiled broadly. "No, in fact, he's already talking about retiring from opera. Other than the Christian concerts he'll be doing, he will spend most of his time at home learning new songs and preparing for his recordings." Jane glanced at the podium then put a finger to her lips. "Shh. It's time for his concert to begin."

The pastor moved to the microphone, surveying the crowded sanctuary. "We're so glad to have you here with us tonight. You are in for a real treat. The name Keene Moray is known all over the world. Keene is a professional and at the peak of his career. But a little over a year ago, God spoke to his heart, and Keene accepted Christ as his Savior. Now a major portion of his time is spent giving concerts like the one you'll be hearing tonight." Gesturing toward Keene, he said, "Ladies and gentlemen, it is my honor and privilege to introduce to you. . .Keene Moray."

With an adoring glance toward his wife, Keene rose and stepped to the front of the platform. "Thank you, Pastor. But before I begin, I must introduce my wonderful, supportive wife. Jane, would you stand, please?"

She stood and waved to the crowd.

"And with Jane is her mother, Lutie Delaney."

His mother-in-law turned and smiled at the audience.

"If it weren't for Jane and her patient and consistent witness to me," he went on, "I wouldn't be here tonight. Her prayers are what brought me to a saving knowledge of Christ. Thank you, sweetheart."

Jane blew him a kiss. Though Keene always introduced her and said the same sweet things about her, she never tired of hearing them.

"Much of the music I'll be performing tonight is from an Easter pageant. Its words and music, plus the prayers of Jane and the other members of Randlewood Community Church in Providence, Rhode Island, are what brought me into God's fold."

He paused, and Jane knew he was remembering that night.

"A little over a year ago, I was invited to sing the part of Jesus in the Easter pageant *Down from the Cross*. At the time, I did not believe God existed. But through singing the part of Jesus and realizing the suffering He endured to take my sins upon Him and die on the cross, I knew I was a sinner and wanted to be saved."

Keene pulled out his handkerchief and wiped at his eyes. "On the final night of the pageant, Easter night, as I hung on that cross, I realized I was a sinner and unworthy to portray the Son of God. I frantically asked the soldiers to take me down. I could not bear to hang there a minute longer. When they stood me to my feet, I fell at the foot of the cross and asked God to forgive me of my sins and accept me into His family."

He bowed his head, his chest heaving silently. When he finally looked up at the audience, tears were streaming down his ruddy face. "I implore each of you: If you have not accepted Christ, do it tonight. Don't put it off like I did."

He nodded to his accompanist, and she began to play.

"Please, listen to the words. Let them touch your heart as they touched mine that night, over a year ago, when I came 'down from the cross' to accept my Lord."

MOTHER'S DAY

Dedication

The very day I finished writing *Mother's Day*, the news of the abduction of an eleven-year-old girl flashed across the television screen. A security camera on a car wash actually captured her abductor grabbing on to her arm and dragging her away. Though he was apprehended a day or two later, the girl wasn't found for over a week. I shuddered as I watched in horror the day they found her body. That could have been one of my granddaughters. Or maybe your daughter or granddaughter. The world is filled with those who would do our children harm. We must be diligent in watching them and training them not only how to keep themselves aware and avoid situations that could put them in jeopardy, but how to defend themselves against such perverts. If you see anything suspicious or have any information about a missing child, please report it as quickly as possible by calling 1-800-THE-LOST. Your tip may save a child's life.

Chapter 1

C huck O'Connor stormed through the door of the house on Victor Lane, slamming it behind him and tossing his set of keys onto the highly polished hall table with a loud thud.

Mindy, who was sorting through the day's mail, spun around to face her husband, ready to scold him for his careless act. But the look on his face told her something was radically wrong. Although she had seen his angry side many times during their troublesome fourteen-year marriage, she had never seen his hands tremble or his face so flushed. She hurriedly placed the mail on the coffee table and rushed toward him. "What's wrong?"

Chuck yanked off his coat, tossed it on a chair instead of hanging it in the closet, as was his usual behavior, and pushed past her with a grunt.

She planted her balled fists on her hips. "Chuck! Are you going to tell me or sulk all by yourself?"

He snatched up the mail and began sorting through it, dropping several envelopes on the floor in the process.

Her patience wearing thin, Mindy crossed the room and yanked on his sleeve, her own anger rising. "All right, don't tell me then," she told him in a stern voice, holding up her hands between them with a frown of frustration.

Tossing the mail back on the table, Chuck plopped his lanky body onto the sofa, fixing his elbows on his knees and cradling his head in his hands. "Jake suspended me."

Thinking surely she had misunderstood his barely audible words, Mindy sat down beside him, placing a hand on his shoulder. "Jake suspended you? I find that hard to believe. You do everything by the book. You're always the top one in sales. Why would he suspend you?"

Chuck sat stone still and didn't respond, his head still resting in his hands, but his rapid breathing told her his anger had not subsided.

"Chuck?" she said softly, gently rotating her fingers across his tense shoulders. "Don't shut me out. I'm your wife. You know you can tell me anything. Why did your boss suspend you?"

Swallowing hard, he slowly lifted his face to meet hers. "You may not want to be my wife when I tell you."

She gave him a puzzled look. Whatever could he mean? They'd had some pretty rocky years, come close to divorce more times than she cared to remember, but they'd struggled through each problem and stayed together. What could be worse than anything they had faced in the past?

"I've"—he paused, still covering his face and pressing his fingertips against his lowered eyelids—"I've been accused of molesting someone."

Mindy stared at him. "What? You? Molesting someone? That doesn't make any sense." She scooted closer, her hand still resting on his back, her fingers splayed. "Who accused you?"

Slowly Chuck pulled his hands away and, with misty eyes, turned to face her. "Jake called me into his office and told me. It—it was one of the women employees. Michelle Stevens."

Mindy tried hard to put a face to the name. Had she met this woman at the company Christmas party? "Is that the little bimbo in the accounting department? The one with the bleached-blond ponytail and the false fingernails?"

He shook his head. "No, Michelle is nothing like that. She's—plain. Kinda ordinary. Has short brown hair and wears glasses."

"Why would she do such a thing? I don't even remember your mentioning her name."

Chuck leaned back and locked his hands behind his head, staring off into space. "I—I never did."

"Chuck? Why?" Mindy's heart sank. "Was something going on between you two?"

His brows quickly furrowing, he glared at her. "Of course not! How can you even ask me that?"

She shrugged, then let out a sigh. "Something must have happened between the two of you to get Jake that riled up. Why else would she make such a statement?"

Though Chuck only lifted his shoulders in response, something about the look on his face gave her cause for alarm. In all the years they'd been married, they'd had problems—many problems—but infidelity had never been one of them. Surely not now—not when their lives had finally settled down into a compatible routine. "Chuck! I asked you a question. I think I deserve an explanation. What did Jake say?"

"It's not true, Mindy. I swear it! It's not true."

She grabbed tightly on to his wrist. "Are you going to tell me what Jake said, or am I going to have to call and ask him myself? I will, you know."

His long fingers clamped her hand. They felt warm. Almost feverish.

"Okay. Let me start at the beginning." He pulled his hand away, rose, and began pacing slowly about the room. "Jake called me into his office, and we talked for over half an hour about business, his family, my family, where we planned to go on vacation this year—all sorts of things that really didn't matter. I could tell he had something on his mind, but I had no idea what. Finally, he leaned across his desk and pointed his finger in my face and asked point-blank if I was having an affair with Michelle."

She blanched at his words. "What did you say? Are you?"

He rammed his fist into the palm of his other hand, glaring at her. "No! I answered an unequivocal no! Of course I wasn't having an affair with Michelle! I told him that."

"Apparently he didn't believe you. He suspended you!" she shot back, half-wishing she had kept her silence until he finished his story.

His eyes flashed. "Hey, where's the trust a wife's supposed to have for her husband? You haven't even heard me out, and you're already finding me guilty," he countered, his voice rising.

"I never said—"

"But you implied it. That's just as bad." He lowered himself into a chair opposite her and, gripping the arm rests, bent toward her, his face contorted with anger. "Now do you want to hear the whole story or not?"

Annoyed by his patronizing behavior and with her heart pounding, she nodded. "Yes, I'm sorry. Go on."

"It appears that Dixie, one of the secretaries in the sales department, was in a stall in the ladies' restroom when Michelle came in and called someone on her cell phone, not realizing Dixie was there. She told whoever she was talking to that she had a new boyfriend and mentioned his name was Chuck but cautioned them to keep it quiet because the man was married. Then when she discovered Dixie was there, she begged her not to tell anyone about the conversation she'd overheard."

Mindy could not help letting out a gasp but kept her silence when Chuck frowned.

"I guess Dixie told everyone."

"Did Dixie or anyone else tell Jake what she'd heard?" Mindy asked cautiously.

"No. Not then. Not until after he talked to Michelle."

Mindy frowned. If Dixie hadn't told Jake, why would Jake talk to Michelle about it?

"I guess I'm not making myself clear." Chuck sent her a weak smile. "This thing has me so upset I'm not thinking straight." He gave his head a frustrated shake, then continued. "Michelle went to Jake early this morning and told him I'd molested her. That's what this is all about."

"Why would she say such a thing?"

"I don't know."

"She had to have said something convincing enough for him to suspend you."

"The sad thing is, he put me on suspension but let her keep her job! Some justice, huh?" The two sat silently staring at one another. There was so much Mindy wanted to know, but she refrained from asking, sure her questions would throw Chuck into a tirade. If he was innocent, he had every right to some righteous indignation. If he was guilty, any words she hurled at him would only fan the flames.

Finally, Chuck turned to face her again, taking her hands in his. "I didn't do it, Mindy. I know at times I have a hot temper and I let it get the best of me, but I'd never hurt a woman in any way. You know that. Over the years we've been together, you've angered me to the boiling point a number of times, but I've never struck you or laid a hand on you."

"Are—are you saying she accused you of hitting her? That kind of molesting?"

Chuck gave a sad shake of his head. "No, the other kind."

"Chuck! This is like a bad dream! Why would she accuse you of something like that if it weren't true?"

He glowered at her, his face flushed and his fists clenched. "So you believe it, too, eh?"

"I—I didn't say that."

"You didn't? It sounded that way to me!"

Mindy bit her tongue, trapping the words that nearly slipped from her mouth, a retort that would have angered him even more.

"I never—let me repeat—I never molested that woman—in any way!"

"I—I can't imagine that you would. Tell me the rest. What happened after Jake asked you about her?" Mindy prodded gently.

"According to her story, I had come on to her, invited her to drive up to Providence and have dinner with me a few times, and things got pretty heavy between us. She even claimed I told her you and I were getting a divorce."

"A divorce? We haven't talked about a divorce for four years!"

He patted her hand. "I know. She went on to say she had decided to break things off between us. She also said that one night after we'd been to dinner in Providence and gone back to her apartment, she told me she was calling it quits and I got really mad. She claims"—he paused and pursed his lips—"she claims I slapped her around, then made advances on her, and when she refused, I—I raped her."

Mindy's hands flew to cover her face. "Oh, no, no, no, no! I can't believe this is happening!"

Chuck held her arms so tightly she squealed in pain. "I didn't, Mindy. I swear it! None of this ever happened."

Mindy felt sick to her stomach. "You never drove that woman to Providence like she said?"

He shook his head vehemently. "Not one time!"

"Then why, Chuck? Why?"

"That's the same thing Jake asked me."

Fighting back a stream of tears and feeling light-headed, Mindy sucked in cleansing breath of air. "I find it difficult to believe she would make up a story like this and then just waltz into Jake's office and tell him!"

Chuck braced an elbow on one knee, cupping his chin in his hand. "Jake said he had a hard time believing it, too. And though he wasn't completely convinced he was telling the truth, he said he had no choice but to put me on suspension until her accusations could be proved or disproved. It's a serious charge. I'm well aware of that. To make things worse, Dixie verified the restroom cell-phone conversation."

Mindy dropped to her knees in front of Chuck, lifting her face to his and gripping his hands. "Look me in the eye, Chuck, and tell me none of this is true."

Her husband of fourteen years trembled. Finally, his eyes filling with tears and his voice breaking, he answered. "Some—some of it is sort of true."

Chapter 2

S ort of true?" Mindy quickly released his hands and rocked back on he heels, wanting to distance herself from him as much as possible. "Some c it is sort of true, Chuck? Exactly what does that mean?"

"Don't get upset until you hear me out."

Mindy stood quickly to her feet and jutted out her chin. "I'm beginning t think I've heard too much already. How could you do this to us, Chuck? To ou family? You're not even old enough to be having a midlife crisis!"

Chuck grabbed her forearm and held on fast. "I did take her to dinner once but that was right here in town, and only because I felt sorry for her."

"You never told me about it!" she screamed back at him, feeling betrayed.

He released his hold and threw his hands up in the air. "Because I knew you'd react just like you're doing right now!"

Mindy stomped her foot. "And you wouldn't behave the same way if I tol you I'd been out playing footsie with some guy?"

"We weren't playing footsie!"

Mindy leaned toward him, her hands on her hips. "Then what were yo doing, Chuck? Tell me that!"

He sucked in a breath and let it out slowly. "A couple of months ago whe you drove to Bristol to visit that friend of yours—"

"While the cat's away, the mice will play, huh?" She was sorry she said it th minute it slipped out.

Chuck spun around and headed toward the kitchen, leaving her standin there, feeling terrible.

Swallowing her pride, she followed him. After pouring them each a cup o the coffee she had put on to brew just before he got home, she handed his cup t him, adding a quiet "I'm sorry. That remark was uncalled for."

He took the cup and seated himself on a stool at the breakfast bar. "It wa raining when I drove out of the parking garage, and there was Michelle, stand ing at the bus stop looking as if she'd lost her best friend. I stopped and askec her what was wrong. She said she'd missed her bus, and another one wouldn't be along for another forty-five minutes. I hated to drive off and leave her there, so offered to take her home. I guess I mentioned it wouldn't make any difference i I got home later than usual, because you were out of town and my daughter wa:

staying overnight at a friend's house and I'd be fixing supper for myself."

"And she came up with this brilliant idea to fix supper for you in her apartment!" Mindy harangued sarcastically, tilting her head at a haughty angle.

Chuck looked as though he would like to choke her. "No, Miss Know-It-All, it wasn't anything like that. She simply offered to buy my supper at a little diner not far from her place."

"And being the gentleman, you took her up on it, right?"

He nodded, the incensed expression never leaving his face. "I couldn't see any harm in it—at the time. Now I know better."

"It must have been cozy. Sounds like something from an old movie. The rain. The diner. The gallant hero who rescues the damsel in jeopardy." Mindy knew her voice had a denigrating tone, but she didn't care. The whole thing upset her, and he needed to know it.

Chuck slammed his cup down, knocking the carton of coffee cream over, splattering it across the countertop. "Think what you like, Mindy. I'm only going to say this one more time. I don't care what that woman says. There was never anything between us."

"You have told me the whole story, haven't you, Chuck?"

He slid off the stool, his dark eyes menacing. "Why should I tell you? You've already tried and convicted me. I can see it in your eyes."

"So?" She turned away and tossed a couple of paper napkins onto the stream of cream that was slowly making its way across the counter. "I think you'd better move into the guest room until this thing is settled. I—I can't imagine sharing a bed with a man—" She stopped midsentence.

"A man you don't trust? Is that it, Mindy? Our years together don't mean anything to you? You're willing to cast me aside, just because a stranger tells a lie about me?"

"A lie? How do I know it's a lie? I'd like to believe you, Chuck—you know I would—but you just told me there was more to the story! I'm afraid to think how much more! I'm only asking you to move into the guest room until this thing is cleared up."

Chuck moved toward the door, his shoulders drooping, and leaned against the doorframe. "I—I guess, if I was honest, I'd admit I'd feel exactly the way you do. I was pretty shaken when Jake told me what she'd said. I knew it wasn't true, but how could I expect you to react any differently when you have only my word for it?" He fingered the slight growth of stubble on his chin, as if debating what to say next. "I'm sorry for blowing up at you, Mindy. I guess, under the circumstances, your request is reasonable. I'll move into the guest room as you've asked. Perhaps it would be best."

"How will we explain it to Bethany?" she asked, suddenly realizing their nearly thirteen-year-old daughter would be coming home soon.

He stroked his forehead thoughtfully. "Since she's usually in bed before we are, she won't even notice. I'll set my alarm a half hour earlier, so I'll already be up when she gets up. No need to get her involved in this."

"Thanks. I sure don't want to upset her. I doubt she's forgotten all the arguments we used to have when she was younger. I think it'd be best if we kept all this to ourselves. I don't want her worrying about it." Mindy walked slowly toward him. "Want me to help you move things?"

He gave his head a sad shake. "No thanks. I can do it myself." With that he turned and disappeared through the kitchen doorway.

Mindy watched him go, feeling as if her world had just collapsed around her. Though Chuck had never been a model husband, he had been a model father. It would not be fair to shake Bethany's trust in him since, she hoped, he would soon be proven innocent and things would get back to normal.

She moved to the sink and wet a clean dishcloth under the faucet, then robotically began to clean up the spilled cream.

Mindy froze when she heard the front door open. Had Chuck decided to leave? Maybe take a motel room somewhere? She hoped not. After all, this was his home, too, and that's where he needed to be.

"Hi, Mom!" a voice called out cheerily.

"In the kitchen!" Mindy dabbed at her eyes with the dish towel. "You're home early!"

Her pretty daughter bolted into the kitchen and plopped her books onto the counter. "The game ended early. Where's Dad? I saw his car in the driveway. He's home early, too. Does that mean we can go out for pizza for supper?"

"I—I don't know. Your—"

"I'm right here, princess." Chuck strode into the room and wrapped his long arms around his daughter, planting a kiss on her forehead. "Pizza sounds fine to me, if it's okay with your mother."

Mindy forced a smile, glad Bethany hadn't wandered into her bedroom before coming into the kitchen and found her father preparing to move his things into the guest room. "Pizza it is!"

Though she felt awkward sitting close to her husband in the crowded restaurant, Mindy did her best to keep their conversation light, making small talk about things that had happened at her office that morning and about an article she had read in a women's magazine about raising teenagers. "You'll be a teenager in a few weeks," she reminded her daughter.

Bethany grinned at her mom, then turned to her dad. "Just think, Dad—I can get my learner's permit next year, and you can teach me how to drive."

Chuck rolled his eyes. "I can hardly wait."

"Dad!" Bethany slapped at his arm. "Some of my friends' fathers are already teaching them to drive."

His eyes rounded. "Not on the street, I hope!"

"Well, not exactly drive, but they're letting them start the car and move it back and forth in the driveway."

Chuck laughed. "Hey, the last thing I need is a big hole in the garage door. I think you'd better wait until you're fourteen and it's legal. Then I'll take you to a big parking lot sometime when all the stores are closed and let you behind the wheel." He jabbed her arm playfully. "Better yet, why don't you just wait until you can take the driver's education class at your school?"

Bethany wiped a string of cheese from her father's chin. "What's the matter, Dad? You afraid I'll wreck that old Corvette of yours?"

"The thought did cross my mind."

Mindy watched the two of them, and despite the bombshell Chuck had dropped on her only hours earlier, she had to smile. If there was one thing she could never accuse him of, it was being a less-than-perfect father. Though she and her husband had disagreed on practically everything about Mindy's upbringing since even before she was born, Chuck had always had their daughter's best interests at heart. He had been there for all of it and had been an integral part of Bethany's life in every way.

"Isn't that right, Mom?"

Brought out of her thoughts by her daughter's question, Mindy gave her a blank stare. "What? What did you say? I'm sorry—I had other things on my mind." She could not help but glance in Chuck's direction.

Bethany let out a giggle. "I said Daddy was funny! Didn't you hear his joke?"

"No—I guess I didn't."

"It wasn't that funny, princess," Chuck said, giving Mindy a shy grin. "Hey, now that we've finished our pizza, how about an ice cream cone? Maybe Rocky Road or Pralines and Cream?"

Bethany leaped to her feet and grabbed her jacket from the back of her chair after tweaking her father's cheek between her fingers. "Or Peppermint Crunch, your favorite, Dad!"

Chuck reached out his hand to Mindy. "That okay with you?"

She nodded and smiled back, but inwardly her heart was breaking. *Oh, Chuck. Sweet, sweet Chuck. Am I crazy to doubt you?*

Later that night as Mindy lay in their bed, her head propped up on a pillow, trying to get her mind off their problems by reading a romance novel, she heard the grandfather clock in the hall chime eleven times, then footsteps in the hall. Chuck was on his way to bed. She ran her hand across the empty pillow beside her, remembering years past, miserable years for both of them, when he had spent much of his time in that guest room. She held her breath, half-hoping h[e] would come in and climb into bed beside her. Though it had taken nearly te[n] of their fourteen years together to cultivate an overwhelming love for her hus[-] band, it had happened. She had hopes of their growing old together and bein[g] grandma and grandpa to Bethany's children. Now this had happened. Chuc[k] had been accused of molesting his coworker. As much as she wanted to believ[e] in his innocence, visions of him with that woman kept playing in her mind. [If] only he had never taken Michelle home that night, perhaps none of this woul[d] have ever happened.

Startled by a soft rap on the door, she grabbed the sheet and pulled it tightl[y] about her neck.

"Can—can I come in?"

Though the voice was barely audible, she knew it was Chuck. "Sure. Com[e] on in."

Still dressed in the shirt and trousers he had worn to work that day, h[e] moved slowly into the room and headed toward the bathroom. "I forgot m[y] toothbrush."

"Oh."

"Sorry to bother you."

"No bother."

He moved quickly into the bathroom, then came out carrying his tooth[-] brush and a new tube of toothpaste. "Okay if I take this?" he asked, holding ou[t] the tube.

"You bought it."

"I think I've got everything else I need."

"There are extra blankets on the top shelf of the closet," Mindy told him a[s] he stopped at the foot of the bed and stood gazing at her. "And clean towels an[d] washcloths in the linen closet."

"I didn't do it, Mindy."

She closed her book and leaned back onto her pillow.

"Somehow I'm going to prove it to you."

"I hope so, Chuck—I really hope so. But it sounds like another one of thos[e] unprovable cases of 'he said—she said,' the kind so many of the sports figure[s] have been involved in lately. Her word against his. How can you prove whic[h] person is telling the truth in cases like that?"

He grabbed hold of the bedpost, pressing his forehead against it. "I know[,] but believe me, this was not one of those consensual things. You have to hav[e] made contact with the person to have that kind of excuse or reason apply. I ha[d] no physical contact with that woman."

Mindy let out a loud sigh. "Seems one of this nation's high public officials[]

made a statement similar to that, and the next day he recanted."

"That won't happen here. I can assure you nothing improper happened," he said firmly, giving her a slight glare. "I have nothing to recant."

"I—I hope that's true, Chuck—" She stopped, unable to speak what was in her heart.

"If our roles were reversed, I'd feel exactly the same way. Even the thought of another man touching you in a more than friendly way sickens me."

"That could never happen, Chuck. Even though our life together has been rocky, I would never cheat on you."

"Nor would I cheat on you! You have to believe that, Mindy. You have no idea how hard all of this is on me!"

He started for the door, stopping halfway across the room to turn back to her. "I'll set my alarm early like I said I would."

She gave him a faint smile. "Thank you. I'm sure you want to protect our daughter as much as I do."

"I am going to prove my innocence, Mindy. Just promise you'll give me some time. I don't know how I'll do it, but I'll find a way. I have to. I—I love you."

"I love you, too, Chuck. That's what makes this so difficult. If I didn't love you, it wouldn't matter, but I do love you. More than you'll ever know. I want you to prove your innocence so our marriage can continue, but—"

He held up his palm between them. "I will, Mindy. I have to."

She flipped over onto her side, turning her face away from him, knowing if she looked at his sad expression one more time, she would break out in tears. "Good night, Chuck. I do love you."

"Good night, Mindy. I love you, too."

A few seconds later she heard the door close softly, and she was alone in the king-sized bed, her tears dampening the pillow.

The strain was still there between them the next morning at the breakfast table, but for Bethany's sake Mindy worked hard at keeping things as normal as possible. And she could sense Chuck was doing the same. The child had suffered enough at their hands during the first ten years of her life, until they had figured out a way at least to appear compatible. But the funny thing was, once they decided to look as if they were trying to get along and live life as a normal family, they had actually begun to like each other. They had even felt some of the same vibes they'd experienced during the weeks they had dated and those first few months after their wedding. That was before Mindy discovered she was pregnant and Chuck lowered the boom on her by expecting her to quit the job she loved and be a twenty-four–seven, stay-at-home mom. Her pregnancy had come as a total shock, and though she had wanted someday to have children, she was not prepared to put her career on hold as Chuck expected her to. At least not until she had reached the top of her profession.

"Why do I have to be the one to give up my job and stay at home? What about you?" she had asked him, fully believing he was an equal partner in their marriage. "Why can't you put your job on hold and stay at home? I'm making more money than you are! We could far better afford to live on my salary than on your commissions."

He had countered by reminding her that God made women to be the child bearers, so He also must expect women to be the caregivers.

In anticipation of the birth of their first child, once they had both accepted the fact that a baby was on its way, and wanting to make sure the baby had a good start in life, Mindy had arranged to take a six-week leave of absence from Health Care Incorporated. She served there as assistant manager—a well-paying position she had worked long and hard to attain. She had known that with that promotion her earning potential would be unlimited, provided she would be available to travel to their many branch offices, spending as much time at each one as necessary. She had hoped that once her six weeks' leave was up, Chuck would change his mind, take over, and become a stay-at-home dad, but that was not to be. Though she resented his pigheaded, unchangeable attitude, she had to admit she loved each minute she spent with their new daughter, soon realizing that being away from her for long periods of time was nearly intolerable.

She glanced to see if Bethany was watching her and, finding her daughter engrossed with her bowl of hot oatmeal, eyed Chuck with a frown. He was dressed in a suit and tie, the way he normally dressed when going to the office. Why was he dressed like that?

As if reading her mind, Chuck took his last swig of coffee and rose to his feet, folding up the sports section of the morning paper and stuffing it under his arm. "See you ladies tonight," he said as cheerily as if nothing had happened and it was a normal day.

Where is he going?

"Got a full day ahead of me." He bent and kissed Bethany's cheek. "Have a good day at school, princess."

"Bye, Daddy."

Stepping up close beside Mindy, Chuck hesitated only for a second before leaning over and kissing her on the forehead. "I'll call you later."

After Bethany left for school and Mindy finished cleaning up the kitchen, she slipped into her dress, checked her appearance in the mirror, then grabbed her briefcase. She was already in the hallway off the kitchen with her hand on the doorknob when the phone rang. After a quick glance at her watch, she rushed to answer it.

"Hi," a male voice said softly. "Is the coast clear?"

"Clear? If you mean is Bethany gone, the answer is yes. Her ride picked her up about ten minutes ago. Where are you, Chuck?"

"I'm at the service station. I—I thought it might be best if Bethany saw me leave for work as usual. I sure don't want to have to explain to her why I'm without a job."

"I was on my way out the door. What are your plans for today?"

"I—I thought I'd come back home. There's no place else for me to go. Somehow I'd like to prove my innocence, but how do you go about doing something like that? Like you said, it's my word against hers."

Mindy nervously twined the phone cord around her fingers. "Have you talked to Michelle about this?"

"No."

"Don't you think you should? If you are innocent, maybe you can talk some sense into her head—let her know what this is doing to your life."

"I've thought about it, but—"

"But what, Chuck? You can't sit idly by and do nothing. You have to take action of some kind."

"I don't want to talk to her in private, not after the kind of accusations she's made, and I don't want to talk to her at the office with everyone listening in on our conversation. I'm furious with her for what she did. I'm not sure I could talk to her face-to-face without losing my temper."

"So? Are you just going to let things ride?"

No answer came.

"Chuck, did you hear me? Are you still there?"

"I—I'm here. I just don't know what to do. Can I meet you for lunch?"

She pulled the phone from her ear and stared into it. *Have lunch?* "I—I don't know."

"Look, sweetie—I can't blame you for reacting the way you are. The whole thing is ridiculous. I can only imagine what it's doing to you, but I—I need you, Mindy. I can't stand this wedge between us. It's miserable in that guest room knowing you're sleeping all alone just a few yards from me. I wanted so much to hold you in my arms and kiss your sweet face. I barely slept a wink last night."

"I had a hard time sleeping, too." She pinched the bridge of her nose between her thumb and her forefinger. "Okay, I'll meet you for lunch, but not at a restaurant. I'll meet you at home and fix us a bowl of soup."

"Thanks, Mindy. You have no idea how much I need you to help me get through this. And don't worry about fixing the soup. I have all the time in the world to do it. I'll open a can of something and have it hot when you get there."

"See you at noon." Staring off into space, she hung up the phone. She loved

Chuck. Though they'd had their troubles, she'd never once thought about him cheating on her. With a lump in her throat, she picked up her briefcase and headed out the door. *What is it they say? The wife is the last to know?*

When she reentered the house on Victor Lane at five minutes past twelve, the enticing aroma of tomato soup greeted her, and she had to smile. For years Chuck had resisted her urgings to keep canned soup in their pantry, reminding her that his mother always made their soups from scratch. She had reminded him that was his mother's choice. Not hers. Mindy was a good cook and spent many hours in the kitchen preparing the things he and Bethany liked, but home-made tomato soup didn't happen to be one of them, any more than his mother would prepare a homemade quiche as Mindy did, which happened to be one of Chuck's favorites. After many an argument Chuck had finally conceded that prepared and fast foods had their place in busy lives.

"Soup's hot, and the table is set," he said, meeting her at the door, taking her jacket from her hands. "How'd your morning go?"

"Okay. I guess." She felt a small smile quirk at her lips as she washed her hands at the sink before sliding into her chair. Wasn't that what June Cleaver always asked Ward Cleaver when he came home from the office? All Chuck needed was an apron tied around his waist, high heels, and a string of pearls.

"I've been thinking about what you said. I'm going to call Michelle and ask her to meet me someplace so we can talk about this." He gave her a shy grin. "Would—would you come with me? I don't want to be alone with her."

She folded her hands on the table and eyed him suspiciously. "You want me to go with you? Isn't it a bit unorthodox to have the little woman go along with the accused man?"

He reached across the table and cupped his hand over hers. "I—I need you there, Mindy. That's why I wanted you to have lunch with me. I want you to hear the entire story before we talk to her."

Her heart sank. "Entire story? You mean there really is more?"

"Everything I've said is true. I—I just haven't told you all of it."

The room began to swirl, making her dizzy. Though Mindy had never fainted in her life, she was sure this was going to be the first time. "Oh, Chuck, I'm not sure I'm up to this."

"Don't worry, sweetheart. I meant it when I said nothing was going on between that woman and me. I think you'll better understand if you hear me out."

She pulled her hands from his and linked them in her lap, her heart doing the fifty-yard dash. "I'm listening."

Chapter 3

C huck rose and walked to the refrigerator. Then, taking out a carton of milk and pouring himself a glass, he returned it to the shelf and closed the door. "What I'm about to tell you is the whole story. As I told you yesterday, I did go to the diner with Michelle, and being a gentleman, I paid for our dinner."

"But that wasn't the end of it?" she asked with trepidation, almost dreading to hear his answer.

Chuck sat down at the table and hung his head. "No, it wasn't. When I got to my car the next evening, she was standing there waiting for me. She said she felt bad because she'd let me pay for our dinner and wanted me to go with her to try out a new pizza parlor in her neighborhood. You were still gone, and I didn't see any harm in it, so I went with her. It was all perfectly innocent."

Mindy nibbled on her lower lip. "On your part maybe, but I'll bet not hers."

"Remember you called that night, and I told you I'd tried a new pizza place? I just didn't tell you I'd gone with Michelle."

Mindy gasped! Of course she remembered that night. She had been surprised Chuck would go alone to try out a new place. She had even kidded him about it, playfully asking him who had gone with him.

"Well, the next day was Saturday. I was messing around with that loose board on the porch floor you'd been wanting me to fix when the phone rang. It was Michelle, and she was crying. She said someone had tried to get into her apartment during the night and she was terrified. She hadn't lived there long and hadn't had a chance to get someone to put a dead bolt on her door. She begged me to come over and put one on. Even offered to pay me for it. Since it was a weekend, none of the places she'd called had anyone on staff to do it. She sounded so pitiful that I agreed. I took that dead bolt I'd purchased to put on our garage door, grabbed up my toolbox, and rushed right over. It didn't take me fifteen minutes to do the job. She thanked me, then offered me a cup of coffee and a piece of her homemade cheesecake. We had a nice visit. She asked all kinds of questions about you and Bethany, and since I like talking about the two of you, I answered them."

"How long did you stay?" Mindy prodded.

"Probably forty-five minutes. No more than an hour—then I left."

"Then what happened?"

"She called Sunday morning to thank me for putting the dead bolt on and said she'd slept soundly because of it. At the time I thought that was nice of her to call. Everyone likes to be appreciated for what they do."

His comment somewhat irked her. "Are you saying I don't let you know you're appreciated?"

He shook his head. "No! That's not what I meant at all. You're very good about thanking me for the things I do for you."

Feeling bad for responding without thinking first, she settled down and forced her tense face to relax. "There's more, isn't there?"

He fingered the salt and pepper shakers on the table without meeting her eyes. "The next weekend you had that meeting in Providence, and Bethany went to stay overnight with a girlfriend. I guess I'd mentioned to one of the guys at the office that I was going to be batching it for a day or two. Anyway, Michelle was waiting for me in the garage again that night. This time she held up two tickets to a Patriots game, telling me she'd heard me say I wanted to go and couldn't get tickets. So she'd called someone she knew whose brother worked in the Patriots' office and arranged with him to get the tickets for her. She said she wanted to take me as a thank-you for putting the dead bolt on her door."

"She sure knew which one of your buttons to push. I'll bet you jumped at the chance."

"Not at first. But I admit I did want to go. I offered to buy them from her, with the idea of taking one of the guys from work, but she wouldn't hear of it. She said she'd gone to a lot of work to get those tickets, that she, too, loved the Patriots, and it was her way of thanking me."

Mindy gave him an indignant stare. "So being the dedicated Patriots football fan that you are, you accepted."

"I tried to say no."

"But she kept at you until you said yes?"

"I didn't realize it at the time, since I really wanted to go to that game, but, yes, I guess she did." Chuck stood, wadded up his paper napkin, and tossed it into the wastebasket as he headed for the family room.

She followed him and seated herself opposite him, folding her hands in her lap. "So you drove her to Foxboro?"

"Hey, it wasn't that far! The Gillette stadium in Foxboro may be in Massachusetts, but it's still only a forty-five-minute drive from here."

Mindy rolled her eyes. "A lot can happen in forty-five minutes. Not to mention the return time."

Chuck gave her a disgruntled look. "We barely talked on the way over there. Most of the time we listened to the pregame show on the radio. And during the game it was so noisy you couldn't talk if you wanted to."

"Did you give her high fives when the Patriots scored, the way you do me when we go to the games?"

"Yeah, but I give high fives to everyone sitting around us—you know that."

"Sometimes you even hug me when they score. Did you hug her?"

With an air of indignation, Chuck leaned back against the sofa and crossed his arms over his chest. "Of course not! What do you take me for?"

"I'm more concerned with what she took you for," she answered coolly.

She could tell her inference upset him, but he did not comment. He just stared at her.

"You want me to continue with my story?" he finally asked in a low, controlled voice.

She could almost see his teeth gritting. "Yes, go on."

"This isn't easy, but I want you to know everything. Okay?"

She nodded. "I'm sure it isn't easy."

He rose slowly, stuffing his hands into his pockets as he moved to the window and stared out into the backyard. "The game was great. The Patriots won. We listened to the coach's postgame interview on the way back home. We got to her apartment, and I was letting her off at the front door before heading on home when she said she'd baked a new cake recipe and wanted me to come up and try it out."

"Come up and see my etchings? That's an old line. Surely you didn't fall for it," Mindy said sarcastically.

"I almost did. I was so excited about their win that I felt like celebrating, and you weren't here to celebrate with me. I thought about it but didn't go. If it had been Jake, it would have been a different story."

"It wasn't Jake, though," Mindy pointed out.

"No, it wasn't." Chuck let out his breath. "What I meant as a friendly gesture, she must have taken another way."

Both Mindy and Chuck turned as the kitchen door opened and Bethany appeared, her face flushed and her hair askew.

Chapter 4

I think I'm getting the flu. The school nurse said I had a temperature. I told her both of you were at work, so since she was going to pick up her lunch at the drive-thru down on the corner, she brought me home. What are you doing here? You guys never eat lunch at home."

Mindy flashed a worried glance toward her husband, then turned her attention back to Bethany, her mind racing for a good excuse, one her daughter would believe.

"It was a spur-of-the-moment idea. We were both hungry for soup." Chuck reached out and placed his palm on Bethany's forehead. "You do feel a bit warm."

"Have you had lunch yet?" Mindy hurried to the range and checked the soup pan. "There's a little tomato soup left."

Bethany squiggled up her face and spread her hand across her abdomen. "I—I don't want anything to eat. My tummy doesn't feel so good. The nurse said there's a bunch of that twenty-four-hour stuff going around. I guess I got it."

Chuck hurried to his daughter and, after taking her book bag from her hands, helped pull off her coat. "I'll check the medicine cabinet. I think we still have some of those tablets the doctor recommended when you had that bout with the flu last year."

Mindy wrapped her arm around her daughter's slim shoulders. "Why don't you get into your pajamas, sweetie, and try to take a nap? Do you feel like drinking a cup of hot tea?"

Bethany winced as her hand covered her mouth. "Hot tea? Yuck! I hate hot tea."

"Then how about some spritzy-type soda pop? Sometimes that'll help settle your stomach."

"I might try to drink a little bit, but not the hot tea."

Bethany was already crawling into her pajamas when Mindy took a glass of soda into her room. "Try to drink this. Your body needs fluids."

"Drink some when you take this tablet," Chuck said, coming into the room. "Do you want me to call the doctor?"

"No, Daddy. I'm not a baby. It's just the plain old flu. It's not that serious. A bunch of the kids at school have had it, and only two of them have died so far."

Chuck's eyes widened. "Some of the kids died? I didn't hear about it! Was it on the news?"

Bethany let out a strained laugh. "Dad! It was a joke!"

Despite her concern for her daughter, Mindy had to laugh. Normally Chuck was the prankster.

He lifted his arms in surrender. "Okay, ladies, you got me!"

"Ohh!" Her face turning an ashen white, Bethany rushed past them into the bathroom, slamming the door behind her.

"I'll go to her," Mindy said, moving quickly across the room.

Chuck hurried past her, beating her to the door. "No, I will. You have a soft stomach."

"But I'm her mother," she insisted, reaching for the doorknob.

"And I'm her father."

"I don't want either one of you," a small, weak voice responded through the door. "Just leave me alone. I'm—I'm about to—"

The two stood staring at each other, listening to the strange sounds coming through the locked door.

Eventually Bethany emerged, her face pale, with damp curls resting on her forehead. "I—I feel better now."

Mindy slipped her hand beneath her daughter's elbow and lovingly helped her cross the room.

"Can I get you anything, princess? More soda pop? Crackers?" Chuck asked, supporting her on the other side as they helped her into bed.

"No, Dad! Don't even mention food, please!"

"Do you need another blanket?" Mindy asked, tucking the quilt beneath her daughter's chin, feeling the need to do something to make Bethany feel better.

Bethany gave her head a slight shake. "Would you put a plastic bag in my wastebasket and set it by the side of the bed? My tummy still feels yucky."

"I'll get a bag," her father volunteered as he rushed out of the room.

"Mama?"

"Yes?"

"Are you mad at Daddy?"

Mindy quickly pasted on a smile. "Mad at Daddy? Whatever makes you ask such a thing?"

Bethany took on a solemn look. "I—I heard the two of you arguing last night. Like you used to argue when I was little. It—it scared me."

"Oh, honey, all parents argue once in a while. We're humans. We can't always agree on everything. I'll bet your friends' parents argue sometimes, too." It was the best answer she could come up with on the spur of the moment.

Bethany let out a sigh. "I know, and some of them have gotten divorces, too.

I remember the many times you and Daddy talked about divorce when I was a little kid. I—I was afraid it was happening again."

Mindy sat down on the side of the bed and began to stroke Bethany's clammy forehead. "Your dad and I always worked things out, didn't we?"

Bethany gave a slight nod.

"I'll be honest with you, sweetheart. Those first ten years were hard for both of us. We were each pretty selfish, and neither wanted to give in to the other. If we hadn't had you and experienced the joy you brought into our lives, we might have split up. But we didn't. We hung in there, and I can honestly say the past four years have been the happiest of my life. I guess your father and I finally grew up and began to act like adults."

"I—I wish you both loved God like I do."

Mindy gave her daughter's shoulder a patronizing pat. "We go to church with you now. Isn't that enough?"

Chuck came back into the room with the plastic bag. "Isn't what enough?" He gave the bag a flip to open it, then picked up the wastebasket.

"I was telling Mom I wished the two of you loved God like I do."

He gave her a puzzled look as he placed the bag in the little basket. "We go to church with you nearly every Sunday."

"That's what I was telling her," Mindy added, suddenly becoming her husband's ally.

"I—I told Mom I heard the two of you arguing last night."

Chuck flashed a glance toward his wife.

"I explained we were just having a slight disagreement." Mindy kept up her fake smile. "Nothing for her to worry about."

Bethany's eyes filled with tears. "I—I don't know what I'd do if you guys got a divorce like some of my friends' parents have. You have to promise me you'll never let that happen."

Mindy's heart sank. How could she make a promise like that in light of what was going on? If she ever discovered Chuck had been unfaithful to her and that woman's accusations were true, she could never live another night under the same roof with him. Not even for Bethany's sake. *Am I being honest with myself? If Bethany begged me to stay in our marriage, would I still leave?*

Chuck reached out and took Mindy's hand, his thumb stroking her knuckles. "I don't want that ever to happen either, princess. I love your mother and can't imagine life without her."

Mindy wanted to burst into tears at his words, her heart soaring up and down on an emotional roller-coaster ride. She did not want a divorce either, but if—

"Mom? You'd never divorce Daddy, would you?" Bethany's pleading eyes pierced straight to her mother's heart.

Pulling free of Chuck's grasp, Mindy rose quickly and grinned at her child. "You need to put this silly kind of talk out of your mind, young lady, and concentrate on taking a nap. Sleep is the best thing for your body right now."

"You're not going to go back to work and leave me, are you? What if I have to throw up again?"

Chuck leaned over Bethany and kissed her forehead. "I'll be here all afternoon. I have some things in my briefcase I can work on. I'll check on you again soon, but call if you need me. I'll be in the family room."

Liar! Mindy had to bite her tongue to keep from reminding Chuck he had no job to go to and certainly no work in his briefcase. "Since your father will be here," she said, trying to keep her hurt feelings under control, "I'm going back to my office. But if you want me to come home, just give me a call, and I'll be here immediately. And, Bethany, stay off that computer. You've been spending entirely too much time on it lately. What you need is bed rest. Okay?"

The two of them backed out of the door, closing it gently behind them.

"Work in your briefcase?" Mindy asked sarcastically in an exaggerated whisper once they were alone in the family room and, she hoped, out of earshot.

Chuck sat down on the sofa, his head in his hands. "You didn't want me to tell her the real reason I'm home, did you?"

She tugged her coat on and picked up her purse from the coffee table, slinging the strap over her shoulder. "Of course not. You heard what she said in there."

"I never thought she'd hear us last night. I assumed she was asleep."

"Do you have any idea what this would do to her if she found out?"

Chuck lifted his face slowly. "The truth will prove my innocence, Mindy."

She put a finger to her lips. "Shh. She may be listening."

"But I never got to finish. I need to tell you the rest of the story."

She gave her head a shake. "Not now. It'll have to wait until we're sure she can't hear us. I'm going to the office. Call if you need me."

He gave a slight shrug, stood, and followed her to the door. "I love you, Mindy."

She turned the knob and stepped onto the porch. "I love you, too, Chuck. More than you know."

"Michelle's accusations aren't true, sweetheart."

She turned and stared at him for a moment, scanning his face for any telltale expression. "I hope not, Chuck, for all our sakes."

Mindy crawled into her car and headed down the street toward her office, but on a sudden whim she turned the steering wheel in the opposite direction.

~≈~

Chuck watched until Mindy's car was out of sight. He loved that woman more than life itself, though those first ten years of their married life had been a love-hate battle almost every day. Mindy had done so many things that irritated him that he'd found it difficult to live with her. Being a neat freak and raised by a mother who was one, his creed had always been to put things away the minute you were finished with them. Toothpaste. Toothbrush. Hang your coat in the closet. Sort your clothing out by type and color when you place it on the closet rod. Suits together. Trousers together. Jackets together. Shirts together—sorted by whites, blues, greens, and so on, starched just the way he liked them. Underwear and T-shirts sorted and folded in the same exact rectangular shapes and piled neatly in the drawers. On and on and on, but everything had been precise and in order, with a place for everything and everything in its place. Both the interior and the exterior of his car were always sparkling clean and devoid of trash. He had never been late to an activity or business appointment in his life, always preferring to arrive early. He retired early and rose early, selecting his next day's attire before going to bed. His life had been thoroughly organized and virtually stress free.

Until he met Mindy.

The pretty little blue-eyed blond with the cute dimples, a button nose, and Southern twang in her voice made him forget everything. It didn't bother him at all that Mindy was the opposite of him, that she was late for every date, making him wait as much as a half hour for her to finish applying her makeup and get dressed. He didn't mind that she left fast-food wrappers in his car, spilled soft drinks on his floor mats, left her apartment in disarray with clothing and shoes strewn everywhere, dirty dishes piled on the kitchen counter, magazines scattered on the tables and floor—leaving it to look as if a tornado had just roared through. Even the fresh bouquets of flowers he brought her remained in their vases for days after they had wilted and lost their fragrance. As long as Mindy was by his side and he could claim her as his girlfriend, none of those things mattered. All that mattered was that they were together.

But all that changed after the wedding and the two of them took up residence in Chuck's apartment, which was considerably larger than hers.

"But, Chuck," he remembered her saying when he'd suggested she take time to organize her belongings, "I simply don't have the time." Then she'd spend hours talking on the phone to her girlfriends about ridiculous things that didn't count, reading those dumb fashion magazines or giving herself a manicure and a pedicure, trying out a dozen colors of polish until she could decide on the right one, the other eleven bottles sitting on the bathroom counter, their lids off, just waiting to be spilled. The laundry never got done unless he did it, and Mindy did not even know where the dry cleaner's shop was located. Even the grocery shopping and most of the cooking were left up to him, though they ate out most of the time because Mindy preferred it. That was the way it was at her house when she was growing up. It was good enough for her mother, and it was good enough for her.

If that was not bad enough, since Mindy hadn't been his mother's first choice for a daughter-in-law, his mother was constantly at him, reminding him he knew what Mindy was like before he married her.

"Daddy."

He startled at the sound of his daughter's voice calling from her bedroom. "Can you bring another clean bag for the wastebasket? I don't feel so good."

∽ৎ৵

Mindy sucked in a breath of air, squared her shoulders, and pushed open the door to Cox Machine and Parts Company.

"Hello, Mrs. O'Connor." The receptionist's eyes rounded as if she was surprised to see Mindy standing there. "Chuck—Chuck isn't here," the woman said, looking embarrassed.

"I know. I'm here to see Clarisse. Is she in?" Mindy asked, trying to act nonchalant, as if everything were fine in the O'Connor household.

"I'll buzz her and tell her you're here." The receptionist gave her a questioning frown, then spoke into her headset to Clarisse. "She said to come on back. You know where her office is, don't you?"

Mindy nodded and headed toward the elevator. She punched three, waited impatiently until the elevator ground its way to the third floor, then stepped out smiling, hoping her face wouldn't reflect the turmoil she felt inside. Clarisse was standing at the door of her office. She motioned her in, closing the door behind her.

"I—I didn't expect to see you here today," she said awkwardly, pointing to a chair and seating herself behind her big desk.

"I have to talk to you." Mindy worked hard at keeping the nervousness from her voice, but it came through anyway. "I—I need some answers, and I'm not sure who can give them to me. I thought maybe you could help."

"You know I'll do anything I can. I'm sick about Chuck's suspension," the woman answered kindly, her face showing sincere concern. "What do you want to know?"

"I assume you've heard the accusations that woman made against him."

"Unfortunately, yes. We've all heard them."

Mindy felt as awkward as a pig on ice skates. "Do—do you believe her?"

"Absolutely not! I didn't like that woman from the start. Had bad vibes about her. From her employment record she doesn't stay anyplace very long. I wish she'd never come here."

Those words were like a soothing salve on Mindy's troubled soul, and she began to cry. "Oh, Clarisse, you have no idea how much it means to me to hear you say that. I–I've wanted to believe Chuck, but—"

"I'd have a hard time believing my husband if someone accused him the way Michelle accused Chuck. You have every right to be angry about this, but please give your husband the benefit of the doubt until you hear otherwise. Chuck's a good guy."

Clarisse pulled a box of tissues from a drawer and pushed it across her desk. Mindy took one and dabbed at her eyes. "I—I don't know the woman. I'm not even sure if I've ever seen her."

"She's not a bad looker, but nothing special. Most of the women in the office dislike her and have from the start. She gets along fine with the men, but the women—?" Clarisse raised her hand and gave a flip of her wrist. "None of us like her. Did you ever get the feeling when you met someone that they couldn't be trusted?"

"Not really."

"I hadn't either until the day I met Michelle, but I felt it then."

Mindy looked up and frowned. "Really? Why? Was it something she said or did?"

Clarisse leaned forward in her chair and linked her fingers together, resting her hands on her desk. "No, just a feeling. She's one of those loners—you know what I mean? Most of us women congregate in the employees' lounge for breaks, drinking coffee or soft drinks, laughing and talking together about the boss, our jobs, our families. Not that one. She stays pretty much to herself or off talking to the men. The rest of us haven't really gotten to know her, and she's been here for nearly six months now."

"Does she dress provocatively?"

"Provocatively?" Clarisse gave her head a firm shake. "No, just the opposite. She dresses very businesslike. Like the proverbial wolf in sheep's clothing, if you ask me."

"I probably shouldn't put you on the spot and ask," Mindy said, lowering her eyes and twisting the tissue between her fingers, "but have you ever seen anything improper going on between Chuck and her? Like a wink or a look that didn't seem right to you?"

"Not a one—from Chuck to her. But I can't say I haven't seen the reverse. I'd say she's had her eye on him from day one."

Mindy's heart sank. This was not what she wanted to hear.

"But Chuck?" the woman continued. "I doubt he ever noticed. All he ever talks about is you. That man is crazy in love with you."

Mindy felt herself blushing. "Clarisse, you've known us for what? Ten years? You know how troubled our marriage was until four years ago. I think Chuck and I honestly loved each other those first ten years, but we sure weren't in sync. We couldn't seem to see eye to eye on anything, from how the house should be kept, to the foods we ate, to when we should have a baby, to who should stay at home and care for her, to everything else that pertained to our lives."

Clarisse gave her a placating smile. "Don't they say opposites attract? Apparently it was true with the two of you. But you worked it out. You're to be commended for that. I've never seen a happier married couple than the two of you these past few years. I don't know if you went to a marriage counselor or what, but I know I've seen a real change in both of you."

"I hate to admit it, Clarisse, but I think we both grew up. We finally realized what our arguments and battles were doing to our family. Poor little Bethany was always in the middle." Mindy smiled through her tears. "Did you ever see that movie about the little girl who decided to divorce her parents?"

Clarisse nodded. "Yeah, I saw it. My husband and I watched it again not long ago on TV."

"That's what happened to us on Bethany's ninth birthday. She watched it on TV at a friend's house. The next morning she came into the kitchen with her little suitcase and asked Chuck for five hundred dollars. She said she was tired of all our arguing and had decided to divorce us. She wanted the five hundred dollars to pay a lawyer to draw up the papers. Chuck, thinking it was a joke, asked her where she planned to live." Mindy paused, the scene playing out in her head. That scene had changed their lives.

Clarisse let out a gasp. "She was serious?"

Mindy nodded, remembering the determination on her daughter's face. "She said she didn't know where she'd live, but any place, even jail, would be better than living with us."

Clarisse leaned back in her chair, her hand covering her heart. "Oh my. That must have upset both of you."

"It did. We knew she didn't like to hear us argue, but we never realized how deeply it affected her until that day."

"What did you do?"

"I remember it like it was yesterday. We threw our arms around Bethany and each other and vowed we would change. And we did. Although we continued to annoy each other with our habits, we kept our complaints to ourselves, and you know what? It wasn't long before we each barely noticed the faults in the other, and we both certainly enjoyed the newfound peace and quiet. We noticed an instant change in Bethany, too. Where she had been an extremely quiet, moody child, she blossomed, a smile constantly on her face. Her teachers noticed it, too, and asked us what had happened to cause such a transformation."

Clarisse clapped her hands together. "That's wonderful! I hadn't realized what had happened, but I noticed a change in Chuck, too. Oh, he's always been a born salesman, and everyone likes him, but there was something about his countenance, a glow, a feeling of self-pride that began to show on his face." She gave Mindy a grin. "Up to that time he talked constantly about Bethany, but he rarely said a word about you. After that, though, he talked about you constantly, saying how happy he was being married to you and what a wonderful wife and mother you were."

"He actually said that about me?"

"Many times. Too numerous to count."

"I—I didn't know."

"That's why it shocked all of us when Michelle made her accusations. It wasn't like the Chuck we all knew and loved, to behave like that. Especially with a woman like her, when he had such a beautiful wife at home."

"But you never saw Chuck do anything improper?"

"Never. Even when Dixie told us what she'd heard in the rest—"

"Dixie told you about that phone call?"

Clarisse nodded. "Dixie is a nice person, but she couldn't keep her mouth shut if her life depended on it."

"I—I don't know what to do, Clarisse," Mindy confided, knowing Clarisse could be trusted. "How do you prove someone's innocence when it's their word against the other person's? I'm beginning to understand how those star athletes feel when a charge like this is made against them. As Chuck said, it's one person's word against the other's, with no witnesses to prove one way or the other."

Clarisse shook her head. "Many a person's reputation has probably been ruined for life for that very reason."

Mindy stared at her hands for a moment, then lifted her eyes to meet Clarisse's. "I have to know the truth. For everyone's sake."

"Know what I'd do if I were in your shoes?" Clarisse asked, her question surprising Mindy. "I'd stalk that woman. I'd watch her every move, even go Dumpster-diving."

Mindy frowned. "Dumpster-diving? What's that?"

"You know, go through the trash she throws away. I heard a trash collector interviewed on TV once on one of those investigative shows. He said he could tell you almost anything you wanted to know about a person just by looking through their trash."

A giggle escaped Mindy's lips. "Dumpster-diving, huh? I may give it a try."

"I figure this isn't the first time she's done something like this, and it won't be the last. I'd talk to the people she worked with before she came here. Maybe talk to her neighbors to see if she makes a habit of inviting men to her apartment. I'd—"

"You'd do all of that?"

Clarisse narrowed her eyes and leaned forward again, anchoring her elbows on her desk. "You bet I would! Why not? What do you have to lose? If I loved my husband the way I know you love Chuck, I wouldn't leave a stone or, in this case, a trash can unturned until I learned the truth. Even if it hurt, I'd have to know what happened and who the guilty party was."

Mindy stared at the woman. She'd never seen her this intense. "I—I wouldn't know where to start. I don't even know where she lives."

Clarisse let a small, mischievous smile curl at her lips. "I know. I have most of that information right here on my computer. All I have to do is punch a few keys on the keyboard."

"But isn't that information confidential?"

"Oh, I didn't say I was going to give it to you." Clarisse tapped several keys and stared at the computer screen for a few seconds, then pulled a yellow steno pad from her top desk drawer, placed a pen on top of it, and, rising from her chair, shoved them both toward Mindy. "But if I just happen to have that information on my screen, and I just happen to go down the hall to the lunchroom to get us a cup of coffee, and you just happen to copy that information on this pad while I'm gone, is that my fault? Have I actually given it to you? Of course not. I wasn't even in the room." She gave Mindy a wink, then made her way out of her office, closing the door behind her.

Mindy's heart pounded so loudly she thought she could hear the sound echoing off the walls of the little office. She circled the desk, sat in Clarisse's chair, and quickly began to copy the information onto the pad. Armed with almost everything she needed to find out more about the elusive Michelle, she nervously pulled the sheets off the pad, folded them, and put them into her purse.

Within minutes the office door opened and Clarisse was back, carrying two cups of steaming hot coffee. With a glance toward the computer screen, the woman lifted her brows, her lips forming a slow smile. "Oh? Did I leave that computer turned on? How careless of me."

After enjoying the hot coffee, which helped to calm her frazzled nerves, Mindy thanked Clarisse, said her good-byes, and moved out the door, heading back toward the elevator. When it arrived, she stepped in and pressed the button marked LOBBY. As the doors began to close, a woman's voice called out, "Hold it, please!"

Instinctively Mindy stuck her arm through the opening, and the door reversed its direction and opened wide as a woman dressed in a beige pantsuit hurried inside, her arms filled with file folders, a pencil stuck over her ear. Though neither woman said anything, Mindy felt the woman's gaze on her, and it made her uncomfortable. *Could this be Michelle?* When they reached the first floor, she waited until the woman was out then stepped out and hurried to her car, clutching the information she needed to do a search on her husband's accuser.

It was nearly six thirty before Mindy finished loading the dinner dishes into the dishwasher. She went into the living room and, trying to appear as casual as possible, moved up to Chuck's chair, hoping the game show he was watching would keep his attention and he wouldn't ask her any questions. "I'm going to go pick up some more toothpaste and a couple of rolls of paper towels. I should be back in an hour or so. Bethany is in her room."

Chuck barely glanced her way. "Could you get me some deodorant while you're there?"

Mindy winced. She had not planned on stopping at a store. Now she would have to if she wanted to cover her tracks. "Sure. Usual kind?"

"Yeah," he answered with a deep sigh, his eyes still fixed on the screen. "You know the kind."

Relieved he did not suggest going with her, Mindy hurriedly snatched up her purse and jacket and headed toward the door.

After rushing into the store and picking up the few items she had mentioned to Chuck, as well as his deodorant, she drove to the address she'd scribbled on the sheet that lay folded in her purse. She'd had no need to check the address; it was etched into her memory.

The neighborhood was much more upscale than she'd expected it would be, filled with lovely townhouses and twin homes. How could a single woman who worked as a secretary afford such nice housing? Maybe she had a roommate to share expenses.

Since the porch light was lit, she easily located the proper address—a two-story, red-brick townhouse done in a colonial style, with black shutters and white trim. Slowly she pulled to a stop across the street and turned off the lights and engine, her heart beating wildly within her chest. *Think, Mindy! You've watched movies with stakeouts before. What did they do? Maybe you should have brought your binoculars.*

This is ridiculous! She stiffened in her seat with a mocking shake of her head. *I feel like an idiot. What did I expect to find? It was a dumb idea to come here.*

She fingered the key in the ignition, intending to get out of there and never come back, when the front door of the townhouse opened and a woman stepped out onto the porch. *Michelle! The woman in the elevator. No wonder she gave me the eye!*

Instinctively Mindy scrunched down in the seat, lowering her head, while at the same time trying to peek through the upper opening in her steering wheel. Other than the few seconds she'd had to observe Michelle at the office, she had never seen the woman before; but considering she was the one causing a rift in her family, Mindy knew she would never forget that face.

She narrowed her eyes into a squint, trying for a better look at the woman. *What is she doing, standing on the porch that way? Why doesn't she either leave or go back inside?* Still peering through the odd-shaped slot in the steering wheel and suddenly realizing how irrationally she was behaving, Mindy uttered a small laugh. *What's the matter with me? I'm being paranoid. It's dark outside. She can't see me!* Relaxing a bit, she straightened and leaned back against the seat, circling her arms about the steering wheel, her eyes once again focused on her rival.

Rival? The word struck horror in her heart! *Is that what that woman is? My rival? For what? My husband's affections? His dedication? His respect?*

So caught up was she in pondering the answers to her questions, she barely noticed the red Mercedes as it pulled into the townhouse driveway and stopped. Michelle closed the door, hurried down the few steps, and crawled into the passenger's side. Though the light from the porch lamp was dim, Mindy could tell the woman was dressed in an attractive beige coat and very high heels and had her hair swept up in a French twist. All sorts of scenarios raced through her mind. Maybe Michelle was having dinner with an old friend. Or perhaps a group of women. Or maybe, just maybe, a man. A man she had made a play for, as she had done with Chuck? Could another unsuspecting wife be sitting at home somewhere in Warren, Rhode Island, unaware Michelle had given up on Chuck and was now after her husband? A shudder coursed through Mindy's body at the thought. *Oh, Chuck, please don't be lying to me!*

As soon as the Mercedes was out of sight, Mindy started her car and drove off, no closer to having answers than when she had come, and feeling very much alone.

The house was quiet when she entered. No doubt Bethany had gone to bed. She slipped out of her coat, hung it in the front closet, and made her way through the darkened family room toward the kitchen, half-hoping, since it appeared the TV was turned off, her husband had retired, too.

"I was beginning to get worried. You've been gone a long time."

Whirling around quickly, she found Chuck sitting in his recliner in the darkness. "I—I"—she fumbled for words, knowing she'd have to cover for herself with a lie—"I ran into a friend at the supermarket, and we got to talking. You know how that is. Time gets away from you." Hoping for a nonconfrontational change of subject, she asked, "Bethany go on to bed?"

Chuck clicked on the lamp beside his chair, bathing the room in light. "Yeah, about a half hour ago. She must be feeling better. She was on the computer talking to one of her friends on that instant-message thing when I went into her room. She said to tell you good night."

"I really don't like her spending so much time on that computer." Mindy faked a yawn. "I'm going to get a glass of water, then turn in, too. Been a long day."

Chuck rose and, walking toward her, closed the gap between them. "I hate sleeping in the guest room."

His expression reminded her of a little boy whose mother had made him sit in a corner until he learned to behave properly. "I don't like sleeping alone either, Chuck, but I think it'd be best until this thing is settled and you've been exonerated."

"But I love you, Mindy. I thought you loved me!"

"I do love you, Chuck! That's why I'm so upset about this whole thing! That's why it hurts!"

He gave his head a frustrated shake. "It hurts me, too! Can't you see that? I'm caught in the middle, and I don't know how to convince you there is not, and never has been, anything going on between me and that woman."

Though she longed to throw herself into his arms, Mindy backed away, holding her palms up between them like a shield. "Then prove it, Chuck. Prove that woman is lying."

Chuck started to say something but turned his head aside and kept his silence. He shrugged, then moved past her toward the bedroom wing of the house, pausing long enough to say a simple "Good night" before making his way down the hall.

She listened until she heard the *click* of the guest room door, then, brushing a tear from her eye, walked into the kitchen for her drink of water.

❧

Dressed in his maroon and navy blue plaid pajamas, the ones he wore only when they entertained overnight company or went on an occasional vacation, Chuck sat down on the edge of the bed and lowered his head into his hands. Never had he felt so rejected.

"Daddy? What are you doing in here?"

He turned quickly to find his sleepy-eyed daughter standing in the doorway. "Hi, princess. I thought you were asleep," he answered sheepishly, not sure what else to say.

"I was, but I heard you and Mom talking. I wanted to ask her if she'd pack my lunch tomorrow. Thursday is pigs-in-a-blanket day in the school cafeteria. I hate the school's pigs-in-a-blanket! No one fixes them like Mom does. I'd rather have a peanut butter and lettuce sandwich."

"Want me to ask her for you?" He moved toward the door. "I came in here to—to get a—ah—an old shirt I keep in the guest room closet. I was about to go back to our bedroom. Your mom is already there." The last thing he wanted was for Bethany to find him sleeping in the guest room.

Bethany nodded, then rubbed at her eyes with a yawn. "Sure. Thanks, Daddy."

Relieved, he watched her go, then hurried to their bedroom to convey her message. Mindy was standing in front of the mirror brushing her hair, wearing the yellow satin nightgown he had given her for her birthday. To Chuck she was a vision of loveliness. The years had been good to her. She was even more beautiful than she had been the day they'd eloped.

"Bethany wants you to fix her a sack lunch tomorrow," he told her, cautiously entering the room. "Guess she doesn't like the school's menu." To his surprise Mindy offered him a pleasant half-smile.

"Must be pigs-in-a-blanket day."

He nodded. "You know our daughter well."

"Very well." She placed the brush in a dresser drawer and turned to face him. "I may not have been the best of mothers her first few years, but I'm trying to make up for it."

"You're a good mother, Mindy. The best. Bethany is lucky to have you."

She moved to their bed and pulled back the lovely handmade Jacob's Ladder quilt Chuck had inherited from his grandmother. "I've always thought she was lucky to have you. You've been a terrific father to our daughter, but now—"

"Now you're not so sure?"

"That wasn't exactly what I was going to say." She picked up the pillow from her side of the bed and gave it two hard jabs with her fist to plump it up.

"But you were thinking it, right?"

Mindy slipped off her scuffies and slid between the sheets, pulling the covers up over her. "Chuck, it's late. Please let's not get into another discussion."

He moved to stand beside her, his arms dangling limply by his sides. "I don't want to argue with you, sweetheart. I just want you to believe me—that's all."

Mindy stared at him for a few seconds, then reached up and turned out the lamp on her nightstand. "On the way to your room, try not to wake Bethany again, okay?"

He stood in the semidarkness of the room, a shaft of moonlight creeping around the edges of the shade its only light, and let out a deep sigh that came from the uttermost part of his being. "Good night, Mindy."

For the next week, each day as Mindy drove home from her office, she managed to swing by Michelle's condo. It was as if the car would not allow her to go home until she had made the out-of-the-way detour. But each time either Michelle wasn't at home yet or she had gone out for the evening or she was simply inside doing whatever single women did when they were home alone, and Mindy never saw her.

"I'm going crazy!" Chuck told her on Friday evening when he came into the house and slammed down his briefcase.

Mindy gave him an impatient frown. "Good thing Bethany has play rehearsal tonight and wasn't here to hear that outburst! What's wrong?"

He pulled off his sports coat and tossed it onto the chair, then yanked his tie from about his neck. "I've been all over town applying for jobs, but do you think anyone will hire me? Not a chance! Not after I tell them I've been suspended indefinitely and the reason why. You'd think I had the plague!"

"I'm sorry, Chuck. I never realized it would be so hard to find another job," Mindy told him. "But in some ways you can't blame them."

Chuck gave her a ferocious stare. "How many times do I have to tell you that woman is lying?"

"Chuck! I'm on your side!" Mindy shot back defensively. "She's made some very serious charges against you! Put yourself in their place."

He grabbed her arms and leaned into her face. "Why should I expect anyone to believe those things didn't happen when my own wife, the woman who should know me best, doesn't believe me?"

His words went right to her gut. Mindy crossed to the sofa and sat down, moved by his obvious pain. "I want to believe you, Chuck," she said in a hushed, controlled voice. "I really do, and I'm trying to believe you, but as yet, other than simply denying the charge, you haven't given me any reason to believe you. Help me here. Give me some hope. So far you've given me nothing but a few denials. I need more. Surely you can understand that."

Chuck sat down beside her, wringing his hands, a deep scowl etched on his face. "I'm sorry, Mindy. I have no right to take my rage out on you, but I'm at my wit's end. I had a talk with Jake today, and although he is sympathetic, he says he has no choice but to keep me on suspension until I find a way to prove my innocence. Michelle is still working at her job, drawing her pay, with probably everyone feeling sorry for her. Meantime I can't even support my family."

Mindy could not resist the urge to place a comforting hand on his shoulder. "It's not as if we're destitute, Chuck. I'm still making good money. We have a sizable savings account and a couple of CDs, and our home is paid for. We have much to be thankful for."

He reached up and capped her hand with his long fingers. "I am thankful for those things, sweetheart, but you don't know what all this is doing to me. Though you make more money than I do, I still feel it's my responsibility as the husband and father of this family to provide for you and Bethany. How can I do that if I can't get a job?"

Mindy tugged her hand away. He made it all sound so hopeless. "I don't know, Chuck. I wish I did." How much longer could this go on? Chuck had become a different man from the one she had known all these years. He'd nearly given up on finding employment and had become the proverbial couch potato, a constant daytime surveyor of news programs and soap operas. Most days he would rise, dress for work, and drive away at his usual time, only to return a few minutes after Bethany left for school, leaving again a few minutes before time for her to return. If dirty dishes were left in the sink, he failed to put them in the dishwasher. If the hampers were filled with dirty clothes, he left them there. His who-cares attitude was driving Mindy crazy. This was not the Chuck she knew.

"Chuck," she would say, trying to hold down her temper, "the least you can do is help out at home!"

But Chuck would only give her a blank stare and nod. Most times she was not even sure he heard her. Each night when she'd come home from her office, those things would still be waiting undone, and she would have to do them. Even Bethany voiced her concern at the way her normally neat-freak father left things these days. But he would laugh and give her a big hug, telling her both he and her mom were too busy with their jobs sometimes to get everything done.

Mindy resented it when he did that. His careless attitude began to rub off on their daughter as Bethany, too, began to leave her bed unmade and clothing lying around. Each time her mother would mention it to her, she would respond by saying, "Daddy does it. Why don't you get after him?"

Saturday morning was the day Mindy usually did the grocery shopping and had her hair done and a manicure. Several years ago she had cautioned her staff to contact her on weekends only in the case of an emergency. Weekends were family time. But today, with Chuck off visiting his mother in Providence and Bethany spending the day at the church practicing for an upcoming Bible quiz, Mindy found herself breaking her usual routine and going by Michelle's townhouse. As she sat in her car outside the woman's home, she pondered her life. Something had to give. Sooner or later Bethany would catch her father sitting at home during the day instead of going off to work as she thought he had, or sneaking into the guest room to sleep at night, and she'd begin to ask questions to which they had no answers.

Unexpectedly the front door of the townhouse opened, and Michelle came out carrying a big white plastic bag. She circled the sidewalk to where a communal Dumpster stood and tossed the bag inside. Instantly visions of one of those TV detectives scrounging through a suspect's trash came to mind, and Mindy could almost see herself crawling into the trash bin to obtain evidence, her feet dangling over the sides.

Again the door opened, and Michelle reappeared; only this time she made her way to her car, climbed in, and drove off. Mindy checked her watch, waited five minutes, then, swallowing her pride, pushed open her door and ran to the Dumpster. It was nearly three-fourths full. There, on the top of the other trash, sat the white bag. She glanced first one way, then the other, and seeing none of the other residents, she reached in and snatched up the bag and ran to her car, fully expecting to hear the wail of a siren and see a police car come rushing down the street with an officer leaping out, gun drawn, ready to arrest her.

A rush of adrenaline almost made her giddy as she sat in the front seat clutching the bag tightly. It was all she could do to keep from opening it, to see if her bizarre behavior was worth taking the risk, but she restrained herself, preferring to go through it in the privacy of her home. Feeling like a thief who had just stolen the world's largest diamond, she yanked the gearshift into the drive position and hit the gas pedal, squealing her tires in the process.

Once back in her kitchen, she spread an old worn-out tablecloth onto the floor and dumped out her treasure. Remembering she had a lightweight pair of plastic gloves in the pantry, she pulled them on and plowed into the mass of eggshells, moldy bread, spoiled coffee cream, smelly paper plates, a few pizza boxes, and numerous other nauseating items, her stomach nearly getting the best of her. Undaunted, she swallowed hard and continued, putting items back into the bag one at a time, wishing she had a free hand to hold her nose. Most of the items she found were the things you would expect to find in the average person's trash. "This has turned out to be nothing but an exercise in futility, a pure waste of time," she said aloud. "It was a stupid idea. Whatever possessed me to do something so foolish?"

She stood in the middle of the room, awkwardly holding the bag in her hands. "Now what? How am I going to get rid of this thing? Chuck is always the one who gathers up the trash, deposits it in the trash can, and places it beside the curb. What if he decides, for some unknown reason, to go through it? It certainly wouldn't do for him to find trash belonging to Michelle in our trash can!" She was crossing the kitchen slowly when an idea hit her. "As awkward as it may be, I'll just have to drop off that bag in a Dumpster at the mall!"

As usual, both Chuck and Mindy were at the Sunday morning church service with their daughter, although they were only there because Bethany insisted they attend. Mindy was sure he felt as awkward as she did as they sat next to each other in the silence of the big sanctuary. Try as she may to concentrate on the pastor's message, all she could think about was Chuck with that woman.

Clarisse, who attended their church regularly, caught up with Mindy in the foyer at the close of the service. "I've been meaning to call you. How are you and Chuck doing?"

Mindy let out a sigh. "Not good. He's so discouraged, Clarisse. He has no idea how to go about clearing his name. And I'm no help."

"I'm keeping my ears open, hoping Michelle will slip up and say something that will be of value. She's a smug one. She struts around that office as if she owns the place. No one likes her. Her overconfidence sickens me. I wish she'd quit and leave town."

Mindy gasped. "We don't want that to happen. She's the only one who could tell the truth."

"Then you believe Chuck's side of the story?"

"I'm trying to," Mindy answered, lowering her head to avoid Clarisse's gaze. "But it's so hard. So hard."

Clarisse reached for Mindy's hand and gave it a squeeze. "As I told you, Mindy, Chuck is a good guy. That woman could never convince me he did anything improper with her. Hang in there. He needs you."

Before Mindy could reply, Clarisse disappeared into the milling crowd of worshippers, but her words lingered, making Mindy wonder if perhaps Chuck was telling the truth.

❦

"I have a math test at school today," Bethany told her mother a few days later as she finished her breakfast and pushed her bowl aside.

"You'll do fine. Knowing you, you've probably studied for it." Smiling, Mindy grabbed her jacket from the hook by the kitchen door and dangled her car keys in front of the girl. "I'm ready when you are. I'll go start the car."

"You're going to have to use my car today, Mindy," Chuck said from his place at the breakfast table, handing her his key ring. "When I went out to get my briefcase out of my car, I noticed your front tire was flat again. I'll change it and have a new one put on for you."

"I should have done it weeks ago. Thanks, Chuck. I'd appreciate it. I have a superbusy day today." She gave him an honest smile as she exchanged keys with him. "I'll be waiting in the car, Bethany."

❦

Chuck sat staring at his daughter a moment later. "Is that red lipstick I see on your mouth?"

Bethany gave him a smile. "I'm nearly thirteen now, Daddy. All my friends wear red lipstick."

"And I don't like that shirt you're wearing either. It's much too short. It shows your belly button. I'm surprised you'd even consider wearing it. I think you'd better go change into something more presentable, and maybe you should take about half of that lipstick off while you're at it."

Bethany gave him a slight glare. "I can't. I'll be late for school."

"No, you won't. You have plenty of time." Chuck rose and with a smile laid his hand on her shoulder. "Look, princess—I know being a teenager brings on a lot of changes. I just want you to be safe. That's all. Now scoot! Run back into your bedroom like a good girl and do as Daddy asks."

Five minutes later Bethany came back all smiles, without the red lipstick and wearing a turquoise polo shirt. "This better?"

Chuck nodded. "Much better. What took you so long?"

Bethany shrugged. "Nothing."

"Run along. Your mother is waiting."

ॐ

Since Bethany usually had her backpack and sometimes a sweater and other items that more than filled up the front seat of Chuck's sports car, Mindy tossed her purse into the backseat.

The two giggled and had a pleasant conversation on the way. Mindy never tired of hearing Bethany laugh and tell stories about the things that happened at school. She let her daughter off at the front sidewalk, waved, and hurried on to her office. When she arrived she parked the car and reached into the backseat for her purse. But when she yanked on the shoulder strap, everything she kept stored inside tumbled out onto the seat, helter-skelter. *Oh, I forgot to zip the zipper!*

With a glance at her watch, she leaped out the door, turned, and began shoving her belongings back into her purse. Finding her compact and her lipstick missing, she ran her hand down the back of the seat cushion to retrieve them. She found them easily, but she also found something else.

A silver and turquoise bracelet, one she'd never seen before.

Instantly red flags began to wave in her mind. *Michelle! The bracelet must belong to Michelle!*

Chapter 5

Her hands shaking, Mindy stared at the bracelet. Had Chuck been lying to her all this time? Was he guilty of the charge Michelle had made against him? Just the thought of her husband and that woman in the backseat of his car made her want to vomit.

Filled with disgust, her eyes dripping with tears of both hurt and disappointment, Mindy clutched the bracelet in her hand and headed for home. All thoughts of her early appointments and her staff waiting for her at the medical office for the customary Monday morning staff meeting vanished as she drove over the speed limit toward their house.

Chuck was still sitting at the kitchen table in his pajamas when she burst through the door. "What are you—"

"Whose bracelet is this?" she shouted at him angrily, waving it in his face. "It sure isn't mine!"

He gave her a mystified look. "I have no idea! I've never seen it before. Where did you get it, and why are you so angry?"

Chafing at his look of innocence, Mindy spat out, "Wedged down in the backseat of your car, that's where!"

Chuck took the bracelet from her hand and examined it. "Maybe it's Bethany's."

She jerked it from him and snarled, "You think I don't know my own daughter's jewelry? I can assure you it does not belong to Bethany!"

Obviously angered by her harsh demeanor and her accusations, Chuck stood quickly and glared at her, his hands planted on his hips. "Are you insinuating Michelle was in the backseat of my car? With me?"

Mindy glared back, her own anger at the boiling point. "Was she?"

Chuck's eyes narrowed, and his face grew red as the little muscle in his jaw ticked with irritation. "I won't dignify that question with an answer."

She seethed at his evasive response. "I've asked you a simple question, Chuck. All it needs is a simple yes or no."

"No!"

"And you expect me to believe that?"

"What you choose to believe is up to you." Chuck headed toward the family room, stopping in the archway to turn and say in a soft voice, "I only hope you know me well enough to make the right choice. If my own wife doesn't believe me, why should anyone else?"

Mindy dropped into a chair at the table, feeling both physically and mentally drained. She wanted so much to believe Chuck, but how could she? So far everything seemed to point to his guilt. Everything, except what Clarisse had said about Michelle the day Mindy visited her at his office. Surely, if Chuck were innocent, there would be some way to prove it.

~~~

The next few weeks were miserable for both Mindy and Chuck. They fought anytime they spoke to each other, except when Bethany was in their presence. At those times they carried on as normally as possible, not wanting to upset her with harsh words.

To Mindy's dismay, Chuck spent most of his days hanging around the house in either his pajamas and robe or the grubbiest old clothes he owned, sitting in front of the TV listening to the same news stories over and over, watching sports and soap operas. Sometimes he would piddle around in the garage trying to repair an old toaster or some such gadget—shaving and dressing just before Bethany came home from school.

"Why don't you go and talk to Jake, plead your case again, and ask him to take you off suspension? At least let him know you're interested in coming back to work," Mindy told him one Saturday morning as she straightened the house and gathered up the laundry. "You're certainly not worth much around here. You could help with the household chores instead of"—she paused and rolled her eyes—"instead of whatever you do, or don't do, around here all day."

Chuck hiked his shoulders. "What good would it do, Mindy? Like you, Jake has his mind made up. He prefers to believe that woman rather than me, the guy who has faithfully worked for him all these years."

"You've turned into a couch potato, Chuck. Look at you. I barely recognize you. You've quit exercising. You're edgy and short on patience. You never go out of the house. This place is in total disarray, with old newspapers, magazines, and such scattered everywhere. Something has to change, or we'll all go crazy! I can't keep covering up for you in front of Bethany."

He shook his head and fumbled with the stubble on his chin. "You don't know what this is doing to me, Mindy. My life is out of control, and I can't find a way to get it back on track."

"Get yourself cleaned up! Go out and find a job, even if it's being a greeter at a department store. Something—anything—that might restore your self-esteem and get you out of the house."

"I've tried, sweetheart—honestly I have. But every employer I've spoken with has asked me for references. Jake is sure to tell them I'm on suspension and the reason why. Would you hire me if you heard I'd been suspended because a coworker accused me of molesting her?"

Mindy did not have to answer. She knew her face told it all.

"I've never been this discouraged in my entire life," Chuck admitted, leaning back in the chair and locking his hands behind his head. "I want my old life back. You and I had a good thing going. Now it's all gone. Sometimes I think everyone, especially you and Bethany, would be better off if I'd just disappear."

Mindy's blood ran cold. The idea of Chuck disappearing from their lives, with no idea of where to find him, frightened her. She had never considered he might do anything that drastic.

Chuck stood slowly to his feet and headed off toward the guest room. "I'm no good to anyone, least of all you."

The words repeated in her head. *I'm no good to anyone, least of all you.*

The ringing of the doorbell cut into her thoughts. She considered not answering it. She certainly was not in the mood for neighborly chit-chat if it was that nice Mrs. Greeley from next door. But since both cars were in the driveway, it was obvious someone was at home. Trying to force her emotions to settle down, she moved slowly to the door.

"Hello, Mindy. I'm Janine Porter." A pretty, dark-haired woman stood on the other side of the storm door smiling at her, holding a plate of cookies. "My husband, Jim, and I live across the street. We moved in about three months ago. We've met Bethany, but we've never met her mother and father. She's such a delightful child. We're both crazy about her, especially Jim. I thought it was about time we met her parents." She lifted the plate toward Mindy. "I made these for you."

Though Mindy wished the woman had come at a better time, she summoned a smile and pushed open the door, accepting the cookies. "Where are my manners? Please come in."

The woman held up a hand. "No, I need to get back—maybe another time. Perhaps we can all go to dinner some evening."

"It was very thoughtful of you to bring these. You said you've met our daughter?"

The woman nodded. "Oh, yes, Bethany found our dog and returned him to us when we first moved in. Those two took a real shine to each other. She's stopped to visit with him several times. She's even helped Jim teach Cocky a few tricks."

"Oh, you're the ones with the cute cocker spaniel. Bethany has mentioned you a number of times. It's nice to meet you. I hope she hasn't been a bother. That girl loves animals. Especially cute little dogs."

Janine shook her head. "A bother? Not at all. We love having her around. In fact, if we had our way, we'd see her more often. You have a lovely, well-mannered daughter. You and Mr. O'Connor should be very proud of her."

Mindy's heart swelled with pride. "We are. Bethany is the delight of our life."

"We don't have children yet. We've only been married a few months, but someday we will. We both love children, but Jim keeps reminding me not all children are as pretty or as well behaved as your daughter."

"Thank you for the compliments. I'll pass them on to Chuck. That's my husband."

Continuing to smile, the woman backed off the porch. "Well, it's been nice meeting you, Mindy. I hope we can become friends."

"Me, too. Thanks again for the cookies. I'm sure we'll enjoy them."

Janine gave her a wave as she turned to cross the street. "You're welcome. See you later."

Mindy watched her go, deciding it would be nice to get acquainted with their new neighbors. She wondered about Janine's husband. She hoped Jim Porter would be as nice as his wife.

⁓⁓

"Mom, can I go home with Tracie after school so we can work on our homework together? I know you have a dinner meeting with someone," Bethany asked when she called her mother during lunch break the next day. "Her mom said it's okay. Her dad is going to drive us to play rehearsal."

Mindy smiled into the phone. "That someone I'm meeting is the chairman of the board. We have to finalize the information for the yearly stockholders' meeting."

"Whatever."

Mindy could almost see her child's face as she used her favorite overworked word. "It's fine with me, honey. Just make sure you get that homework done. What time is play rehearsal over? I'll pick you up."

"Probably by nine."

"I'll be waiting at the main door. See you at nine."

"Line two!" Erica, one of the secretaries, called out as soon as Mindy hung up the phone. "The chairman of the board. He said he needs to change the time for your dinner meeting."

Ever the competent employee, Mindy quickly answered line two. "Changing the time will be no problem," she told the man. She was sure Chuck could pick up Bethany in her place. "I'll meet you at seven thirty at the restaurant."

She tried the house and, guessing he had gone to the grocery store or maybe to get a haircut, left her message on the answering machine, asking him to pick up Bethany at nine.

She planned to call again and remind him after she reached the restaurant, but the chairman and his wife were already waiting for her when she arrived. The three had a lovely dinner as they talked over some business dealings and discussed the agenda for the yearly meeting. He even hinted he thought it was about time they gave Mindy a nice big increase in salary. It was ten after nine and pouring down rain by the time Mindy left the restaurant and crawled into her car. She was tempted to drive by the school, but knowing Chuck and his tendency to be early wherever he went, she headed on home. Sure enough, his car was in the driveway. He and Bethany were already there.

After gathering up the few papers she'd brought home to go over and slipping them into her briefcase, she opened her umbrella and ran the few steps to the porch. Mindy let out a loud gasp as she entered the house. Chuck was in his pajamas, sitting in his recliner, staring at the TV! "Where's Bethany? You did pick her up, didn't you?" she screamed at him as she tossed her briefcase onto a chair and rushed to his side, yanking the remote from his hands.

He gave her a dazed look. "You said you were going to pick her up."

"Chuck!" She grabbed on to his sleeve, giving it a hard shake. "No! I asked you to do it. I left a message on the answering machine. Didn't you get it?"

"I've been home all day! Why would I check the answering machine?" He sat up straight, his eyes wild, the footrest on his chair plummeting down with a loud thud.

"You weren't here when I called!" She felt herself trembling.

"I was here! I never left the house, not once! I did go out into the garage to find a screwdriver, but I was only gone a few minutes!"

Mindy raced toward the door. "It's nine thirty, Chuck! Our child has been waiting nearly thirty minutes, and you know how she hates storms! I'm going after her."

"I'll go with you."

"No, you stay here. She might try to call!"

Paying no attention to the speed limit, Mindy raced her car toward the school, pulling up to the front entrance in record time despite the heavy downpour. But with the exception of the security lights, the school was dark, and not a soul was in sight. Not taking time to grab her umbrella, she pushed open the door and ran up the steps, banging loudly on the glass with her fists and calling out Bethany's name.

But Bethany didn't answer.

Lightning flashed across the sky, and thunder rolled overhead, giving the night an eerie look.

Not sure what else to do or where to turn, Mindy pounded on the door again and again, continuing to scream out Bethany's name. Finally, a face appeared behind the glass—a weathered face—framed by scraggly white hair. "I can't find my daughter!" Mindy yelled out as the man unlocked the door and pushed it open a crack. "I was supposed to pick her up at nine."

"No one here now," the man, who explained he was the night watchman, said sympathetically. "A girl was waiting when I made my rounds about a half hour ago. I offered to let her wait inside, but she refused to come in. Said her mom would be here any second. She was gone when I checked about twenty minutes later."

Mindy watched helplessly as he closed the door and disappeared into the darkness. Grabbing her cell phone from the holster on her waistband, she frantically dialed Tracie's number.

"She was still waiting for you when my mom picked me up, Mrs. O'Connor," the girl told her. "We offered to take her home, but she wouldn't go. She said she was supposed to wait for you."

Mindy punched the end button and dialed her home number. Chuck answered on the first ring.

"She's not at the school! Have you heard from her?" she yelled into the phone, trying to make herself heard above the claps of thunder belching overhead.

"No, I was hoping she was still there."

Mindy began to cry. Where was Bethany? Her baby? Her only child? "Oh, Chuck, if only you'd checked the answering machine!"

∽∾

Chuck clutched the phone tightly between his palms, his mind in a whir. "I'm calling the police," he told her in a take-charge manner. "Stay right where you are. I'm coming over there."

After phoning, without even taking time to change from his pajamas into jeans and a T-shirt, Chuck grabbed his jacket and his keys from the hall table and ran to his car. He arrived at the school in a matter of minutes, as two police officers moved up onto the porch. Mindy was crying hysterically and trying to explain what had happened. He joined in the conversation but found he was of no more help than his wife.

Mindy flailed an accusing finger in his face. "He was supposed to pick our daughter up after play rehearsal, but he—"

"I would have if I'd known my wife put a message on the answering machine," Chuck countered, feeling guilty for letting Mindy and his daughter down.

The officer who was doing most of the questioning held up his hand between them. "Look, folks—I know you're both upset, but let's quit all this blaming and concentrate on finding your daughter." Turning to Mindy, he asked, "Have you contacted her friends or anyone she might have ridden home with?"

Mindy nodded. "There's only one person she would have ridden with, her best friend, and I've already called her. She said Bethany was still here when she left."

"And you've talked to the night watchman, right?"

Again she nodded. "Yes, he said she was here when he checked about ten after nine. He tried to get her to wait inside out of the rain, but she refused. When he—"

"When he checked about twenty minutes later," Chuck inserted, pulling his wife into his arms and pressing her head against his chest, "she was gone. We've cautioned Bethany over and over not to accept rides from people she doesn't know. I can't imagine she'd accept a ride with a stranger."

"The best thing you folks can do for your daughter is go on home. She may be trying to call you right now," the officer said kindly.

"She has my cell phone number." Mindy's flattened palm went to her waist. "She knows I keep it with me at all times. Why hasn't she called me?"

"I don't know, ma'am, but there is nothing you can do here. You need to start calling all her friends, her teachers, your neighbors, anyone who may know of her whereabouts."

Chuck wiped the rain from his face with the back of his hand. "What about the night watchman? It seems he was the last one to see her. Shouldn't you talk to him?"

"That's exactly what we plan to do, sir." The officer nodded his head in Mindy's direction. "I suggest Mrs. O'Connor go on home and wait by the phone, in case your daughter tries to call there. I'll have another officer follow her and stay with her. You can stay and cruise the neighborhood with me." He placed a consoling hand on Mindy's shoulder. "We'll do our best to help you find your daughter, ma'am. Both my partner and I are parents. We know what you're going through."

Less than ten minutes later, Mindy and the officer entered the house on Victor Lane. She let out a shriek of joy when the phone was ringing and hurried to answer it.

"Mrs. O'Connor, this is Tracie's mother. I was concerned about Bethany and wanted to see if you'd found her yet."

Aching with disappointment, Mindy braced herself against the desk, her hand on her forehead. "We were hoping this was a call from her."

"I'm so sorry. I'll get off the line. Please let us know if we can do anything to help."

After thanking the woman for her concern, she placed the phone back in its cradle.

"Mrs. O'Connor, try to concentrate," the officer said. "Is there anyone else your daughter might have trusted enough to ride home with? A neighbor, maybe a friend you haven't seen in a long time? Possibly an older boy she met at school?"

"No, of course not! She's not quite thirteen. She's certainly not old enough to be thinking about boys!"

He gave her a slight grin. "My daughter is thirteen, and she's plenty interested in boys."

Mindy pulled off her jacket and sank down on the sofa. "Maybe I don't know my daughter as well as I thought, but I doubt she'd do something like this knowing we were coming to pick her up."

"Even if everyone else had gone and she was the only one standing there in the rain?" he prodded gently.

"Maybe, if it was someone she thought she could trust. She's terribly frightened by storms," she conceded, hating to consider such a thing but knowing there was a slight possibility something like that had occurred. "Sometimes when the weather is bad, she's so frightened she crawls into bed with us."

She listened as the officer used his cell phone to call in and report his whereabouts, then waited, hoping he would have something to tell her.

"My partner and your husband are still combing the neighborhood," he explained as he fastened the phone back in the holster on his heavy black belt.

Mindy stared at the clock on the desk. It was well past ten. Flashes of lightning still brightened the room, and thunder continued to roll overhead. Wherever Bethany was, she had to be terrified.

At eleven Chuck and another man he introduced as Captain Wyatt appeared at the door. Mindy threw herself into her husband's arms and pressed her face against his chest. "Oh, Chuck, you didn't find her?"

He shook his head sadly. "No, but we'll keep looking."

"It's your fault!" Now in hysterics, Mindy beat her fists against his chest. "You were supposed to pick her up! Can't I count on you for anything?"

～⚬～

Filled with more guilt than Mindy could ever heap on him, Chuck grabbed on to her wrists and held them tightly in his grasp. "Look—there's nothing you can say to me I haven't already said to myself. You're right. I should have checked the answering machine, and I should have picked her up! If anything has happened to our precious Bethany, I'll—I'll—" Slowly he released his hold; then, tilting his wife's chin up and meeting her gaze with his, he whispered softly, "We'll find her, Mindy. We have to."

The two jumped when the doorbell rang and two additional officers entered their home. One of them, a woman, introduced herself as Lieutenant Terry and gestured toward the sofa. "Please sit down. I need to ask you some questions."

Mindy's eyes widened. "Why? We've already told you what we know. Shouldn't you be out looking for our daughter?"

Chuck cradled the small of her back with his hand. "Let's do what she says

Maybe we'll think of something that might help."

Once the three were seated, the lieutenant pulled a pad from the case she was carrying and made a few notes. Then, looking at them in a kind, understanding way, she asked, "Has your daughter been upset about anything lately? Maybe been grounded for having low grades or for not coming home on time?"

Mindy's eyes flashed. "No! Not Bethany! She's a model student. Makes straight As!"

The woman scribbled a few notes, then turned to them again. "Has she ever run away from home or threatened to run away?"

"No!" Chuck answered firmly. "Not once. Bethany is a happy, easygoing child who rarely complains about anything."

Lieutenant Terry peered at them over her half-glasses. "That may be so, but your child is missing, and it's nearly midnight. You have to give us something to go on. We need your complete honesty here. Is there anything going on in your family that might affect your daughter? A fight between the two of you? Money problems? Maybe a job situation?"

Mindy cast a quick glance at Chuck.

"I've been suspended from my job, but Bethany doesn't know. We haven't told her yet."

"Maybe you only think she doesn't know. Kids are often more perceptive than we realize."

Captain Wyatt moved up beside Lieutenant Terry, his thumbs locked into his belt. "You said suspended. What exactly does that mean?"

Chuck's gut hurt as he drew in a deep breath. "I was falsely accused of something."

"Must have been pretty serious for your boss to place you on suspension." The man stood waiting for Chuck's explanation.

"One of the women in our office accused me of—" He swallowed hard, finding it impossible to say the word.

"Of what, Mr. O'Connor?"

The look on Mindy's face broke Chuck's heart.

"Of molesting her."

"And you're sure your daughter doesn't know about this?"

"We've been keeping it from her," Mindy said. "We're trying to find a way to prove my husband's innocence."

Her words of support surprised Chuck, and he suddenly didn't feel as alone anymore. "I didn't do it. Honest, I didn't," he said adamantly. "I have no idea why she would accuse me of such a thing."

The officers cast a glance at one another, which Chuck interpreted as saying they doubted his story.

"I'll need several recent photos of your daughter," Lieutenant Terry said, rising. "And we'll need to know if she has any distinguishing marks, like a birthmark or an unusually placed mole, and a description of what she was wearing."

Once the officers had each been given a recent snapshot of Bethany, along with a description of her clothing, they conferred with one another, then left to continue their search, leaving Lieutenant Terry behind. "I'll be staying with you," she told them. "Just in case you get a phone call."

"From Bethany?" Mindy asked quickly, feeling a new ray of hope.

The officer frowned slightly. "Her or anyone else who may know her whereabouts."

"You think someone has taken her?" Mindy nearly screamed out. "Kidnapped our daughter? But why?"

"No, I'm not saying that, Mrs. O'Connor, but we have to be realistic. Your daughter has been missing for several hours now. From what you tell me, she is not the type of child who would stay out with friends without telling you or run away from home. The best thing you and Mr. O'Connor can do is try to come up with the names of others who may know of Bethany's whereabouts."

"But we don't—"

"Why don't you fix a pot of coffee, Mrs. O'Connor? I think we could all use a cup."

"I'll help you," Chuck said, sensing his wife's need and wanting to comfort her. "Coffee sounds good."

The lights blinked as a gigantic clap of thunder roared overhead. Mindy grabbed on to Chuck's arm and melded herself to him, her tears flowing freely. "Oh, Chuck, where is Bethany? Where is our baby girl? Is she huddling somewhere, terrified of the storm?"

She paused, her eyes rounded with fear, then let out a pitiful cry that ripped at Chuck's heart. "Or is she going through something much worse?"

Chapter 6

The morning dawned gray and cloudy, with an almost ominous feeling. Sleep had eluded Mindy, as well as Chuck, each crash of thunder and each bolt of lightning bringing on a new set of fears. Over ten hours had passed since their daughter disappeared. Ten long, painful hours, and the wear and tear of the experience was showing as they huddled together in the semi-darkness of the family room, waiting, hoping for the phone to ring or the door to open and Bethany to come walking through.

But it did not happen.

Mindy's mother arrived from Newport about seven, her face tired and haggard from her all-night vigil near her phone.

By eight they had received more than six calls from radio and TV stations or newspapers that had heard about Bethany's disappearance and wanted to do stories on it.

By nine Mindy left her mother in charge of the phone and joined the search with Chuck, going from house to house in the four-block area around their home, personally begging their neighbors for any scrap of information that might lead them to Bethany.

Though several people told the two how much they loved their daughter and what a sweet kid she was, none of them offered any concrete information. Not even Treva Jordan, Bethany's Sunday school teacher and mentor, or Tracie, her best friend, who had attended the play rehearsal with her, could think of anything to help. Though several of her classmates remembered seeing Bethany on the porch, waiting for her parents after the practice, none of them had actually seen her leave.

"Jim and I will be glad to help in any way we can," Janine Porter told them when Mindy appeared at her door asking about Bethany. "You name it—we'll do it."

"Thanks," Mindy told her as she backed off the porch, pulling her jacket collar up around her neck. "If some news doesn't turn up soon, we may have to ask you to help us canvass a larger area. Someone in Warren has to have seen our daughter."

"Are you planning to pass out flyers or put up posters around the community? I could help with that, and I'm sure Jim will want to help, too. He's home

171

today. He wanted to play golf all day, but I refused to let him go. It might sound silly, but I'm afraid to stay home alone. I had to shed a few tears to accomplish it but I actually managed to keep him here. I told him if he went, I was going with him. That kept him here. He knows what a terrible golfer I am." Janine rambled on, seemingly uncomfortable and unsure what to say.

"At this point I'm not sure what we should do next. Almost everyone we've talked to has offered to help in any way they can. We just keep hoping Bethany will call and say she's all right."

"Oh, Mindy, I'm praying that will happen."

"So am I, Janine. So am I."

～～

Chuck was waiting for her at the corner. "No one knows anything," he said sadly his tone somber.

Mindy slipped her hand into the crook of his arm and let out a sigh. "I didn't get anywhere either. Now what?"

"I think it's time to talk to Captain Wyatt again." Chuck pulled out his cell phone, dialed, and waited for an answer.

Mindy wept softly as she listened to the one-sided conversation, all the while her mind fixed on Bethany.

"Let's go," Chuck said after placing his phone back in his pocket. "He's going to meet us at the house."

Mindy's mother met them at the door with reddened eyes and an anxious look on her face. "Any news?"

Both Mindy and Chuck shook their heads.

"Captain Wyatt is in the kitchen," Mrs. Carson said, brushing away a tear from her cheek. "He's such a nice man. I know he's doing everything he can to help find our little girl."

"She's not a little girl anymore, Mom," Mindy said, wiping her eyes with a tissue as she followed her into the kitchen. "She's a lovely, responsible teenager I'm so afraid some—"

"Now, dear, don't be thinking those kinds of thoughts." Her mother took her by the arm and motioned her toward a chair at the kitchen table. "I'm going to fix you a piece of toast. I'll bet you haven't eaten a thing today. You must keep your strength up."

～～

Chuck extended his hand as he entered the kitchen. "Any word?"

Captain Wyatt rose with a shake of his head. "Sorry. No. If we don't hear something soon, you two might want to consider doing an interview and showing pictures of Bethany on one of the Providence TV station's news reports. I'm sure they'd send one of their reporters and cameramen here to do it."

"It has to be the night watchman," Chuck replied, trying desperately to come up with a viable solution to his daughter's disappearance. "She knew him. She might have gone inside with him."

"The man has been at that school for nearly thirty years. His reputation is impeccable. There's never been a single complaint lodged against him. He's sick about this and has offered to help in any way he can."

"But he might be covering up," Chuck insisted.

The captain nodded. "Yes, he might be, but so far nothing has indicated he is."

"Who else could have had the opportunity?"

He motioned for Chuck to come closer, then said in a low voice, "I don't want your wife to hear this, but I have to tell you. Thirteen is the prime predator target age. You can't imagine how many thirteen-year-olds have twenty-two-year-old boyfriends, and their moms and dads are clueless."

Chuck winced, his mouth suddenly going dry. "Bethany has never even had a boyfriend!"

"As I said, parents often have no idea what is going on with their daughters when they are supposed to be spending the night with a friend or attending one of those slumber-party things. I just thought you should know."

"I'd never even considered something like that. Though Bethany is maturing, she's still very young. I guess I hadn't realized my baby is no longer a baby."

"Mr. O'Connor, in cases where a child is actually abducted—"

Chuck felt his heart clench at the word. "Abducted? You really think someone has taken our daughter?"

With another glance toward Mindy, who was still in conversation with her mother, Captain Wyatt went on. "Your daughter has been missing since last night. It's a possibility we have to consider at this point. Anything you can remember, even the tiniest thing, maybe a comment Bethany made or some type of unusual behavior, might be valuable to us as we search for her."

Shocked by the idea of someone taking Bethany, Chuck felt himself reel. He wanted to ask the captain much more but dropped the subject when his wife approached with a fresh cup of coffee.

"Wh—what are you two talking about?"

"Just going over a few things." Captain Wyatt stretched first one arm and then the other, gazing at Mindy for a moment before going on. "I hate to ask this again, ma'am, but are you absolutely sure your daughter hasn't run away? Statistically, that's what happens with most missing teenagers."

"No, not our Bethany!" Mindy rubbed the back of her hand across her sunken eyes, smearing bits of mascara onto her cheeks. "You don't know her. She'd never run away."

The captain gave his head a sad shake. "I hope you're right. It's tough to find a girl who doesn't want to be found. Too many people out there who are willing to help her hide."

The ringing of the doorbell sent Mindy racing to the door, with Chuck following close behind.

"Hi," Janine said with a smile. "When I told my husband I'd offered to help you, he suggested we come right over."

"Hi, I'm Jim Porter." The man opened the storm door and stuck his hand through. "I've heard so much about the two of you from Bethany. It's nice to finally meet you."

Chuck gave the man's hand a vigorous shake.

"That girl said you two are the best parents ever." The smile left the man's face as they moved inside and Chuck closed the door. "You guys have to be worn out. Janine said you've been helping the police canvass the neighborhood."

Weeping quietly, Mindy motioned them to the sofa and chairs in front of the crackling blaze in the fireplace. "We are, but we have to keep going, for Bethany's sake. We stopped long enough for a cup of coffee. Can I get you some?"

"No thanks." Jim nodded toward Captain Wyatt, who had come into the room. "Is there any news at all?"

The man gave him a slight frown. "We're still hoping to hear from her."

"So," Jim said, briskly rubbing his hands together, "tell us what we can do."

"Jim suggested putting posters up all over town with Bethany's picture on them," Janine said. "I think that sounds like a good idea, don't you, Chuck?"

Chuck nodded. "Sure wouldn't hurt."

"I can make the posters for you," Jim volunteered. "I'm pretty good on the computer. All you have to do is let me know what you want the text to say. If you can give me a recent picture of Bethany, I'll scan it in, then take the whole thing to the copy center and have it blown up in color."

"That's very kind of you," Mindy replied, blotting at her eyes. "We can't thank you enough for wanting to help."

Jim stood and hurried across the room to the desk, pulling out the chair. "Chuck, you come over here and write what you want the poster to say while Mindy gets me Bethany's picture, and I'll get right on it."

Fifteen minutes later, after Captain Wyatt approved the wording for the posters, the Porters were out the door with the promise the posters would be ready by four o'clock and they would help put them up all over town.

"They seem like a nice couple," Mindy said, blowing her nose as she gazed out the window, watching the pair cross the street. "It's amazing how willing people are to help one another in a crisis."

"It sure is." Chuck moved up close and slipped an arm about her waist. "Why don't you stay here and rest? I'll start knocking on doors over on Water Street."

Mindy took one final glance out the window before turning to face her husband, her sobs uncontrollable. "I'll go with you. I don't care how tired we are; we have to spend every minute looking for our daughter. No telling where she is, Chuck, but I know wherever she is, she's frightened, and I can't rest until we find her."

After an uneventful afternoon of knocking on doors, Chuck walked with Mindy into their house just minutes before the Porters arrived with the stack of posters.

"I added a brightly colored border," Jim said, pulling several posters from the stack and placing them on the coffee table. "I thought they might attract more attention that way. And I also had some flyers made that we could pass out to everyone we meet."

Mindy picked up one and touched her finger to her daughter's picture. "My beautiful Bethany," she said in a teary whisper. "I love you so much."

Chuck took her hand and linked his fingers with hers. "We'll find her, babe. Have faith."

She whirled into him and pressed her face to his chest. "Faith? I don't know how to have faith. I wish I'd paid attention to Pastor Park's words all those Sundays we attended church with our daughter. She's the one who has faith. I wish I knew how to pray like Bethany does."

"Wherever she is, she's fine, sweetheart. We have to believe that."

"I do believe it, Chuck. Honest I do, but it's been so long. Where could she be? Is she cold? Hungry? Frightened? Is she calling out to us for help?"

"You can't talk like that," Janine said, putting an arm around her shoulders. "It's not good for you or for her."

"I say we get these posters up as soon as we can." Jim divided the stack in half. "A couple of our neighbors have volunteered to help, too. We'll take part of the stack to them so they can get started. I think we should put them in any store windows we can, tack them to posts, place them wherever there's a spot, besides giving the small flyers to everyone we see." He pulled a folded piece of paper from his pocket, laying it on the table before them. "I've made a rough map of the area. Chuck, if you and Mindy take this small part from here to the east edge of town, Janine and I and the other volunteers will take care of the rest. If we haven't heard something by tomorrow, I'll have more posters printed, and we'll fan out even farther."

"You don't mind staying by the phone?" Mindy asked her mother.

"Not at all, dear. You two get those posters up. That's the important thing right now. If I hear anything at all, I'll call you on your cell phone."

Three hours later, feeling discouraged, Mindy stood in front of the bathroom mirror holding a warm washcloth to her face, trying to soothe her jangled nerves. Every bone in her body ached. But the worst ache of all was in her heart. Her baby girl was still missing, and they had not found one shred of evidence as to where she was or whom she was with.

Though she had tried, other than the piece of dry toast that she had eaten for breakfast, she hadn't had a thing all day except for countless cups of hot coffee.

After drying her hands and rubbing on a bit of lotion, Mindy walked slowly down the hall. Never had she felt so helpless. There seemed to be nothing else to do other than what she had already done. Her efforts seemed futile.

"Feeling any better?" Chuck asked as she sat down beside him on the sofa. "You really ought to get some sleep."

"Sleep?" Mindy snapped at him, the strain of the situation telling on her. "With my daughter missing, you think I can sleep?"

"Dear, Chuck is as upset about this as you are," Mrs. Carson told her daughter, reaching to pat her hand.

Turning to her husband, Mindy rallied a slight smile. "I'm sorry, Chuck. I had no business jumping at you like that. I know you love her as much as I do."

Without a word he slipped an arm around her and pulled her close, planting a kiss on her forehead.

Lieutenant Terry studied her clipboard for a moment, then checked her watch before raising her narrowed eyes to the pair. "It's after nine o'clock. Your daughter has been missing for twenty-four hours. I know you've checked her room, but it's time we do a thorough search."

Mindy leaned forward with a frown. "Why? I've already told you what she was wearing."

Captain Wyatt stood, locking his thumbs into his belt. "Lieutenant Terry is right. A thorough search of that room needs to be done now."

"Bethany's room is hers. In this house we respect one another's privacy."

Lieutenant Terry's brows climbed a notch. "You mean, Mrs. O'Connor, you never go into her room?"

"Of course I do," Mindy said defensively. "I take the clothes out of her hamper, and after they're washed I hang them in her closet and place the other things on her bed so she can put them where she wants them."

"You never take a peek in her drawers? Or check out what CDs she plays?"

"I've never felt the need to do those things. Bethany is a model child."

The officers gave each other guarded glances.

Chuck stood, his shoulders slumping. "You'd have to know our daughter to understand what my wife is saying. I can't even remember the last time we had to discipline Bethany."

"That may well be, and I'm sure you're telling the truth about Bethany, but she is almost thirteen, and from my experience," Lieutenant Terry said in a sympathetic voice, "girls that age are eager to try their wings. Plus, they're easily influenced by their peers. It's estimated over a million young people run away from home every year."

Mindy stared at her, unable to comprehend such a vast number. "Surely that's not true."

Lieutenant Terry nodded. "Yes, ma'am, I'm afraid it's not only true, but many runaways go unreported because the parents are too embarrassed to admit it or they're glad to have the children out of their hair."

Captain Wyatt stepped forward, nodding his head in the direction of the hall. "Why don't we have a look at her room? More than likely we won't find a thing. But if something there would give us the slightest clue, I'm sure you'd want us to find it, right?"

Both Mindy and Chuck gave a nod of surrender. Chuck led the way, with Mindy following and the two officers behind her.

"She loves pink," Mindy said as she sat down on Bethany's bed, sobbing. "We did this room just the way she wanted it."

"Did she spend much time in her room, Mrs. O'Connor?" Lieutenant Terry asked as her eyes surveyed the room's contents.

"Oh, yes," Mindy said proudly. "She loved this room. Most evenings she did her homework in here."

Captain Wyatt picked up a Bible from the nightstand. "This hers?"

Chuck nodded. "Yes, Bethany is a Christian, and she's on the church's quiz team. You wouldn't believe how many verses of scripture she's memorized."

"How about this jewelry box?" Lieutenant Terry asked, picking it up and handing it toward Mindy. "I know you said you've already checked it once, but would you take another look? Is anything missing? A piece of jewelry she was particularly fond of or one that had a special meaning to her?"

Mindy lifted the lid and fingered through the contents. "No, not that I'm aware of." She pulled a fine gold chain from the box and held it up for them to see. "This was what she loved most. This gold chain with the tiny diamond cross on it. Her father gave it to her on her twelfth birthday. That just shows you she didn't run away. She'd never leave it behind."

"Has she had this computer long?" Lieutenant Terry pressed the ON button and watched as the computer booted up and the screen illuminated. "I noticed you had a computer on the desk in the family room. Is this her personal computer?

Does anyone else use it?"

"No, she's the only one." Mindy watched as the woman pulled out Bethany's desk chair and sat down. "Is something wrong?"

"I just want to have a look and see what sorts of things she keeps on here."

"I'm not sure Bethany would want you doing that."

"Even if it will help us find her if she's in trouble?" Lieutenant Terry asked, her eyes fixed on the screen.

Captain Wyatt pulled out the top drawer of a tall chest. "Does she keep a diary?"

"She used to, but I don't think she does anymore. I never see her writing in one." It irritated Mindy to see them going through her daughter's things in this way, but she kept her silence.

"Where did she keep it when she was writing in it?" the captain asked. "In one of these drawers?"

"I'm not sure," Mindy conceded.

The officer motioned toward the chest. "I think you'd prefer to handle her personal items yourself, ma'am. Would you come over here and lift the things out of the drawers one at a time?"

Mindy sent Chuck a bewildered look, and when he nodded she moved up next to the officer and began removing Bethany's things from the drawer. When they finally reached the bottom, he told her she could put them back in. They continued the procedure until each of the drawers in the chest, the nightstands, the dresser, and a small cabinet had been searched.

Captain Wyatt closed the last drawer and stood back, looking disappointed. "Well, it doesn't look like there's anything here to help us."

"I may have something." Lieutenant Terry stared at the screen as she made a slight move of the mouse. "Have you ever heard your daughter mention someone she calls Trustworthy?"

Both Mindy and Chuck shook their heads as they moved up to stand behind her.

"I'm not sure yet, but I found a folder marked TRUSTWORTHY. That's a pretty unusual name. Like a name one would use as a nickname or a screen name in a chat room or on one of those instant-message programs."

Captain Wyatt placed his hand on the desk and leaned over her, peering at the screen. "Are there any documents in the folder?"

"Only one."

"What does it say?"

"It's a short message. Looks like it has been copied and pasted from somewhere else. It's time stamped. I have my computer set up the same way."

"Time stamped?" Chuck asked, looking confused. "What does that mean?"

"When you talk on one of those instant-message services, you can set your computer to list the actual time, right down to the second, along the left side of each entry," Captain Wyatt explained, still bending over the computer.

"I'm not sure you'll want to hear this," Lieutenant Terry said, straightening in the chair.

Chapter 7

The message is from someone named Trustworthy, the name on the folder. He's talking to someone who calls themselves Twinkletoes. I assume that's your daughter, since this is her computer."

Mindy moved closer and gawked at the screen. "I've never heard her mention anyone named Trustworthy."

"How about Twinkletoes?"

Chuck let out a gasp. "That's the nickname I used to call Bethany when she was a little girl, but I rarely call her that now! From the time she could walk, she danced anytime music came on the radio or I played an audio tape!"

"Evidently that's what she chose for her screen name."

Mindy felt light-headed and sick to her stomach. "What's the message say?"

"I won't read it to you line by line, but Trustworthy is telling her he is a talent scout for a major Hollywood movie producer who is looking for a young girl to play the lead part in his upcoming movie. He's telling her he thinks she'd be great for the part, if only she could get to California for an audition."

"She's never mentioned a thing about this to me," Chuck said, backing away from the desk with a questioning glance toward Mindy. "Did she tell you about it?"

Fighting off fresh tears, she shook her head. "Not a word. I can't imagine why. She tells me everything."

"His next line will tell you why," the lieutenant said. "He warns her most parents are reluctant to let their daughters go to Hollywood and become a star. He tells her to keep things quiet, and he'll try to work out a way to pay for her trip. If that works out, then she can tell her parents."

Feeling faint, Mindy grabbed on to the edge of the chest, her head reeling.

After rushing to Mindy's side and wrapping his arm around her waist to support her, Chuck asked, "When was this written?"

Lieutenant Terry paused, as if checking to make sure Mindy was all right before answering. "Two weeks before your daughter disappeared."

The room fell into a petrifying silence, the steady hum of the computer's hard drive the only sound.

"That's all I've discovered on the computer so far. There may be more. I'll keep looking."

"But you found that one message," Chuck said, looking hopeful. "If she talked to this person, wouldn't all of his messages be on her computer, too?"

Captain Wyatt shook his head. "You must not spend much time on the computer, Mr. O'Connor. Once an instant-message conversation is over, the participants click out of the window, and that conversation is gone forever."

"But that one was on there. How did it stay?"

"She must have wanted to save that one. Your daughter highlighted that portion, hit COPY, transferred it over, and saved it to a document, then put it in this file folder. Unless she has saved others, any talks she had with Trustworthy are not retrievable. But I can have one of the computer geeks we occasionally use take a look at her hard drive. If she's saved others then deleted them, he might be able to find them."

Chuck rubbed at his forehead. "I use computers for a lot of things every day at work, but I guess I know very little about them."

"I—I don't know much about them either. I use the one in the family room only to send e-mail to my friends and family and write a few letters now and then." Mindy sucked in a deep breath of air, hoping it would help her head to clear. "I've never gotten into this message thing. I have no idea how it works. Bethany is our computer whiz."

"Do you suppose this Trustworthy has anything to do with her disappearance?" Chuck asked.

Captain Wyatt shrugged. "Without knowing exactly how chummy the two of them have become, it's hard to say."

His words made Mindy furious. "Bethany would never leave with someone she met on the Internet!"

"Mrs. O'Connor, you have no idea how persuasive these people can be. We're not saying your daughter ran away with him. What we are saying is, we have to explore every possibility. Your daughter has been gone over twenty-four hours now."

"You don't think I'm aware of that?" Mindy barked back. "Don't you people know how hard this is on us?"

Mrs. Carson, who had been standing quietly by the doorway, moved quickly to her daughter and gently took hold of her arm. "You're worn-out, dear. You have to get some sleep. Why don't you let me fix you a nice cup of hot tea and—"

Mindy jerked her arm away. "Don't you see, Mother? Until Bethany is found I can't sleep! She may be lying out there somewhere, cold and hungry. How can I sleep without knowing where she is and if she's all right?"

Mrs. Carson backed away with a look of exasperation. "I want Bethany found, too, but you can't keep going without rest. You can't think straight, and your body will rebel."

Mindy felt heartsick at the way she'd snapped at her well-meaning mother. "I'm sorry, Mom. I hope you'll forgive me, but I doubt I'll sleep again until my baby girl is safe at home."

"We haven't searched her closet yet," Lieutenant Terry reminded them. "Maybe something in there will help us. From my experience, girls Bethany's age like to keep mementos in a box or a bag. That'd be a great place to hide anything she didn't want you to see."

Mindy had to bite her tongue to keep from lashing out at the officer. How dare she think Bethany would keep things hidden from her? "I've already told you—all that is missing is the clothing she was wearing last night."

"Let them have a look," Chuck said softly, nudging her toward the mirror closet doors.

She nodded and, following his lead, slid open one of the doors.

"Looks like the typical teenage girl's closet," Lieutenant Terry said. "Filled to the brim. This may take awhile."

Mindy leaned into Chuck's arms as the two stood off to one side and watched as the officers pulled the garments from the rod, one by one, checking the pockets, then placing them on the bed.

Once the rod was emptied, they began taking things from the two overhead shelves, going through numerous shoe boxes and bags, checking the contents of each one before stacking it by the garments.

"Nothing so far," Captain Wyatt said while pulling a rather large box from the back of the top shelf.

"Be careful. Those are her Barbie dolls!" Mindy stepped forward and reached for the box.

Lieutenant Terry moved it from her grasp. "I'll need to check the contents just to make sure there's nothing else here. Sometimes these guys manage to get presents to their intended victims."

"Presents? What kind of presents?"

"Jewelry. Fancy T-shirts. That sort of thing. Those gifts become a tangible bond between the two."

Mindy grabbed hold of Chuck's hand, needing something stable to hold on to. "This is too much! I'm sure Bethany would never take a gift from someone she didn't know."

Captain Wyatt gave a slight shrug. "Let's hope you're right."

Finally, all the clothing had been removed from the rack, and all the shelves had been emptied. Mindy stared at the pile on the bed, her heart breaking. "I was hoping you'd find something."

"We're not through yet." Lieutenant Terry knelt and began taking the many shoes from the closet floor. "Your daughter must like shoes the way my daughter does," she said with a slight snicker.

Mindy gazed at the pile. "Bethany loves shoes. We try to get her a pair for each of her birthdays and Christmas, not to mention the ones her grandmother buys for her or she buys herself."

"Well, that's about it," Lieutenant Terry said, placing the last shoe by its mate. "That pair of cowboy boots is all that's left."

"She loved those boots. We bought them for her at the state fair," Chuck explained as the woman reached into the far back corner of Bethany's closet. "Always kidded me, saying she needed a horse to go with them."

"Oh, oh. What have we here?"

Captain Wyatt quickly squatted down beside his partner. "Got something?"

She nodded as she reached into the boot and pulled out a pink diary. "Looks like our girl kept a diary after all."

Mindy's hand went to her chest as she let out a loud gasp. "I didn't know she was still keeping one!"

Lieutenant Terry rose. "Which probably means there are things in here your daughter would prefer you didn't know."

As Mindy reached for the diary, Captain Wyatt stepped in between the two women. "I'm sorry, Mrs. O'Connor, but your daughter's privacy is no longer a concern here. Why don't you and your husband go on in the other room while we have a look at it?"

Crazed, Mindy pushed past him. "No! If there's anything in that diary that will help us find Bethany, we want to know about it."

"She's right." Chuck took hold of his wife's arm and pulled her out of the way. "We need to know what's in that diary."

Captain Wyatt shrugged. "Your call." Then, turning to Lieutenant Terry, he said, "Go ahead. Check it out."

The three stood silently, their attention fixed on the woman as she leafed through the pages. Suddenly she stopped on a single page, her brows rising. "Bingo!"

"You found something?" Mindy asked quickly.

The officer nodded. "It appears your daughter and Trustworthy have been carrying on a conversation nearly every night for well over a month. Her first entry about him said she'd met a really nice man on the Internet who was a talent scout. And after he'd asked her a number of questions about her age, her size, and the color of her hair, he told her she sounded like the kind of girl he'd been searching for to play the lead part in a movie."

Mindy clutched at Chuck's arm. "Why didn't she tell us this?"

"I can answer that one." Lieutenant Terry thumbed back a few pages. "She says right here that he told her she shouldn't tell anyone, especially not her parents, because she wouldn't want them to be disappointed if things didn't work out. And he also said that if any of her friends found out about it, they'd all want to be movie stars, too, and he didn't have the time to talk to each one, especially when he felt Bethany would be perfect for the part."

Mindy burst into tears. "How could she have believed him?"

"These guys are pros at this, Mrs. O'Connor. They know what to say to these kids to get them to trust them."

"What else does she say?" Captain Wyatt interjected.

Lieutenant Terry read a few more pages, then lifted her eyes slowly. "He told her he had decided it was time for her to come to Hollywood for an audition. He asked her if she thought her parents would pay for her flight out there and for the hotel room during the week she would have to be there, learning lines and meeting with the movie producers."

"She never said a word to me about this." Chuck gave his head a sad shake.

"Apparently she told him she was sure you would say no because you still thought of her as a baby, instead of a maturing young woman as Trustworthy did."

"She is our baby!" Mindy nearly shouted, her nerves to the breaking point. "She's not even thirteen!"

"Well, she says here that he was so certain she was right for the part, he decided to pay for things himself. He said—" Lieutenant Terry stopped reading aloud and shot a quick glance toward Captain Wyatt.

"What? What did he say?" Chuck reached his hand toward the diary, but the officer pulled it away.

"He said that since most parents are reluctant to let their daughters become movie stars, it would be best if she didn't tell you he had decided to pay for everything. He told her she should go on to Hollywood with him, and once they were there she could call you and tell you where she was. He'd convinced her that when you heard how much money she was going to make doing the movie, you would be sorry you tried to stand in her way."

"She's with him?" Mindy felt the room swirling about her as the reality of Bethany's words hit her full force. "In California?"

Chuck grabbed on to her and held her fast. "Surely not! Not Bethany. She's so levelheaded! I can't believe she'd go off with a stranger!"

"He may have been a stranger to her, but believe me, he knew all about her. Guys like this look for young, naive, inexperienced girls, usually girls with no siblings. They have a way of winning their confidence and belittling their parents, to the point the girls think this guy is the only one in the world who understands them and wants to see them become a star. It's an old story. Been done time and time again."

"How can we find out who he is? Where he might have taken her?" Mindy threw herself onto Bethany's bed, crying hysterically.

"It's doubtful he took her on public transportation. He probably drove." Captain Wyatt turned back to Lieutenant Terry. "Finding anything else in there that might be helpful?"

"Most of it is going over the same thing. Telling her how lucky he is to have found her. Emphasizing how excited her parents are going to be when she shows them the amount of money she'll make. He tells her she may want to buy her parents a big house in Beverly Hills so they can be close to her. It looks like she's told her diary nearly every conversation she's ever had with the guy."

Finding it almost impossible to breathe, Mindy gasped for air. "She'd never believe lies like those!"

"Oh, no!" Lieutenant Terry handed the diary to Captain Wyatt. "You'd better take a look at this."

He took it, read it for a moment, then gave them a look Mindy would never forget as long as she lived. "In the last entry, the morning before she disappeared, she writes that she and her father had an argument because she was wearing too much lipstick and because he didn't like the shirt she had on and made her change it."

"I did," Chuck confessed, looking quickly toward Mindy. "It wasn't a real argument. I just insisted she take some of that lipstick off and change her shirt."

"She must have taken time to write in her diary when she came back into her bedroom. She says she was putting the shirt you complained about in her backpack so she could change back into it when she got to school."

Mindy glared at the captain. "Bethany would never go against her father's wishes like that!"

Lieutenant Terry held out the diary toward her. "Read it for yourself. She also told Trustworthy she wouldn't be able to talk to him on instant message that night because she'd be at play rehearsal until nine."

"You think this Trustworthy picked her up? I thought he lived in California!" Mindy said, trying to find her voice through her tears.

Lieutenant Terry latched on to Mindy's hand. "Mrs. O'Connor, when you talk to someone on that instant-message thing, there is no way of knowing where that person actually is. They could tell you they were in Africa and be just a few miles from your home. You have to take their word they are telling you the truth."

"I'm going to contact a few people who have dealt with missing children and see if they've ever heard of Trustworthy." Captain Wyatt turned quickly to Lieutenant Terry. "When you're finished going through that diary, sign on to Bethany's computer. Run a search through Google and some of the other search engines for Trustworthy and see if anything comes up. It's a long shot, but it might be worth it. When you're finished, pull that hard drive out and bring it to the station. I've got a guy lined up who'll be able to check out the files and documents she deleted."

"Wait a minute!" Lieutenant Terry held the diary up in front of Captain Wyatt. "I found something else. An entry written several weeks ago. She says she lost the silver and turquoise bracelet he left for her in a box in the flowerbed in your front yard. The guy was right here! In Warren!"

Chuck and Mindy exchanged worried glances.

"We—we found that bracelet in the backseat of our car," Chuck said with a sheepish look toward Mindy.

Mindy felt sick. Not only was her daughter missing, but now she knew she had falsely accused her husband of being with Michelle in the backseat of their car.

"Shouldn't we call the FBI or something?" Chuck asked, turning back to the officer.

Captain Wyatt moved toward the door. "I've already called them. An agent should be here anytime. Don't mention anything to the press or anyone else about anything, especially about the diary or what it says. If someone has taken your daughter, we don't want them to know we've found it. If any reporters call you, refer them to me. I'm going to set up that interview with the TV station; then we'll go over what you should say before it's videotaped. I'm sure they'll come to your house for the taping. I'll get back to you with a time."

Mindy and Chuck followed him as far as the family room. As soon as she heard the front door close, she rushed toward Chuck and wrapped her arms around his waist, unable to control her crying. "Can you ever forgive me? That bracelet didn't belong to Michelle! It was Bethany's!"

He nestled his chin in her hair. "I told you that, but you wouldn't believe me."

She pressed her face against his chest and let the tears flow. "I know, and I'm so sorry."

Sliding the tip of his finger beneath her chin, he lifted her watery gaze to meet his. "I do love you, Mindy. You have to believe that. There's never been anyone but you."

"I want to believe you, but—" She leaned into him, loving the feel of his arms around her, the smell of his sweater, the touch of his fingers as they caressed her cheek. "I'm so tired, Chuck. So confused."

"I know, honey—so am I."

"Can we just forget about this Michelle thing until we find Bethany? I need you, Chuck. You've always been my fortress."

"I'm here for you, sweetheart. I'll always be here for you." Chuck took her hand and led her to the sofa.

She leaned back against the cushions and closed her eyes. "My eyes burn," she said in a half-whisper as drowsiness nearly overtook her.

"We both need sleep."

"But how can we sleep, knowing our daughter may be out there somewhere with a lunatic? Or maybe even worse—a child molester?"

Before he could answer, the cordless phone on the coffee table rang. Mindy snatched it up quickly. It was Janine.

"No, no word yet," Mindy told her.

"Is there anything else we can do? Jim wanted to go see one of his buddies in Providence today, but I refused to let him leave. I'm scared, Mindy. Is there anything else we can do to help? I told him while we were waiting for your call, he might as well paint the bedroom like I've been asking him. He's in there grumbling about it right now. If you need us, we can drop everything and give you a hand." She paused. "Oh, here's Jim. He wants to talk to Chuck. Can you put him on the phone?"

Mindy handed the phone to her husband. After a short conversation with the man, he hung up. "Both Jim and Janine said they are praying for Bethany's return."

～∞～

The front door opened, and Captain Wyatt stepped in, holding one of his shoes in his hand. "You got any rags? Some dog left a pile in your front yard, and I stepped in it."

"Sure, out in the garage." Chuck stood and motioned the man to follow him. "There should be a bag of old rags on my workbench." He opened the door, flipped the light switch, and moved toward the opposite wall.

"Never mind. I see a rag hanging out of this trash can. I just need something to wipe this smelly mess off my shoe. I was afraid it would stink up the whole squad car." Captain Wyatt grabbed the rag and began to wipe at his shoe. "Oh, oh!"

Chuck spun around, wondering what had caused his reaction.

Chapter 8

There's blood on this rag!"

"Blood?" Chuck leaned in for a better look. "I use that old shirt to wipe my hands when I change the oil in our cars, but there wasn't any blood on it, and I sure didn't put it in the trash."

"You're telling me this isn't your blood?"

"Captain Wyatt? The FBI agent is here," Mindy called out as she opened the door into the garage.

"Tell him he'd better come out here," the officer said, eyeing Chuck suspiciously.

A man with graying temples, wearing a dark sports coat and gray trousers, moved quickly into the garage. "I came as soon as I could. I'm Agent Cliff Rogers. You're Captain Wyatt?"

Captain Wyatt shifted the rag to his other hand. "Yes, and this is Chuck O'Connor, the father of the girl who is missing. I just made an interesting discovery. This rag was in the trash can. It has blood on it, and though Mr. O'Connor admits it's the one he uses when he changes the oil, he claims he didn't put it there and has no idea who did."

"I didn't put it there," Mindy said from her place in the doorway.

"How about your daughter?"

Chuck appeared thoughtful. "I can't remember the last time Bethany came out into the garage, except to get into the car. She never spends any time here."

The FBI agent reached out and took the rag. "Can you get me your daughter's hairbrush, ma'am? We'll need to check her DNA."

Chuck grabbed on to the man's arm. "You think that blood might be Bethany's?"

The man gave him a hard look as he pulled a plastic bag from the case he was carrying and slipped the rag into it. "We'll know when we check it."

With Captain Wyatt leading, the group moved back into the living room. After a short briefing, Agent Rogers questioned both Mindy and Chuck, taking notes and asking all sorts of questions that upset Mindy, personal questions about Bethany, which he explained had to be asked if they were to find her.

"I'll be honest with you," he said finally, closing his notebook. "The possibility of finding your daughter unharmed diminishes with each passing minute."

Shocked by the man's words, Chuck stood helplessly as Mindy went into hysterics. "Did you have to say that?" he asked angrily as he wrapped his arms around his wife. "She's about at the breaking point."

"I'm sorry, Mr. O'Connor, but you have to be prepared. I'm sure you've gone over things a dozen times, but you must do it again. Somewhere there has to be something that will give us a lead as to your daughter's whereabouts."

"You found out about Trustworthy! Isn't that enough?" Chuck snapped back, his own nerves shattering. "Are you working on that lead?"

"We're checking on that right now," Captain Wyatt said with a sympathetic look. "In addition to Lieutenant Terry, several top-notch computer experts are searching the Internet right now, looking for Trustworthy. The Center for Missing Children is going through their records, trying to find other girls who may have had contact with this person. Unfortunately, these guys usually change their nicknames with each new victim."

"Stop calling our daughter a victim!" Mindy shrieked at him.

"Look," Captain Wyatt said in a low, quiet voice. "You're both worn-out. There's nothing more you can do tonight. The important thing right now is to get some sleep. Surely you have something in the medicine cabinet to help you relax. A number of people are working around the clock trying to find Bethany. Go to bed and try to sleep. You'll feel a lot better in the morning."

Chuck gave his wife's forehead a gentle kiss. "He's right, honey. Why don't we try to get some sleep? When Jim called, he said Bethany's Sunday school teacher, Treva Jordan, is at their house right now, and the three of them are calling all the volunteers and asking them to meet at the community center in the morning at nine. He suggested we fan the search out even farther and cover the outskirts of town. He's already drawn up another grid so we can make sure every property is covered."

With eyes so swollen she could barely see, Mindy let out a deep sigh. "You're probably right, but I'm not sure I'll be able to sleep, knowing our daughter is out there some—"

Chuck put a finger to her lips. "Don't even say it."

"You do need to sleep, dear." Mindy's mother bent and patted her hand. "I doubt I'll sleep much either, but I am tired. I'm going on to bed. Let me know if you need me. Good night, everyone."

As soon as the officers and the FBI agent were out of the house, Chuck walked Mindy to their bedroom, kissing her good night in the doorway.

"Chuck?"

"Yes."

She gave him a demure smile that set his heart singing, despite the dreadful ordeal they were experiencing. "I—I don't want to sleep alone tonight. I need your arms around me."

Without a word Chuck swept her up in his arms and carried her into their room.

About three in the morning, he was awakened by Mindy tugging frantically on his arm.

"She called to me, Chuck! I heard her! Bethany was calling to me."

Even in the dim light from the moon, Chuck could tell his wife was smiling. "Go back to sleep, sweetheart. You must be dreaming."

She shook his arm even harder. "No, it wasn't a dream. I'm her mother! It was Bethany! I'm sure of it. She was calling out to me for help. She's alive, Chuck. I know she's alive!"

"Shh, shh." He pulled her to him and held her trembling body close, trying to calm her down.

Finally, the trembling stopped, and her breathing became almost normal. "Our baby is alive, Chuck," she said in a near whisper. "Bethany's alive."

Though they endured a troublesome night, with sleep coming in bits and snatches, both Mindy and Chuck crawled out of bed at six, feeling somewhat rested. He placed a call to Captain Wyatt, who told him there had been no further developments.

❧

At exactly eight o'clock the doorbell rang. Mindy's mother hurried to answer it.

"My wife and I have been out of town. We just heard about Bethany," Pastor Bob Park explained as she motioned him inside. "We'd like to do anything we can to help. Bethany is very special to us. The ladies of our church are organizing a prayer chain."

Mindy's mother patted her daughter's arm. "I'll be in the kitchen if you need me. I'm going to put a roast in the oven."

Mindy nodded, then turned and gave the pastor a questioning look. "A prayer chain?"

"Within minutes of receiving a major prayer request," he explained with a gentle smile, "our church ladies start calling the team prayer captains, who in turn call their assigned groups. Everyone drops what they're doing and goes to the Lord in prayer. Right now hundreds of our church members are praying for the safe return of your daughter."

"That's so sweet of them. Please thank them for us." Mindy swallowed at the lump in her throat, overwhelmed by the kindness and concern of people who did not even know them.

"I'd like to pray for her, too. Let's form a circle." Pastor Park reached out his hands, linking them with theirs, and lifted his face heavenward. "Lord, I come to You asking You to keep Bethany safe, wherever she is, and to return her to her home and to her parents and to those of us who love her. And be with whoever might be preventing her from coming home. Keep them from harming her in any way. She's Your child, God. She's accepted You as her Savior and turned her life over to You. And I ask You to be with Mindy and Chuck. They need Your touch of comfort, Lord. Speak to their hearts. Make Yourself real to them. We love You, God, and we ask these things in Jesus' name. Amen."

Mindy tried to hold in her emotions, but she couldn't. The pastor's words touched her in a way no words had ever before. She grabbed his arm, weeping so hard it was nearly impossible to form the words she wanted so much to say. "Oh, thank you, Pastor Park," she managed to get out finally. "I—I don't even know how to pray, and I'm not sure God would want to hear from me anyway."

The man put a comforting hand on her shoulder. "God is always ready to listen to His children, Mindy. Have you ever accepted Him as your Savior? Turned your life over to Him, the way Bethany has?"

"You know we've been attending church with her," Chuck said.

Pastor Park gave Chuck an understanding smile. "I know you have, Chuck, and you have no idea how much it means to Bethany to have you both there. But attending church doesn't make you a Christian. Getting right with God does. Your daughter has been concerned about both of you. She has been praying for your salvation."

"We've heard your messages on sin, but we've never thought of ourselves as sinners," Chuck said defensively.

The ringing of the phone put an end to their conversation. It was Jim Porter telling them the volunteers had all been briefed and given their assignments.

"We'll be right there." Chuck punched the OFF button on the phone. "Jim said it might help if we came over and talked to the volunteers before they left."

"I'll go with you," Pastor Park said. "I want to help."

❧

By three o'clock all of the volunteers had returned, but most had little to report. A few had been told about a blue van several had seen cruising through one of the neighborhoods; some mentioned a man on a motorcycle who had been riding up and down a side street, making lewd comments to anyone who would listen. But other than that no one reported anything out of the ordinary.

Agent Rogers arrived at their house about the same time Mindy and Chuck turned into their driveway. "I've brought some pictures. I'd like you both to take a look at them. See if any of them look familiar." He followed them into the house and placed the big book on the coffee table. "Take your time. If you see anyone the least bit familiar, let me know."

"Who are these men?" Mindy asked as she and Chuck sat down and stared at the first page.

"Child molesters."

Mindy's breathing quickened, and she had a difficult time swallowing.

"These guys move from place to place. Maybe one of them came to your door posing as a salesman, a repairman, something of that sort. Or maybe you saw him around Bethany's school. Sometimes they just sit in their cars and watch until they find a likely victim."

With a frown Chuck held up his flattened palm. "I've asked you not to use that word. It upsets my wife."

"Sorry, but that's exactly what these men do."

"Why aren't they in prison?" Mindy asked, gazing at the pictures.

"Most of them have already served time, and they're either out on parole or have been released," he answered matter-of-factly. "There's no way to keep them off the streets or from doing the same thing again."

Nearly an hour later Chuck closed the book and handed it back to Agent Rogers. "Sorry. Neither of us recognized anyone."

When the phone rang, both Mindy and Chuck grabbed for it, hoping it was good news, but it was only a reporter from a tabloid trying to get an exclusive interview.

Agent Rogers set up shop in the little den Chuck used as his home office, leaving Mindy and Chuck alone in the family room.

"Mindy, I've been thinking about what Pastor Park said—you know—when he asked us if we'd ever accepted Christ as our Savior, the way Bethany did." Holding on to the cup of coffee his mother-in-law had brought to him, he crossed the room and sat down by his wife. "Did you hear the way that man prayed? It was as if he was having a conversation with God Himself. I half-expected God to answer him right then and there."

Mindy, cradling a framed picture of her daughter, nodded. "I know what you mean. That's the way Bethany prays when I tuck her in at night. I—I wish—" She stopped and stared at her daughter's image.

"I know. I loved to hear her pray, too, but I figured God really didn't care about the prayer of a child. I"—he gave her a hangdog grin—"I guess I always thought praying was something preachers did, not kids."

Mindy dabbed at her reddened nose again. "I hate to admit it, but when Bethany would talk to me about becoming a Christian, I actually made fun of her."

"I guess I did, too. Now I wish I had her faith." Chuck smiled as he remembered several conversations he'd had with his daughter about that very thing. "She tried to convince me that all people were sinners and needed to go to God and ask Him for forgiveness, then turn their lives over to Him. I scoffed at her words. Now I'm ashamed of myself." He sat staring at the photograph in his wife's hands. "I wish I would have listened to her."

"She told me I was a sinner, too, but because of my silly pride, I scolded her for talking about me that way." Mindy turned to face him, and he could see the hurt in her eyes as a tear made its way down her cheek. "I—I wish we'd asked Pastor Park to show us how to become Christians. I want that kind of faith, Chuck. I need it! I want to be able to call out to God and know I'm His child. I just don't know how."

"He said to call him if there was anything he could do for us." Chuck picked up the remote phone from the coffee table. "Shall I call him? I'm sure he'd come right back."

Desperate to ease the pain of her loss, Mindy lowered her head and pressed the photograph to her heart. "Yes, Chuck, call him."

Pastor Park rang their doorbell a half hour later.

"You didn't say why you wanted me to come," he said as he rushed into the room. "Have you heard anything about Bethany?"

"No, Pastor Park, no news, but that's not why I called you." He turned to Mindy with a smile. "My precious wife and I are ready to become Christians. We're tired of playing church on Sunday mornings. We want the real thing. Like our daughter has."

"That's the best news I've heard in weeks. Bethany has been praying for your salvation. She never lost faith that this would happen."

"Mindy and I have discussed this at length. We want the same kind of faith Bethany has, and we're willing to do whatever it takes to get it."

Giving them each a warm smile, Pastor Park sat down between them and opened his Bible. After reading and explaining a number of scripture passages, he asked, "Are you sure you understand what it means to become a Christian? You're not going to be suddenly perfect, with everything going exactly the way you'd like it to—believe me, it won't work like that. But as a child of God, if you let Him and want His perfect will for your life, He'll take control. Remember— God has promised never to leave or forsake His children." He closed his Bible, placing it on the table in front of them. "Are you ready to make that decision?"

"Yes, Pastor, we are." Chuck stood and, crossing over to Mindy, reached for her hand, then knelt beside the sofa, pulling his wife down beside him.

"Then pray with me," Pastor Park said, placing a hand on each head.

When he finished praying for both Chuck and Mindy, he prayed for Bethany's safe return. Somehow, hearing Pastor Park pray so fervently for their child gave Chuck new hope. "Thank you, Pastor Park. We're very grateful to you for being so good to our Bethany and for coming over like this."

Pastor Park slipped an arm around Mindy as they all stood. "Have faith in God. You're in His hands. Whatever happens, you must accept as His will for your life. To draw close to Him, read your Bible and pray." He gave them a grin. "And attend our church every Sunday." Then with an outright laugh he added,

"That last part wasn't from the scriptures. I added that one. We love seeing the O'Connor family lined up in the pew on Sundays."

Chuck, along with Mindy, walked Pastor Park to the door, once again thanking him for coming and for treating them in such a loving way.

"Well, we did it!" Chuck said, grabbing Mindy up and whirling her about the room.

Mindy threw her arms around his neck and held on fast. "We did, didn't we? Oh, Chuck, I feel really good about what we have done. I've wanted so much to pray for our daughter's safe return, but honestly I didn't think God would want to hear from me. I've turned my back on Him all these years, feeling totally self-sufficient. Who did I think I was?"

"I was the same way." He stopped whirling and set her down on her feet. "Maybe if we'd done this a long time ago, when we were first married, we could have spared ourselves all those troubled years when we would only fight and disagree." He tightened his grip around her waist and stared lovingly into her eyes. "I know you still have misgivings about Michelle and me, and you have every right to. I haven't been able to prove my innocence yet, sweetheart." He paused and lifted the flat of his palm to her. "As our God is my witness, I never did anything indecent with that woman. Just trust me. Please—trust me."

∽≈∽

Mindy stared up at him, her eyes misting over. She wanted so much to believe him; but she still had too many unanswered questions, and right now her focus had to be on finding Bethany. She did not have the will or the strength to deal with the Michelle thing at this moment. "I want to trust you, Chuck. You mean everything to me, but—" She bit her lip, choosing her words carefully. "Let's forget about that woman for now and pretend she never existed, and then we'll deal with your suspension after we find our daughter." She stood on tiptoe and gently kissed his lips. "I promise I'll help prove your innocence in any way I can."

"You mean it? You'll help me?"

"Yes. I want to help you, Chuck." *Even if it means going Dumpster-diving again!*

Chuck glanced at his watch. "I had no idea it was so late. The TV crew will be here in an hour."

Mindy turned toward the clock on the wall. "I was going to put a load in the washer, and then I want to freshen up."

He nodded. "I need to take a quick shower, but first I'm going to jot down a few things I want to make sure we cover when we do the interview."

Mindy had barely left the room when the phone rang.

"I'm glad I caught you, Chuck," a male voice said on the other end.

Chuck pressed the phone tightly to his ear. "Hello, Jake."

"I spoke with your mother-in-law last night, and she told me you'd had no further word about your daughter's disappearance. I'm so sorry, Chuck. I wish I could do something to help."

"Thanks, Jake. There seems to be nothing anyone can do. This waiting is terrible." Chuck rotated his stiff neck.

"Well, I may not be able to do anything about finding your daughter, but I do have good news. I fired Michelle this morning."

Chuck sucked in a deep breath and held it, afraid he'd misunderstood his boss's words. "Does that mean—"

"It means you have your job back, and I owe you an apology."

"You have no idea how glad I am to hear you say that. But why? How?"

"From the glowing reference her former boss, Alexander Delmar, of the huge Florida-based Delmar Industries gave her, I had no reason to feel otherwise, but I thought it might be worthwhile to call Mr. Delmar. I wanted to ask him about Michelle's former work record and see if perhaps there had been any problems with her we hadn't heard about. I've been trying to phone that man for over two weeks but was told he was on his annual African safari and unable to be reached until he returned. Today was the first day he was back in his office, and after the hard time I gave his secretary by calling her nearly every day, she put me through to him."

Beads of perspiration broke out across Chuck's forehead as he sat down on a nearby chair. "What—what did he have to say?"

"At first the man was reluctant to talk to me, but I explained that my best salesman's reputation was at stake and I needed any information he could give me."

Chuck's heart pounded wildly. Dare he hope Jake had discovered something about Michelle?

"Finally, after I explained about the charges Michelle had filed against you and how I'd had no choice but to put you on suspension, he began to open up. He asked me about your work record and how well I knew you. I could tell the man was not being completely honest with me, so I told him about Bethany's disappearance and the horrible time you and Mindy were having waiting, with no word of her whereabouts."

Jake nervously cleared his throat. "Chuck, she did it there, too. In Florida. Only that time Mr. Delmar was the victim."

Chuck straightened in his chair, shocked by Jake's words. "You mean she falsely accused him of the same thing she did me?"

"Yes, but he asked me to keep it quiet. It seems Michelle played on his sympathies just as she did you, asking him to drive her home, taking him out for dinner, inviting him to a sold-out NCAA game because she had two tickets that were going to go to waste unless she could find someone to go with her, and other things, too. Even called him saying she was afraid someone was trying to break into her apartment. His words sounded like a carbon copy of what you'd told me. Finally, she made her play for him, and like you he turned her down. The next day she showed up in his office, threatening to accuse him of raping her if he didn't give her a good severance package, which he considered as a payoff, and an excellent letter of reference. He said he hated to do it, but he knew what an accusation like that could do to his marriage, his reputation, and his business, so he did it. He hoped meeting her demands would put an end to it all."

"Amazing," was all Chuck could say.

"The poor man said he hasn't had a good night's sleep since the day she walked out of his office. The guilt of letting her get away with her lecherous scheme has nearly ruined his life. He's been consumed with the possibility she'd do the same thing to someone else. And unfortunately she did. To you."

"I—I don't know what to say. I was so afraid I wouldn't be able to prove my innocence. You have no idea how happy this makes me, Jake."

"As I said, Chuck, I owe you an apology. I only hope you can understand why I had to suspend you until this thing was cleared up. I intend to do everything I can to make things right. You've not only been the best salesman I've ever had, but you've also been a good friend. I—I hope we can continue to be friends."

"Who is it, Chuck?" Mindy asked, hurrying into the room with an armful of freshly laundered towels.

Chuck couldn't hold back the wide smile that erupted across his face. "It's Jake," he told her, covering the mouthpiece. "It's over, sweetheart. I have my old job back! I'll tell you all about it as soon as I finish talking to him."

Setting aside her load, Mindy dropped down beside him, smiling as she placed her arm around his shoulders and gave him a squeeze.

"I don't expect you to come back to work now, Chuck," Jake went on, "but I am anxious to meet with you. I said you had your old job back. That's not quite true."

Chuck's heart sank.

"I've hired another man to fill your job."

"But you—"

"Hear me out, Chuck. I hired that man because I'm making you sales manager. I hope you'll accept the position, because you've earned it. There's not another person who deserves it more. Of course you'll have a substantial increase in pay, a nice office, and a number of other perks."

Chuck had cried only three times in his adult life: when his mother found out she had cancer, when Jake put him on suspension and Mindy asked him to move into the guest room, and when they realized their precious Bethany was missing. Tears filled his eyes now and ran down his cheeks as he cradled the phone in his hands. "Accept the position? Of course I'll accept it. I've looked forward to being sales manager since the first day I came to work for you."

Chuck slipped an arm around Mindy and pulled her close. "Thanks, Jake. Thanks for everything, and thanks for believing in me and going to all that effort. I owe you."

"You owe me nothing, Chuck. It's a pleasure to help and promote a man like you. I won't keep you. I'll be praying for you and Mindy and the safe return of Bethany. Keep me posted and let me know if there is anything I can do."

Chuck rested his cheek against Mindy's. "I will, Jake, and thanks again."

Mindy gazed into his eyes. "Oh, Chuck, this is the best news we've had in a long time. Did I understand it right? Jake gave you a promotion?"

Feeling he almost needed to pinch himself to make sure he wasn't dreaming, Chuck planted a kiss on Mindy's cheek, then smiled at her. "Yes, he did. Mindy, my love, you're looking at the new sales manager. Our prayers about my suspension have been answered." He rose, pulling her up with him, feeling more encouraged than he had in a long time. "Maybe God will answer our prayers about our daughter, too. Let's get ready for the interview!"

❧

Though Chuck was fairly successful at fighting back tears, Mindy wept openly throughout the entire interview.

"I'm sorry," she told the reporter as he and the videographer packed up to leave. "I had promised myself I wouldn't cry like that, but I'm so concerned about Bethany that I couldn't help it."

The reporter placed his hand on her arm and gave her an understanding smile. "Of course you cried. I'm sure my mom would have cried, too, if I'd been missing. Moms do that. You did fine. I just hope this interview will bring your daughter back to you. Maybe someone in our viewing audience will have the lead you're looking for."

She and Chuck thanked the two young men. But even before their news cruiser was out of sight, Captain Wyatt's squad car pulled into the drive, and he and Agent Rogers stepped out. From the look on their faces, it was obvious they were the bearers of bad news.

Chapter 9

W e're going to have to ask you to come with us," Captain Wyatt said firmly as he took Chuck by the arm.

"Why?" Mindy screamed out, grabbing on and clinging to her husband's hand. "What's happened? Have you found Bethany? You have to tell us!"

"No, ma'am," the captain replied, his face void of expression. "I'm sorry. We've had no further news of your daughter's whereabouts."

"What's going on here?" Mrs. Carson asked as she came in from the kitchen. "Why are you holding on to my son-in-law's arm like that?"

Captain Wyatt motioned her aside with a nod of his head. "Just step back, ma'am."

"Where are you taking me, and why?" Chuck asked as he struggled to pull his arm free.

Agent Rogers took over. "The blood on the rag found in your garage matches your daughter's DNA. We're taking you to the station for further questioning."

"I'm coming with you," Mindy said resolutely as she headed for the closet to get her jacket.

"No, you stay here. I'm sure I'll be back soon. I have no idea how Bethany's blood got on that rag." Chuck gave Mindy a tender smile. "Please, Mindy, stay here with your mother. Pray they'll find our daughter and this nightmare will end."

It broke her heart to see her husband being herded off to the police station like some criminal, and as soon as the squad car was out of the driveway, Mindy dropped to her knees and began to pray.

Two hours later Chuck returned, looking exhausted.

"What did they do to you?" Mindy asked, rushing to him as the door closed behind him. "You look awful!"

He circled her waist with his long arms and rubbed his cheek against hers. "They all but accused me of having something to do with our daughter's disappearance. I think they're clutching at straws since they haven't been able to find any other evidence."

"You'd never harm Bethany!"

"You know that, but they don't. To them I'm a suspect, the only one they've been able to turn up. I told them I had no idea why her blood would be on that rag, but since it was one of the rags I use in the garage, they don't believe me."

"Oh, Chuck, this is too much. I've been praying almost all the time you've been gone."

He cradled her head in his hand and pressed it to his chest. "We have to have faith, sweetheart. Remember what Pastor Park said? God has promised never to leave us or forsake us. We have to trust Him to take care of our little girl, wherever she is, and bring her back to us."

At ten that evening the two sat huddled in front of the TV set, watching the interview they'd taped that very day. It ended with a plea directly to the audience from Mindy as she held Bethany's picture to her breast. Chuck turned off the TV, then reached out and took his wife's hand in his. "Honey, no one could resist that plea. If anyone knows anything, I'm sure they'll call the authorities."

Mindy leaned against him, absorbing his strength. "I know wherever our daughter is—with her strong faith in God—she's praying, too. Probably for us. She knows how much we love her."

"She also knows we won't quit until we find her. We have to be strong for her sake."

❧

The interview generated hundreds of phone calls to the command center that had been set up in the community building, but none of them seemed promising enough to offer much hope of finding her or her abductor.

Three more long, arduous days went by, with still no clues as to Bethany's whereabouts. Chuck had watched Mindy cry and cry, until there seemed to be no more tears for her to shed. Her stomach ached, her head hurt, and she said every bone in her body felt as if it were on fire.

She had not mentioned it to him, but he knew in his heart that this was the day his wife had been dreading.

Mother's Day.

Mindy smiled at him as she came out of their bedroom, dressed and ready for the day. Despite the lack of sleep and the dark circles under her eyes, she was beautiful. He had tried to be a rock to her through all of this, hoping his displays of love and devotion would make it hard for her even to consider that he'd had anything to do with Michelle.

Moving quickly to her side, he took both her hands in his and lifted them to his lips, kissing them as he gazed into her swollen, watery eyes.

"You don't need to avoid mentioning it, Chuck. I know it's Mother's Day. I'm just hoping and praying this will be the day Bethany comes home to us."

"Bethany couldn't have asked for a better mother, sweetheart. Just remember that." He slipped an arm around her. "Let's go to the Center. We have work to do."

To their surprise, despite its being Mother's Day, the day most folks spend with their families, a number of volunteers were already at the Warren Community Center when they arrived. After greeting everyone and thanking them for their diligence in helping them look for Bethany, Chuck moved to the big gridded map on the wall, gazing at the hundreds of colored ball-headed pins the many volunteers had placed there to show the houses and buildings they had canvassed. He carefully scanned each area that had been covered. "Hey, Jim," he called out when he checked an area at the extreme lower end of the grid. "Why hasn't this area down here by Bristol been covered? There isn't a single pin in it."

Jim Porter placed a stack of papers on the table and hurried over to him. "Hey, don't worry about that area. I know it very well. Me and a buddy of mine have hunted and fished there a number of times. Take it from me. Sending the volunteers down there would only be a waste of time. I think we'd be better off having them backtrack some of the areas where they've already been." He rushed off to answer one of the many ringing phones.

Treva Jordan moved up beside Chuck as he continued to gaze at the map. "I was raised in that area, Chuck. I just assumed it had been searched. My aunt's in a care home in Bristol, but she still owns a house there. I remember a number of old, abandoned outbuildings and barns not too far from her. She even has two or three on her place. Want me to take a couple of the volunteers and go down there?"

Chuck nodded as his index finger traced the edges of the uncanvassed portion on the map. "That's a great idea, but I can't ask these people to give up the entire day. It's Mother's Day. I have a better idea. I'll go with you. We'll get two or three other people to go with us."

"How about Jim?" Treva asked. "He seems to want to be in on everything that's going on."

Chuck glanced toward the table where Jim was sorting out a new batch of flyers and shook his head. "No, let's give him a rest. He and Janine have been working way too many hours on this. Don't even mention it to him, or he'll want to go."

"Did I hear you say you were going to search the area around Bristol?"

Chuck recognized the voice. "Hey, Pastor Park. What are you doing here on a Sunday morning? Aren't you supposed to be at church?"

"It appears both Treva and I are playing hooky today." The pastor nudged Treva's arm, then gave Chuck's hand a warm shake. "Normally I would be, but we have a special speaker this morning to commemorate Mother's Day. A woman from our congregation who has quite a story to tell. I left things in her capable hands. I've taken practically no vacation time in the past few years, so I told our church board I wanted today and tomorrow off so I could help you and Mindy. I'd like to go to Bristol with you. I've held some evangelistic meetings there, so

fairly familiar with that area. My wife is here, too. I'm sure she'd like to come
ong. We can take my Durango."

Chuck gave him a grateful smile. "I'd be mighty happy to have you both along,
stor."

"I heard you. I'm going, too."

Turning, Chuck faced a look of determination on Mindy's face. "You need
stay here, sweetheart. You're worn-out. You can drive our car on home."

Mindy held on tightly to his arm. "I'm going with you."

He could tell by the set of her jaw that there was no way he could discourage
r. "Okay, that makes five of us. Let me get one of the single men to go along,
d we'll be on our way."

⁓❦⁓

ven after five hours of searching abandoned buildings and talking to local resi-
nts, nothing new turned up. Standing before the tired, hungry group, Chuck
lled off his cap and ran his hands through his hair. "I guess Jim Porter was
ght. Maybe we'd better give up and head back to Warren."

"But we haven't checked out my aunt's place yet," Treva said. "It's only about
mile from here."

Mindy tugged on his arm. "We're already here. Let's check it out, Chuck."

He cupped his wife's chin with his hand. "You sure? It's been a long day
ready."

She sent him a weak smile. "Yes, I'm sure."

⁓❦⁓

'd never say this to anyone but you, Pastor," Chuck said in a low voice as they
lled into the yard of the house owned by Treva's aunt and the two men climbed
ut of the vehicle. "I've spent quite a bit of time on the Missing Children's Web
te, and from what I've read we have very little chance of finding our daughter
ive."

"Chuck, don't give up hope!" The pastor placed his hand on Chuck's shoulder.

"I'm not, Pastor Park, but I have to face the possibility."

"I understand what you're saying, Chuck, but let's not give up hope yet. God
able."

"Treva and I are going to check out the house," Mindy told her husband as
e crawled out of the backseat and pulled her scarf up around her neck. "She
ows where the key is hidden."

"Just be careful," he called after her. "And don't take too long. We need to
ead back to Warren." After sending Pastor Park and his wife off to the west to
eck out a shed Treva had told them about, he and Cal Rivers, the single man
'd asked to come with them, headed off toward the old, dilapidated barn out
hind the house.

Their search of the old barn yielded nothing more than a few broken gall
jugs, a ball of heavy twine, and a couple of rotten wooden crates. "Nobody's be
here in years," Chuck said, brushing his hands on his jeans. "This is a beauti
piece of property, but the buildings sure aren't much. I hope the house is in bet
shape. Let's walk on toward the east a couple hundred more yards. Then we
head for the Durango."

Treva and Mindy arrived back at the vehicle minutes after the men g
there. "Nothing in the house, but you should see the view of the bay from the
It's beautiful!" Mindy told him as she crawled in beside him. "Aren't the Pa
back yet?"

"No, not yet."

"I'm so sorry you're having to do this on Mother's Day," Mindy told Cal a
Treva, holding back her tears. "You should be home with your families on a d
like this."

"I love that daughter of yours," Treva said. "She's very special to me. I w
there when Pastor Park led her to the Lord."

Mindy's brows raised. "I didn't know that!"

"Mindy and I finally accepted the Lord," Chuck said with a big smi
"We're so anxious to tell Bethany about it. Pastor Park led us to the Lord, to
just like he led her."

"That news is going to make your daughter one happy girl." Treva's voi
was filled with excitement. "She's really been praying for the two of you, and s
had faith that God would answer her prayer."

"You know her well, Treva. Do you think Bethany would go away wi
someone she didn't know?"

Treva's eyes rounded. "Bethany? Never, Mindy! That girl has a good he
on her shoulders."

Mindy let out a relieved sigh. "That's what I was hoping you'd say."

"What could be taking them so long?" Chuck scanned the area off to t
west. "I'm going to go find them. We need to get back." He pushed the do
open and crawled out.

Suddenly Pastor Park's voice rang out from a dense grove of trees about
hundred yards from where they were parked. "Chuck! Mindy! Come over her
quick!"

Chapter 10

"Is it Bethany?" Chuck screamed out, racing toward the pastor's voice. "Is she alive?"

"I can't tell!" he called back. "Hurry!"

Chuck ran as fast as he could, pushing his way through thick boughs and ergrowth, his heart pounding with both joy and fear. "She has to be alive!"

"Look through this crack!" Pastor Park yelled out excitedly as he pointed to eparation between two weathered boards in the old shed. "I can see her! She's der that pile of dirty old horse blankets. You can barely see her face!"

Chuck squinted his eyes and peered through. "It's her. Oh, dear God, it's r! You've answered our prayer!" He tugged on the padlock securing the door, t it would not give.

"I'll get my tire iron." Pastor Park hurried away toward the Durango.

"Oh, Chuck, is it really her?" Panting for breath, Mindy reached for his arm. —is she alive?"

"I—I don't know." He shoved her toward the space between the two boards. ake a look. Can you tell if she's breathing?"

Mindy pressed her face against the opening. "Bethany, baby, Mama and addy are here! Can you hear me? Oh, baby, please say something!"

Pastor Park tossed the tire iron into Chuck's hand. "Here—try this."

Chuck shoved the tip of the tire iron under the hasp and gave it a sharp nk. It budged slightly but did not open. He tried it a second time and the hasp ve way. He jerked open the door and rushed to Bethany, dropping onto his ees at her side, bending and listening for any signs of life.

"Oh, Chuck, we've found her!" Mindy screamed as she threw herself down side Bethany and began to stroke her beloved child's hair. "Oh, thank You, od! Thank You! This is the best Mother's Day present I could ever ask for!"

"She's breathing, but barely, and she has a nasty cut on her head." Chuck pulled f his jacket and threw it on top of the blankets covering the still, small body curled on the dirt floor of the shed. "We've got to get her to the hospital."

Cal bent down and began to take the girl's pulse. "I've already used my cell one to call for an ambulance. They should be here shortly. She may not have d food," he added, looking around, "but she had water, thanks to that hole in e roof. Looks like that rain we had a few days ago must've run right off that roof into this old bucket."

Slowly Bethany opened one eye and peered out through the slit. "Dadd she whispered faintly.

He shot a smile to his wife. "I'm here, princess. So is Mommy." Caref Chuck slipped his hand beneath her shoulders, bracing her head with his ar "You're safe now."

The girl simply nodded as her eyes closed again.

"We're going to take you home, sweetheart," Mindy told her, her fing stroking the girl's matted hair. "You're going to be just fine."

Chuck silently thanked God as he heard the wail of the ambulance's sir *Lord, I know I don't deserve it, but thank You for answering this father's prayer.*

After examining her, the EMTs agreed to take her back to Warren, whi was only a five-mile trip, instead of into Bristol. Chuck and Mindy were allow to ride to the hospital with their daughter.

Chuck glanced impatiently at his watch as he and Mindy sat in the hospit: waiting room. "What's taking so long? She's been in there for nearly two hours

Mindy crossed her arms over her chest and leaned back in the chair. "I do know, but I think we should be with her. I know she's still terrified."

Agent Rogers rose to his feet and began to pace around the waiting room. don't want to frighten you, Mr. and Mrs. O'Connor, but Bethany is still in gra danger. She's the only one who can identify the person who did this to her." I pushed one of the upholstered chairs in front of them and sat down. "I've plac one of my best men here at the hospital to guard her room. We don't want take any chances."

Mindy's hand went to her chest. "You think he'd actually come here? To t hospital?"

"We don't know, but until we find whoever it was who kidnapped yo daughter, we have to take as many precautions as possible."

"Your daughter has been through a terrible ordeal," the doctor told Min and Chuck as he stepped into the waiting room. "I doubt she's had any foc She's been exposed to the cold, even though I've heard her abductor did lea some old horse blankets for her, and it appears she's been either hit or shov into something. She has a broken rib and bruises over her entire body."

Mindy let out a gasp and buried her head against Chuck's chest. "Oh, r not my baby!"

Chuck knew what his wife was thinking. Though they had never voiced to each other, it had been his worse fear, too. "Was she—"

"Raped? No."

Chuck could not help it. He burst into tears right along with Mindy. "Prai You, Lord!"

The doctor placed a comforting hand on Mindy's shoulder. "She's going to e sore for a while, but give her a little time, some good food, and a lot of love, nd she'll be fine. I've already stitched up that cut on her head. She wants to see ou. But don't expect too much. She's still in a bit of a stupor and maybe will be or some time to come. It may be several days, maybe even weeks, before she's nore like her old self, and even then she'll no doubt have nightmares. In fact, he may not want to sleep at all. More than likely she hasn't slept since she was aken. I've given her something to sleep, so we'd better hurry if you want to talk o her before she drifts off."

"Has—has she said anything about what happened to her?"

"No, Mrs. O'Connor," the doctor said, with a glance toward Agent Rogers. Nothing. I doubt she'll want to talk about it. Victims seldom do. Now follow ne. I'll take you to her."

❧

Mindy and Chuck moved quietly up to Bethany's bed.

"Baby, are you awake?" Mindy whispered, bending over to stroke her daugh-er's cheek. "It's Mama. Daddy's here, too."

Slowly Bethany opened her eyes and gazed at them, squinting and blinking s if she were having trouble focusing.

"We love you, princess," Chuck said, smiling at his daughter. "And we have omething to tell you."

Mindy bent and kissed her daughter's cheek. "Treva told us you'd been pray-ng for us, that we'd accept God like you had."

"We did it, sweetheart. Your mama and me. We accepted Christ as our avior."

"Pastor Park helped us. He led us to your Lord."

Bethany opened one eye as a smile took birth on her dry, chapped lips. "Really?" he said faintly.

Chuck nodded. "Really. We'll talk more about it later. There's so much we vant to tell you. Right now you need to rest."

They hadn't noticed that Agent Rogers had followed them into the room. Ask her who did this to her."

Chuck nodded at the man and leaned in closer. "Who took you from us, 3ethany? Can you tell Daddy?"

Bethany turned her head away, and her entire body began to shake violently. No! Leave me alone!" she shouted, her eyes widening and taking on a glassy laze. "Don't let him hurt me! Please—don't let him hurt me again!"

"You'll have to leave," the doctor said firmly, motioning them toward the loor. "This child has had a terrible shock. I won't have her upset." He ushered hem out of the room, with all three protesting.

"She's my daughter!" Mindy nearly screamed at him, refusing to be separated from Bethany. "I have to be with her!"

"Once she's asleep," he told them, his voice now kind and gentle, "if you promise you won't upset her, you can stay in the room with her—but no more questions tonight. Understood?"

Agent Rogers whipped out his badge and presented it to the man. "We're talking about a kidnapping here. The person who did this is still out there, running loose, maybe already planning to kidnap some other child. I need answers."

The doctor stepped forward and stood nose to nose with the agent. "And you'll get them, but not until that child is ready to talk to you. I'm sorry, Agent Whatever-Your-Name-Is, but the health of the little girl comes first. Right now she needs rest."

"I think one of us should be with Bethany at all times," Mindy told Chuck. "I'd like to stay with her tonight. You go on home and get some rest. Maybe by morning she'll feel like talking to us. I don't even care if she knows I'm in the room. I just want to sit and watch her breathe."

"I should be the one to stay. You're exhausted. You go—"

"Please, Chuck, it's Mother's Day. Let me spend the rest of it with my daughter."

Chuck smiled as he nodded his head. "Okay, sweetheart, you stay. I'll come back first thing in the morning."

The doctor reached out to Chuck's arm. "I'm sorry. I didn't mean to sound harsh. I know both you and your wife want to stay with your daughter. I have a daughter of my own. I'll permit it if you promise not to ask her any more questions. I'm sure you understand why."

Chuck's heart did a leap at the news. He hated the idea of having to leave. "We can both stay?"

"Yes. Just remember my words. I'll be checking on her the first thing in the morning."

The two sat quietly, holding hands and watching the rhythmic rise and fall of Bethany's chest. About two in the morning, Chuck stood to his feet and stretched. "Want to go with me to see if we can find a vending machine? I'm thirsty." He was glad when she nodded and reached out her hand.

"Good evening. I'm Officer Kirkpatrick."

Mindy startled as she stepped into the hall, having forgotten about the guard posted by the door.

"Oh! Hello. We're Bethany's parents."

"Got any idea where the vending machines are?" Chuck asked the man after shaking his hand.

Before the officer could answer, a nurse called out to them from the nurses

ation. "Mr. and Mrs. O'Connor. There's a bag over here for you and your wife. A
an, I think his name was Park or Parks, left it for you. He said he knew you and
ur wife hadn't eaten all day, and he brought you some sandwiches and some other
ings. There's a small lunchroom and a coffee machine at the end of the hall."

Chuck hurried to retrieve the bag; then he and Mindy made their way
ward the lunchroom. "Good old Pastor Park. What a thoughtful guy."

"God really answers prayer. The way he kept Bethany alive and the way He
d us to her—now this! Food when we really need it."

"Mr. O'Connor!"

Both Chuck and Mindy turned as a man stepped up beside them.

"I'm Bill Dayton from WBBB radio. I wondered if I might ask you a few
estions. I know your daughter was found somewhere not far from here." He
ent on without giving Chuck time to answer. "Can you tell me where and who
d this to her?"

Chuck shook his head and gave him a menacing stare. "I think you'd better
lk to Captain Wyatt or Agent Rogers about that."

"I couldn't help overhearing Mrs. O'Connor make some comment about
od answering your prayers. You really don't think God had anything to do with
ur finding her, do you?"

Chuck glanced at Mindy, then squared his shoulders. "Yes, I do. My wife
d I are both Christians now, and we believe in prayer. We're confident God
ok care of our daughter while she was away from us and led us to find her."

The man gave him a mocking frown. "If I were a Christian, which I'm not,
would be furious with God for letting something like this happen to one of
y family members. Are you telling me this tragic kidnapping didn't shake your
ith in God?"

Chuck silently sent up a quick prayer. *Let me answer this man in a way that
ill honor You!* "No, not at all. I can honestly say that finding our daughter has
eepened our faith in God. I feel sad for you if you don't know Him and would
ggest you get yourself right with Him. If you'd like, I'd be happy to provide a
ible for you."

"Ah—thanks for your time. I'll check with the police." The man nearly
ipped over his feet getting out the door.

"You were wonderful," Mindy said, smiling up at Chuck, her weary eyes
ow sparkling. "I'm so proud of you." She giggled as she gave his arm a pinch.
For a brand-new Christian you did very well."

Her melodic giggle made him smile. What a joy to see his wife happy again.
ven the worry lines on her face had begun to relax. He playfully tapped the tip
f her nose with his index finger. "Only because I sent up a prayer to God, asking
Iim to give me the right words."

Bethany struggled to open her eyes. Why hadn't they left a light on? She hated the darkness. *Oh, I hurt.* Painfully she shifted her weight a bit, turning toward the two empty chairs beside her bed. *Mama! Daddy! Where are you?*

Carefully she rolled onto her back, wincing at the stifling pain in her chest from the broken rib. *Mama! Daddy! Come back. I don't want to be alone. Please come back!*

She stared at the narrow shaft of light wedging its way through the nearly closed door as it suddenly widened and the silhouette of a man appeared.

"Daddy, is that you? Where's Mama?"

But her father didn't answer.

"Daddy?"

Chapter 11

The figure closed the door, rendering the room in near darkness again. Though he was not nearly as visible now, with only the light filtering in through the closed Venetian blinds, she could still see him as he crept stealthily toward the bed.

That's not my daddy!

Panic gripped her heart as the experiences of the last few days flooded her mind and soul. *Is it him? The man who kidnapped me?* She wanted to scream out, to yell for help, but the words were trapped in her throat and would not come.

As he moved closer, instinctively, with trembling fingers, she grabbed the sheet and pulled it tightly around her neck, her heart clenching with fear and pounding so loudly she was sure he could hear it. She tried to back away as his hot breath scorched her cheek, but it was impossible.

There was no place to run.

No way to escape.

～∽～

Mindy took Chuck's hand as they made their way toward Bethany's room after they had consumed the delicious sandwiches and pieces of cake Pastor Park had brought. "I'm so glad the doctor said we could both stay the night with her."

Chuck gave her a doting smile as they came to Bethany's room. He reached for the door handle, then pulled back. "Where's the guard?"

A bloodcurdling scream sounded from the room!

Chuck rushed in, momentarily blinded by the semidarkness. Someone was leaning over Bethany! "Get help!" he yelled at Mindy as he hurled himself at the figure, grabbing the person around the shoulders and wrestling whoever it was to the floor.

"Help! Someone, help!" Mindy yelled at the top of her lungs.

Instantly two orderlies appeared and rushed through the door. With their help Chuck was able to subdue the man.

"Jim!" He couldn't believe his eyes. It was Jim Porter, the man he had thought to be a newfound friend. The man who had worked so diligently as a volunteer!

"It's him, Daddy!" Bethany, her face contorted with fear, pointed a shaky finger at Jim. "He's the one who took me away!"

Mindy raced toward her daughter, scooping her up in her arms and holding her close to her breast, barely noticing when Bethany winced in pain. "Oh, Bethany, my Bethany. My poor, poor baby!"

"He told me you'd sent him to pick me up at school that night because you'd had a car wreck. I believed him! He tied my hands together and took me to that awful place!"

"You did that to my daughter?" It was all Chuck could do to keep from wrapping his fingers around the man's neck and choking the life out of him.

"He—he told me that if anyone found me before he came back for me and I told them he was the one who had taken me—" Gasping for breath, Bethany stopped and stared at Jim. "He said he would kill both of you! That's why I didn't want to answer that man last night."

"You lowlife! You don't deserve to live!" Chuck pulled back his arm and took a swing at the man, but one of the orderlies restrained him.

Within minutes he and the two orderlies had Jim's hands and feet secured with medical tape, immobilizing him.

A nurse hurried into the room. "We found the guard in a storage room down the hall. He's unconscious."

Chuck shook his head with disgust, then bent over Jim and spit on him. "Someone call 911 and ask for Captain Wyatt. Tell him we've got our man."

❧

"Well, you're certainly looking better," Dr. Born told Bethany as he came into her room the next morning, chart in hand. "Nice to see you're eating, but take it easy. Your tummy has been without food for a few days."

"How long before we can take her home?" Mindy asked.

"Probably tomorrow. She's much better today than when she was brought in last night. Her rib is going to give her fits for a while, and it will take a couple of weeks for her head to heal, but her bruises will soon fade, and she'll be fine." He gestured toward the door. "Why don't you two go have some breakfast while I check her over?"

Smiling, Bethany shooed them toward the door. "Yeah, Mama, you and Daddy go eat. I'll be okay. I'm not afraid anymore."

"What'd Jim have to say when they questioned him?" Mindy asked as she and Chuck moved into the hall outside Bethany's room. "You haven't had a chance to tell me since you got back from the police station."

Chuck rolled his eyes. "I'm glad you weren't there to hear it. When confronted with the evidence, the guy actually spilled his guts, almost as if he was proud of what he'd done. Captain Wyatt said it was because he was hoping to plea bargain by giving the FBI the names of the people who mail him child porn."

"I can't believe he got Bethany to go with him."

"Agent Rogers said these guys spend days planning something like this. It seems one time when Bethany had stopped by the Porters' house to play with their dog, she told them how she and her friends talked to one another on that instant-message thing. She even told them the code name she used. Jim got on his computer and began talking to her as—"

"Trustworthy!" Mindy shook her head in disbelief.

"Yep, Trustworthy. He even admitted he was the one who left that bracelet in our flowerbed. Remember how in her diary she mentioned she'd told Trustworthy she wouldn't be able to talk to him that evening because she'd be at that play rehearsal? He knew exactly what time it would be over, and he was sitting in his car waiting when she came out of the school, hoping he could get to her and convince her to get in his car before you got there."

"But how could he be in two places at once? Everyone we knew, including the Porters, were questioned as to their whereabouts that evening. Janine swore he was at home with her all evening, watching a football game."

"That's the sad part. Janine had no idea her husband was involved in anything like this. He had fixed her a cup of hot cocoa laced with three high-powered sleeping pills. Then, once she dozed off, he slipped out and went to the school. She actually woke up just as he was coming in the front door after he'd taken Bethany to Bristol, but he said he'd been able to convince her he'd just stepped out onto the porch because he'd heard a noise out front and had gone to investigate."

Mindy closed her eyes, gulping hard. "Why—why did he want to take Bethany since he didn't—didn't—?" She couldn't say the word.

"He planned to, but he knew he had to get back before his wife woke up. So he took her out to that old shed, meaning to come back the next day and do it. He'd even called a friend on his cell phone while he was driving, pretending to be at home watching the game, so he'd have that as a second alibi, in case he needed it later. But you know what? I think Bethany's prayers were what kept him from coming back. God was protecting her from further harm. I should have been suspicious when the guy spent so many hours passing out those flyers and putting up posters and the way he was constantly at my side, asking questions about the investigation. Especially when he made up that grid and didn't assign any of the volunteers to search the area where Bethany was found!"

"That's hindsight, Chuck. There's no way you could have known. Don't blame yourself. He had us all fooled."

He let out a heavy sigh. "That's what Captain Wyatt said."

It took Mindy a few minutes to absorb it all. "While you were gone, Bethany told me he had tried to pull her shirt off, but she hit at him and kicked him real hard—right where they told her to in the self-defense classes she took at school. It made him so angry he kicked her back several times with the toe of his boot, then grabbed up a piece of an old barrel stave and hit her with it—once across her ribs and the last time over her head, knocking her to the ground. She said she thought if she just lay there, he'd think she was dead. When she finally opened her eyes, he was gone, and the door was padlocked."

"Yeah, he told them he'd hit her and how she'd fallen to the floor with blood gushing from her wound and running down her face. He did think maybe he'd killed her, but he decided to leave her there and come back later. He never expected her to fight the way she did. I guess that kick of hers really hurt the guy—in the right place."

"I feel sorry for Janine. She told me she'd only known Jim for about two weeks before they got married."

"Yeah, I guess she was the one who messed up his plans to go back. She was so scared, with a crazed kidnapper on the loose, that she stuck to him like glue, and he couldn't shake her off long enough to drive back down to Bristol without raising suspicion. Agent Rogers said he asked Jim if he'd kidnapped any other girls. He laughed and said that was for them to find out. But when they confronted him with a number of pictures of young girls they'd found in his house, he actually bragged about the number he'd molested, most of them too embarrassed to let their parents or the authorities know. The FBI is hoping, armed with the pictures found in Jim's house and the information he has given them, that some of the other missing children's cases may be solved. Jim had met most of the girls on the Internet. Our precious, innocent, naive little girl has been at the mercy of this cunning, lecherous pervert for weeks, and we didn't even know it."

Mindy reached out and touched her husband's arm, then bowed her head. "Thank You, God, for keeping our baby safe while she was in the hands of that madman."

"Amen." Chuck pulled her hand to his lips and kissed it tenderly, gazing at her with eyes full of love. "Isn't it amazing the way God not only brought our Bethany back to us, but cleared my name, as well, and I ended up with a big promotion?"

Mindy released a slight giggle. "I tried to help clear your name, Chuck. I did a bit of sleuthing on my own, but I wasn't very good at it."

Chuck tilted her face upward. "You? Sleuthing? How? What did you do?"

Mindy could not contain a full-fledged chuckle as she remembered what she had done and how foolish it seemed looking back on it. "I paid a visit to Clarisse and got her to pull up Michelle's file on her computer screen."

He reared back, his jaw dropping. "Clarisse gave you information on Michelle? That kind of stuff is confidential! I can't believe she gave it to you!"

"She didn't exactly give it to me. She left the room for a few minutes, and I copied it down myself."

"So? Did you find anything?"

"Not really. Nothing of any use."

"What exactly do you mean—nothing of any use?"

A smile curled at Mindy's lips. "I went Dumpster-diving in her trash."

Chuck's jaw dropped as he threw his arms into the air. "You what?"

"I pulled a big plastic bag out of her trash and took it home with me. It was a dumb thing to do. I actually sifted through Michelle's garbage. It was disgusting!"

Laughing, Chuck grabbed her up in his arms. "My prissy little Mindy—Dumpster-diving? Now that is a picture!"

"I guess I naively hoped I'd find a note or a scratch pad where she'd written some heinous plan to discredit your name. I wanted to prove your innocence. I may not have acted like it, but I loved you!"

Chuck let out a belly laugh as he lifted her and whirled her around the hospital corridor. "Dumpster-diving. I never would have believed it!"

≈≈≈

"Michelle's gone, and I'm the new sales manager, Mindy! Can you believe it?"

Mindy leaned into Chuck's embrace. She had her family back, and it felt so good. "Yes, dearest, I can believe it. This week has been filled with miracles." She let her expression go somber. "But I think we should keep this to ourselves. There's no reason for Bethany to know about your suspension. She has enough to deal with."

The feeling of Chuck's lips on hers was delicious as he bent and kissed her. "I love you, Mindy O'Connor."

"I love you, too."

Chapter 12

I s my hair okay? Do I have on enough lipstick?" Mindy asked as she and Chuck sat on their sofa, staring into the lens of the portable TV video camera.

"You look beautiful, sweetheart."

"Heads up. We're ready." The WKRI-TV videographer behind the camera began his countdown, "Five, four, three, two, one," then pointed a finger at them.

"Hello, I'm Chuck O'Connor, and this is my wife, Mindy. Our daughter, Bethany, was kidnapped this past week and held captive for several days. But thanks to God, she has been found and is now home with us."

A bundle of nerves, Mindy cleared her throat and took a deep breath. "We want to thank all of you for your assistance in finding our daughter. Some by praying, some by actually helping in the search. We're fortunate. Our child has been returned to us. Many families are still waiting for news of their child." Mindy stared directly into the camera lens, speaking from her heart. "Cherish each minute you have with your children. Tell them how much you love them as often as you can. None of us knows what a day may bring."

Chuck gave her hand a squeeze as he took over. "If you have any information about a missing child, please call the Missing Children's hotline at 1-800-THE-LOST. Your information could be the lead that brings a child home to their anxious, waiting family. Thank you."

"Cut!"

Captain Wyatt gave them a smile. "You both did great. From what I've been told, your public service announcement will run not only in Rhode Island, but also in a number of the surrounding states. It may be the means of bringing other missing children home to their parents."

Chuck slipped an arm around Mindy. "We're both praying it will be."

～～

Two days later Chuck stood in the middle of their family room, rubbing his chin and looking thoughtful. "I still don't understand one thing. How did that rag with Bethany's blood on it get into the trash barrel in our garage?"

"You mean that piece of your old shirt?" Bethany asked from her place on the sofa, looking surprised. "I put it there."

Mindy frowned. "When? You never bother the things on Daddy's workbench!"

"Tracie and I were skateboarding, and one of those boltie things in the bottom of my board was loose. I went to Daddy's workbench and got one of those wrenchie-type things and tried to tighten it. But my hand slipped, and I cut myself. I wiped the blood on Daddy's old shirt and put it in the trash. I didn't think I'd get in trouble for it. I didn't mess up Daddy's toolbox, and I put the wrench back where it was supposed to be."

Chuck raced to his daughter. "You're not in trouble, princess. In fact, if it wasn't for your broken rib, I'd give you a big bear hug!"

"Your dad and I have an idea. We want your opinion. What would you think about us renewing our vows?"

The girl screwed up her face. "What does that mean?"

"Getting married again. We eloped the first time, and neither Grandma Carson or Grandma O'Connor got to attend our wedding," Chuck explained. "It wasn't much of a wedding. No one was there except the man who married us and his wife and some woman who played the organ."

"I didn't even have real flowers," Mindy confessed with a laugh. "I had a silk bouquet. I still have it, though it's probably a bit dusty. It's been up in the attic all these years."

"Wow! Some of my friends got to go to their mother's or father's wedding 'cause they got divorced and married someone else. But they've never been to their own parents' wedding. I think that'd be cool!"

"We've already talked to Pastor Park about it. He's going to perform the ceremony in three weeks," Mindy said with a loving glance toward her husband. "I want you to be my bridesmaid."

Bethany's eyes sparkled. "Really? A bridesmaid? Wow!"

"We'll have to buy you a new dress for it, but I'm going to try to get into the champagne-colored lace dress I wore at our first wedding. That dress cost me a whole two weeks' salary!"

Bethany clapped her hands together. "Wow! I can't wait to tell Tracie. Me— a bridesmaid!"

Mindy gazed at her daughter as she lay on the sofa covered up with the Jacob's Ladder quilt. "Are you sure you're up to this, sweetie? You've been through quite an ordeal. We don't want to push you. The wedding can be put off until—"

"No! I'm doing okay, honest. I want you and Daddy to get married!"

Mindy stroked her daughter's beautiful, silky hair. "Go call Tracie. Maybe she'd like to be a candlelighter."

"I will in a minute, but Daddy and I have a surprise for you." Bethany gave her father an exaggerated wink. "Could you get it for me, Daddy?"

With a mischievous smile exploding across his face, Chuck snapped his fingers, then hurried out of the room.

Mindy cocked her head to one side and frowned. "What was that all about?"

Bethany let out a giggle. "You'll see."

Chuck sauntered back into the family room and knelt in front of Mindy. "Bethany and I did a little shopping a couple of weeks ago, didn't we, princess?"

A wide smile blanketed their child's sweet face.

"This is for you, with all our love." Chuck handed Mindy a small red-velvet jewelry box. "Sorry, we didn't wrap it."

She glanced from one smiling face to the other.

Bethany's eyes sparkled. "It's for Mother's Day! I'm sorry we couldn't give it to you then."

With trembling fingers and a heart overflowing with love, Mindy lifted the lid. "Oh! A gold locket! It's beautiful!"

"Daddy and I picked it out," Bethany said with pride, her face beaming. "You can wear it to your wedding! Look inside."

Carefully using the tip of her fingernail, Mindy popped it open. "Oh, pictures of the two people I love the most in all the world. You and your daddy." A tear clouded her vision.

"Do you like it, Mama?"

Mindy smiled at her daughter. "No, baby, I love it!"

Bethany cradled herself up next to Mindy. "I love you, Mama. Happy Mother's Day."

The next three weeks flew by as Mindy and Bethany shopped for Bethany's dress, arranged for flowers, called the caterer, and performed an array of other tasks necessary to plan a wedding.

While on a business trip to Providence, Chuck ran into an old friend, Keene Moray, an opera singer who had quit the opera to sing full-time for the Lord, and asked him to sing at their wedding. Knowing Keene's busy schedule, he'd expected him to say he wouldn't be able make it; but to his amazement the man agreed and even said he'd be bringing his wife, Jane.

Mindy shrieked when he told her Keene had accepted his invitation. "Keene Moray! The famous Keene Moray is going to sing at our wedding?" She threw her arms around Chuck's neck and, giggling like a schoolgirl, planted dozens of kisses all over his face.

"Wow! I'd have asked him long ago if I'd known I was going to get this kind of treatment!"

Finally, the day arrived. "I'm going to throw my bouquet to you, Treva. You need the love of a good man," Mindy told her friend as they stood before the mirror in the bride's room of the church.

Treva laughed out loud, then handed Mindy the bouquet of yellowed silk flowers from Chuck and Mindy's first wedding. "You think catching a bouquet of flowers will snag me a man?"

Mindy cocked her head coyly. "Well, you do have to do your part. You can't just sit and wait for him to come knocking on your door. You have to get out there and circulate."

"Circulate, huh? I'll give that piece of advice some serious thought." She lifted the bouquet and touched one of its blossoms. "Hey, these silk flowers don't look too bad, considering they're fourteen years old. But I know they're precious to you, so if I catch them, I promise to give them back to you so you can save them for Bethany."

To Mindy's surprise, every seat in the church sanctuary was filled, as friends, church members, Bethany's teachers and classmates, both Chuck and Mindy's business associates, and countless volunteers who had helped find Bethany crowded into the pews.

Mindy's joy was uncontainable as she stood between her handsome husband and her beautiful daughter, listening to the rich baritone voice of Keene Moray as he sang the words of "I Love You Truly," which had been sung at their first wedding.

God had blessed her more abundantly than she could ever ask or imagine He would. *How quickly life can change. In the twinkling of an eye,* Mindy thought as she held tightly to her husband's arm, *the things I've taken for granted—the most precious things in my life—were nearly taken from me. I came so close to losing both my husband and my daughter. But thanks to God's goodness and His everlasting love, I didn't, and my little family has been reunited.*

She wiped away a tear of joy with her gloved hand and listened carefully as Pastor Park challenged the two of them to live for God and for each other, and in her heart of hearts she knew she'd found her calling.

With a warm smile Pastor Park took Mindy's hand and placed it in Chuck's. "By the power vested in me by the state of Rhode Island, I now pronounce you husband and wife. You may kiss your bride."

A tingle ran through Mindy as Chuck slowly lifted her veil; then, gazing into her face with eyes filled with love, he kissed her. This time, though, it was different from when he'd kissed her in the little wedding chapel in Las Vegas. Now they were experienced adults who had faced tremendous challenges in their lives, not silly twenty-year-olds with pie-in-the-sky ideas. And they knew, without a shadow of a doubt, their love was real and would last a lifetime.

"I love you, my darling," Chuck whispered against her lips. "I'll love you forever, and I promise always to be there for you."

"I love you, too, sweetheart. With God as my witness, I'll strive to be the best wife I can be. The wife you deserve."

As Mindy felt a small hand slip into hers, she pulled away from Chuck's embrace. Bending, she kissed Bethany's shining face. "And I love you, too, baby. Thanks for praying for us. Your faith is what brought us here."

As the organ began to play, Chuck grabbed Mindy's hand, then reached out his free hand toward Bethany. "Come on, princess. We want you with us."

Mr. and Mrs. Chuck O'Connor and their daughter, Bethany, together again, walked down the aisle to begin life anew—this time with God as the head of their family.

THE FOURTH
OF JULY

Chapter 1

Along with the other happy onlookers, Treva Jordan waited anxiously, her gaze pinned on Mindy O'Connor. Her friend stood at the head of the stairs in front of the church where she and her husband, Chuck, had just renewed their vows.

"Here it comes!" Mindy's mirth-filled laughter echoed above the crowd as she tossed her bouquet. It soared through the air, hit a branch on a nearby tree, then fell into Treva's hands.

"Good catch, Treva!" Mindy called out, clapping her hands with glee. "I told you I was going to throw my bridal bouquet in your direction!"

"I never thought you'd actually do it!" Treva looked down at the bouquet, clutching it to her breast with an embarrassed laugh, still in shock that she was the one to catch the coveted cluster of flowers. "It's going to take a whole lot more than this bridal bouquet to help me find a man. Besides, I'm not even sure I want one!" she called back, grinning.

Her friend threw her a playful kiss. "That's what I said before I met Chuck!"

Treva responded with a shake of her head. "Not many men in this world are like Chuck. You got lucky!"

Holding on to the railing, Mindy quickly descended the stairs, shaking a few well-wishers' hands on the way as she hurried over to stand by her friend. "You and I both know it wasn't luck that brought Chuck and me together. It was God's hand. I can see that now, but way back then, when we were dating and behaving like two spoiled children, impulsively deciding to elope, the last thing on my mind was God."

"Congratulations, Mindy." A pretty woman walked up to them and patted Mindy's shoulder. "I'm so glad you and Chuck were able to work out your problems. I just knew you would. It's nice to see you back together again, and I'm sure your daughter is happy about it, too."

Mindy leaned forward and kissed the woman's cheek. "Thanks, Clarisse. Your encouragement really helped."

"She works in Chuck's office," Mindy explained to Treva when the woman moved on. "She's a real sweetie."

"This is the third wedding bouquet I've caught in the past two years," Treva admitted, giving her a doleful smile, her fingertips tenderly fondling the faded petals of a yellow silk rose. "You think there's hope for me?"

Mindy grabbed Treva's hand and gave it an affectionate squeeze. "As beautiful as you are? Of course there's hope. You just have to be patient until the right man comes along."

Tiny frown lines worked their way across Treva's forehead. "You make it sound as if I've been out there looking. I haven't. Oh, maybe I did a few years ago, when I was in college, but I've been on my own for several years now and doing quite nicely. I've seen too many of my eager-to-be-a-wife college classmates jump into the marriage thing, wishing afterward they'd gotten to know the guy a whole lot better before committing themselves to him. Their lives have been pretty miserable. I don't want to end up like that. *If* and *when* I get married, I want it to be to the right man, the one of God's choosing, and I want our marriage to last forever."

"That's very wise, Treva. You have a good head on your shoulders. But if you're going to meet that guy of your dreams, you have to get out there and circulate. You'll never meet him by keeping your nose stuck in that third-grade classroom where you teach."

Treva gave her a wink. "I don't know. Some of my students have pretty terrific-looking fathers!"

Mindy harrumphed. "You? A home wrecker? Never!"

Treva's face became somber. "I want more than a terrific-looking guy, Mindy. I want a man who loves the Lord as much as I do, and those are few and far between."

"That may be—but it only takes one, and if God wants you to marry, I'm sure He'll send that man into your life. I'm going to keep praying for you. You're very special to Chuck and me and to our daughter. You're Bethany's role model."

"Thanks, Mindy. I do want that husband, two kids, house, dog, white picket fence, minivan thing—but there aren't many guys my age who are still unattached. The ones who are available are often weird, and I surely don't want them. Guess I'm too picky."

"You're still planning to spend the summer in Bristol fixing up your aunt's house, aren't you?"

"Yeah. With Thursday being the last day of school, I plan to drive down to Bristol on Saturday. Most of my things are already boxed and ready to go. I didn't have that much to pack since I've been living in a furnished apartment. I'm hoping to get a nicer place when I come back in the fall."

"How is your aunt doing?"

"Not well at all. I went up to the nursing home to visit Aunt TeeDee last weekend. She was too weak even to speak to me. I hold my breath each time the phone rings, thinking it's them calling to say she's passed away. Besides Robert, her stepbrother who hasn't had anything to do with either of us for years, she's the only relative I have. I can't imagine life without her."

Mindy gave her a puzzled look. "If her health is that bad, why are you going to fix up her old house? It doesn't sound as if she'll ever be going home again."

"Originally the main reason I decided to spend the summer in Bristol was so I could be near her and visit every day. She's leaving the property to me, and I thought I'd have a head start on getting it ready to sell as she wants me to."

"Whew! There for a minute I was afraid you might stay in Bristol permanently, instead of coming back here to Warren."

"No, my plans are still to come back in the fall."

"Maybe you'll meet some nice guy in Bristol. It could happen, you know."

Treva responded with a snort. "Not likely, but I'll keep my eyes open."

"Our family is going to miss you. Especially Bethany. Our daughter thinks you're the greatest Sunday school teacher in the world. She really looks up to you."

"I'll miss her, and you and Chuck, too. But I'll be back in time for school to start in the fall. With all I have to do I'm sure the three months will go by pretty quickly."

"Hey, quit monopolizing my bride!" Chuck wrapped an arm about his wife and planted an exaggerated kiss on her cheek, ending with a loud smack. "I want you ladies to meet someone." He nodded his head toward a handsome, muscular-looking man standing beside him. "This is Tank LaFrenz. I'm sure you've both heard me talk about him. I met him at that men's conference when they had their regional meeting in Providence."

Mindy nodded as though she recognized the name, but Treva drew a blank. Perhaps Chuck had mentioned him, but she'd been too preoccupied to remember.

"Nice to meet you ladies." Tank nodded toward Mindy then turned to Treva with a toothy-white smile that sent goose bumps up and down her spine. "I see you caught Mindy's bouquet."

She felt her cheeks grow warm like a schoolgirl's. "She aimed it at me."

"My darling wife, your chariot awaits," Chuck told Mindy, bowing low as he gestured toward the shiny black limousine parked at the curb.

Mindy's eyes sparkled. "Chuck! You old romantic! You didn't tell me you'd ordered a limousine!"

"Only the best for my best gal!" With hoots and hollers from the many friends and business associates who had gathered, Chuck swept her up in his arms and rushed toward the waiting limousine. "Not every day a guy gets to remarry the love of his life!"

"Bye, all, and thanks!" Mindy yelled out the open window as the car pulled away from the curb. "We love you!"

With Tank LaFrenz still standing at her side, Treva watched until the couple's car disappeared from sight. Then she gazed at the bridal bouquet, remembering how close Mindy and Chuck had come to losing everything they held near and dear. *Lord,* she prayed, lifting her eyes heavenward, *thank You for letting me become part of that sweet couple's life. How I long to have the same kind of love Mindy and Chuck have. If it is Your will for me to get married someday, please guide me to the man of Your choice. I sure don't want to make any mistakes.*

"Doesn't that Keene Moray have a great voice?"

She looked up quickly and found Tank smiling at her. "Yes, he certainly does. I've never heard anyone sing 'I Love You Truly' the way he did at the wedding. I'm glad they videotaped the ceremony. I'm sure the O'Connor family will play it over and over."

"Have you heard his testimony? Chuck and I heard it at that conference. He has quite a story."

She shook her head. "No, I haven't, but Mindy told me about him. Isn't it amazing what God can do when a man opens his heart as Mr. Moray has?"

"I hear he's cut his opera schedule to a bare minimum and now spends most of his time doing Christian concerts. I'd sure like to go to one sometime."

Treva turned as someone grabbed onto her arm.

"Treva, you'd better come with us."

She stared up into the pastor's face.

"I hate to be the one to tell you. Someone from the nursing home in Bristol just phoned. Your aunt passed away."

❧

"Miss Priss!" Treva yelled at her big mouser cat who skittered past her and headed for a nearby grove of trees. "You come back here this instant!" But Miss Priss kept right on going, without so much as slowing down or giving a backward look. "You independent cat! Just because you're pregnant doesn't mean you get to have your way about everything. I'm sure you'll come and find me when you're hungry."

She glanced toward the front seat where her German shepherd, Groucho, sat staring at her. His haunches were on the seat, his front feet resting on the floor, and she could almost see a look of disgust on his face. Though Groucho hadn't been pleased when Miss Priss appeared at their door cold, tired, pregnant and hungry, he'd come to accept her presence and the antics that kept her in continual trouble. "Okay, you can get out, too. I know you're as anxious as Miss Priss to have a look around." The big dog climbed out slowly, stretching like an ld man who'd fallen asleep in his recliner. "Come on. I don't have all day!" she old him, giving his collar a slight yank.

She closed the passenger door, leaned against her car, and stood gazing at Aunt TeeDee's old house, thinking about the work ahead of her and feeling very much alone now that her aunt had gone to be with her Lord. *From a wedding to a funeral in less than a week. Life sure is filled with ups and downs.* "Well, Groucho, ld boy, I guess we'd better get at it. It'll be dark soon."

Her enthusiasm waning, Treva lifted the hatchback door and, pulling out her overnight bag and suitcase, carried them up the broken sidewalk and across he sagging porch. Though she and Mindy had visited the house less than a month ago, somehow today it seemed darker, almost foreboding, as she pulled he key from the hiding place where her aunt always kept it. After twisting it in he lock and giving the heavy door a push with her foot, she watched it slowly reak open. A stagnant musty smell assaulted her nostrils. *Yuk! This place stinks! You can tell it's been closed up for a long time. When Aunt TeeDee lived here, it always melled like freshly baked cookies or roses from her garden. Not like this!*

Her breath caught, and she gave a backward leap as Groucho let out a bark nd darted past her. Something furry scurried across the room and disappeared ehind a chair. "A mouse! I hate mice!"

She glanced at Groucho, who had apparently decided to forget about finding he elusive mouse and returned to sit at her side, his tongue hanging out and his yes scanning the room. "Where is that cantankerous cat when we need her?"

Leaning against the doorframe, her heart still pounding erratically, she reonsidered her plan to redo her aunt's place. *Maybe I'd be wise to chuck the whole hing and head back to Warren. Sell the place as is. But where would I go? I've already given up my apartment.*

Looking around, Treva shrugged off her dismay and allowed herself to be pulled into the magic of the old house. Despite its run-down appearance it eemed to be beckoning to her, inviting her to take another taste of yesteryear. She'd spent many happy days here as a child. Picnics on a quilt spread out under he old shade tree in the backyard, walks through the meadow on a summer day, playing house up in the spacious attic with Aunt TeeDee's fragile collection of china-headed dolls, dressing up in her aunt's old dresses and hats, having lavshly planned tea parties with her aunt. Just remembering those wonderful times brought a smile to Treva's face. *Stop being such a baby! Be brave! You knew this job wasn't going to be a piece of cake.*

Lifting her chin and squaring her shoulders, she marched into the semidarkness of the room with an air of authority, setting her bags on the dusty, faded sheet covering the nearly worn-out frieze sofa.

"Listen, Mr. Mouse, or Mrs. Mouse—whichever you are—this house belongs to me now, and I'm issuing you an eviction notice. If you want to live, you'd better be out of here pronto, 'cause once I get to the hardware store in town, I'm going to buy something that will make you wish you'd left when you had a chance. Plus, I want you to know I'm armed with the most vicious cat in the animal kingdom, and she'd like nothing better than a mouse steak!"

Smiling to herself, she located the wall switch, and the room was instantly bathed in light. "Once I get those heavy drapes yanked down from the windows and let in a little air, the place will look—and smell—a whole lot better." Treva shook her head and let out a hearty laugh as Miss Priss came prancing into the room as if she owned the place and jumped onto a pile of pillows, making herself comfortable. "Well, Miss Priss, did you decide to join us?"

"Not safe for a single woman to be living here at the edge of town all alone," a man's voice said.

Shocked, Treva whirled around, her hand going to her heart. Before she could stop him, Groucho raced toward the stranger, snarling and scaring the man half out of his wits.

His face contorted with sudden fear, the man retreated a few steps, holding his arm up in front of him. "Mean dog you got there. He should be on a leash."

The shriveled-up little man looked as though he could be in his eighties, but with the look of panic on his face it was hard to tell. Keeping his attention centered on Groucho, he hobbled in through the door without being invited, pulling a faded ball cap from his bald head and rotating it nervously in his hands.

Still upset by his sudden appearance, Treva asked, "How dare you come into my house like this? Who—who are you?"

Groucho's upper lip curled, a low rumble coming from deep within his chest.

"Homer Jones," the man answered, keeping his gaze trained on the big dog. "My property adjoins this one. I occasionally did odd jobs for your aunt. She was a nice lady. I tried to talk her into selling this place to me, but she wouldn't do it."

Treva eyed him suspiciously. "Why would you say it's unsafe for me to live out here? I've heard nothing but good about Bristol and its people."

"Bad things happened here."

Her brows rose. "You mean the kidnapping of Bethany O'Connor?"

He nodded. "That's one of them."

Treva felt herself relax. "I know all about that kidnapping, Mr. Jones. I'm Bethany's Sunday school teacher. I've known the family for years. In fact, I was with her parents when they found Bethany locked in my aunt's old shed. Hundreds of people were praying for her safe return. Though she went through a terrible ordeal, other than her kidnapper hitting and kicking her a few times, he didn't"—she stopped and cleared her throat—"you know. God answered prayer. That man is in jail now. He's probably going to serve a long prison sentence. I doubt he's going to bother anyone for some time to come."

"Ghosts," the man said simply as he and Groucho held a staring match. "You'd better worry about them ghosts."

Treva let out a laugh. "Ghosts? Surely you don't believe those silly rumors."

"They're true."

"Who says they're true?"

He gave her a blank stare as his hand went to cup his ear.

She stifled a giggle then spoke up a bit louder. "I asked, who said the rumors were true?"

"Lots of folks have seen them ghosts. I've seen them myself. Right there on my own property."

Poor, senile old man. Treva tugged a dusty sheet off one of the chairs and hiked her head toward it. "Would you like to sit down, Mr. Jones? I'd offer you a cup of coffee, but I haven't been to the store yet to purchase groceries."

He ran a hand over the top of his head then put his ball cap back in place. "Nope, got to git home. Gonna be dark soon. Just wanted to warn you. Sorry about your aunt, but if you decide to sell this property, give me first chance at it."

"I do plan to sell it eventually but not until I get it fixed up. Thank you for your warning, though I doubt there was any need for it."

He gave Groucho a worried look. "That dog of yours won't bite, will he?"

Fighting to hold back a grin, she quirked up her lips. "I guess he could, if someone made him mad enough, but I doubt he's afraid of ghosts." She motioned toward the door after telling Groucho, "Stay."

The man made a wide arc as he passed Miss Priss. "That's a mighty mean-looking cat you've got there, too."

Treva bit at her lip to avoid an outright snicker. "She's not afraid of ghosts either."

He paused in the open doorway, shaking a bony finger at her. "Make fun of my words if you want, but just remember, I warned you."

"I'm a Christian, Mr. Jones. I don't believe in ghosts."

"You will when you see one."

She watched before closing the door until she was sure he'd made it down the rickety steps and to his old pickup truck. "That'll teach me to leave the door standing open."

After making two trips to her car for her vacuum sweeper, a clock radio, and boxes containing the essentials she'd need to make it through her first night in Aunt TeeDee's house, Treva set about cleaning the bedroom that had been hers when she'd come to visit. Two hours later she finally ventured into the kitchen where she was greeted by a sink full of dirty dishes, a refrigerator stocked with spoiled food, and mouse droppings everywhere.

"Well," she told Groucho, throwing up her hands in frustration, "looks as if I'll be having my peanut butter sandwich in the bedroom." Grabbing two dented aluminum cake pans from a nearby shelf, she filled one with water and one with dog food, placing them both on the floor in front of him. "But you, my friend, are going to have your supper in here."

Miss Priss jumped up onto the kitchen table and meowed, leaving a trail of paw prints through the dust.

Treva swatted at her. "You know you shouldn't be up there. Now scoot! I opened your bag of cat food. Help yourself. It's right over there in the corner, but what I'd prefer you to have for supper is mouse! Doesn't that sound yummy?"

Miss Priss tilted her head to one side, her green eyes darting from Treva to Groucho and back, as if to ask, "Can't I have mine in a pan, too?"

"You stay down here in the kitchen and keep those mice at bay," Treva told her, wagging her finger in the cat's face. Then turning her attention to Groucho, who was more interested in his food than what she had to say, she told him, "I'll be in the bedroom. Come up as soon as you're finished. I don't want to spend my first night in that bedroom all alone." She turned the light off over the sink and gave each pet a loving pat as she left the room.

She had done the final cleaning on her apartment before turning the keys in to her landlord that morning; then she'd loaded her car and made the drive to Bristol with Groucho and Miss Priss fussing at each other. After arriving, she'd cleaned her new bedroom and put fresh linens on the bed. Exhausted, she finished her sandwich and crawled between the sheets.

How she missed Aunt TeeDee. The house didn't feel the same without her. Her aunt always kept it immaculate. *Now look at it.* Treva gave her head a disgusted shake. *I should have made a special effort to come in here and clean things after she was taken to that nursing home. My aunt would never have allowed her home to look this way.* She flipped over onto her side and stared at the streak of moonlight filtering in around the edges of the blind, giving the entire room a soft glow. *Well, I'm here now, and with a little elbow grease I'll have the place cleaned up in no time. Then I can start on the remodeling.*

Groucho sauntered into the room and, after making a few circles, curled up on the throw rug next to her bed. She hung her arm over the side and patted his head. "Keep an eye out for those ghosts, okay?"

Groucho gave her hand an affectionate lick then lowered his head onto his paws and closed his eyes.

"Fine watchdog you are."

Weary from her tiresome day she finally fell asleep, only to be awakened several hours later by Groucho's loud growl. "What is it, boy?"

Groucho moved quickly to the closed bedroom door and stood poised as still as a statue, his head cocked to one side.

"What is it?" Clutching the sheet up about her, Treva felt her breath catch in her throat. Had something alarmed him, or was he merely restless being in unfamiliar surroundings? "Don't tell me that old man's tale has you spooked, too?"

What should I do? Should I venture downstairs? With her heart pounding, she grasped Groucho's collar, put on her slippers, cautiously opened the door, and tiptoed out into the hall, listening for any sound that might indicate someone may be in the house. Though Groucho tugged toward the stairs, she held on fast. Finally, after listening for a short time, she decided all was well, and perhaps a tree branch rubbing against a window or some such thing had spooked Groucho. She let out her breath, moved back into the bedroom, and crawled into bed. "Good boy," she told Groucho with a pat to his head as he settled down again on the rug beside her bed. "You have no idea how nice it is to have you with me."

Though she feared she might stay awake the rest of the night, she fell asleep almost at once.

∼❧∽

"Stop, Groucho! Stop licking my hand. The alarm hasn't gone off yet, and I don't want to get up again until it does!"

The big dog hurried across the room and began whining and scratching at the door.

Aggravated by his antics Treva sat straight up in bed. "Stop it this minute! You know you shouldn't be scratching at the door like that!"

But Groucho didn't stop and began to scratch even more furiously.

"You want out? Is that what's the matter?" She gave the covers a disgusted toss and climbed out of the bed, shivering as her bare feet touched the cool floor. "But don't expect me to let you back in anytime soon. You want out—you stay out. And quit that whining!"

Halfway across the room she stopped and sniffed the air. *Smoke!*

Her heart raced as she grabbed up her robe and slippers and dashed down the stairs to the first floor, with Groucho barking at her heels. She hadn't used the gas stove in the kitchen. Surely it wasn't the furnace. It was too hot for it to be coming on.

The heavy, pungent odor seemed to be coming from somewhere in the rear part of the house. Treva rushed into the back hall and flung open the basement door. A cloud of heavy black smoke wrapped itself around her, causing her to cough and gasp for air. She slammed the door and, her pulse pounding in her ears, ran to the front hall to retrieve her cell phone from her purse.

"Help! My house is on fire!" she screamed into the phone when the 9-1-1 operator answered on the first ring.

"Calm down, ma'am. Give me the address."

"I—I—" Her mind clouding with fear, she fumbled for words. "It's the Martin Gunther place. I think the number is 6333 DD Road."

"I'm dispatching help right now. They'll be there soon. Are you in the house now?"

Treva nodded, momentarily forgetting the woman couldn't see her.

"Ma'am, if you're in the house, I advise you and anyone who is with you to get outside as soon as possible. Help is on its way."

She hit the OFF button and stuffed the phone into the pocket of her robe.

"Oh, why did this have to happen? Especially now. Could that be why Groucho was growling during the night? Did he really hear something?" She yanked on her slippers and pulled her robe close around her before heading for the front door. She stopped only to grab her purse, car keys, and jacket. "Where is Miss Priss?" she asked the big dog, who tilted his head to one side quizzically.

"Miss Priss!" she called out loudly. But the cat didn't come. "Here, kitty, kitty!" Still Miss Priss didn't come. "She has to be in the house. I'll prop the screen door open so she can get out," she told Groucho as she grabbed onto his collar and dragged him out into the early morning's gray haze.

In the distance she could hear the mournful, wailing sound of a siren, and her heart quickened. If the fire was confined to the basement, surely they could put it out and save the house. "Hurry! Please hurry!"

Groucho barked when the big fire truck roared into the yard and pulled up close to the house, its siren still wailing. A police car was close behind.

"Where's the fire, ma'am?" one of the firemen yelled, leaping from the cab's passenger door and hurrying toward her.

"In the basement!"

"Is there an outside entrance?"

She racked her brain, trying to remember. "Yes, on the east side, but it's locked. My aunt always kept it locked and dead bolted from the inside."

"Stay back out of the way, ma'am. We'll take care of it." He motioned toward the driver, who immediately pulled the truck across the lawn in the direction she was pointing. "Are you the home's owner?"

Treva turned quickly as a uniformed police officer approached. "Yes, well, I am now. My aunt left it to me."

A low rumble echoed in Groucho's throat, but to her surprise the hair didn't tand up on his back as it usually did when a stranger, especially a uniformed tranger, approached.

Treva glanced at him over her shoulder as she moved closer to the house, her nind riveted on the fireman who was about to pull open the basement door.

"Do you have any idea how the fire started?"

"No. My dog woke me up. Then I smelled smoke."

"You're the one who turned in the 9-1-1 call?"

Treva let out a gasp as the basement door was pulled open and Miss Priss arted out. Wild-eyed, the cat ran toward the woods.

"The 9-1-1 call? You're the one who made it?"

She tried hard to focus her scattered brain. "Yes. Right after I discovered he smoke was coming from the basement." Treva felt dazed. She'd never been round a house fire before.

One of the firemen motioned them to move farther away from the truck. Then, speaking over the noise of the pump's engine, he said, "We've got the fire nder control. It was pretty well confined to an area at the bottom of the steps. Good thing you caught it in time." He gave her a slight frown. "When was the ast time you were down in that basement?"

Her hand went to her chest as she let out a sigh of relief. "I was so afraid it vas worse than that. I had visions of the whole house burning to the ground."

"The basement, ma'am. The last time you were down there?"

Her eyes widened. "It's been at least six months. Why?"

He sent a quick look of concern toward the police officer. "Because that fire vasn't caused by faulty wiring or a gas leak. It was set deliberately."

Chapter 2

Treva stared at him, barely able to comprehend his words. "Someone s
the fire?"

"Are you sure about that?" the officer asked.

"There was a big pile of trash and oily rags right in the middle of the floo
and an empty gas can nearby. We've called for the fire investigator. He'll be he
soon."

Frightened and astounded by his words, Treva asked, "Who would do suc
a thing? My aunt didn't have an enemy in the world. Besides, she always ke
that outside basement door bolted from the inside, and I checked all the oth
doors before I went to bed."

The man fidgeted for words. "I—I'm sorry to have to tell you, ma'am, bu
someone used a crowbar to gain entry. You'll have to have a new door put o
The old one is in pretty bad shape."

Treva felt a numbness creep into her bones. "Are you saying someone wa
actually in that house and set fire to it while I was asleep upstairs?"

"Looks that way." He dipped his head and backed away. "I'm sure Lieutenar
LaFrenz has some questions for you. I'd better get back to my men."

"I do need to ask you a few questions, Mrs.—"

Her heart still pumping frantically at the thought of being alone while
stranger set fire to the house, Treva turned toward the officer. "I'm—I'm sorr
What did you say?"

"I know you're upset, ma'am. But I need to ask you a few questions befor
the fire investigator arrives."

"It's Miss. I'm Treva Jordan, Theodora Gunther's niece. I—" Staring at him
she paused and tilted her head. "Do I know you? Your face seems familiar."

A slight smile crept across his handsome face. "We have met, though I'
forgotten your name. My friend, Chuck O'Connor, introduced us at his an
Mindy's wedding."

"Oh, yes, I remember now! He said the two of you met at a conference
His friend, Keene Moray, the man who sang at their wedding, was at that sam
meeting."

"Yes, ma'am, that's exactly where we met. Chuck's a good man. So is Keen

The three of us had a great time together."

Treva raked her fingers through her hair. "I'm sorry I didn't recognize you. This whole thing has really upset me."

"I'm sure it has." His brows furrowed. "I hadn't realized you were Theodora's niece. I was sure sorry to hear about your aunt. She and my mom were close friends. When I was a kid, I used to ride my bike out here and cut the grass for her. She always had a plate of cookies or a piece of freshly baked pie and a tall glass of lemonade for me when I finished."

"I can't believe she's gone. It felt strange walking into her house with all her personal things still there." Treva paused, struggling against her tears. "She left the house to me."

"You're going to stay here? In Bristol?"

"No, the house is way too big for me. My aunt suggested I fix it up a bit, sell it, and use the money to buy myself a house in Warren. I teach grade school there."

"We need good teachers in Bristol. Maybe you should stay."

She stared into a pair of dark brown eyes the color of a semisweet chocolate bar. "I love teaching in Warren, but the main reason I have to stay there is because of my church."

"We have good churches here, too. I go to a great church."

Despite the gravity of her situation, she allowed a slight smile to curl at her lips. "Since I'll be here all summer, you'll have to give me the address."

"Be happy to." He motioned toward the clipboard in his hand. "Maybe I'd better get back to filling out this form. It is part of my job, and you'll have to have it for insurance purposes. I'll need your name and address and a number where you can be reached."

She nodded and gave him the information.

"What's your zip code?"

"Ah—June 20."

The man laughed. "I said your zip code, not your birthday."

Treva stared at him for a moment then, realizing her error, felt very foolish. "I'm sorry. It's ah—ah—"

He gave her an understanding smile. "That's okay. I'll look it up. You mentioned you'd arrived at the house late yesterday. When you entered, did you notice anything unusual? Maybe signs someone had been here since your aunt moved permanently to the nursing home?"

She closed her eyes, trying to visualize the house's interior when she arrived and opened the door. "No—I don't think so."

"Did you hear any noises during the night?"

"Not really. I was dead tired by the time I cleaned up my old apartment, told a few friends good-bye, and drove here. But I think my dog did." Even now Treva shuddered at the thought. "He woke me up—probably about two o'clock—growling at the bedroom door. It scared me at first, but when I ventured out into the hall and listened, I didn't hear anything and eventually went back to sleep. Do you suppose that's when someone broke into the house?"

"It sounds likely."

A cold chill coursed through her body.

"You said you hadn't been in the basement for about six months. When you smelled smoke and ran to the basement, the door was closed, right?"

She nodded. "Yes, I'm sure it was closed, because when I opened it, I nearly strangled on the black smoke that poured out at me."

His eyes narrowed, and he took on a serious expression. "Think hard. Was that basement door open or closed when you went to bed last night?"

Terror seized her heart. "It was open!"

"You're sure?"

"Yes! I left it open purposely because I'd seen a mouse run across the floor. I was hoping Miss Priss would find it and maybe go down in the basement looking for other mice. Yes, it was definitely open. No doubt about it."

He tilted his head quizzically. "Miss Priss? I thought you said you were alone in the house."

"Miss Priss is my cat. The one who came running out the basement door when the fireman opened it." Her heart thundered against her chest viciously as the realization hit her. "She must have already been down in the basement when someone closed that door at the head of the basement stairs!"

Lieutenant LaFrenz's hand gripped her wrist. "Calm down, ma'am. Maybe you need to sit down. I know you've been through a frightening experience, but it's important that I ask you a few more questions."

"No, it's okay. I'm too nervous for sitting." Treva took two deep cleansing breaths, hoping her heart would settle down and she could make sense. "I'm sorry. Go ahead."

He slowly released his hold on her arm. "Can you think of anyone who would want to do this to you? Maybe an old boyfriend you dumped? A coworker?"

She searched her memory. "No. No one."

"You think about it, and if anyone comes to mind, please let me know." He pulled a card from his shirt pocket and handed it to her. "You seem a little unnerved. Do you have a close friend or maybe a relative you can call? You really shouldn't be alone at a time like this."

Treva shook her head. "My aunt was my last living relative, except for a few shirttail cousins. Aunt TeeDee had a stepbrother, but I haven't heard from him since he walked out of her life and refused to help take care of her when she got sick."

"Well, the fire investigator should be here soon. I'm sure he'll have some questions for you, too." He backed off with a tip of his hat. "My shift is over, so I guess I'd better head to the station."

Treva watched him go, suddenly becoming aware of how alone she was. Oh, she'd met some of Aunt TeeDee's friends when she'd visited her for the weekend, and she knew a number of the nursing home residents by name, but no one she could actually call on for help.

Seeing an old log lying nearby, she crossed the yard, sat down, and began stroking Groucho's back. "Thanks for waking me up this morning, old pal."

The dog looked up at her, his ears pointed skyward, his long pink tongue hanging free.

"Well, look who's coming to see us," she told him when Miss Priss wandered out of the trees and jumped into her lap.

Groucho stood, moved a few feet away, and sat down, as if to say, "Keep that cat away from me. I don't trust those claws of hers."

"Are you and those unborn kitties of yours okay?" Treva cradled the big cat in her arms, rubbing her chin against her soft fur. "I wish you could tell me what happened last night. You're the only one who knows. Did whoever set that fire know you were there, or were you hiding?"

Ignoring her question, Miss Priss snuggled up close and began to purr.

"We could have all died if Groucho hadn't wakened me when he did. I'll need to have some smoke detectors installed. I can't believe Aunt TeeDee lived here all these years without them."

Not wanting Groucho to be jealous, she reached out and gave his head a pat. "You're a real hero, you know that?"

She turned as a black sedan rolled into the driveway and a man in a suit and tie headed toward her. "Must be the fire investigator."

༺ঌଙ༻

It was nearly ten when Treva walked back into the house. The firemen, the fire investigator, and Lieutenant LaFrenz were gone; and she was alone again, alone except for Groucho and Miss Priss. Though the firemen had shoveled up the charred remains of the oily rags, trash, and cardboard boxes, carried them outside, and doused them with more water, a putrid odor remained, smelling up the entire house.

She changed into an old pair of jeans, a stained T-shirt, and a worn pair of tennies, then stood at the foot of the basement stairs, broom in hand, wondering where to start. The water they'd used to put out the fire had seeped under boxes, old furniture, broken-down appliances, and other things that had accumulated over the forty years Aunt TeeDee had lived there.

Propping the broom against a nearby wall, Treva sat down on the bottom step and began to cry. When she'd arrived at the old house yesterday, she'd been filled with enthusiasm and excitement about the remodeling job she was about to take on; but now it all seemed so hopeless.

She jolted when a knock sounded on the outside basement door.

"Miss Jordan? Are you down here?"

Groucho's ears perked up, and he gave a low growl.

Her heart raced as she tugged on his collar, pulling him closer to her. Who could it be? Why would anyone be knocking on that door? It was nothing but splinters and tatters, with only a few boards still holding it on its hinges. All someone would have to do was give it a slight shove, and it'd fall in by itself.

She drew back when a second knock sounded.

"Miss Jordan, it's me. Lieutenant LaFrenz."

She let go of the big dog's collar and raced to the door. The knob fell off in her hand. "You scared me."

"I'm sorry. I didn't mean to."

She barely recognized him, dressed in jeans and a plaid shirt and without his hat.

"I knocked at the front door several times, but I guess you didn't hear me." He stepped inside and began running his fingers up and down the edge of the doorframe. "Umm, not too bad. I was heading over to the lumberyard to get a towel rack to mount in my mom's bathroom, and I thought about you and that busted-up door. I wondered if you wanted me to get you a new door while I was there. This frame is still in fairly good shape. It wouldn't take me long to put the new door in for you. I've got my toolbox in my pickup."

His generous offer nearly rendered her speechless. "I can't ask you to do something like that!"

"You didn't ask. I volunteered. Free, gratis. I'm pretty good at handyman jobs. Kind of a hobby with me now, but I worked for a contractor building houses for a couple of years while I was waiting to get on the police force." He pulled a tape measure off his belt and held it up against the opening. "Just as I thought. It takes a standard thirty-six-inch door. I noticed in the Sunday paper that they're having a sale on steel entry doors. That's what I'd recommend, since I know you're worried about safety."

"Only if you'll let me pay you whatever it would cost to hire someone to come in here and do it for me."

He twisted his mouth to one side, fingering his chin thoughtfully. "Okay, but instead of paying me, let's barter."

She frowned. Though she'd heard of bartering, she'd never done it.

"I'll fix the door for you today"—he paused—"and you go to church with me next Sunday! Is it a deal?"

In spite of the dirty mess around her, she had to laugh. "You're crazy. You know that, don't you?"

"Maybe. Maybe not. You get your door fixed, and I get to have all the folks at my church wondering what such a beautiful young woman is doing with me! Sounds like a fair trade to me. If you don't go, my mom will be highly disappointed. I told her all about you when I went by her place to see what size towel rod she needs and said I was going to invite you. She's eager to meet you."

She eyed him suspiciously. Surely a good-looking man like him had better things to do with his time. "What's the catch?"

He let out a chuckle. "Uh-oh. You found me out."

"So I was right. There is a catch."

"Yes, I'm afraid so." He let the tape measure rewind with a loud snap then clamped it back onto his waistband. "You have to go to lunch with me after church."

"That's it? That's the catch?"

He crouched and began rubbing Groucho's ears. "Yep, that's it. It's a good, solid offer. I suggest you take it."

She did need a new door installed, and he did say he'd do it today. Even if she called someone else to come and put one on, it'd probably be a few days before he could get there, and she certainly couldn't sleep in that house knowing anyone could come waltzing into the basement anytime he wanted. "I accept."

He gave her a shy grin as he rose to his feet, glancing at his watch. "Look—it's a little after ten. After I leave the lumberyard, I'll stop by a little diner I go occasionally and pick up—"

She couldn't resist. "Is that the place you and the other officers go for doughnuts?"

He screwed up his face. "Yeah, that's where we all meet for doughnuts instead of chasing the bad guys. Old joke and not true, believe me. But I do like doughnuts!"

She grinned. "Me, too. The big glazed ones, with loads of sugar and fat grams."

He let loose with a belly laugh. "That reminds me. Did you hear the one about the cop who stopped a guy because he was speeding and weaving all over the road?"

She grinned back. "No, I didn't."

"When the guy rolled down the window, the cop said, 'Your eyes look a little bloodshot. Have you been drinking?' The guy looked up at him and, slurring his words, answered, 'No. Your eyes look a little glazed. Have you been eating doughnuts?' "

The punch line surprised her, and she, too, let out a belly laugh. "That's hilarious!" His sense of humor washed over her, taking some of the fear of her frightening experience away, at least temporarily.

"We cops take a lot of razzing, but that's okay. We expect it. As I was saying, I'll stop by the diner and pick up a couple of burgers and some fries on the way back. You want everything on yours?"

"I can't let you do that!"

He moved a step closer and looked down at her, his face growing serious. "Look, Miss Jordan. You've—"

"Treva."

"Treva. I like that name." He reached for her hand and gave it a pat. "You've had a horrendous morning. Your basement door is half off its hinges, making it impossible to lock. You have a monumental mess to clean up down here, not to mention the overwhelming task ahead of you in remodeling this old house. You haven't even been here long enough to clean up the kitchen or go shopping for groceries, and you probably haven't taken time to eat a bite of breakfast. I think you deserve a burger and fries, and I'm going to bring them to you. Now tell me. Do you want the works?"

How could she resist such an offer? "Thank you. A burger and fries sounds great."

"With onions?"

"Are you having onions?"

"Only if you are."

She gave him a demure smile. "Yes. Onions."

He sent her a mock salute and headed for the door. "I should be back in an hour or so."

"Oh, Lieutenant LaFrenz!" she called after him. "Mayo, too!"

He stopped in the doorway and spun around. "Only if you call me Tank."

"Mayo, too, Tank."

She smiled to herself as she heard his pickup start. It was nice to have a new friend.

⌒⌒

Tank leaned back in the seat, keeping an eye on the traffic moving in front of him as he headed his pickup toward the lumberyard. Yes, he wanted to help Treva

Jordan by putting a new door up for her, but to be honest about it, he was worried about her. She was lucky last night. Whoever broke into the basement and started that fire wanted to harm her. No doubt about it. It was arson. Plain and simple.

He pulled over into the left lane and came to a stop, waiting for the light to turn green.

That beautiful young woman was sleeping in an upstairs bedroom. Why hadn't the perpetrator gone up there? She was alone and virtually defenseless. She said that big dog of hers was sleeping on the floor beside the bed, but taking care of him would have been relatively simple if the guy wanted to—

He banged the heel of his palm on the steering wheel. *Stop! I don't even want to think about what he could have done.*

"Hey, Marty, I need a thirty-six-inch exterior steel door," he told the clerk as he entered the lumberyard. "What's the best deal you have?"

"For you, Tank? Fifteen percent off anything I have in stock. Even the sale stuff." The man gave his arm a nudge as the two walked to the back of the store. "The big, brave cop afraid somebody's going to break into his house?"

Tank gave the man a playful shove. "Not me! I keep my gun under my pillow."

The man nodded. "Oh, I see. Then this must be for your mom's place."

"Nope, not for my mom, but I do need to pick up a towel rod for her while I'm here."

Marty gave him a sideways grin. "Well, I've heard of guys giving their girl-friends some strange gifts, but never a steel door!"

Tank became serious as he checked out the steel door display. "There was a break-in out at the old Gunther place last night. Whoever did it broke down the basement door then purposely set a fire in the middle of the floor."

"Whew! Good thing no one's living there now."

Tank pulled a door from the display, leaned it against the wall, and looked at the price tag. "Someone *is* living there. Theodora's niece. She arrived yesterday."

"Do tell."

"Yes. Theodora left it to her. She's going to give the old place a face-lift and try to sell it this fall." He motioned toward the door. "This one should do the trick."

"Any idea who did it?"

"Not a clue or why he did it. It didn't appear anything was missing. Only things there of any value were the pieces of antique furniture her aunt owned. I guess they would bring a few bucks but certainly not enough to go to all that trouble. Fortunately they didn't lay a hand on the niece. Her dog woke her up when he smelled smoke."

"So you're gonna put this door in for her?"

"That's the plan."

Marty gave him a gentle shove. "I didn't know part of a policeman's job was repairing the damage done to a citizen's home. I'm betting that niece is a pretty woman."

"Hey, let it rest. I've probably already told you more than you need to know." Tank pushed the door into the man's hands. "Take this up front. I'm gonna take a look at the towel rods."

~~~

By the time she heard Tank's pickup pull into the drive, Treva had the kitchen countertops cleaned and sanitized, a pot of coffee brewing, and the table set with the paper plates and silverware she'd brought from her apartment. She'd even picked a few wildflowers from her aunt's yard and placed them in a glass of water in the center of the table.

"Here ya go! The best burgers and fries in town." Tank placed the bag on the table and headed toward the kitchen sink to wash his hands. "We'd better eat them while they're hot."

"I can't thank you enough, Tank. It was very thoughtful of you to go after the door and bring lunch."

He held up his palm. "No thanks necessary. I hate eating alone. You're doing me a favor by having lunch with me." He reached out for her hand. "God's the One we should be thanking. Want to pray?"

She nodded and slipped her hand into his. It felt warm, secure, safe.

"Lord, our great provider, we thank You for this food we are about to eat. But even more than that, we thank You for keeping Treva safe last night. We ask that You will continue to be with her and guide her as she endeavors to remodel her aunt's house. In Jesus' name we pray. Amen."

She lifted misty eyes to his. "I've been thinking. Maybe I should just put the house on the market as is, after all."

"You know you won't get nearly as much for it that way." Tank gave her a reassuring smile. "You'll feel better after I install that steel door in your basement. No one will be able to get in through that baby."

"I'll admit I've been pretty shaken up by this whole thing, but that's not the only reason I'm thinking of turning it over to someone to sell for me. I did some looking around while you were at the lumberyard. I had visions of coming in here with a scrub brush, cleaning the place as best I could, wallpapering a few of the rooms, painting the others, and generally giving it a good sprucing up. It's amazing what you don't see when you're not looking for it. I never realized until now what bad shape Aunt TeeDee's house is in."

She uttered a sigh and shrugged her sagging shoulders. "A lot of the woodwork will have to be replaced, as well as most of the light fixtures. A number of the windows are cracked, the kitchen needs to be gutted and new cabinets and appliances added, the bathrooms are outdated, and the porch needs to be fixed. This house has ten rooms! I must have thought I was Wonder Woman to consider taking on this project. I'd even planned to redo that observation platform out on the cliff."

He glanced around the room. "This place looks to me like a project worth taking on. I've always loved this house. So did your aunt."

"I love it, too, but the whole thing is impossible."

"Why?"

"For a number of reasons, the biggest one being money. I've been saving some each month with the hopes I'd eventually be able to buy my own home. There'll be several thousand dollars left from the insurance money after I pay off the mortuary and the nursing home; but that, and the little money I've saved, may not be enough to hire someone to do the things I can't."

He pushed her plate toward her. "Structurally this house is as sound as they come. Seems to me it's well worth fixing up. Especially with the view of Narragansett Bay you have from here."

She picked up her burger and took a small bite. "I'm wondering if it might be a whole lot smarter just to give the place to one of the local Realtors and go back to Warren. I might even be able to get my old apartment back."

"Well, that decision is up to you, but I'll guess this place would bring a much higher selling price if it was remodeled before it was put on the market."

She leaned back in the chair and stared at the ceiling, emitting a heavy sigh. "I thought so, too. I was sure I was doing the right thing. I had my summer all planned out, with visions of selling the place to some affluent couple ready to retire and make their home in Rhode Island. I never anticipated someone breaking in and setting my house on fire."

"Guess no one can decide that, except you." He rose, picked up his paper plate, and tossed it in the wastebasket beside the refrigerator. "If I'm going to install that door, I'd better get at it."

"Thanks for both the lunch and the company, Tank, and for your willingness to help me like this. It means a lot to me. I'll be down in a minute."

❧

Tank stood in the doorway watching as Treva slowly rose and finished clearing the table. *She sure is a pretty little thing. She's got to be in her late twenties. I can't believe some guy hasn't come along and married her before now.* With a smile he tilted his head to one side. *Beautiful dark hair and pale blue eyes and, best of all, she seems as beautiful on the inside as she is on the outside. Can't say that about too many women And I should know with the experiences I've had with females.*

He hurried down the basement stairs and out to his truck to retrieve the steel door. She was already at work clearing a path from her uncle Martin's cluttered workbench to the doorway when he returned. "Any old rags there?"

She turned quickly. "Rags? There's a roll of paper towels."

He held out his bleeding thumb. "I cut it on the bottom of the door."

She yanked a couple of towels off the roll and hurried over to him, taking his hand in hers and blotting away the blood. "Is it deep? Do you think it needs stitches?"

He stared into her blue eyes and found himself mesmerized. How long had it been since a gorgeous woman had held his hand?

"I could drive you to the emergency room."

"No, it's fine. It's not deep at all. Just a surface wound. Don't worry about it. I just didn't want to bleed on your new door—that's all."

She examined his hand with great concern. "I have a couple of little bandages in my purse. I'll see if I can find some antiseptic in Aunt TeeDee's medicine cabinet."

"Don't bother. See—it's stopped bleeding already."

She let go of his hand and wagged her finger in his face. "You stay right there and don't do a thing until I get back. I don't want you to get dirt in that cut."

He watched as she climbed the stairs. *I sure wish I could do something to help her. It'd be nice to keep her around.*

❧

Treva had barely reached the top of the stairs when the doorbell rang. Through the lace curtains she could see a man dressed in a navy business suit, who looked to be in his midsixties, standing there holding a black briefcase in his hand. Deciding he looked harmless, she opened the door.

"Miss Jordan? I'm Benson Cordell. Perhaps your aunt has mentioned my name."

"Ah—no. I don't believe so. You knew my aunt?"

He gave her a pleasant smile. "Oh, yes. As a matter of fact, she and I were about to complete a business deal."

Still holding onto the knob, Treva gave him a questioning frown. "What kind of deal? She never mentioned anything about a business deal to me, and I've been taking care of her checkbook and handling most of her affairs for the past several years."

His eyes rounded. "I own Cordell Realty. She listed this house with me. I already have several buyers who have expressed interest in the place."

"That's odd. You must have misunderstood her." She eyed him suspiciously. "Listing this house with you would have been impossible, Mr. Cordell. She signed it over to me six months ago."

Seeming surprised by her words, he shrugged. "Perhaps I misunderstood. Maybe what she meant was that you would be selling the house, and she wanted *me* to be the one to list it, since she knew I would do a good job for you. Your aunt was a very perceptive woman."

"I—I—" She paused, not sure what she should say since she hadn't yet made up her mind whether to go back to Warren or stay in Bristol.

"You can ask anyone in Bristol about me and my company. We've been in business for over thirty years and have sold homes to hundreds of satisfied buyers." He pulled open the screen and, smiling, handed her his card. "My reputation is impeccable. No one can sell it faster or get you a better deal than I can."

"I *was* planning to fix it up before I sold it. I thought—"

"That you'd get a better price for it? I doubt that. Many buyers want to fix up a place themselves—like they want it. You'd be better off selling it as is, believe me."

She stared at the card. Perhaps he was right. Why go to all the trouble to fix up the place when new owners might come in and want to remodel it their way? Maybe she should just go ahead and list it with him.

"I have the listing agreement right here," he said, patting his briefcase. "We could have this taken care of in a matter of minutes. Just think of the time and work it would save you."

"I thought I heard the doorbell." Tank moved up beside her. "Hello, Benson."

The man frowned. "Tank, what are you doing here?"

"He's putting a new door on for me. Someone broke in here last night and started a fire in the basement."

Mr. Cordell's hand went to his mouth as he let out a gasp. "I hope no one was hurt! How terrible! Have you found out who did it?"

Tank moved closer toward her, protectively. "Not yet, but we're going to. We have a couple of leads."

Treva stared at him. *Leads? What is he talking about? No one told me about any leads.*

"You don't suppose this has anything to do with that O'Connor girl, do you? The one who was kidnapped a few months ago and kept locked in that old shed on the back of this property?"

Treva gave her head a vigorous shake. "I doubt there's any connection."

The man leaned forward conspiratorially. "There's a lot of talk around town about her. Several folks have said they've seen ghosts out there in the woods. One of them said the ghost had on the same pink blouse that girl was wearing when she was found."

Tank huffed. "I don't believe in ghosts. Besides, Bethany O'Connor was found very much alive. Treva even helped find her. Why would a ghost be wearing the blouse of someone who is still alive?"

The man cocked his head to one side. "All I know is people have seen that ghost. Just ask anyone. We've all heard about it."

"I think those ridiculous ghost stories are made up by people who live dull lives and have way too much time on their hands."

"You're probably right. I do hope you catch the person soon. Someone who would do something like that should be locked up for good. I've always thought of Bristol as a safe place to live. Did whoever broke in here take anything of value?"

Treva shook her head. "There wasn't anything worth taking."

The man gave his head a shake. "I hope you weren't here at the time."

"She wasn't quite alone. Her big German shepherd was up in the bedroom with her. If he got hold of a perpetrator, that'd be the end of the guy. He's a pretty vicious dog."

Treva shot another quick glance at Tank. *Groucho may be big and look threatening, but he's certainly not vicious! Why would you say such a thing?*

"I'm certainly glad to hear that." Benson Cordell backed away from the door, his eyes scanning the area. "He isn't loose now, is he?"

"No, Treva usually keeps him locked up when someone comes to the door. She wouldn't want anyone to get hurt."

Tank, he's not locked up! He's roaming around outside somewhere, and though he may growl, I don't think he'd ever hurt someone, unless they were hurting me!

Mr. Cordell, seemingly satisfied Groucho wasn't anywhere near, reached into his case and pulled out a paper. "I'm sure, after an experience like that, you're anxious to get out of here as soon as possible. Let's take care of this listing, and I'll start finding you a buyer immediately."

Treva stared at the paper. If she signed it as he asked, she could pack up and go back to Warren tomorrow. Maybe even get her old apartment back, or at least one in the same building.

Tank shook his head. "She needs some time to think it over, Benson. Why don't you call her in a day or two? A decision like this shouldn't be rushed."

"But I could—"

Treva leaned forward, one hand resting on the screen's handle. "He's right,

Mr. Cordell. At this point I'm not sure what would be best. You've given me your card. If I decide to list it, I'll call you. Thanks for coming by."

"I'm sorry, Miss Jordan. I hope I didn't come off too strong. It's just that I feel quite confident I can find the right buyer for your home. Now that we're able to list properties on the Internet, not a day goes by that I don't get an e-mail or a call from people who have visited our wonderful Rhode Island and want to make their home here. I have quite a backlog of qualified buyers."

Treva pushed a lock of hair from her forehead and gave him a smile. "I'm sure you do, Mr. Cordell, and if I decide to list, you'll be the one I call."

"Thank you. It's been nice meeting you. Your aunt talked about you all the time." He nodded toward Tank as he backed off the porch. "Nice seeing you, too, Tank. Give my best to your mother."

"I will. See you later, Benson." Tank grabbed onto Treva's wrist and pulled her inside, closing the door.

"What was that all about? Groucho is a vicious dog? That'd be the end of the guy?" Treva's balled hands went to her waist. "Why would you say such a thing? And leads? We don't have *any* leads!"

Tank held up his hands in surrender. "Look—I like Benson. He's a fine man, but he's also a gossip. I just figured it would be good sense to let him spread the word around town that we have several leads. And that story about Groucho being vicious? It might make whoever broke in here think twice before doing it again."

Her knees went weak at his words. "Why would that person come back here a second time?"

They locked gazes as Tank grabbed onto her arm. "Why did anyone come here the first time?"

She pulled away and seated herself on the sofa, her heart racing. "I don't know, but just the idea of someone coming back a second time—"

"You want to spend the night at my mom's? When I told her what had happened, she said to tell you you're welcome to stay. She'd love to have you, and you could stay as long as you like."

"No, that is asking too much of her. She doesn't even know me."

"She knew your aunt. I told you the two of them were best friends."

Treva mulled over Tank's mother's generous offer. It was tempting. Even if she decided to go back to Warren, she'd have to stay around for a week or so, just to make the place presentable. She couldn't stand the idea of someone coming to see the house and finding spoiled food in the fridge and mouse droppings everywhere. No, if she were going to stay, even long enough to do some cleaning, it would be right here in this house. Tank would soon have the steel door installed in the basement, the windows and doors on the main floor had locks, she had her cell phone, and she had Groucho—and the Lord.

Tank's brows lifted as he picked up his phone. "Shall I call Mom and tell her you're coming?"

Chapter 3

I can't, Tank. I appreciate her offer, but I'm a big girl. I have to stay. I can't let some fruitcake scare me off. Maybe this person was only a vagrant looking for a comfortable place to spend the night."

Tank's warm brown eyes searched her face. "You may be right, but it seems highly unlikely he'd build a fire in the basement. No, I don't mean to frighten you, but my cop's instinct tells me this is far more serious than a random hunt for a comfortable place to sleep."

She squiggled up her face and winced. "Those aren't exactly comforting words."

"They weren't meant to be comforting. I want you to realize the gravity of what happened. If Groucho hadn't wakened you—"

She closed her eyes tightly as the scene replayed in her mind. "I know. You don't have to say it."

He reached out for her hand again. "Then say you'll stay at my mom's house?"

"No. I told you before I'm going to tough it out. I may not sleep a wink, but I'm staying right here. This is my house now, and I refuse to leave, even if I *am* terrified."

He relaxed his grip and turned loose of her. "In that case, Miss Stubborn, I'd better get that door installed. Think you could help me? I need you to put your foot on the crowbar to help hold the door in place while I slide the pins into the hinges."

She nodded, and they headed down the stairs. "Oh, wait!" She fished something out of her pocket. "I found a tube of antibiotic for your hand."

"It's really not that bad. I forgot all about it."

"Well, I didn't! You cut your thumb on my door, and I'm going to see to it you have a little antiseptic and a bandage on it."

He held out his thumb. "Have at it, if it'll make you feel any better, but it's really not necessary." He gave her a wink. "I'm a big boy!"

Once the bandage was in place, he headed for the open doorway. "When I lift the door, slide that crowbar under it, just about in the middle. Then when I tell you, put your foot on the end of the crowbar, and apply a little pressure."

"Like this?"

"Yes, but don't push down until I tell you." He moved the door a little to the left. "Okay, now. Easy."

She watched his muscles flex as he lifted the door ever so carefully. It was obvious the man worked out. His shoulders were broad, but his waist was slim. That door had to be heavy. The ease with which he lifted it amazed her.

"Okay. Keep the pressure on it. I have to line up the holes." He shifted the door a fraction of an inch. "There! All lined up. Keep the pressure on until I slip the pins into place."

Treva couldn't keep her eyes off him. Since he'd come on the scene, she'd been so caught up in her troubles she hadn't noticed, until now, how handsome he was. She had to admit that, though he was gorgeous in his uniform, he was even better looking in his worn jeans and stained T-shirt.

"There, all done." He added some lubricant and closed and opened the door a few times. "No one is going to get through that door." Tank glanced around the basement. "I'm glad to see someone was smart enough to board up those windows."

"Uncle Martin did that a number of years ago. He got kind of eccentric there at the last and did a lot of strange things. Aunt TeeDee and I thought maybe he was in the beginning stages of Alzheimer's, but since he died of a heart attack, we never knew for sure."

"Well, between this new door and the boarded-up windows, you don't have to worry about someone getting into this basement again."

"How can I ever thank you? You've been so kind to me. You have no idea how much it's appreciated. I'd have fallen apart if it hadn't been for your coming here and fixing my door like this."

"Think nothing of it. I've enjoyed being here with you." He reached over and touched her arm then followed her up the stairs. "Since you insist on staying here, I'll be checking on you several times during the night. My shift is from eleven until seven in the morning. If you need someone to talk to, turn your porch light on, and I'll stop by. Okay?"

"Can you do that?"

He gave a slight chuckle, his face so close she could feel his warm breath on her cheek. "Sure I can. Unless I'm out chasing bad guys, I spend most of the night cruising the streets of Bristol. You may be pretty isolated out here, but you're still in the city limits."

"It would make me feel better to know you are checking on me."

"Checking on you will make me feel better, too. I'm concerned about you." He turned toward the front door. "Now I'd better get going. I promised Mom

I'd have that towel rod up for her before her ladies' prayer group comes over tomorrow."

"Tell your mother I appreciate her invitation, but I feel as if I need to stay here." She gave him a shy grin. "And tell her thanks for raising such a wonderful, thoughtful son."

After returning her smile, he reached for the knob and opened the door. "I'll tell her."

Groucho darted in the door past him, nearly knocking his feet out from under him. Tank chased him and grabbed onto the dog's collar then squatted down and patted his head. "Hey, fella, where were you? Don't you know you have a job to do? You're supposed to be guarding this little lady. Do me a favor and stick to her like glue, will you?"

The big dog's tongue shot out and licked him on the face. "Groucho, no!" Treva shook her head. "I'm sorry. I don't know what's gotten into him. He's never friendly like this to someone he's just met."

Tank cradled the dog's head between his palms, his thumbs stroking his ears. "He knows I like him. We're buds, aren't we, Groucho?"

Groucho leaned into Tank's side, shifting his head slightly, as if saying, "That feels so good. Scratch this part over here."

Tank stroked his ears a few more times then stood. "Sorry, Groucho, but I have to leave. I'm putting you in charge, though. Watch Treva for me, okay?"

Groucho barked loudly.

Tank threw back his head and let out a laugh. "I'll take that as a yes." Turning to Treva he added, "Remember to switch on the light if you want me to stop."

Treva couldn't keep the smile from her face. "I will. I promise." She watched until his pickup truck disappeared out of sight.

Once again she was alone, except for the big straggly dog she'd rescued from the animal shelter and one very independent cat. The house seemed so quiet. Maybe she should turn on the radio or the TV—something, anything, to keep her mind off the problems that seemed to appear without warning.

After going into the kitchen for a drink of water, she grabbed the broom, headed down the basement stairs again, and began sweeping the few shards that remained into a pile in the center of the floor. Using the dustpan she'd brought down with her, she bent to brush them into the pan. That's when she noticed something shiny under the bottom step.

What is that?

Getting down on her hands and knees, she stuck her arm under the step and pulled out her find. It was a money clip! She stared at the shiny object. *How did you get here?*

Though it had no distinguishing marks on it, it was stamped eighteen-karat gold and obviously quite expensive. Being careful not to tear them, she pulled a thick group of bills from the clip and unfolded them. They were all one-hundred-dollar bills! Six of them! She clutched at her heart. *This clip had to have been dropped by whoever broke into the house. There isn't a speck of dust on it.*

Her hands trembling, she sat down on the bottom step, clutching the money and the clip with both hands, tears of anguish rushing down her cheeks as she bowed her head in prayer. "I don't understand any of this, God, and I'm scared out of my wits. Thank You for protecting me from whoever did this awful thing. Show me what to do. I'm so confused. Should I pack up and go back home and turn this place over to that Realtor? Is that what You want me to do? I can't do this alone. I had no idea there was so much to be done. There's too much work for one person to accomplish. How did I ever think I could do it by myself? Help me! I need Your guidance."

Groucho sat down beside her, his fur touching her leg. She threw an arm around him and pulled him close. "Oh, Groucho, thank you for protecting me, too. You're a good doggy."

Both she and Groucho turned their heads as Miss Priss darted past them across the basement floor, a plump gray mouse just inches ahead of her. Treva smiled at her dog and ruffled the thick fur on his back. "I guess, in Miss Priss's own way, she's protecting me, too!"

She finished sweeping the open areas of the basement then carried the money clip upstairs, placing it on the hall table so she could show it to Tank.

～◆～

It was a little after five o'clock when she made her way into the kitchen in search of something to eat. Though she'd brought a few things from her cupboards in her old apartment, the selection was pretty sparse, and the stove had to be cleaned before she could cook on it. Aunt TeeDee had never wanted a microwave, so she couldn't heat anything in there. Her own microwave was buried beneath a stack of boxes in the back of her car. "Umm, peanut butter and crackers? Grape jelly and crackers? Apple butter and crackers?" she asked herself aloud.

She decided on peanut butter and crackers with a thin topping of grape jelly and was about to take the lid off the jar when the doorbell rang. Her heart did a flip-flop! Who would be coming at this time of night?

Warily she peered through the lace curtain.

"Pizza man!" a voice called out.

She yanked the door open, and there stood Tank, all cleaned up, his hair slicked back with gel, wearing a pale blue polo shirt and a pair of khaki trousers. Instinctively she looked down at her grubby clothes, knowing her hair was a mess, and she hadn't taken time to put on a dab of lipstick all day. "I—I didn't think you'd be coming back tonight."

All smiles, he pushed past her. "I was trying to figure out what I wanted for supper, and you came to mind." He placed the box on the coffee table with a laugh. "That didn't exactly come out right. What I meant was—I knew you hadn't had time to get the kitchen shipshape, so I took a chance, hoping you hadn't eaten yet and you'd share a pizza with me. I can't eat a whole one by myself, so you'll be doing me a favor."

Miss Priss twined herself around his legs and began to purr.

"What's with you anyway? Both my pets seem to like you better than they do me!" Miss Priss arched her back as he bent down and stroked her.

Tank gave Treva a wink. "What can I say? I don't know about Groucho, but all the females love me!"

She crossed her arms over her chest and gave him a coy smile. "*All* the females love you? Okay, then, why haven't you married one of your many admirers?"

He dipped his head shyly. "Because I haven't found the right one yet. The one God has prepared to be my wife."

Treva felt the heat rise in her cheeks. That was the same answer she gave people when someone asked her why she'd never married. Because God hadn't sent the right man into her life.

"I almost forgot! I have to show you something I found when I was sweeping the basement floor after you left." She hurried to the hall table and brought back the money clip. "It was under the bottom step."

He took it and turned it over slowly. "Eighteen-karat gold. No special markings, but this thing had to have cost a few bucks."

"Look at the money."

He let out a low whistle as he unfolded the bills. "Six one-hundred-dollar bills? Who would carry around that kind of money? I'll bet whoever dropped this thing would sure like to get it back."

She grabbed onto his arm. "That's what scares me. I'm so afraid whoever it belongs to will come back again."

"I'm taking you to my mother's."

"No. I admit I'm frightened, but I'm staying right here."

"Did anyone ever tell you that you are a stubborn woman?"

His expression made her momentarily forget how frightened she was. "Occasionally," she admitted.

"I'll take this money clip into the station tonight." He gestured toward the box on the table. "Our pizza is getting cold."

She hurried into the kitchen and filled two mugs with coffee, thankful she'd

brought the pot along with her, then sat down on the sofa beside him. "You'r
too good to me. I was about to make a supper of peanut butter and jelly on crack
ers. This is much better."

"You can't beat pizza. It's the all-around American food." He grabbed he
hand and bowed his head. She listened as he thanked God for their food an
for keeping her safe; then he asked Him to continue to watch over her and giv
her wisdom as to what she should do about the house.

"Thank you," she said softly, her heart full of admiration for a man wh
could pray so easily.

"You're welcome." He opened the lid and, using his fingers, pulled out
piece of pizza and placed it on her plate. "I thought you looked like a supreme
pizza type of girl."

She grinned as she lifted the piece and bit off a big bite. "I love supreme. It
my very favorite."

"Tell me about yourself, Treva," he said between bites.

"Not much to tell. I've lived a fairly boring life." She allowed a nervou
giggle to escape her lips as she pulled a string of cheese from them. "Until now
I've had more excitement in the past fifteen hours than I've had the rest of m
life combined."

"You've never been married?"

"No."

"Engaged?"

"Umm, no."

"Did I detect a bit of hesitation there?"

She lowered her eyes and took a sip of coffee. "I thought a man was goin
to ask me to marry him—once—but it never happened."

"Any regrets?"

She tilted her head thoughtfully. "No. I realized later the two of us woul
have been miserable together. He turned out to be a gambler. The woman he di
marry left him a year later because of it."

"Too bad. Some guys really get hooked on gambling. From what I hear, it
like an addiction. What a waste. Did you always want to be a teacher?"

"Not always, but like so many kids when they go off to college I didn't hav
a clue as to what I wanted to be when I grew up. So, for lack of anything tha
interested me, I chose elementary education as my major."

He placed another slice of pizza on her plate. "And?"

"And I found my niche. I love teaching grade-schoolers." Feeling uncom
fortable having the conversation focused on her, she asked, "What about you
You never married?"

"Nope. Never even came close."

"I'm sure you've had plenty of girlfriends, though."

With a wide, toothy grin he nodded. "I've had a few but none I wanted to get serious about."

She picked up the piece he'd placed on her plate and waved it through the air. "A handsome guy like you? I find that hard to believe. I would imagine you could have your pick of women."

The smile left his face. "Although I admit I enjoy female companionship from time to time, I've never found that special someone."

"God's choice for you, right?"

He bobbed his head. "Right. And not every woman wants to be married to a cop. I can't tell you the number of guys who work with me who are divorced. Their wives were fine with the idea of their being policemen until after they'd said, 'I do.' Then it all changed. Too dangerous. Too many odd hours. Too little pay. The complaints are endless."

"You can't blame a woman for being upset about her husband's life being in danger. I know I'd feel that way."

"Oh, I understand, but those women should never have married a man with that kind of occupation in the first place. Several of my best friends have quit the force, and now they're working at dead-end, boring jobs they hate!" He placed his slice of pizza on his plate and leaned back against the cushions, his eyes pinned on her, his face solemn. "Being a cop is who I am, Treva. I not only chose it. It chose me. My dad was a cop. My two older brothers are cops. One in Baltimore and one in Chicago. I know it sounds silly, but I was born to be a cop. I knew from the time I was old enough to say the word *policeman,* that's what I was going to be. Sure, the danger is there, and so are the long hours and the low pay; but those things are secondary to me. Being a cop is worth whatever it costs. At this point in my life, if I had to make a choice over a woman and being a cop, I'm afraid being a cop would win out."

"But you have to admit, it is dangerous. That's the part I think most women would worry about. You have to understand it from the woman's point of view, too."

"I know it's dangerous. My best buddy was killed on a routine stop one night. When he walked up to the car, the driver shot him. We got the guy a few days later, and he's serving time in prison, but that won't bring my buddy back. You never know what's going to happen from one minute to the next. It's also part of the reward. If you're in danger, it's because someone is doing something they shouldn't. It's up to you to protect the innocent. Sometimes you win, and—"

"Sometimes you lose," she said with a melancholy tone.

"Yes, that happens, but we are well-trained. A good cop reacts automatically to a bad situation. We don't go barging in—guns blazing—like you see on TV. We follow certain policies and procedures. If you keep your head and do things the right way, you're less likely to—"

She shuddered. "Be killed?"

He pursed his lips and nodded. "Yes, be killed. But someone has to do it. I'm that someone. I feel God has called me to be a cop as surely as some men are called to be missionaries. We need godly cops."

They sat silently, each nibbling at their pizza.

"I never thought of it that way."

"I'm afraid most folks don't."

They ate all they could then gave what was left to Groucho, who downed it in barely one gulp.

"Hey, it's seven o'clock. I'd better be going. I have to grab a couple hours of z's, shower, and change into my uniform."

Her eyes widened. "A couple of hours? Is that all the sleep you get? I feel terrible! You should have been sleeping instead of bringing pizza to me."

"You didn't like it?"

"Of course I liked it, and I liked your company, too." She patted nervously at her hair. "I just wish you'd warned me you were coming so I could have made myself presentable. I must look awful!"

"I think you look fantastic."

"You're only saying that because you're a gentleman."

His expression sobered. "You're still determined to put your house on the market and go back to Warren?"

She gave him a slow nod. "I've been thinking about it ever since that Benson Cordell was here this afternoon. Maybe it would be best for everyone if I just packed up and left Bristol."

"Not for me. I like having you here."

"But, Tank, don't you see? I've finally realized I can't remodel this place all by myself. And even though I've brought my life's savings with me and have some insurance money left over after paying for Aunt TeeDee's funeral and the few outstanding bills she had, it isn't nearly enough to hire someone to come in and do the work."

His eyes sparkled. "What if you could get someone to do those things, someone qualified to do the work, and you wouldn't have to pay them until the house is sold? That'd make it possible for you to get the roof fixed and buy the appliances and the other items you'd need with the money you have, wouldn't it?"

She stared at him, not sure what he meant. "You mean, take on a partner?"

Giving her a mysterious grin, he shook his head slowly. "Not exactly, but I guess you could call that person a partner. I was thinking of someone who could do it in addition to his regular job, so he wouldn't be dependent on any income until the house sells."

She huffed. "Work and not get paid for it? Only a person without any sense would offer to do something like that."

Chapter 4

Tank bowed low in front of her. "Say hello to a senseless person!"

Treva stared at him. "You? You're kidding, right?"

He straightened and gave her a winsome smile. "Nope. I'm willing to do whatever it takes to get this house remodeled and ready to go on the market. You won't have to pay me a penny until the sale closes and you get your money."

"But—"

"Look—I told you I worked with a contractor for a couple of years while I was waiting to get on the police force. I know how to do almost everything you need to have done, and I'm good at it. I hope to build my own house someday. This will be a great experience for me. I've got the tools, the know-how, and the time. And I'm more than willing. What else could you ask?"

"You can't—"

"Oh, but I can. I'm on duty from eleven at night until seven in the morning. I can work here until three or four in the afternoon and still get in six hours of sleep. Besides, it'll be fun. I've always loved this old house. I'd like to see this grand lady restored to her original beauty. Come on—what do you say?"

"But—"

"I don't want you to go back to Warren. Please say yes."

His offer was too good to be true. Was there a catch, and she was too enthralled with him to see the obvious? Her head swam as her emotions fought with one another. She wanted to stay, but she wasn't sure she could stick it out—that she'd be brave enough to spend nights alone in the house. But she really didn't want to leave. She'd never thought of herself as a quitter.

"Treva?" he prodded softly. "Will you stay and let me help you? I'm willing to work for sweat equity."

"You're crazy, you know."

"I'm waiting."

What am I getting myself into? I barely know this man. But he's so sweet, and he is a police officer. Surely I can trust him.

"You won't get many offers like this."

"Okay, yes! I'll stay! If you're crazy enough to offer, I'm crazy enough to accept!"

"Good!"

Had she made the right decision? Was Tank LaFrenz too good to be true, or s she going to wake up and find out this had all been a dream?

"I have to go. But I'll be back bright and early in the morning, and we'll get rted. Remember—I'll be cruising by your house a number of times during the ht. If you need me to stop, turn on the porch light."

She stood in a daze as he backed toward the door.

"Make sure this lock is set when I leave, and keep Groucho at your side all ht. You have my cell phone number, right?"

She nodded.

"Good night. Sleep tight. I'll be praying for you."

"G—good night." She watched the door close behind him and then heard : sound of his pickup pulling out of the driveway. "Groucho," she told the dog h a victorious smile as she twisted the dead bolt on the door, "it looks as if 're staying after all!"

∽

eemed Treva heard a thousand noises during the night as untrimmed branches bbed across the screens and Miss Priss prowled the downstairs kitchen in search mice. Though she closed her eyes and covered her head with her aunt's lovely pliquéd, red and white album quilt, sleep refused to come. At two o'clock she wled out of bed and padded to the window. Pulling back the curtain, she stared the road in front of the house. Had Tank been cruising by as he'd promised? veral cars had sped up and down the road, but none seemed to slow down, so : assumed he hadn't been among them.

Where is he? What is he doing? Maybe helping with a domestic dispute? They say se are the worst kind. How would I feel if I were married to a cop, knowing he was there risking his life? Would I react like the women he told me about?

In the distance she could see the headlights of an approaching car. As it ared the house, it slowed down and came to a stop in front of her driveway. r heart thudded against her chest. It was too dark to tell if it was a police car. as it Tank coming to check on her? Or was it the person who broke into her use, set the fire, and left his money clip behind?

The car door opened, and someone stepped out, approached the house, and od in the driveway near the front porch, gazing up at her window. It was nk!

She quickly lifted the sash. "I was hoping that was you."

"I didn't wake you, did I?"

"No, I can't sleep."

"But you're all right?"

She leaned her head against the screen, suddenly feeling safe and secu "Yes, I'm fine."

"Okay, don't forget what I said about the porch light. I'll be by every h or so. I have to go by my apartment and change clothes when my shift is over I'll see you around seven thirty."

She gave him a smile, although she knew he couldn't see it in the semida ness. "I'll be waiting for you."

"Put on the coffeepot. I'll bring doughnuts," he added with a chuckle. "The this neat little doughnut shop over on Fourth Street that keeps us cops in doughnuts. They're pretty good, too."

"I'll have the coffee ready."

"Good. See you in a few hours."

"Okay."

"Treva."

"Yes?"

"I'm glad you're staying."

"So am I."

&

Wearing a leather tool belt around his waist, Tank placed the bag of doughn on the kitchen table then pulled off his jacket, draping it over a chair. "So problems last night?"

Treva sent him a triumphant smile as she filled his cup with steaming coffee. "Not a bit. How about you? How did your night go?"

"Fairly quiet. Picked up a couple of teenagers out joyriding in a car the stolen from a parking lot, issued a few speeding tickets, stopped a fight at a b usual stuff. Pretty routine." He lifted his cup and took a big whiff. "Umm, not ing smells as good as freshly brewed coffee."

"I love a good cup of coffee." She pulled a heavily glazed doughnut from t sack and took a big bite. "Umm, these are good."

"Told you so."

She dabbed at the corners of her mouth with her napkin. "I sure appreciat your driving by and checking on me during the night."

"My pleasure and part of my job. I'll be doing it every night from now o He pulled off a chunk of doughnut and tossed it to Groucho, who caught it midair.

"I don't want to get you in trouble!"

He huffed. "Hey, the Bristol Police Department's motto is Protect and Ser That's what I'm doing!"

"I still feel bad about our arrangement. Your working on this house a not getting paid for it until it sells. It's not too late to change your mind," she told him.

"And let you go back to Warren? Not on your life." He downed his last swallow of coffee then stood, smiling at her as he rubbed his hands together briskly. "I'm ready to tackle this place. Where do you want me to start?"

She gave him a blank stare. "I—I don't know. Where do you think we should start? I'm wide open to suggestions."

He pulled a small notebook and carpenter's pencil from a pouch on the tool belt and began flipping through the pages. "I jotted down a few notes when I took my supper break last night. You mentioned the roof needs new shingles. Why don't you call Gerry Roofing—the number is in the phone book—and have them come out and give you a bid. They're reputable and do a good job."

"I was hoping you'd know a good roofer."

"I think the best place for you and me to start is that upstairs bathroom. I was thinking maybe we'd pull out that old tub and put in one of those fiberglass shower–tub combinations."

She contemplated his idea. "I was thinking the same thing."

"While we're picking out the tub, you'll probably want to decide on a new stool and lavatory; maybe one of those long oak vanities would be nice. Of course, we need to replace that old galvanized pipe with PVC, and wire in a few more receptacles. As soon as the bathroom is done, maybe you should let me replace the ancient hot-water tank in the laundry room. It needs to be taken care of before we tackle the kitchen." He continued to run his finger down his handwritten list.

Treva stared at him in amazement. The man was a human dynamo.

"Are you good at painting?"

Before she could answer, he went on. "What do you think about painting all the woodwork white? It'd sure lighten up the place."

"White would be nice. I could do that. I like to paint."

He stared off in space. "It's been a long time since I've been upstairs, but it seems I remember the ceiling in that northeast bedroom had some water damage from a leak in the roof. I know your aunt got that part of the roof repaired, but what about the ceiling?"

"The damage is still there."

He jotted a few notes on the page. "Maybe I can take that plaster ceiling down and replace it with Sheetrock without disturbing the walls. Probably ought to add a few more receptacles to all those upstairs bedrooms. Most of these old houses only have one or two in each room." He closed the notebook and stuffed it back into the pouch. "Remind me to have the roofer take a look at the gutters while he's here."

Treva sank back down in the kitchen chair. "Oh, Tank, what would I have done if you hadn't come along? I had no idea so much needed to be done when I decided to fix up my aunt's house. You must think me very foolish."

He dropped into the chair next to her and covered her hand with his, giving it a pat. "Foolish? Not at all. In fact, I admire your spunk. Not many women would have the guts to take on a project like this."

"Only because they're a whole lot smarter than I am!"

"No, because they don't have your drive and ambition. You have a dream, and you're going after it. That's always commendable."

She gazed up into his eyes. "I couldn't do it without you. I realize that now."

He rose and pulled her up with him. "Well, that's one worry you can put out of your mind. I'm here, ready to go to work, and I plan on staying until the SOLD sign goes up in the front yard." He released her hand and snapped his fingers. "Oh, I nearly forgot. I brought you something." Reaching into his jacket pocket, he pulled out something orange. "Your very own nail apron. I picked it up at the lumberyard when I went for the basement door. Turn around." He slipped the apron about her waist and tied the strings. "Looks good on you."

She laughed. "I'm not sure orange is my color. I've never worn orange before."

He stepped back, sizing her up. "You look pretty official. Maybe you should go into the carpentry business."

"Yeah, right."

"Well, I'm going to call the lumberyard and check on our order. Then I'm off to work on that upstairs bath."

She stood in the kitchen doorway watching as he climbed the stairs, whistling as he took them two at a time. After calling the roofer and setting up a time for him to come and take a look at the roof, she went to the sink and filled a bucket with hot soapy water and headed toward the refrigerator.

By three o'clock Tank had the fixtures removed from the upstairs bathroom and part of the galvanized plumbing replaced. "The lumberyard is supposed to deliver the new tub and stool in the morning. Maybe we can run down there when we take our lunch break tomorrow and pick out that oak vanity and lavatory." He unfastened the tool belt from around his waist and placed it on a chair. "Time for me to go play policeman." Leaning toward her, he smiled. "You gonna be okay tonight?"

"I think so," she answered in an almost whisper, enjoying his closeness. "I hope you can get to sleep right away. I hate the idea of your having to work all night."

He cuffed her chin playfully. "Hey, I'm used to this crazy schedule. I've been working nights ever since I joined the force."

"I can't begin to tell you how much I appreciate what you're doing for me."

His gaze still locked with hers, he pulled his key ring from his pocket and backed toward the door. "My pleasure, ma'am. See you in the morning, but don't forget to turn on the light if you need me."

She nodded then watched as both Groucho and Miss Priss walked him to the door. By bedtime she'd cleaned up both the refrigerator and the stove, taken the rest of the sheets off the furniture in the living room, and given the entire room a good going-over with the dust cloth and vacuum cleaner. Dead tired from all the work, she climbed into her bed and slept, barely waking up even when the trees brushed against the window.

Tank arrived at exactly seven thirty the next morning, all smiles. "One of my policemen buddies does drywalling on his days off. He said if I'd help him hang the Sheetrock, he'd tape it, mud and sand it, and have it ready to paint. And, best of all, he owes me a favor, so he's gonna do it cheap. I told him I'd let him know when we were ready."

His enthusiasm contagious, she clasped her hands together. "That's wonderful! That should really speed up things."

"Yeah, I was pretty excited about it. In fact, I've decided to tear all the lath and plaster from the bathroom walls and go ahead and Sheetrock them, too, if that's okay with you. That'll make it easier to get to the rest of the plumbing. But before I do that I'm going to take up the dark green asphalt tile on the floor. We can replace it with sheet vinyl in maybe a light cream or white. What do you think?"

"I like the idea if you're sure it won't be too much work."

He picked up his tool belt, fastening it about his waist. "Maybe more work now, but in the long run it'll save time and look a lot better." He glanced at his watch. "Let's plan on going in to the lumberyard about noon, okay?"

She couldn't conceal a smile as she leaned against the counter. He looked so cute in his worn jeans and torn T-shirt with that leather tool belt wrapped around his waist. "Noon is fine. I'm going to start working on the other upstairs bedrooms. That old wallpaper pulls off pretty easily. I think all they're going to need is a couple of coats of white paint on the ceiling, the woodwork sanded a bit and painted, and some pretty new paper."

"Good idea. We can get the upstairs work done first then tackle the downstairs." He frowned. "It might be a good idea for you to move into one of the downstairs bedrooms. Once we start pulling off that old lath and plaster, it's going to be pretty dusty up there. Not good on the old lungs. We can hang a sheet of plastic at the head of the stairs to try to keep as much of that stuff from filtering down as possible."

"Good idea. I'll move my things downstairs tonight."

He tilted his head sideways and listened. "There's the truck with the tub and stool. I'd better go help them unload."

As soon as the delivery truck left, they headed into town. Once they had selected the fixtures for the bathroom and run a few errands, they stopped at Al's Diner for lunch.

The fry cook waved his spatula at them as they entered. "Hey, Tank, I hear you've been working out at the old Gunther place."

Tank gave him a nod. "Yep, we're remodeling it from top to bottom."

The man moved from behind the counter, one hand cupped around his mouth as if he were getting ready to tell a secret. "Seen any ghosts? Homer Jones saw one. Said it was floating along the ground and wearing a pink shirt, just like that O'Connor girl was wearing when they found her. Scared the stuffing out of him. A couple of other folks said they'd seen it, too."

Tank cuffed his arm. "Don't believe everything you hear, Zeke. You know there aren't any ghosts. I guess it makes a good story, though. Gives gossipy folks something to talk about."

The man frowned. "Guess that means you haven't seen any."

"Nope. 'Fraid not, and I don't expect I will."

Treva scooted into the little booth and gave her head a shake. "I can't believe people believe in ghosts."

"Me either." He gestured toward the menu. "You want to take a look at it or do you want to go for the burger and fries?"

She snickered. "The burger and fries, of course!"

In no time the waitress brought their order, placing big platters in front of them. Tank folded her hand in his and prayed.

"Now this is what I call food." He added the pickles, tomato, and onion slices to his burger, then slathered on a layer of ketchup.

"It smells wonderful," she conceded, reaching for the little paper container of mayo. "These fries are delicious. No wonder you come here so often."

Tank picked up a fry and twirled it at her. "We make a pretty good team, don't we?"

She gave him a shy grin. "I think we do."

"You've surprised me."

"Oh? How?"

"The way you've dug right in on those bedrooms. You're pluckier than I'd

lized." He dipped the fry in ketchup then popped it into his mouth. "But I'm
d you're not trying to do the whole thing by yourself."

"If it weren't for you, I probably wouldn't be doing it at all. Instead Mr.
rdell would be out beating the bushes for a buyer, and I'd be heading back to
arren."

He picked up the saltshaker. "You're not sorry you're staying, are you?"

"No, of course not, now that you're helping me. But when I'm lying in the
d in that dark house, staring at the ceiling, knowing someone deliberately set
e to it, I have to admit I have my doubts."

He leaned across the table and took hold of her hand again. "Try not to be
aid, Treva. You're never alone. God is with you."

"I know He says He is, but sometimes I—wonder."

"You do know I'm praying for you while I cruise the streets on my shift, don't
u? You have to remember God has promised never to leave us or forsake us."

"I know that's true, but when I think about what other Christians go
rough, it makes me wonder why God would allow such things to happen. I
uld never let those things happen to my child."

He gave her hand a squeeze then leaned back in his chair, his expression
mber. "I don't have the answer, Treva. I wish I did. All I know is that we have
take God at His word."

When they arrived back at the house, Tank finished taking up the tiles while
eva worked at pulling off more wallpaper. At three he left for his apartment,
anning to get in his six hours of sleep before reporting for duty. She lingered in
e doorway, hoping maybe he'd hug her good-bye, but he didn't.

She finished pulling the paper from the first bedroom; then she gathered it
up and stuffed it into the trash can she'd brought upstairs with her and carried
down to the kitchen. Rather than go out into the darkness and put it in the big
rrel, she decided to leave it there until morning.

Groucho stared up at her while she pulled a TV dinner from the freezer
ction of the clean refrigerator, one of several she'd purchased that day on the
ay back to the house, popped it into the microwave, and waited for the bell
sound. As she placed the hot container on the table, she glanced at the dog's
sh and, seeing it empty, reached into the cabinet beneath the sink, took out
e bag, and filled the dish. "Sorry, Groucho. I guess I have too many things on
y mind." Then, glancing around the kitchen, she asked, "Where's Miss Priss?
rely I didn't lock her out."

She hurried to the back door and, after making sure the screen was still
cked, called out to the cat several times. She was about to shut the door when
iss Priss darted up onto the porch. "You'd better get in here, lady. I sure didn't

want you to spend the night outside."

Looking unconcerned, her head held regally, her tail pointed high, Miss Priss sauntered across the kitchen floor to her open bag and began nibbling her cat food.

Treva glanced from one animal to the other. "You two have no idea how it is to have you here."

She ate her meal in silence. After supper she moved her personal items from the upstairs bedroom to the downstairs one at the front of the house. Smiling herself, she glanced around the room, absorbing every detail. It was like taking a step back in time. The high ceilings, the old waterfall bed, chest, and dresser. The yellow and turquoise chenille bedspread, the iron floor lamp, the fringe shades on the dresser lamps. There was even an old, chipped enamel bedpan the top shelf of an ancient storage chest.

She gathered her robe, pajamas, and slippers and padded down the hall the bathroom. After lighting a scented candle she'd brought from home adding a couple of scoops of bubble bath to the tub, she filled it with water slipped into it, relishing the feel of the hot water as it engulfed her body. The sweet scent of honeysuckle filled the room while she lay in the claw-footed with her head resting on its back, her mind wandering in all directions.

Groucho ambled into the room and stood staring at her.

"We're sleeping in a different place tonight, boy, but I'll expect you to s right by my side again, just like you did last night."

He tilted his head, lapped at his chops, and turned a complete circle bef lying down on the little rag rug beside the tub, his chin resting on his fr paws.

When the water cooled off, Treva reluctantly climbed out of the tub, towe dry, and donned her pajamas. After blowing out the candle and turning off light, she headed toward the bedroom that would be hers until the upstairs rem eling was finished. Once she was settled under the quilt and Groucho was at side, curled up on the little rug she'd put there for him, she closed her eyes in pra thanking God for bringing Tank LaFrenz into her life.

❧

She awoke with a start and stared at the glaring red numbers on the clock sh placed on the dresser: 3:15. Groucho let out a low growl and hurried to the do scratching on it much as he'd done the first night she'd spent in the old hou "What is it, boy?" With her pounding heart echoing in her ears, she yanked her robe and slippers and hurried to open the door.

Groucho pushed his way past her, doing a combination of both barking a whining as he bolted down the hall toward the kitchen.

Smoke! I smell smoke! Surely not again!

With feelings of panic rushing through her, Treva raced toward the kitchen. Flames, nearly reaching the ceiling, were leaping out of the metal container where she'd placed the old wallpaper she'd torn off the upstairs bedroom. Terrified, she braced herself against the wall: *9-1-1! Call 9-1-1!*

Tentacles of fear wrapped themselves around her vocal cords as she grabbed up the wall phone and dialed the number. "Fire! There's a fire in my kitchen," she blurted out when the operator answered. She gave the woman the address then begged, "Hurry—please hurry!"

I've got to do something! I can't just let it burn! Glancing around frantically, she noticed the metal lid that came with the trash can leaning against the wall. Grabbing up an oven mitt to protect her hands, she reached out and slapped the lid onto the can, trapping the flames inside.

She felt weak, numb, and sick to her stomach. She'd put that same lid on the trash can last night after stuffing the wallpaper into it! Someone had taken it off and deliberately set the old paper on fire!

Chapter 5

Treva rushed to the door as the fire truck turned into her driveway with Tank's patrol car right behind it. Waving her arms from the front porch, she called out, "The fire is out!"

The same fireman who responded to the first fire crawled out of the truck and headed toward her. "Where was it this time?"

Tank hurried to join them, slipping his arm about Treva's waist. "Are you okay?"

She nodded. "Other than being shook up, I'm fine." She gestured down the hall. "In the kitchen. I—I filled that big metal trash can with the old wallpaper I tore off yesterday, then put the lid on it before I went to bed. Someone took that lid off and set the paper on fire."

Tank gave her a vacant stare. "You didn't use a match to light a candle and then toss it into that can? Maybe the flame wasn't completely out."

She pushed herself away and glared at him. "I did not toss a match into that can, and I certainly didn't leave the lid off. I distinctly remember having to crush the paper down to get the lid on!"

"Ma'am, have you taken a look around? Is anything missing or out of place?" the fireman asked kindly.

With a heavy sigh Treva sat down in one of the kitchen chairs and rested her arms on the table. "I haven't checked out the entire house, but everything in here looks fine."

Tank cautiously placed his hand on her shoulder. "Did you lock up the house as I told you?"

Still miffed by his question about the trash can, she answered without looking up. "Yes. There is no way I'd sleep in this house without making sure all the doors were locked up tight."

The fireman lifted the lid a crack and peered into the trash can. "But none of the locks had been forced and none of the windows broken?"

"As I said, I haven't gone through the whole house."

"I'll do it." Tank checked the outside kitchen door then hurried out of the room to check the others, leaving Treva and the fireman alone.

"Do you have any idea who would do this, ma'am? I mean, this is the second fire in this house in three days."

"No. I can't think of a soul." Treva licked her dry lips nervously then sat quietly waiting for Tank's return.

He came back a few minutes later. "I've gone through every room in the house, even the basement. Not a window is broken, and every lock is intact."

The fireman stared off in space and rubbed at his chin. "The first time, whoever set the fire broke down the basement door to gain entry." He paused thoughtfully. "How did they get in this time? Does anyone, besides you, have access to the house? Maybe a neighbor, a gardener, or a repairman?"

"The old man who lives down the road mentioned he did odd jobs for her aunt occasionally. Maybe she gave him a key," Tank inserted quickly.

Treva shook her head. "I doubt my aunt would do that."

"How about other neighbors who might have a key?" Tank asked.

"None that I'm aware of, and my aunt never had a gardener. She always paid one of the teenagers from her church to cut the grass and weed the flower beds. She would never have given them a key."

Tank frowned. "How about repairmen? Maybe she had some work done on the furnace or her appliances and let them have a key."

She gave him a slight smile. "You must not have known my aunt as well as you thought you did. She was a very cautious person, and although she'd lived in this house by herself for years after Uncle Martin passed away, she never got over being afraid. No, unless it was a sheer emergency, my aunt would never give a key to her house to anyone."

The fireman shrugged. "Well, it seems the only other explanation is that someone was in the house before you locked it up for the night."

Assailed by fear, panic ripped through Treva, and she felt faint. Could that be true? She *had* carried a few of the emptied boxes out to her car after Tank left. Could someone have slipped onto the porch and into the house without her seeing him? If a person had, that meant that all the time she was reclining in the bathtub someone had been in the house with her!

"I'm going to carry this trash can outside and dump the contents so we can make sure there's nothing still smoldering in the bottom." The fireman grabbed onto the handles and lifted the can. "I wish I had some answers for you, ma'am. I can only imagine how frightening this is for you." He nodded toward the trash can. "Let's hope this will be your last fire."

"I'm going to hang around awhile," Tank told the man, walking him to the door. "Thanks for the quick response. See you later." He stood in the open doorway until the fire truck was out of sight.

"Do you think someone could have come in while I was putting those things in my car?" Treva asked as he turned to face her. She tried not to cry, but she couldn't help it. Fear was holding her in its grip.

He walked slowly toward her then took her hands and lifted them to his mouth, kissing them as he stared into her eyes. "I don't know, but what other explanation could there be? You said the house was locked up tight. This thing has me baffled."

It took several restorative breaths for her to calm down. "Tank, I'm trying to be brave, but how can I live like this? I'm jumping at my own shadow!"

A voice barked out from the small radio clipped to the epaulet on his shoulder. He listened, responded, then pulled away from her. "Got a robbery going on in town. I have to go. I'll get back as soon as I can. Will you be all right?"

"I—I guess so."

He hurried to the door, opening it wide. "Make Groucho stay with you, and call my cell phone number if you need me."

"I will."

With Groucho at her side she walked to the door, engaged the dead bolt, then stood watching out the window as he climbed into his car and drove off. Once again she was alone.

She huddled under the covers in the big bed and stared at the shadows on the ceiling, going over the events of the day, trying to figure out how someone could have gotten into the house and set the fire without breaking in. Whoever it was had to have had a key and must have gone out the front door, locking it behind him. The men who'd delivered the tub, stool, and a few other supplies had come in the house just long enough to carry the items up the stairs; then they walked out the door and drove off. No one else had even been in the house, except Tank.

Tank!

Treva felt a sudden chill. Tank knew where she kept the spare key! He'd been with her when she'd checked to make sure it was still in the place Aunt TeeDee always kept it. *What a stupid thought! That man has been nothing but kind to me!*

Whoa. Slow down. She tugged on the quilt, pulling it up beneath her chin. *Think this thing through. Who answered the call when the first fire was set? Who answered the call tonight? Who knew the layout of the house, including the basement, the kitchen, and the bedrooms? And had every opportunity to come and go whenever he chose? Who could get by Groucho without his barking or growling?*

Tank LaFrenz!

But why? What would he have to gain? Besides, the man is a Christian!

"Who told you he was a Christian?" a still small voice seemed to ask from deep

inside her. *"What do you really know about him? Do you think just because he's a cop you can trust him? Come on—get serious! What guy in his right mind would want to come in here and help you get this place all fixed up and not get paid for it until the house sells? There has to be an ulterior motive here somewhere. The guy's too good to be true."*

But I prayed and asked God to send me the person I should hire to do the work I couldn't do, she shot back defensively. *I was sure Tank was my answer to that prayer!*

None of this made any sense. She had been in the house both times someone had set the fires. If the person meant to harm her, they'd had two perfect opportunities; yet they hadn't. Was there something in the house they wanted? If so, where was it? And what could it be? Had they searched the house while she was sleeping? If they had, why set the fires? They could have left, and she would never have known they were there.

God, she called out from the depths of her heart, *show me what to do. I don't know who to trust. Protect me—please protect me!* Still trembling, she slipped her hand from beneath the quilt and leaned over the side of the bed, reaching out to pat the sleeping dog.

Though she heard Tank's patrol car pull into the driveway and stop several times during the remainder of the night, she didn't get up and go to the window.

By the time he arrived the next morning, she was feeling much better and had decided the idea of even considering that Tank could be the one responsible for entering the house and setting the fires was ludicrous. He was the kindest and most considerate man she'd ever met, and he knew too much about God's Word to be faking it.

"You sure you feel up to helping me tear that plaster and lath off that upstairs bedroom ceiling?" he asked as the two of them sat down at the kitchen table to enjoy the doughnuts he'd brought. "I could see how frightened you were last night. I was almost afraid you'd be gone back to Warren by the time I got here this morning. I felt like a heel running off on you like that last night, but that robbery was on my side of town." He grinned victoriously. "We got the guys, too. They won't be robbing any more convenience stores anytime soon."

She avoided his eyes by staring into her cup. "I considered leaving, but the more I thought about it, the madder I got. Someone is trying to run me off, and I'm not going to let them!"

"Good girl. But I have to admit, I'm worried about you staying here alone. You don't want to accept my mom's invitation and stay with her?"

She lifted her chin, trying to appear braver than she felt. "And leave this house empty for whoever seems to come and go whenever they please? Not on your life. I'm staying right here."

"Okay, if that's what you want to do, but remember—the offer still stands."

She stood and, picking up the work gloves she'd found in the basement, squared her shoulders and hitched her head toward the stairway. "Let's get to work."

It took them less than two hours to tear the old plaster and ceiling lath down. She watched Tank out of the corner of her eye as they worked side by side, cleaning up and picking the pieces off the floor and tossing them out the open window into the bed of his truck, which was parked below.

"There's a lot of dust in here. Don't take that mask off until we go back downstairs," he told her as he scooped up an armload and carried it to the window. "And leave the heavy stuff for me. I don't want you lifting it."

What a man! she thought as she gazed at him. *How could I have ever mistrusted him? Tank is everything I'd ever want in a boyfriend. I love the way he plays Christian music on his boom box while we're working, singing along with the artist, and the way he always prays before we eat.* She chuckled to herself. *Even if it is only leftover Chinese take-out that has already been prayed over!*

When the time came for him to go back to his apartment to get some sleep, they'd not only taken down the ceiling in that room, but they'd also finished stripping off the wallpaper in it and two others.

"You are going to church with me in the morning, aren't you?" he asked as he took the tool belt from around his waist. "You promised."

"Do you want me to?"

"Of course I do. I already told you I want to show you off to my friends—make them jealous." He slipped an arm about her as they walked to the door. "I'll pick you up about nine."

She felt her toes curl as he bent and lightly kissed her cheek. "I'll be ready," she managed to say. She took a couple of quick breaths to get oxygen to her addled brain as he backed away.

He turned and playfully touched the end of her nose with his fingertip. "If I don't get out of here, I'm not going to get any sleep before my shift starts. The captain frowns on his officers taking naps while they're on patrol."

"Please be careful, Tank. Don't take any unnecessary chances."

He took her hand in his as they walked toward the door. "Don't you take any chances either. Keep that door locked at all times—even lock it behind you if you make a trip to your car."

∽∾

Standing next to Tank as they sang praises to God during the morning service at his church and seeing the way he interacted with his fellow believers made Treva wonder how she could have ever doubted him. He seemed to be one of the pillars of the church. She felt a warm welcome when he introduced her to his mother and many of the churchgoers. Almost all of them had good things to say about Aunt TeeDee, and that made her feel happy, too. And she loved Mrs. LaFrenz. She was a beautiful woman and every bit as nice as her son.

"So? What'd you think? Did you enjoy the service?" he asked as they walked hand in hand to his pickup. He paused before opening the door and stepped away from her, giving her an exaggerated look from head to toe. "I intended to tell you earlier. You look beautiful! Do you realize this is the first time I've seen you in a dress and wearing makeup?"

She felt the heat in her face. She had gone to great lengths to get ready, changing her dress at least four times and taking an inordinate amount of time to apply her makeup. She'd even used the curling iron on her hair, something she rarely did.

"Umm," he said, cocking his head to one side. "I don't know which one I like best. Treva in jeans and a T-shirt, with paint smears on her face and plaster in her hair, or the Treva I'm looking at now, with the rosy cheeks and mouth and dressed in that soft, fluffy dress. Maybe I'd better try to keep them both."

Keep? Does that mean he enjoys being around me as much as I enjoy being around him? She offered a demure smile. "Thank you for your compliment."

He treated her to lunch at his favorite seafood restaurant then dropped her off at her house, saying he had promised a buddy he'd watch a ball game on TV with him. Though she was disappointed they weren't going to spend the afternoon together, she was glad to see he was taking a little time off for relaxation.

❧

The next few days went by swiftly, with no more incidents, as the two labored hard on the old house. Tank finished changing out the plumbing, putting down the sheet vinyl floor, installing the tub–shower combo, the stool, and the oak vanity while his friend finished taping and sanding the new Sheetrock they'd put up in the bathroom and the northeast bedroom. Treva sanded the residue off the walls where they'd removed the old wallpaper; then she painted every inch of the upstairs woodwork and doors a brilliant white, giving the entire second floor a light, airy look.

"I can't believe the change," she told him as he prepared to leave. "The paperhangers will be here in the morning. Once that's done, I think I'll have the carpet layers go ahead and install the carpeting up there."

He nodded as he unfastened his tool belt. "Good idea. Now that we've about whipped the upstairs pretty well, I'm really excited about tackling the downstairs."

"Me, too. Thanks. I could never have done this without you."

He stared at her for a moment, as if wanting to say something but deciding against it.

"You, my lovely lady, are habit-forming!" He gave her a mischievous grin. "Maybe I should just hang around the rest of the day and go without sleep. Just think how much work we could get done."

She reached over and touched his arm lightly. "I'd like that, too, but you have to get some sleep. You need to be at your best when you tackle the bad guys."

Letting his hands fall to his sides, he let out a long, low sigh. "I hate to leave you."

Giving him a demure smile, she took his hand and led him to the door. "I don't want you to leave either, but you have to go."

Groucho darted past him as he pulled open the door and backed out slowly. "Hey, boy! Where've you been? You're supposed to be here looking after my girl."

Treva's heart pounded erratically. *My girl?*

He bent and stroked the dog's fur then looked up at her, his face taking on a serious expression. "I don't want to alarm you, but you must keep those doors locked at all times, okay?"

She nodded. "I will. I haven't said much about it, but I'm still scared every time I hear a noise in the house."

"Even though you tried to hide it, I knew you were afraid. Keep that cell phone handy, and don't hesitate to call me." He stood and kissed her cheek then closed the door behind him.

~

Treva climbed out of bed earlier than usual the next morning. She hadn't slept well. Not only because she was afraid, but also because she couldn't get Tank off her mind. In her heart of hearts, she knew she was falling in love with him, and it felt wonderful. But did he feel the same way?

She hurried into the kitchen, deciding to peel and section the cantaloupe and honeydew melons she'd bought at the store several days before. But as she reached for a long knife she discovered the entire cutlery tray was gone! She scanned the kitchen, thinking perhaps Tank had moved it when he'd fixed a sandwich, but it was not to be found.

"Have you seen my cutlery tray?" she asked him when he came in a few minutes later. "I can't find it anywhere."

He shook his head with a frown. "It was there yesterday. I used that long bread knife. Are you sure you didn't put it somewhere else and forget about it?"

"Tank! I might forget leaving a knife somewhere, but a whole cutlery tray? Not likely!" She raised her chin a notch and eyed him defiantly. "You just admitted you used it last."

"Are you accusing me of taking it?" He opened his hands as if he had noth-
to hide, a deep scowl cutting into his forehead. "Is that what you're saying?"

"I'm not saying anything. I just want my knives back."

He approached her slowly, his gaze never leaving her face. "I can see fear
our eyes, Treva. I saw it another time, too. The night the fire was set in the
:hen. You're afraid of me, aren't you? You think I had something to do with
se fires."

She tried to back away, but the cabinets behind her prevented it. "I—I don't
w what I think, Tank. I'm suspicious of everything and everyone. Besides
, you are the only one who has access to this house. You know where I keep
extra key. Even Groucho lets you come and go as you please. I've never heard
n bark or growl at you once."

He stood and stared at her for a long time. "I could never hurt you—don't
: know that?"

She fumbled with her fingers, avoiding his gaze. "You have no idea how
ch I want to believe that."

He took a cautious step toward her. "Look, Treva—I'm a Christian and have
n since my early teens. I'm a deacon in my church, and I'm on the church's
lding committee. I've mentored a number of young people who've accepted
Lord. More important, I love God with all my heart, and I'm not ashamed to
nit it. Does that sound like the kind of person who would purposely set fires
l frighten you? Can you come up with a single, good reason I'd want to hurt
? Or do damage to your house?"

Her heart sank. What was the matter with her? Why was she letting her
rwhelming sense of fear dominate her life? This man had been nothing but
d to her. "No, I—I can't. I'm not thinking straight." She lifted her head slightly,
barrassed at her hasty accusation. "I'm sorry, Tank. I had no business accusing
like that. Of course you didn't take the cutlery tray."

"And the fires?"

She gave her head a shake. "No, I know you didn't have anything to do
h those either. Why would you? With all the hard work you're putting in
ry day?"

"I wouldn't. You have to believe that. Each minute I'm away from you, I
rry. I still hate the idea of your being here alone at night."

"At least I know you're checking on me. That helps."

He gave her a shy grin. "I wish I could tell you how important you are to me,
I've never been one for fancy words. You just have to take my word for it."

"You're important to me, too."

He reached out his arms, and she ran into them, burying her face in his strong chest. "Can you ever forgive me?"

"Nothing to forgive." He paused and cleared his throat loudly. "Ah—thi[s] really hard for me to say. I've never said it to another woman." He hesitated a[nd] raised one dark eyebrow. "I guess the easiest way to say it is just to blurt it out. I think I'm falling in love with you."

His warm breath against her skin sent shivers snaking down her spine. H[ow] could she have ever suspected him of such awful things? "Oh, Tank, I feel [the] same way," she whispered, afraid to say the words out loud. "I never thought [I'd] feel this way."

He gave her a boyish grin. "You're sweet, you're wonderful, you're beauti[ful] both inside and out, and you love my Lord. What more could I ask?"

They parted as a truck turned into the drive. The paperhangers had arriv[ed]. As Tank went to open the door, Treva bowed her head in prayer. *Dearest Fath[er], I want so much to believe in Tank. I'm still tingling at his words, but at the sa[me] time I'm not totally convinced I can trust him. Help me, Lord. Don't let my mind [be] so clouded with love for this man that I miss the obvious. And may I not be so eage[r to] place the blame on someone that I jump to unfounded conclusions.*

❧

The next few days their work progressed even better than they could have im[ag]ined as the paperhangers finished sooner than expected and were gone by l[ate] Thursday afternoon. Treva stood in the upstairs hallway along with Tank, a[d]miring the newly finished walls. "This looks even better than I thought it wou[ld]. I love the white woodwork. I'm glad you thought of it."

"It does brighten the place, doesn't it?" Smiling and looking proud of hi[m]self, Tank brushed the dust from his hands onto his shirt.

"Oh, you'd never guess who called awhile ago. That real estate man."

Tank laughed and rolled his eyes. "Let me guess. I'll bet he has a buyer j[ust] ready to sign on the dotted line."

She gave him a playful smile. "How did you guess?"

"I hope you told him to forget it!" He glanced at his watch. "Oh, no! It's nea[rly] six o'clock. I have to get some shut-eye before I go on my shift." He gave he[r a] quick peck on the cheek and hurried out the door. "See you in the morning."

The carpet layers arrived on Friday morning, their truck loaded with seve[ral] rolls of the carpeting Treva had selected to match the wallpaper she'd chose[n]. Tank watched with interest as they carried their supplies into the house. "I ca[n't] get much done with these guys going in and out of the house all day. Unless y[ou] have something you want me to do, I think I'll take the day off. I have so[me] business to attend to."

He was glad when she merely nodded and didn't ask any questions. "I m[ay]

back before I go to work, but I doubt it. I'll probably try to sleep a little earlier
this afternoon than I did yesterday." He gave her a wink. "Hard to catch the bad
guys when you're yawning from exhaustion."

"Where do you want this green carpet?" one of the men asked, leaning over
the railing.

Treva gave Tank a wave and a smile then made her way up the stairs.

He hurried out the door, glad their conversation had been interrupted. He
didn't want to have to lie to her.

Chapter 6

I t was a gorgeous day as Tank maneuvered his truck through the narrow overgrown road at the far end of the property. The sky was a clear blue, an the winds were nearly nonexistent. A marvelous day to work outside. H grabbed hold of the two-by-fours and the other lengths of board he'd brough tugged them out of the truck bed, and carried them to the observation platform pausing to admire the spacious view of beautiful Narragansett Bay before return ing to his truck for the other supplies. *This place is so special. I can hardly wait t bring Treva here. She's gonna love it once I get this platform repaired. I'm sure glad sh accidentally told me when her birthday was the day of the fire. This is going to be th perfect birthday present for her.*

Checking the stability and safety of the anchoring before stepping out ont the platform, he carefully began removing the rotted boards, replacing them wit new pressure-treated lumber, as well as new nuts and bolts. He also took tim to check all the other boards and their bolts, making sure the nuts were screwe on tight, especially those on the railings that covered three sides of the deck as i clung to the side of the hill. Though it took most of the day, by five o'clock no only was the observation deck finished, but he'd also built a bench into one sid and covered everything with a fresh coat of redwood paint.

After making sure his tools and the remainder of his supplies were safel back in the truck, he carried the old boards to a place where he could burn ther later then headed back into town.

～∾～

Tank gave Treva a mischievous grin when he stopped by her house for lunch th next day. "I see the carpet layers are already here and at work. How about havin a picnic lunch outside?"

She gave him a mystified frown. "Why?"

He lifted his brows and shrugged. "No reason. It's a beautiful day. I jus thought it might be nice."

She headed toward the refrigerator and pulled open the door. "We have loaf of bread, but other than peanut butter, there really isn't anything to mak sandwiches. I was going to heat up some of that spaghetti I made yesterday."

"I stopped by the deli and picked up a couple of subs and a carton of potat alad on my way here." He tried to sound casual but was afraid his face was giving him away. He had never been good at keeping secrets.

She closed the fridge and turned to face him, her hand still on the door handle. "You did?"

"Yeah. Don't you like the idea?"

"Sure, I like the idea. I love picnics, even impromptu ones. You caught me off guard. That's all." Treva opened a cupboard door and stared at its contents. "I thought maybe there were a few cookies left, but I guess not. How about potato chips? I think there's still an unopened bag in the pantry."

Tank grabbed onto her arm. "Don't worry about it. I have plenty of food in the cooler." He was so amused by the surprised expression on her face, he nearly laughed out loud. "Even dessert."

"Even dessert?"

"Yep."

"We'll need a blanket to sit on. There's one—"

"All taken care of."

"Should I fix a pitcher of iced tea? Or lemonade?"

"That's taken care of, too."

She gave a little disconcerted shrug. "Paper plates?"

"All I need is you," he said with a tender smile, hoping she'd pick up on his double entendre.

A faint pink flush rose to her cheeks. "I can't believe you went to all this trouble."

"No trouble." He reached out his hand.

She took it, her gaze still resting on his face. "I—I guess I'm ready."

Tank whistled for Groucho then lowered the tailgate so the dog could jump in while Treva locked up the house, and soon they were on their way.

"Where are we going? I had thought we'd probably have our picnic out on the porch."

He reached across and squeezed her hand. "You'll see soon enough. Close your eyes. It's a surprise."

She giggled. The sound went straight to Tank's heart.

"You're teasing me. Really? It's a surprise?"

He nodded. "I mean it. Close your eyes, and don't open them until I tell you."

Within minutes he turned off onto the narrow dirt road leading to the bay. "Keep them closed!"

"I am!"

"No fair, peeking."

The truck rocked back and forth as it crossed over the weathered washboard road.

Treva kept one hand over her eyes but used the other to grasp onto the truck's armrest for support. "Where are you taking me?"

"We're nearly there. Just a few seconds more."

He brought the truck to a stop a few feet from the rebuilt platform.

"Can I open them now?" she asked, a huge smile blanketing the little bit of her face that wasn't covered by her hand.

"Not quite. Wait a sec. I want to get you out of the truck first." He opened his door and hurried around to the other side then pulled her door open and grabbed on to her hand, helping her exit. "Keep them closed." Tank released her hand and wrapped an arm about her, leading her to the edge of the platform. "Now you can open them."

Treva let out an animated gasp. "The observation platform! You've fixed it! No one has ever done something this nice for me!"

Before he knew what was happening, she spun around and kissed him on the cheek, her eyes sparkling with tears. "Oh, Tank! How can I ever thank you? I've always loved this place."

He pulled her close, his smile turning to a satisfied grin. "Happy birthday, Treva."

Placing her hands against his chest, she pushed away slightly and gazed up at him, her eyes rounded. "How did you know it was my birthday? I never told you."

"Yes, you did."

"I did?"

He gave her a lopsided grin. "The day of your basement fire. I asked you for your zip code, and you were so flustered that you gave me your birth date, June 20."

She leaned her head against his chest. "I was pretty much out of it that day. I doubt most of what I said made any sense."

He nestled his chin in her hair, enjoying their closeness. "It worked out well for me. That very night I circled the date on my calendar so I'd remember it."

Standing on tiptoe, she kissed his cheek again then pulled away from him and stepped onto the platform, admiring the breathtaking view stretched out before them. "You did this yesterday, on your day off."

He moved up behind her and circled his arms about her waist. "You thought I'd run out on you, didn't you?"

She reached her hand up and caressed his face. "I wasn't sure."

"Do you like your birthday present?"

Leaning her head back against his chest, she let out a sigh of contentment. love my birthday present. This is wonderful, Tank. I know what bad shape this platform was in. You made it look like new and even added the bench. What marvelous idea."

He gave her a gentle squeeze then pulled away. "While you try out the nch, I'll set up our lunch."

"I can—"

He pointed to the bench. "Sit."

They both laughed when Groucho obeyed his order and sat down on the ck, the order meant for Treva, not him.

Tank pulled a card table from the pickup's bed and snapped open the legs, acing it directly in front of the new bench; then he returned to the truck, nging back a paper tablecloth with the words *HAPPY BIRTHDAY* printed all er it in bright colors. Next he brought matching paper plates and cups, plastic-re, and napkins.

"You've thought of everything," Treva said, grinning at him from her place the bench.

"Not quite." He gave his head a disgusted shake as he placed the bag of bmarine sandwiches and the carton of potato salad on the table. "I forgot the lt and pepper."

He placed a small ice bucket, a jar of iced tea, a sack of potato chips, and carton of baked beans onto the table, then scooted next to her on the bench. Jungry?"

Treva leaned her head on his shoulder. "I am now. This all looks delicious."

Tank enfolded her hand with his and bowed his head. "Lord, we come to ou on this gorgeous day, a day only You could have made. I thank You for Treva d for making it possible for me to help her celebrate her birthday. Be with her, ve her many more years to serve You, and keep her safe. We love You, Lord. men."

∽◌◞

er heart touched by the sincerity of his words, Treva fought back tears of joy. hank you, Tank. Your prayers mean a lot to me." She lowered her head and zed at him through her lashes. "You mean a lot to me."

He gave her hand a squeeze. "The feeling is mutual. Now let's eat."

They talked and laughed their way through lunch, telling silly things that d happened during their childhood. Finally, after Tank had cleared the table everything but their glasses and plasticware, he leaned into one of the lockup xes in the truck's bed, pulled out a large white box, and carried it to the table.

"What is that?" Treva asked, trying to lift a corner of the lid.

He slapped at her hand playfully. "Close your eyes."

She tilted her head coyly. "Again?"

"Again."

Her heart pounding with excitement, she opened her eyes and squea[led] with glee when he began to sing, "Happy birthday to you, happy birthday to y[ou], happy birthday, dear Treva! Happy birthday to you!"

There, before her on the table, was the most beautiful birthday cake sh[e'd] ever seen, all done in pinks, pale blues, and yellow and green, with her na[me] written in a lovely script. "It's—it's—" Words failed her. He'd done so much [to] make her birthday special. How could she have suspected he had anything to [do] with the mysterious things that had been happening to her? "Beautiful!"

He put his finger to her lips. "Don't get all teary-eyed on me. Birthdays [are] supposed to be happy." Pulling a book of matches from his pocket, he lit [a] single candle. "You didn't tell me how old you were—I'm guessing about twen[ty]-eight. Don't hit me if I'm wrong."

She linked her hands together on the table and sat staring into the flame [as] it wiggled back and forth in the nearly nonexistent breeze. "You're exactly rig[ht.] I'm getting to be an old lady."

Tank leaned over and gently rubbed his smoothly shaven cheek across he[r.] "I sure wouldn't call you old, but you are indeed a lady and a beautiful one, [at] that. Your eyes are as blue as that bay out there, and you have the cutest smile[.]"

"When I got out of bed this morning, I reminded Groucho and Miss Pr[iss] that they were the only ones who knew today was my birthday, and I felt a lit[tle] sad. I always knew there would be a birthday card from Aunt TeeDee in [my] mailbox, and now she's gone. Oh, it isn't that I mind getting older, but I feel [so] alone." She linked her arm through his. "Now you've turned this sad day into o[ne] of the happiest days of my life."

"Only because you deserve it." He pulled a plastic knife from the box a[nd] cut two generous wedges of the delicious-looking cake, placing them on pa[per] plates. "We should have ice cream with this, but I couldn't figure out any way [to] keep it frozen."

She pulled away from him and lifted her fork. "As full as I am, I doubt [I'll] have room for cake and ice cream. There's some vanilla ice cream in the freez[er.] We can have it later."

They feasted on the sumptuous dessert; then, after cutting Groucho a sm[all] wedge, Tank slipped the remainder into the box and placed it back in the truc[k's] lockup area. "I know sweets are hard on dogs, but he's a very special dog. [He] deserves a piece of your birthday cake." He gathered up the trash and put it i[n] the large plastic trash bag he'd brought with him, placing it in the bed of t[he] truck alongside the folding table.

Treva stood and stretched her arms, enjoying the sun on her face and the majesty of their surroundings. "I just don't understand how anyone could look at this place and doubt there is a God." Gazing at the sparkling blue water and the little boats bobbing out on the bay, she moved to the railing. "What a spectacular view."

"It is pretty awesome, isn't it?" Tank answered from the back of the truck, lowering the tailgate for Groucho.

"Yes, awesome doesn't even begin to describe it." She braced her hands on the railing as he walked up to join her. "Don't you ever wonder how God could do it all in one day? Just think of—

"Tank! Help!" Treva screamed out as the railing gave way. She grabbed onto an upright board as she began to fall over the edge, but it, too, began to pull away.

≈≈≈

In one swift movement Tank grabbed Treva's arm. With the other he anchored himself by slipping his fingers into an open space between the floor boards. "I've got you!" he yelled out, straining with all his might to hold onto her. He sat down on the platform and, after testing it by giving it a kick, wrapped his leg around the base of the upright board and reached out his other hand. "Grab hold!" he called out, leaning toward her as far as he dared. "I can pull you up!"

"I—I can't!"

"Don't look down, Treva!" The fear on her face ripped at his heart as she dangled precariously over the side of the platform with nothing below her to catch her fall. He had to hang on. "Go on—grab!"

"I—I can't—reach it!"

He shifted his weight a bit, leaning farther over the edge. The upright board leaned with him. "Hurry! I don't know how much longer this board is going to hold. Grab my hand!"

She closed her eyes tightly and, gritting her teeth, thrust out her hand.

He wanted to cry when he finally felt her hand in his. He'd never been so frightened. "I'm going to pull you up now. Don't be afraid. I have you." He pulled her up slowly, holding on tight until she could get one leg up on the platform; then with one big yank he pulled her up beside him and wrapped her trembling body in the safety of his arms. "I—I'm so sorry, Treva. I don't know how that happened."

She leaned into him, sobbing from the depths of her being, her breathing erratic and labored.

Tank stroked her hair as she rested against him. A fall from that high up could have killed her. "I replaced all the rotten boards and added new nuts and bolts to the entire platform. I double-checked to make sure they were all as tight as possible, using my wrench."

She lifted watery eyes and stared at him. The look of fear and mistrust he saw there broke his heart.

"All I know is that railing gave way when I leaned on it."

Tank helped her to the bench and, once she was seated and holding on tight to its edge, moved cautiously to the fallen area in the railing. The nuts were gone! Missing! So were the bolts! He felt numb as he ran his fingers over the empty holes. How could this be? Just yesterday he'd put those new bolts in that railing, as well as every other joint. Being careful to stay away from the edge, he moved along the rail, checking each area where there should have been a nut and a bolt. Several more were missing! His heart plummeted. Gasping for breath, his hands shaking, he stared at the open portion of the railing. Someone had to have done this! Nuts didn't unscrew themselves, not after he'd tightened them with the wrench. He sent a glance toward Treva and found her glaring at him in a way that unnerved him. "What? You think I did this?"

She hugged her body with her arms, half-turning away from him, her face contorted with fear. "I—I'm sorry, Tank. I don't know what to believe. All I know is—I came very close to dying today. I would never have come out here if you hadn't brought me."

"This whole platform and its railings were rock solid when I left here yesterday. You have to believe that!" He rushed to her, grasping her hands, his mind in a whirl. "I would never do anything to harm you!"

She turned her face away as if the very sight of him repulsed her. "Then who would, Tank? You seem to be near every time something dreadful happens to me. What should I believe?"

"No! Not me! It was just a coincidence I was there. Maybe it was that old codger, Homer somebody, who lives down the road. It'd be easy enough for him to come over here and do all these things."

"Homer Jones is an old man. What motive would he have?"

"He mentioned he tried to buy your house several times, but your aunt wouldn't sell it!"

She glared at him. "That was years ago!"

Be gentle with her. She's been through a horrendous ordeal. "Look," he said, making his voice as soft and nonthreatening as possible. "I don't have any idea who did this or why they did it. I only know I had nothing to do with it." When she didn't protest, he sat down on the bench beside her and warily slipped his arm about her shoulders, resting his forehead against hers. "You have to believe me, Treva. Please say you do."

A sob caught in her throat. "I want to go home."

He rose and took her hand, leading her to the truck, safely depositing her into the passenger seat, then he crawled in behind the steering wheel and turned the key in the ignition.

They rode silently back to the house, with Tank searching his mind for something to say that would convince her of his innocence. But from the look on her face, anything he could say at this point would only upset her even more.

Treva tried to control her shaking but couldn't, the horrible experience of the railing giving way still too vivid in her mind. She ventured a quick, sideways glance toward Tank and was glad to find his gaze was fixed on the road. *Oh, Tank, I'm so confused. You were the one who repaired the platform; yet, when that railing gave way, if it hadn't been for you and your quick action, catching hold of my arm and putting your own life at risk, I might have been seriously injured, maybe even killed. I want to believe you, but these doubts keep pulling at me.*

"I—I have about an hour before I need to get back to my apartment. I thought I might finish putting that baseboard—"

"Let's forget about doing any more work today," she said, interrupting as he pulled the pickup into the driveway and brought it to a stop. "I have a headache, and I'm not feeling very well. I think I'll take a nap." She pushed open the door and jumped out before he could turn the key to the OFF position.

"Don't you want me to check on the carpet layers?"

"No, I'll do it." She could feel his eyes on her as she crossed in front of the truck and headed for the house but resisted turning to look at him.

"I'm sorry," he called after her, his voice breaking with emotion. "I tightened the nuts on all those new bolts when I put them in. Someone else took them out. You have to believe me, Treva. I'd never hurt you. You mean too much to me."

When she reached the porch, she turned long enough to watch as he climbed out of the truck and lowered the tailgate, allowing Groucho to jump out.

He gave her a slight wave. "I'll be here first thing in the morning. We need to get started on the downstairs."

Her emotions still in an upheaval, she simply nodded before opening the door and going inside. *Please, God,* she said in her heart as she closed the door and leaned her forehead against the lace curtain, watching until the pickup was out of sight. *Only You know the truth, Father. Why are all these awful things happening to me? Somehow give me a sign. Let me know what I should do. I really want to believe Tank. I love him. I thought he loved You. Surely, if he is a Christian as he says he is, he would never deliberately hurt someone like this. I'm begging You for guidance.*

Miss Priss stood eyeing her, her head cocked to one side.

Treva knelt, lifted the cat, and cradled her in her arms, stroking her soft fur. "You like him, too, don't you, Miss Priss? Even Groucho likes him. That has to be a good sign, doesn't it?"

The big cat purred and licked at her arm.

"That belly of yours is getting pretty big. Isn't it about time for you to have your babies?" With Groucho at her heels, Treva carried the cat into the kitchen and filled her dish with milk before setting her on the floor. Then, with a sigh of frustration, she poured herself a glass of the cold milk. Raising it into the air as if to make a toast, her eyes misting up again, she said, "Happy birthday, Treva. What started out to be one of the happiest days of your life has turned out to be one of the most terrifying."

"Miss Jordan."

Hurriedly wiping at her eyes with her sleeve, Treva turned toward the voice.

"All the carpeting is down if you'd like to come and take a look at it. My men and I are about to leave."

"Oh, fine. Thank you." She trudged up the stairs behind the man. The carpeting was finally down, the crowning jewel of the work she and Tank had labored over for the past few weeks, and he wasn't even there to see it.

❧

He showed up the next morning as promised, and though the strain was still there between them, they worked amicably, with neither bringing up the near disaster from the day before. He worked at tearing out some of the old cupboards in the kitchen while Treva ripped the wallpaper off the downstairs bedroom walls. Though they met in the kitchen for lunch, very little conversation passed between them.

When it came time for Tank to leave that afternoon, he paused in the doorway then turned to face her. "I don't know what to do, Treva. We can't go on like this. I'm miserable, and I get the feeling you are, too. Maybe I'm only a partner to you, someone to help you get this place ready to sell. But you're far more than that to me." His gaze fixed on her face, he approached her slowly, his hand extended. "I'll do whatever you want me to. Stay and help you, or leave and never come back. It's up to you, but I love you, and I can't stand the idea of your not trusting me."

Her heart raced. "I love you, too, Tank. That's what makes this so difficult. I can hardly stand it when you're away from me, and I can't wait to see you again. But then something happens, and the old doubts take over. And even though I want to, I'm afraid to trust you. I constantly ask God for wisdom and discernment, but so far"—she paused and lowered her face into her hands—"He's not answering."

"Could we ask Him together?"

She allowed him to take hold of her hand. It felt warm, comforting, and secure. "I guess so."

His grip tightened as he bowed his head and began to speak in a low voice. "Lord, help! We have a real problem here. Bad things are happening, and we don't know what to do or how to put a stop to them. Though we don't deserve it, You've promised never to leave us or forsake us, and You're our protector, Father. Our rock, our shield. Forgive us for our lack of faith. Show us Your presence, God. Answer our prayer. We ask these things in Your name. Amen."

An overwhelming love and sense of peace washed over Treva's heart. How could she even consider Tank would betray her? She lifted misty eyes and found him gazing at her lovingly.

"I love you, Treva. I've never said that to a woman before—never wanted to."

She threw herself into his open arms and pressed her head against his chest. "I love you, too, Tank. Can you forgive me for doubting you?"

"As I said before, there's nothing to forgive. If I had all the things happen to me that have happened to you, I would have felt exactly the same way." He lifted her face to his. "You're the light of my life, sweetheart. I think of you day and night."

"I feel the same way about you. I can hardly stand the hours we have to be apart, especially when I think of the dangers you're facing out there every night."

He lowered his lips to hers, his touch as light as a feather.

A thrill of pleasure rippled through her, leaving her breathless, caught up in a love she'd never expected to experience. For the first time she felt desirable. Her prince had finally come.

"Treva, I know a lot is going on in your life right now, but I have to let you know how I feel." He took both her hands in his and lifted them to his lips, his gaze locked with hers. "I've dated a number of women. Some of them didn't share my faith, I'm ashamed to say, and I'd almost given up on finding the right one. All the guys at the station tease me about being an eligible bachelor. But the day I met you at Chuck and Mindy's wedding, I knew you were something special. I'd hoped to get your phone number, but then your pastor came and told you Theodora had passed away, and I never got the chance. You can't believe how excited I was when I answered that house fire call and found you again." His finger trailed her cheek, coming to rest on her lips. "What I'm trying to say, and not doing a very good job of it, is that you're everything I've ever hoped to find in a woman. I feel—finally—God has answered my prayers and my search is over. I've found the girl of my dreams."

A wave of euphoria swept over her. "Oh, Tank, those words are so sweet. I've been saving myself for the man of God's choosing. I never expected Him to send me someone like you. You're—you're wonderful!"

"No, dearest, it's you who are wonderful. Sweet. Beautiful. Caring. I'm no poet, and words like this don't come easily for me, but I could think of dozens of words to describe you."

"I'm glad this is your night off. You've been working way too hard," she whispered. "We can spend the whole evening together."

" 'Fraid not, sweetie. That phone call I got this morning was Chad Morgan, one of the guys on my shift, asking me to work in his place tonight. I couldn't say no. His wife has gone into labor."

Disappointed, she gazed dreamily up into his eyes. "I will miss you."

He pulled her close, cradling the back of her head in his hand. "I'll figure out a way to make it up to you."

"Tank."

"Uh-huh?"

"Thank you for my birthday picnic, that beautiful birthday cake, and for rebuilding the observation platform. I know how hard you must have worked to get it ready."

A heavy sigh coursed through his body. "I wanted your birthday to be special. I guess it was kind of fouled up."

Reaching up to cup his face, she gave him an adoring smile. "It was special. You did it for me. That made it special."

"I didn't get a chance to give you your real birthday present."

Her eyes widened with surprise. "Real present? What do you mean?"

"I left it at my apartment. I'll bring it tomorrow." He glanced at his watch. "Oh, no. If I don't get out of here right now, I'm going to be late!" Giving her another quick kiss, he backed away. "Don't ever doubt my love, Treva, please."

She followed him to the door then waved as he drove away. *Thank You, Lord.*

When the phone rang fifteen minutes later, she snatched it up, hoping it was Tank.

"Hi, Treva. This is Mindy. I just wanted to see how things are going with your aunt's house. I heard about her death. I'm so sorry. I know how much you loved her."

Treva sat down on the couch and drew her legs up beneath her. "I've had quite a few problems, but let's not talk about them now. How was the honeymoon?"

"Divine. I know it sounds silly since we've been married for over fourteen years, but it was like falling in love all over again. Chuck was so sweet. We spent every minute together doing all sorts of fun things."

"Is Bethany getting along okay? How did she make it with the two of you gone?"

"She's doing amazingly well. Much better than any of the psychiatrists thought she would after being kidnapped and kept locked in that old shed." There was a slight pause. "Oh, Treva, I'm so thankful that man didn't—didn't—"

"I know. Only God could have protected her from that, since that dreadful man admitted that's what he'd planned to do."

"She misses you, Treva."

"I miss her, too. Maybe I can make a trip to Warren soon." Treva smiled as she gripped the phone tightly. "I have something to tell you. Tank LaFrenz has been helping me with the house. I–I'm falling in love with him."

"Oh, Treva! That's wonderful! I figured something like this would happen when you caught my bridal bouquet. You won't find a better man than Tank. Chuck thinks he's just about the greatest, and Tank loves the Lord."

"We'll see what happens. I've put it all in God's hands."

"Well, sweetie, I won't keep you. Just wanted to check on you. Try to come for a visit soon. Bring Tank with you. The two of you can stay at our house. We have those two extra rooms, you know. And Chuck will be glad to see you, too."

"I'd love that. Give Bethany a big hug for me."

"Will do. I'll be praying about you and Tank. Bye for now."

"Bye." How good it was to hear from her friend. Though Warren, Rhode Island, was only a few miles up the road, at this moment it seemed very far away.

It was nearly nine o'clock by the time she made a trip to the grocery store and prepared herself a light supper of grilled-cheese sandwiches and coleslaw. She cut a piece of leftover birthday cake, filled her coffee cup, and carried them out onto the porch. It was a beautiful summer evening, with not even the faintest hint of a breeze. She had to laugh when—with great effort—Miss Priss jumped up onto the porch railing and began preening herself. "You certainly look different from the way you did the day that woman dumped you out onto the road in front of my apartment house. Why didn't you tell me you were pregnant? Were you afraid I wouldn't want you either?"

Treva's breath caught as a car came down the road and turned into her driveway, and a man crawled out.

"Evening, Miss Jordan. I was out this way meeting with a client, and I happened to remember your aunt had an antique Hoosier cabinet in her kitchen. I always liked that old piece. I was wondering if you'd be interested in selling it?"

"No, Mr. Cordell, I'm not interested in selling it. I wouldn't think of parting with it. It was my aunt's favorite piece of furniture."

He gave her a pleasant smile. "Well, if you ever decide to sell it, I do hope you'll give me first chance at it. As I recall, it's a wonderful piece of antiquity."

Wishing he'd leave, she wrapped her arms about herself and faked a shudder.

"I really need to get back in the house."

A low rumble echoed through Groucho's chest. He lifted his head, sniffed the air, then barked several times.

"Looks like your dog is spooked," he said, jutting his chin forward as he peered out into the darkness.

Panic seized her, clutching her heart in its grip. Though she didn't like having Mr. Cordell appear on her doorstep uninvited, she was glad she wasn't alone. "What is it, boy? Is something out there?" But she only heard the stillness of the night and the beating of her own heart.

Carefully picking up her dish and cup, she moved slowly across the porch with Benson Cordell at her heels as Groucho continued to do a combination of growling and barking. Something, or someone, was out there.

Squinting against the darkness, she peered across the vast lawn toward the old barn. That's when she saw it!

Chapter 7

The form seemed to be floating in space as it moved slowly across the field toward the barn. A figure. A girl, maybe? And she was wearing pink! From that distance Treva couldn't tell for sure, but it looked very much like a girl. Whatever it was, it was wearing a pink blouse like the one Bethany had been wearing when they'd found her in that old shed out behind the barn!

Mr. Cordell leaned over the railing, his eyes wide, as he pointed toward the barn. "It's that ghost! Did you see it? It was wearing a pink blouse like that O'Connor girl had on when they found her! I told you this property was haunted. Now maybe you'll believe me!"

Her heart thundering against her chest, Treva stood transfixed, stunned by what she was seeing, her feet glued to the porch. She tried to cry out, but the words wouldn't come. *Lord, what is this? I don't believe in ghosts, but something is out there, and I'm afraid!*

Benson Cordell stepped into the yard, his eyes trained on whatever it was they were seeing. "Look—it's going toward the shed!"

Tank! I've got to call Tank! Willing her feet to move, she rushed into the house, her plate and cup crashing onto the porch floor, but she barely noticed.

"Tank!" she screamed into the phone when he answered. "I've seen it! Mr. Cordell saw it, too!"

"What? Take it easy, sweetheart! What did you see?"

She sucked in a deep breath. "The ghost! The one everyone has been talking about. It was in the field out by the barn! Even Groucho saw it!"

"Treva, you don't believe in ghosts. It had to be someone trying to scare you. I'm not far away. Don't let Cordell leave. I'll be right there."

"Hurry, Tank! Please! I need you!"

When he arrived minutes later, she was waiting at the door and trembling so hard she could barely twist the dead bolt to the OPEN position.

"Are you all right?" He pulled her into the safety of his arms and held her close. "I'm glad you called me." He turned toward the man seated in a chair. "Thanks for staying until I got here, Benson."

Mr. Cordell placed his coffee cup on the table and stood. "I saw it, too, Tank. It looked like that O'Connor girl. And this isn't the first time I've seen it."

"That's stupid. Bethany O'Connor is alive and well. Besides, there are no ghosts!"

Benson Cordell gestured toward Treva. "I'm not sure you'll be able to convince your friend of that. She and I both saw that ghost." He gave Treva a slight wave. "I'll be going now. Remember what I said about that Hoosier cabinet."

Treva waved back. "Thanks for staying, Mr. Cordell. I'm glad you were here."

As soon as the man was off the porch, Tank grabbed Treva's hand and led her to the sofa. "Now try to tell me exactly what happened."

Through quivering lips she told him all of it. "I know there is no such thing as ghosts, and I know it wasn't Bethany. She's safe at home in Warren with her parents—I talked to Mindy—but, Tank, what was it? I've never seen anything like it before. And don't say I imagined it, because I didn't. I saw it, Mr. Cordell saw it, and so did Groucho. Just like I've told you."

He sat down beside her and began stroking her hand. "Or you saw what someone wanted you to see. This thing has to have an explanation."

She snuggled up close to him, needing his strength. "There can be only one explanation. Someone wants me out of here. But why?"

"I don't know, sweetheart, but I will get to the bottom of this, one way or the other. I won't have you going through this."

He stayed with her as long as he could, forcing himself to leave when a call came through about a three-car accident in the downtown area. "I can take you to my mom's house."

"No, I can't, Tank. Don't you see? It'd be admitting I'm too frightened to stay here. If someone is trying to scare me off, I'd be playing right into his hands. I don't think he wants to harm me. He's had plenty of opportunities to do that. If he was going to hurt me, surely he would have done it before now."

"Here." He reached into a holster-type pocket on his belt and placed something in her hand. "Keep this with you at all times. It's pepper spray. Don't hesitate to use it if the need arises. And keep Groucho by your side. No one likes to tangle with a big dog."

She opened her hand and stared at the container.

"I have to go. Maybe you'd better go with me. I can't stand leaving you alone like this."

She hated for him to leave her, but she had to stay. Trying to steady her voice, she said, "I'll be fine. Go. The people involved in that accident need you, too."

Tank backed out the door slowly, closing it behind him. Treva twisted the dead bolt as once again fear clutched her heart and squeezed it. Though Groucho stayed by her side, Miss Priss was nowhere to be found. "She'll just have to stay outside all night," she told Groucho as the two made their way up the stairs. "I'm sure not going to open that door and call her."

What little of the night she slept, Treva held the container of pepper spray tightly in her hand.

Morning dawned cool and gray with the threat of rain from a cloud-filled sky. Treva stepped out onto the front porch and breathed in the fresh air, her gaze going toward the area where she'd seen the ghostlike figure. She shuddered and wrapped her arms about herself as a chill cooled her body. *Surely it wasn't my imagination, was it? Was I so tired and shaken by the railing giving way that my mind played tricks on me?*

She gave her head a shake. *No, I saw what I saw. I know I did! And Mr. Cordell saw the same thing.*

A bird soared gracefully through the air and landed on a scraggly bush by the mailbox, catching her attention. *I forgot to get the mail yesterday! Probably nothing there except junk mail, but I'd better get it out of there before the mailman comes.* She motioned toward Groucho. "Come on, boy."

She bent and picked a small bouquet of wildflowers as they walked along, lifting each one and gently taking a whiff of its sweet fragrance, remembering how beautiful Aunt TeeDee's flower beds had been before she became too sick and weak to look after them.

"Where do you suppose Miss Priss is, Groucho? I hope she isn't off some-where by herself having those babies." She gave him a quick pat then reached for the handle on the front of the mailbox.

"Aaghh!" she screamed out. "Miss Priss!"

The big cat was crammed into the mailbox with one of Treva's silk scarves wound tightly around her neck, her eyelids half closed, and she was gasping for breath.

Reaching into the box as gently as she could, Treva unwound the scarf from about Miss Priss's neck then tugged the cat from her place of imprisonment and held her close. "You poor baby! Who did this to you?"

In her heart she knew exactly who it was.

The same person or persons who were trying to frighten her.

"I have to get you to the vet." She was about to run back to the house to grab her purse and car keys when she spotted Tank's pickup coming down the road.

❧

"She's fine, but I'll bet those claws of hers gave fits to whoever put her in there," the veterinarian told them after he had examined Miss Priss. "Apparently the scarf wasn't wound tightly enough to completely cut off her supply of oxygen, but you'd better keep a close eye on her. She could give birth to her kittens any-time now." His brow furrowed. "I'm surprised you haven't had her spayed."

"Oh, I would have, and I plan to after she has this litter, but she was already pregnant when some woman dropped her off in front of my door. I considered taking her to the animal shelter, but she looked so pitiful I just couldn't."

The man stroked Miss Priss then lifted her toward Tank. "I hope you can find a home for her babies."

"I'm so glad you found her when you did," Tank told Treva as they climbed into his pickup. "She must have been scared out of her wits."

"I know just how she feels." Treva cuddled the cat to her breast, resting her cheek against Miss Priss's soft fur. "No telling how long she'd been there. I couldn't find her when I locked up last night."

Tank reached across and placed his hand on Treva's shoulder. "Look—I know you don't want to do it, but I'd feel much better if you'd stay nights at my mom's house. Please consider it."

"I can't, Tank. I have to be there. We've put way too much work into Aunt TeeDee's house to have someone come in during the night and trash it. If I'm not here, they'll have free rein. At least if I hear noises, I can call you and 9-1-1. I wouldn't want to go off and leave Miss Priss and Groucho, and I certainly wouldn't expect your mother to take them in, too."

He stared out the windshield, as if in deep thought, then let out a sigh. "I guess you're right. Someone does need to be in the house at night. If I wasn't working the late shift, I'd do it."

When they reached the house, Miss Priss leaped out of Treva's arms and ran to the porch, pressing herself against the screen door. Tank grabbed onto Treva's hand as she walked up the steps. "Just promise me you'll be careful."

He went upstairs to check out the new carpeting while Treva opened a can of Miss Priss's favorite cat food.

"Those guys did a great job, didn't they?" he asked when he came into the kitchen. "If we keep working the way we have, it won't be long before they can lay the carpet down here."

"I'm glad you talked me out of letting Mr. Cordell sell this place before we remodeled it. I know it's going to bring a much higher price once it's finished," she said with pride. "None of this could have happened if it hadn't been for you."

"And I could never have fallen in love with you if you hadn't stayed." He gave her a tender smile. "Do you get the feeling God's hand has been in all of this?"

She leaned against the doorframe, her face becoming somber. "Yes, not only because He brought the two of us together, but also for the way He has protected me through this turmoil."

"Well, I'm ready to get at it. How about you?" He tugged off his long-sleeved shirt. "It's hot in here. All I need is this T-shirt. Maybe we should open some windows."

She fanned her hand across her face. "Good idea. The weatherman said on last night's news that the temperature was going to be unseasonably high for the next few days." She moved to the refrigerator and pulled out the iced-tea pitcher then filled two tall glasses with ice before adding the tea. "Here—this'll help cool you off."

As he reached for the glass, she let out a gasp. "Where did you get those scratches?" she asked with a crisp edge to her voice.

He gave her a puzzled look. "Didn't I tell you? I got them at the care home the other night. I answered the 9-1-1 call when one of the residents had a panic attack and couldn't breathe. The EMTs were trying to give her oxygen, but she was in such a state she was fighting them. When I tried to help, she grabbed onto my arm and scratched me. Why?"

The innocent look on his face was almost more than she could bear.

He twisted his head to one side and stared at her. "Surely you don't think Miss Priss did this."

How should she answer? His excuse seemed valid enough.

Grabbing onto both her arms, he stared into her eyes. "I didn't put Miss Priss into that mailbox, Treva."

"I—I didn't say you did."

"But you thought it, right?" He backed off, pulled his cell phone from his pocket, and held it out to her. "Would you like to call Bill Shaffer, one of the EMTs, so you can ask him where I got these scratches? She scratched him, too."

Feeling terribly embarrassed even to admit she'd suspected him, Treva quickly shook her head. "No, of course not. I believe you."

He pulled her into his arms and held her close. "Look, babe, with everything that has happened to you, you have every right to question the source of these scratches."

She leaned her head on his shoulder. "Thank you for being so understanding. As you well know, I go a little berserk sometimes, over nothing." She gazed up into his kind face. "Can you forgive me?"

"Only if we kiss and make up." Slowly he lifted her face to his and claimed her lips.

"Wa–was the woman okay? The woman at the care home?" she asked, a little frazzled when they separated.

"Yeah, the nurse said she gets these anxiety attacks when her family doesn't come to see her. It's really sad."

"I know. I tried to visit with some of the lonely residents when I went to see Aunt TeeDee. I can't believe the way some people stick their loved ones into a care home and forget about them."

He snapped his fingers. "I almost forgot! I'll be right back."

Treva watched as he hurried out the front door, raced to his truck, and returned, closing the door behind him.

A broad grin covered his face as he handed her a thin, blue velvet box. "Happy birthday, sweetheart."

"Tank! You've already given me my birthday present!"

He placed the blue box in her hand. "Humor me, okay?"

Her heart soared as she lifted the lid. "A locket!"

"Bet you don't know what's inside."

"A picture of you?"

"Nope. Check it out."

Carefully slipping the tip of her fingernail into a small indentation, she snapped the locket open then threw back her head with a laugh. "Groucho and Miss Priss! Where did you get these pictures? Oh, Tank, I love it!"

He gave her a smug smile. "I took them with my digital camera one of those days when you were stripping off the upstairs wallpaper. Do you really like it?"

"I really like it."

"Do you like me?"

"I really like you, too."

"Then quit talking and let me kiss you."

～∂⌒～

The next week went smoothly with no more unusual happenings as Treva and Tank worked on the house's first floor. They attended church together on Sunday then had lunch with Tank's mother at her favorite restaurant.

"I'm so glad you came into my son's life," Mrs. LaFrenz told Treva as they walked slowly across the parking lot. "He's needed a woman in his life. I kept telling him he was too picky, but now I understand why. He was waiting for God's choice, and you finally arrived."

"I feel as if God did lead the two of us together. Your son is all I could ever ask for and more. You did a good job of raising him."

"Thank you. Though his father was a great role model, his job kept him away from home nights. He was a police officer, too, you know." Her voice took on a melancholy tone. "I spent many a night on my knees begging God to protect him. Be sure, Treva, if the two of you do become serious, you're ready to take a backseat to his job. He's as dedicated to his career as his father and is grandfather were. All three of them felt being in law enforcement was their alling from God. His brothers, too. I doubt that Tank could be truly happy if e weren't wearing that uniform."

Treva listened carefully to her words.

"Each day when a police officer leaves for work, his wife has to accept the ict that he may never return home or that he might sustain injuries that could npair him for life. Take it from me—it's not easy. When you marry a career oliceman, you marry not only him but also his job. It's a part of him."

"Hey, what are you two talking about?" Tank asked as he caught up with 1em after paying the bill.

His mother gave him a smile. "Just getting acquainted, son. That's all."

Treva couldn't get the woman's words out of her mind. She was already orried about Tank and the danger he was in each time he put on that uniform. Vhat if she were married to him and they had a family? Would she be able to ut her fears aside and accept his dangerous lifestyle?

"Look—I don't want any flack about this, but since I have the entire night ff, I'm trading places with you," he told her when it was time for him to leave. I doubt you've had a good night's sleep since you arrived. You're staying in my partment tonight, and I'm staying here."

"But—"

Grabbing onto her arm, he ushered her toward her room. "Mom came over o my place yesterday, changed the sheets, and picked up things, so my apart- 1ent looks pretty decent. Here are my keys, and I've drawn you a map to my lace. Now go get whatever you need, and I'll have breakfast ready in the morn- 1g when you come back."

"I can't do that. You need your sleep, too."

He pointed to the stairway. "Take Groucho with you, if you want. Miss 'riss and I will hold down the fort."

She climbed onto the first step and slipped her arms about his neck, leveling er gaze at him. "You're too good to me."

⁓

'ank waited patiently while she packed her overnight bag; then he walked her to er car, leaning into the open window to kiss her good-bye. "I'm glad Groucho is oing with you, but you are taking that pepper spray with you, too, aren't you?"

"It's in my bag. Maybe I should leave it here for you."

He smiled confidently. "I'm a cop, remember? I have a gun."

Tank watched until the taillights of her car disappeared, then, after parking is truck in the old shed, he headed back into the house, carrying Miss Priss 1 one arm. If someone was messing around the house, it might be best if they thought no one was at home. "Looks like it's just you and me, kid," he told th fidgeting cat. "Don't you go having those babies tonight. I'm no midwife."

After putting a fresh pot of coffee on to perk, he made the rounds of th house, checking to make sure each door and window was locked. Then, carryir a cup of coffee into the living room, he settled down on the sofa and used th remote to turn on the ten o'clock news.

He woke up an hour later, the TV still blaring, the remote in his hand, wit Miss Priss curled up in his lap. "We're a fine pair. Do you suppose Treva is fa asleep by now? I sure hope so. This has been a real strain on her."

After turning off the lights downstairs, he made his way up to the roor Treva now called hers since they'd started working on the lower floor. Befor crawling into bed, he turned out the lights, crossed to the window, and stare out toward the old barn. Had she actually seen someone out there, or had sh imagined it? Well, nothing was there now.

He shoved the gun between the mattress and box spring and climbed int bed. A couple of yawns later Tank turned over on his side, his arm sprawle across the pillow, and allowed sleep to overtake him, dreaming of sitting in th porch swing with his arm around Treva as they gazed at a full moon.

Suddenly he awoke with a start. *What's that? It sounds as if someone downstairs.*

He pulled the gun from beneath the mattress and made his way acros the new carpet. He was glad for the small amount of moonlight filtering i around the edge of the blinds that kept him from running into things in th dark. Moving halfway toward the door, he flattened himself against the wa and listened.

Nothing.

He was about to go back to bed, deciding the noise he'd heard was no mor than the wind blowing a branch against the side of the house, when he hear another noise. *Is someone coming up the stairs?*

Moving cautiously, he pressed himself along the wall and slipped behind th nearly closed door and waited. *Come on, fellow. I'm ready for you.* In the silenc of the old house, he heard one of the stairs creak, then another. Whoever wa out there was headed toward the room where he was, the room where Treva ha been sleeping since the carpet had been installed.

Tank bided his time, waiting for the intruder. The last thing he wanted t do was frighten the guy off by letting him know he was in the house, not Trev If he could catch this guy, maybe all this craziness would end.

His eyes narrowed as he crouched low, ready to spring the second the in truder entered the room.

Slowly the door opened.

Tank's heartbeat quickened as adrenaline rushed through his body.

In the dim light of the moon, he could see the figure of a man. With one mighty leap he grabbed him and threw him to the floor.

Chapter 8

D on't hurt me!" the man yelled out as Tank pinned him to the floor, straddling him and holding his gun against the man's back.

Tank shoved his gun back into his waistband and yanked off the man's ball cap. Even in the dim light of the moon, he recognized the face. "Zach Foster? What are you doing here?"

The man twisted his neck, stared up at Tank, and began to cry. "No one wuz spoozed ta be home," Zach answered, slurring his words.

"You're drunk!" Tank eased his hold, helped the man to his feet, then switched on the ceiling light. "Okay, Zach, stop your bawling, and tell me why you're here. I want the truth, and it had better be good."

"I din't wanna come, but sum guy said I'd git fifty bucks if I did."

Tank shoved the man into a chair and leaned over him, pointing his finger in his face. "Who said they'd pay you fifty dollars?"

Zach wiped his nose with his sleeve then gazed at Tank through bloodshot eyes. "Dunno. Called me on da phone. Said he'd leave half in my mailbox." The man paused long enough to hiccup then continued. "Wif a note and key."

"What else?" Tank asked, his patience wearing thin.

"Told me use key. Cum in house. Leave note on da bed in room at top of stairs. Dat's all."

"He left you a key to this house? In your mailbox?"

Zach nodded. "If I dun it, he wuz goin' leave th' udder half money in mailbox ta nite."

Tank stuck out his hand. "Give me the note and the key."

Zach handed him the key but not the note. "No. Hav ta put it on bed."

"I said, give me the note. You're in enough trouble already."

Reluctantly the man shoved his weathered hand into his pants pocket and pulled out a folded piece of paper.

Tank grabbed it from his hand, unfolded it, and stared at it. " 'Boo!' That's it? Boo?"

The man shrugged. "Dunno. Didn't read ut. The guy said he wuz playin' a joke on sum one."

Tank grabbed the man by his shirt lapels and rammed his body against the vall. "You'd better be telling me the truth, Zach. I've had about all of this I can ake."

Zach held up a flattened palm. "Ah swear, Tank. Thas it."

Tank pulled his cell phone from his pocket and called the station. "I caught Zach Foster breaking into the old Gunther place. Send someone to pick him up. He needs to spend a night or two in jail. I'd bring him in myself, but I'm vatching over the place for Mrs. Gunther's niece—" He paused. "She's staying n town tonight. Oh, and keep it quiet about my catching Zach in the act. I want vhoever sent him here to think he did what that guy told him to do."

Fifteen minutes later Tank stood in the open door, watching as the patrol car headed down the long drive and out onto the road. *Thank You, Lord, that Treva wasn't home when this happened. You must have put the idea in my mind for me to stay here tonight in her place.*

He raced back upstairs and pulled on his clothes, once again stuffing his gun nto his waistband, and headed his pickup across town to the run-down trailer park where Zach lived. As many times as he'd driven the old drunk home, he knew exactly where to find his dilapidated trailer house.

After parking about a block away, he wandered down the street, his cap pulled low on his brow, trying to appear as if he belonged there. He stood in he shelter of the low-hanging tree branches and scanned the area. Once he vas sure no one was watching, he casually walked up to the gang of mailboxes mounted on a long steel pole and located the one marked Zach Foster. Sure enough, just as Zach had said he'd been promised, two ten-dollar bills and one five were tucked inside. He was too late. Whoever had sent Zach to leave the note and scare Treva had already been there and gone. He gazed at the money. *Whoever left these here was probably smart enough to wear gloves. Coward! Not even brave enough to do his own dirty work.* If Zach didn't know who he was, since he'd only spoken to him on the phone, why did the guy leave the twenty-five dollars? He could have just left the first half, and Zach would have done the job. If he hadn't left the second half, Zach wouldn't know who to come after to claim it, and the guy would be twenty-five bucks ahead. Tank drew in a deep breath. *Unless the guy planned to use him for another project!* That's why he'd paid him off in full. He must have had another scare tactic in mind for the old drunk!

He slammed the lid with a vengeance. *I can't let Treva stay in that house by herself any longer. It's too risky.*

∽

Treva pulled into her yard at seven thirty the next morning and hurried into the house. After sticking her keys in her purse, she headed for the kitchen, where she found Tank sitting at the table. "I don't know when I've slept so soundly. I hope you had a good night."

He turned and stared at her, his face void of the smile she'd expected. "Pour yourself a cup of coffee then come over here. I have something to tell you."

For the next few minutes Treva sat staring at him, listening, a shiver of fear snaking down her spine, hardly able to believe what she was hearing. "Oh, Tank, what if I'd been here alone when he came in? The man was drunk! No telling what he would have done." When he scooted his chair close to her, she leaned into him and rested her head on his shoulder.

"God had to have intervened in this, honey. I wasn't supposed to be off last night, but Chad Morgan volunteered to work in my place. You remember him, the guy who asked me to work for him on my day off because his wife was in labor?"

She gave a slight nod.

"I made up my mind right then that I was going to insist you let me stay here in your place for at least one night so you could get a solid night's sleep without being afraid."

Treva raised her face to his. "I've already made up my mind, Tank. I'm through. I'm not spending another night in this house. I'm calling Mr. Cordell."

Tank grabbed her hands as she rose. "You're going to sell the house before we finish? After all the work we've done?"

She pulled her hands away and waved them in the air in frustration. "You have a better idea? From my vantage point I see no other option!"

"Look, sweetheart—your life's savings are wrapped up in this house. You've had a new roof put on, the upstairs is finished, the painters are coming today to paint the outside trim, we've torn the fixtures out of the downstairs bath, and we have most of the cabinets and appliances out of this kitchen. We're on the downhill now. The worst of the work is behind us. You can't quit now." He wrapped an arm tightly about her. "Just think what this property will bring if we can hang on for a few more weeks."

He was right. The way the house was now—with the main floor looking like a war zone—would turn off many of the home buyers she hoped to attract. "I know what you're saying is true, Tank, but I can't spend another night here."

Tank laid a restraining hand on her arm. "I think I have a solution."

"What?"

"I didn't want to tell you until I had things worked out, but one of the men on first shift has decided he wants to go back to college and get his degree in law enforcement. The only way he can do it is by moving to the late-night shift. He's asked me to change shifts with him. If I do it, I'll be able to stay here nights until the remodeling is completed, and you can sleep at my apartment."

She tilted her head a little, regarding him thoughtfully. "But you said you liked being on the late-night shift."

"I do, but moving to days wouldn't be so bad. I'd be—"

"Wouldn't he rather work the late-afternoon shift?"

Tank shook his head. "Nope. Two of the classes Jay has to take are only offered in the afternoon, and he'd have to be at work by three. It'd never work. He's already checked into it."

"But the fall college classes won't start for nearly six weeks."

"I know. I explained that if I changed with him I'd want to do it now, even before his classes started. He said he was so glad I was willing to take his shift, he was ready to trade anytime." Tank nodded his head toward the wall phone. "He's waiting for my call."

Though excited by his offer, she was also concerned. "I can't ask you to rearrange your life because of me."

Tank captured her face between his hands, kissing the tip of her nose. "I'm willing to rearrange it because of *us*, Treva. You and me—and the future I hope we'll have together."

Her gaze locked with his, a slight curl of amusement on her lips. "And so I can pay you the money I owe you?"

He gave her an impish grin that set her heart in motion. "You weren't planning to abscond with the proceeds, were you?"

She straightened the collar of his shirt then smoothed his hair. "The thought had crossed my mind. There's this sixty-thousand-dollar foreign sports car I've had my eye on."

He reared back with a laugh. "You? I've always had you pegged as more the minivan type."

His grin was pure masculine charm and made her feel like a queen. "You know me well."

"Not nearly as well as I'd like." Cautiously he lowered his mouth to hers.

"I—I want to know you better, too," she uttered when they parted.

His gaze skimmed her face. "So what's your answer? Do I tell him I'm ready to switch shifts?"

His offer was too good to resist. "Yes, tell him."

She busied herself by preparing a roast and then carrying it out onto the glassed-in back porch where they'd moved the range while the kitchen was being remodeled. By the time she came back into the room, Tank had already hung up the phone.

"That guy thanked me over and over for changing shifts with him. I tried to tell him we were the ones who were thankful, but I doubt he even heard me. All he could talk about was how excited he was about getting his degree. We decided to start tonight. He's going in at eleven in my place, and I'll be reporting to work at seven in the morning in his. It's really going to seem strange. I've been on that late shift since the day I finished my training."

"It's wonderful you were able to work it out so easily, Tank, but I still feel bad about your having to give up the late shift."

"Don't you worry your pretty little head about it. Keeping you safe is all that matters to me." He cupped his hand behind her head and pulled her face to his, planting a kiss on her cheek. "Now you'd better let me get busy, or we'll never get this house finished."

They worked until nearly eight o'clock then had a light supper of delicious sandwiches made from the roast beef left over from lunch.

"Have you seen Miss Priss lately?" Treva asked as she bent to fill the cat's dish.

Tank shook his head. "Not since about noon when she followed me out to the truck."

"She may be upstairs. She likes to curl up on that new carpet and take a nap. I hope she's all right. I thought for sure she'd have her babies before now."

"Well, don't worry about her. I'll check around outside before I go to bed." He raised a brow. "You'd better be headin' out of here. I have to take a shower and get to bed. Full day tomorrow."

She released a weary sigh. "You will be careful, won't you?"

"Hey, you're talking to a big, brave police officer. The bad guys run from us. I'll be fine." He gave her arm a gentle swat. "Now get out of here so I can get some z's."

"You're not going to have to tell me twice. I'm beat. I can't believe how many hours we worked today." She grabbed her overnight bag and headed toward the door.

Tank let out a big yawn as he stretched his arms wide. "I'll walk out with you and see if I can find Miss Priss. I don't want you worrying about her."

❧

Tank waited until Treva called to assure him she'd reached his apartment and was safely tucked inside before making sure the cat was in the house and heading upstairs.

After his shower he settled down under the quilt for a good night's rest. He'd only been asleep a few hours when he heard a loud meow coming from one of the other bedrooms.

"Go to sleep, Miss Priss!"

The cat meowed a second time, a strange drawn-out meow, not at all the way she usually sounded, and he became concerned. "Okay, I'm coming."

He checked the bedroom next to his, but she wasn't there. He checked the two bedrooms across the hall, but she wasn't there either. "Okay, lady. Come out, come out, wherever you are. I'm tired of playing this game."

The third meow sounded like a cry for help. He sprinted to the far end of the hall, to the fifth bedroom. There, tucked into the corner of the closet, was Miss Priss and four little babies.

"Well, aren't you something!" He squatted down and stroked the big cat's head. "Congratulations! You have yourself a fine-looking family."

Though it was the middle of the night, he couldn't wait to get to the phone and call Treva.

She answered on the first ring with a yawn. "What's wrong? Is someone trying to break into the house?"

Tank grinned into the phone. "Everything's fine, but I have some good news and some bad. Which do you want to hear first?"

"Umm, I guess the good news."

"Miss Priss is the proud mama of four little baby kittens."

He could almost see the joy on Treva's face.

"Oh, and I missed it! Is she all right? Is that the bad news?"

He snickered. "She's fine. The bad news is—she delivered her kittens on the new carpet in one of the upstairs bedroom closets. I think it may have to be replaced. You did say you were going to have her spayed, didn't you?"

"Yes. There are too many unwanted animals in this world already. I only hope we can find good homes for her babies. Can you handle Miss Priss and her family, or do I need to come back?"

"She's doing just fine. A perfect little mother. Don't worry about her. My neighbor's cat had kittens when I was a kid. I'm an old hand at this."

"Sure, you are! Tell her I'll see her in the morning, but if she needs me during the night, you have to promise to call me."

⤜⤛

Anxious to check on Miss Priss, Treva arrived earlier than usual the next morning. Though she knew she should get busy stripping the rest of the paper off the downstairs bedroom walls, she had a hard time keeping away from the doting new mama and her precious kittens.

Other than the inordinate amount of attention both Treva and Tank gave the new arrivals, the rest of the week went by without incident, their new arrangement working out better than either of them had anticipated. With Treva's staying in Tank's apartment at night and his staying at the house, she could work on her projects during the day while he was at work; then they worked together in the evenings. She enjoyed being with Miss Priss and watching the growth of her babies.

"I really like the way this bathroom is shaping up," she told Tank one evening as she stood in the doorway holding one of the kittens and watching him anchor the new towel bars to the wall.

He gave her a teasing wink. "I especially like the new wallpaper. You surprised me with your newfound talent. I thought you were teasing when you said you'd decided to wallpaper this bathroom by yourself, instead of waiting for the paperhangers."

"I only did it because I was so anxious to see how that pattern was going to look on the wall. Besides, the only part I had to do was the part above the wall tile. It really wasn't that hard. Not as hard as papering those bedrooms with their high ceilings." She stepped into the room to admire her work. "I was afraid maybe it was too bright, but I like it."

"You made the perfect choice." He took the last sip of coffee and handed her his empty cup then gave his fingers a loud snap. "I nearly forgot. I know you've been concerned about what you were going to do with Miss Priss's kittens. Mom called and said she would like to have one, and three of the ladies in her Bible study group would each like one when they're old enough to be taken away from Miss Priss, unless you have other plans for them."

Treva's face brightened. "This is wonderful news. I've been so afraid I wouldn't be able to find good homes for them, and I couldn't bear to have them put to sleep. I'll call her later."

"There's something else I've been meaning to tell you. My day off this week happens to fall on Saturday, Independence Day. Every year several of us policemen volunteer to work during the annual Bristol Fourth of July Celebration, patrolling it to make sure things don't get out of hand. It's a pretty big thing around here. This celebration has been going on in Bristol since 1785."

"I'm familiar with it. The singles' group from our church in Warren usually comes. I came with them last year. We had a great time. We were here for the parade, too."

"I thought I'd head over to Popasquash Road as soon as I get off Friday afternoon and help them barricade the area where the professional fireworks company will be setting up their night works displays. Then I plan to spend all day Saturday helping the other guys patrol the grounds."

She gave him a coy smile. "If you think you can take time off to eat, I might be persuaded to fix us a picnic supper. I'm sure we could find a place to spread out a quilt. I might even make that slaw you like so well."

He tilted his head and wiggled his brows, a mannerism that always made her laugh. "And some of your famous fried chicken?"

"Sounds good to me."

"With baked beans?"

She gave him a gentle nudge. "Don't push it. I said a picnic supper, not a feast."

He feigned a disappointed look, extending his lip in a pout.

She rolled her eyes. "Okay. Baked beans, too. And if you treat me right, I might even bake your favorite cake."

"You'd bake a carrot cake just for me? With cream cheese frosting?"

Treva offered him her most dazzling smile. "Only for you."

When the clock chimed ten, Tank led her to the door and kissed her good night. "I hate to rush you off," he told her as he stood in the doorway watching her go down the steps with Groucho at her heels. "But 7:00 a.m. comes early, and I have to get some shut-eye. Keep your doors locked, and call me when you get to my place. I want to know you made it okay."

She turned and gave him a flirtatious smile. "Yes, Mother."

∾⦾∾

Treva smiled Saturday afternoon as she closed the lid on the picnic basket Tank's mother had loaned her. "Sorry—you two have to stay home," she told Groucho and Miss Priss as she headed for the door. "You, Groucho, have to guard the house, and you, Miss Priss, have to take care of your babies."

When she reached the area on Popasquash Road, she parked the car then found a grassy place under a tree and spread out Aunt TeeDee's old nine-patch quilt, hoping Tank would be able to find her. She scanned the crowd but couldn't locate him.

"Well, hello, Miss Jordan."

She turned to find Benson Cordell standing beside the quilt, mopping his brow with his handkerchief. "Hello, Mr. Cordell."

"How is the house coming?"

"Things are going quite well, thank you."

He pulled off his sunglasses and stuck them into his shirt pocket. "I was going to phone you tomorrow. I have a new client, an out-of-town buyer, who is really anxious to buy a house in Bristol. Cash buyer. How about letting me show him your place? I'm sure I could get you a good price."

"No, Mr. Cordell. As I told you I don't want to put it on the market until I finish remodeling it, but thanks for thinking of me." *How many times do I have to tell you?*

"You might want to reconsider. He's driven by your property and is really taken with it. We could have the sale closed in a week, and you'd be on your way back to Warren with a tidy sum in your pocket. Cash buyers like this don't come around every day."

"If I change my mind, you'll be the first to know," she told him, trying to keep the agitation from her voice. "But I doubt you'll be hearing from me anytime soon."

The man shrugged then pulled his sunglasses from his pocket and waved them at her. "I sell more property in and around Bristol than any other broker. Listing with me means a sure sale."

"I can guess that's true. I'll keep you in mind."

She was relieved when he nodded and backed away. He was a nice man but like so many salesmen, way too pushy.

Suddenly and without warning, someone's hands slipped over her eyes, causing her to involuntarily flinch as she let out a gasp.

"Guess who!"

Her fear changed to laughter as she reached up and caressed familiar hands. "The handsome man who has allowed me to turn his life upside down?"

"Aw, how did you know?" Tank pulled his hands away and seated himself beside her. "I waved at you when you crossed the parking area, but you didn't see me. Was that Benson Cordell I saw walking away from you?"

She nodded. "He had some story about a cash buyer. I never know when to believe that man. How's it been going? Anyone causing you trouble?"

He lifted the picnic basket's lid and peered inside. "Not really. A bunch of teenagers got into a fight over some dumb thing, but we broke it up pretty quickly. A father locked his baby and his keys in his car, but I used a bent coat hanger and got it open for him. Other than curious people trying to wheedle their way into the danger zone, wanting to get an up close and personal view of the fireworks, it's been a nice, uneventful afternoon. But we're sure not letting our guard down. The way the crazies of this world are now, we have to be on our toes every minute. We don't want Bristol, Rhode Island, put on the map because of some catastrophe."

Smiling at his comment, Treva reached into the basket and pulled out two plates, cups, and silverware. "I don't suppose you're hungry."

"I'm starved!"

He helped her set out the platter of chicken, the bowls of slaw and baked beans, and the other things she'd brought.

She put out the container holding the carrot cake. "With the long hours you're working on the house, I should never have asked you to fix all this. Deli food would have been fine."

"Oh, you'd rather have deli food?"

"No, it's just—"

"You're somethin' else, Tank." She leaned across and kissed his cheek. "How can I ever thank God enough for being so good to me and sending you into my life? I am indeed blessed."

He grabbed hold of her hand and brought it to his cheek then cupped it to his face and kissed her palm. "I'm the one who is blessed, Treva. You're everything I could ever want. Thanks for letting me share your life."

After Tank thanked God for their food, they dug in, laughing their way through their meal as they enjoyed the fried chicken and other delicacies she'd made.

When the last morsel disappeared from his plate, Tank lay back on the quilt, his hands splayed across his stomach. "That was wonderful, but I am stuffed."

"I don't know why you should be." She poked her finger at his tummy. "You only had four pieces of chicken, humongous servings of everything else, and three pieces of carrot cake, not to mention the hard rolls, pickles, and potato chips you consumed."

He groaned. "Don't even talk about it, please. And to think I have to be back on patrol in five minutes so the other guys can have supper."

She grew serious. "Tank, please be careful. I couldn't bear it if anything happened to you. I worry about you."

He pulled himself up into a sitting position. "Better get used to it, sweetie. Your boyfriend is a cop. Danger is our business."

Tank's mother's warning popped into her mind. *When you marry a policeman, you marry his job, too.*

He stood, smoothed out his trousers, then bent and kissed her. "I'll meet you right here after the fireworks. Don't leave until I get here. Okay?"

She nodded. "Be—"

He put his finger across her lips to silence her. "Don't even say it. I'm always careful."

She watched him go. If only he could stay and watch the fireworks with her. After asking the lady on the blanket next to her to watch the quilt while she was gone, she carried the picnic basket to the car and transferred the things that needed to be kept cold to the ice chest in the trunk.

~

Tank took over the post at the edge of the area marked off by wide bands of yellow vinyl tape strung from pole to pole. It should have been obvious it was an off-limits area by the color of the tape alone, which just happened to have the words DANGER ZONE—KEEP OUT written across it in big bold letters. But still people ducked under it as if it meant everyone, except them, should stay away.

He constantly scanned the area for anything or anyone that looked suspi cious in any way. Rumors had been floating around town all week that there wa going to be trouble. *Probably only rumors some kids started to see how far they'd g* he told himself with a smile. *How many years has this Fourth of July celebratio been going on without a mishap? Why should this year be an exception, especially wit the amount of both firemen and police officers who are volunteering their time to kee things under control?*

"How goes it, Tank? Anything happening?"

Tank watched as one of the volunteer firemen walked toward him. "Naw, it been pretty quiet. Almost too quiet."

The man glanced at the darkening sky. "Showtime in fifteen minutes. Look like they planned the time just right." He ducked under the tape. "I'm going ou into the field and see if I can help with anything. See you later. Hold down th fort."

"Yeah. See ya." Tank narrowed his eyes, giving the area another thoroug once-over. He stiffened when someone set off a package of firecrackers in a area near the parking lot then checked his watch again. Five minutes to go. Af ter glancing toward the blastoff area, he pulled his cell phone from his belt an dialed Treva's cell phone number. "Hi, honey. I just called to say I love you."

"Hi, I miss you. How much longer before the fireworks start?"

How he loved the sound of her voice. He checked his watch again. "No quite two minutes by my watch. Well, I'd better hang up. Remember to stay righ there until I come for you."

"I will. I'll be thinking about you as the sky lights up with all those beautifu colors, wishing you were here with me."

"I'll be thinking about you, too. Less than one minute until blastoff. Bye."

As he placed the phone back in its holster his attention was drawn to a youn boy walking toward him with a box in his hands. "Go away. This is a restricte area," he told the boy gruffly, concerned for his safety. "You're not supposed to b here."

The boy ignored his warning and kept coming. "A man told me to give thi to you. He said you were waiting for it."

Tank frowned. "What man?"

The boy pointed across the field. "He was over there by those trees. He sai it was really important. That you'd be mad if I didn't give it to you."

The first rockets flew into the air, sending umbrellas of colorful sparks int the night sky as the crowd cheered.

Leaning toward him, Tank glared at the boy. "Get out of here *now*. You shouldn't be here. It's dangerous!"

The boy lowered the box onto the ground then ran back toward the trees as fast as he could, never looking back.

Suddenly the sky was filled with a zillion colors, and rockets sounded as the fireworks display officially began. Tank let his gaze wander heavenward for a moment, thinking about Treva and how she was watching the same display, then looked back down at the box. *I never asked anyone to bring anything to me.* He walked over to it and gave it a kick. It was heavy. Curious, he pulled his flashlight from his belt, crouched, and yanked open the lid.

Chapter 9

A loud *pop* sounded from inside as something excruciatingly hot struck his face. Instinctively he closed his eyes and tried to shield them with his hands as he fell backward onto the ground, unable to see. Pelts of heat began to pierce his face and body as explosions sounded all around him. He struggled to his feet, disoriented and not even sure which way to run. The pain was agonizing! Tank grabbed at the radio fastened to the epaulet on his shirt, screaming for help, the pain nearly unbearable. The noise from the crowd and the shrill whistles and explosions of fireworks were so loud he could barely hear his own voice.

Pain! I've got to get help—before—before I pass out!

∽◈◈∽

Treva leaned back on the quilt, bracing herself with her arms, and stared upward as breathtaking colors in every shade and hue danced across the sky. How she wished Tank could be there with her to enjoy it, but someone needed to keep the area secure; and Tank—good, dependable Tank—was always there when he was needed. She smiled as she visualized how handsome he looked in his uniform, his dark hair trimmed close, his hat low on his brow. What was it he'd said was their motto? *Oh, yes. To protect and serve. Well, that's exactly what he's doing tonight. Protecting and serving, while I'm here wishing he were by my side.*

She glanced around at the crowd. *I wonder if these people realize the firemen and police officers they see here are all volunteering their time, instead of enjoying the show with their families.*

Oohs and aahs sounded from the onlookers as rockets boomed and flashed, and another round of glorious colors filled the sky, this time in shades of green, blue, and yellow. Treva watched, in awe of its magnitude.

"Isn't this the most beautiful thing you've ever seen?" a young woman who looked to be in her early twenties asked her boyfriend as she snuggled up next to him.

Treva looked away quickly. *Oh, Tank, I miss you.*

"Treva, I'm so glad I found you!"

She turned at the sound of her name as Tank's friend and coworker knelt down on the quilt beside her. "Hi, Jay. Have you seen Tank?"

310

He grabbed onto her hand. The serious look on his face sent shards of terror ɔ her heart.

"There's been an accident. They've taken Tank to the hospital. He asked me ɔ find you and let you know."

She jumped to her feet, speaking almost incoherently. "What happened? ou have to tell me. I have to go to him!"

He reached out his hand. "I'll take you. Come on."

Clinging tightly to the man's hand as they wove their way through the rowd, she tried to ask more questions, but the noise from the fireworks and ιe applause of the crowd made it impossible to hear. Finally they reached the arking lot and his car.

"He's been pretty badly burned, especially on his face and hands. No one knows ow it happened. Fortunately he was able to radio for help. The EMT's ambulance ʾas parked no more than three or four hundred yards away, so they got to him right way," Jay explained as he maneuvered the car across the lot and onto the street.

Treva's hands trembled, and her heart felt as though it were being squeezed s she bowed her head in prayer. *Lord! Great Physician! Father! Be with Tank. Ɔon't let me lose him. Touch his body. Comfort him and protect him from pain. He's ʾours, God. Your child. I'm trusting in You. I have faith that You will bring him back ɔ me. Please, Lord! I love Him so!*

"We're nearly there. I'll let you out at the emergency room door. Someone ιere will help you. I'll park the car then come in. Is there anything I can do? ʌnyone I can call?"

"Tank's mother. She should know," she answered between sobs.

He gave her a frown. "Maybe she shouldn't be told until we know more ɓout his condition."

"She's his mother. She needs to be with him. Call her, please."

He nodded. "Better than that, I'll go by her house and bring her to the ᴏspital."

Tears flooding her eyes, she gave him a brief smile. "Thank you, Jay. I know ʾank will appreciate it."

Barely slowing down, Jay turned into the parking lot and brought the car to screeching halt in front of the big glass doors. "You going to be okay, or do you ʾant me to come in with you?"

She wiped her sleeve across her face, clearing her vision. "I'll be fine. Get ʌrs. LaFrenz."

Treva entered the emergency room, and a nurse approached her. "Tank ɑFrenz! He was just brought in. Where is he? I have to see him!" she screamed ʏsterically.

"Are you Treva?" the woman asked with a kindly smile, taking hold of h arm.

"Yes."

"He told me you'd be coming. I'm sorry. You can't see him right now. Th doctors are examining him, but the minute they're finished and give me the oka I'll take you to him." She led Treva to a chair in the waiting area, promising t check on Tank.

"Miss Jordan? I'm Captain Dillon, Tank's boss."

Treva blinked hard, trying to focus on the man who seated himself besid her. "Have you seen him? Do you know how he is?"

He took hold of her trembling hand. "No, I haven't seen him yet, but I'r sure they're doing everything for him they can."

"What happened? Jay said he was burned, but that's about all he knew."

"We're not sure what happened." He gave her hand a reassuring pat. "Tan radioed he needed help. It was hard to hear him with all the noise going on a the fireworks show. By the time someone reached him, he was staggering aroun with his hands covering his face and was badly burned. He wasn't close enoug to where the fireworks were being set off to have been injured there. We dor know how he was burned. Only Tank can tell us."

Treva leaned her head against the back of the chair, her heart poundin fiercely in her ears. "All he ever wanted to do was protect and serve."

"Tank is one of the finest police officers I know. He's a dedicated man jus like his father and his grandfather before him. They don't come any better tha Tank LaFrenz."

Treva swallowed a fresh supply of tears. "I know."

He gave her hand another pat then stood. "I have to make a phone call. Wi you be all right here by yourself?"

She nodded as a new wave of tears took over.

It seemed like an eternity until a man dressed in blue scrubs circled th receptionist's desk and headed toward her.

"Miss Jordan? I'm Dr. Smithson."

"How is he?" She rose quickly, fighting back the panic in her heart. *Lor please, let it be good news!*

"He has second-degree burns on his face, arms, and hands. But it's his eye I'm most concerned about at this point. I've—"

"His eyes?"

"Yes, I've called an ophthalmologist to come and take a look at him. H has quite a few burns to his upper body, but they're minor in comparison to th burns on his face and hands."

Terrified by his words, she grabbed onto the doctor's sleeve. "But he will be all right, won't he?"

"His injuries aren't life threatening. They should heal without causing him too much trouble, but he's going to be quite miserable for the next week or so, maybe longer."

She stared up into the man's face. "But he will be able to see again?"

"Let's wait until Dr. Mason has a chance to look at him. He's more qualified than I am to answer your questions."

"Did Tank say what happened? How he got burned?"

He gave his head a sad shake. "He keeps saying something about a box, but his pain is pretty intense, and his lips are in bad shape. It's difficult for him to speak."

Treva felt herself floundering for breath. "Can—can I see him?"

"Yes, but try to keep control of your emotions. He won't look much like himself. Keep a positive tone to your voice. Just talk to him—let him know you're there." He nodded toward the area from which he'd come. "Follow me."

As they walked, Treva sucked in several cleansing breaths, trying to brace herself for whatever might lie ahead. *Father God, thank You for sparing Tank's life. He is such a good man. Even now as we wait for the specialist to come, touch his eyes. Please don't let him lose his sight. I have faith that You will answer prayer. I'm calling upon Your promises. You are the Great Physician.*

They passed several curtained-off cubicles before Dr. Smithson opened one and motioned her to enter. The sight that greeted her made her sick to her stomach, and she felt faint. Tank's eyes were nothing but puffy, shiny blobs of crimson red. His eyebrows and lashes were gone, the hair at the edge of his forehead nearly nonexistent, and his lips looked like two thick hot dogs that had been left on the barbecue grill too long. This man didn't look a thing like the man she knew and loved. If it hadn't been for the charred trousers of the uniform he was still wearing, she might not have recognized him.

"Miss Jordan is here, Officer LaFrenz," the doctor told him.

Treva rubbed at her eyes. "Hi, sweetheart."

Tank gave his head a slight nod then mumbled something, which sounded like, "Glad you're here," but she could not be sure.

"Don't talk, honey. They've gone after your mother. She should be here anytime." Not sure what else to say, she continued to stare at him, fingering the locket at her neck. "I'm praying for you."

The doctor nodded in Tank's direction and gave her a smile, as if directing her to continue speaking to him.

Carefully reaching out and finding an area on his arm that appeared free of burns, she touched her fingertips to the spot. "I love you, Tank."

She nearly burst into tears when he slowly lifted his elbow as if to let her know he heard her and whispered, "Love you, too."

Both she and the doctor turned when the curtain opened and Mrs. LaFrenz rushed to Tank's side.

"My baby! How are you?" The woman, whose face was already red from crying, looked as if she was going to faint.

"Hi, Mom," Tank said in an almost whisper, barely moving his lips.

Treva could only imagine how it felt for her to see her son lying in a hospital bed with such serious injuries. She touched Mrs. LaFrenz's arm and put her finger to her lips, hoping she would understand they shouldn't upset Tank. "I'm glad you're here," she inserted quickly, trying to sound upbeat. "I told Tank they'd gone after you."

Mrs. LaFrenz closed her eyes tightly, drew in a deep breath, then said almost calmly, "Thank you for sending Jay for me."

Treva pointed to the area on Tank's arm where she'd put her fingertips and motioned for his mother to do the same thing.

Looking relieved, Mrs. LaFrenz touched the spot and smiled. "I've been praying for you, son. I know Treva is praying for you, too. God is able, Tank. Don't ever forget that. He can heal you completely."

Tank lifted his elbow again. "Keep praying," he struggled to say.

"I'm sure he's glad to have you here, Mrs. LaFrenz," Treva told her, smiling through her tears.

The curtains parted again, and a man who introduced himself as Dr. Mason stepped inside, eyeing first Tank, then Dr. Smithson, then Treva, and Mrs. LaFrenz. "I'm sorry, but I'm going to have to ask you to move out into the waiting room. I want to have a look at our patient."

⟳

The two women sat huddled in the waiting room, their hands locked together, their hearts joined in prayer. Several minutes later Captain Dillon hurried to their side. From the look on his face, it was obvious he had something to tell them.

"Tank told the EMT, the first person on the scene after he was injured, about a boy bringing him a big box of fireworks. He said it exploded in his face."

Treva's eyes widened. "A boy caused Tank's injuries? But why?"

"Apparently he didn't do it deliberately. Seems some man gave him a ten-dollar bill to deliver that box to Tank, saying Tank was waiting for it. When the boy saw the explosion go off, injuring Tank, he ran to a nearby police officer and told him what had happened. I guess the poor kid was crying hysterically, afraid he was going to spend the rest of his life in prison because he'd had a part in

Tank's injuries. He gave us a description of the man. It wasn't detailed enough to do us much good, but we're working on it. I thought you'd want to know. I'll keep you posted when we learn anything else. Believe me, Treva—we'll find the person responsible for this."

She thanked the captain for letting her know what they'd learned then turned back to Mrs. LaFrenz. "Tank's going to be all right. He has to be."

Finally Dr. Mason appeared again.

"Officer LaFrenz is a lucky man. His eyelids took most of the damage. At this point I doubt his vision will be impaired. We'll keep a close watch on him for the next twenty-four hours, but I'm quite hopeful. The two of you should be, too. I'll look in on him again before I leave the hospital, and I'll be back early in the morning."

With grateful hearts Treva and Tank's mother thanked him then wrapped their arms around each other, praising God and thanking Him for answered prayer.

As soon as Tank was moved to a regular room, they were allowed to stay with him.

Treva had to touch him. There was something comforting about being able to feel the warmth of his skin. Carefully she placed her hand over his ankle and gave it a squeeze. Tank responded by whispering, "Stay. Need you." Her heart soared.

"Tank, I know you don't feel like talking, but I have to know. Did you know the boy who brought you the box?"

A faint "no" came from an open corner of his mouth.

Treva's heart sank. *Is Tank's relationship with me the reason someone did this to him? What other reason could there be?* She had to know. "Do you think this has anything to do with me or my house?"

He moaned in pain then answered carefully, "Don't know."

Afraid she might be upsetting him with her questions, she changed the subject, trying for something more cheerful. They could talk about his accident later. "Do you know I love you?"

"Love you—too."

She smiled toward Mrs. LaFrenz. "Your son is one sweet guy."

Mrs. LaFrenz began to cry. "I know. He's just like his father."

"We'd better let you get some rest, dearest," Treva told him, needing to get out of the room where she could have a good cry unobserved. "I'll be back to check on you soon."

"You're not going to stay in that house tonight, are you?" his mother asked with concern as they stepped out into the hall.

"No, Groucho will have to take care of things by himself tonight. I'm staying right here with Tank." She slipped her hand into the crook of Mrs. LaFrenz's arm while they walked toward the lobby. "The nurse said they were giving him something to help him sleep. It's late. Why don't you go on home and come back in the morning?"

"I hate to leave him."

Treva forced herself to smile. "I know, but there's nothing we can do for him tonight. He's going to need both of us until his burns, especially his eyelids, heal and he's able to see again. I'll ask the receptionist to call a taxi for you." She gave the woman a nudge. "It's what Tank would want you to do."

Mrs. LaFrenz stared at her for a moment as if contemplating her decision. "All right, if you promise to try to get some sleep yourself. I know this has been hard on you, too. My boy loves you."

"I love him, too, Mrs. LaFrenz. We both feel God brought us together. With all the trouble I've had since I came to Bristol to remodel my aunt's house, I can't imagine what I would have done without him."

"Since Tank was a little boy, I've asked God to lead him to his life's mate. I'd about given up. Then Tank came to see me, all excited about a woman he'd met when he answered a call to a house fire. That very day I asked God if this was the woman I'd prayed for. The minute I met you and saw the look of love in both yours and my son's eyes, I knew my prayers had been answered."

Too choked up by his mother's words to speak, Treva simply kissed her on the cheek then gave her a hug.

Treva waited inside the big glass doors until the taxi pulled out of the parking lot then headed quickly for Tank's room, happy to find he was sleeping soundly. She sat down in the chair, lovingly watching the rise and fall of his chest and listening to the rhythmic sounds of his breathing.

Feeling a bit chilly, she looked around the room and located a folded blanket on the upper shelf in the closet. She wrapped herself in it and snuggled down into the chair, folding her legs up close. *Oh, no! I forgot to get Aunt TeeDee's quilt! It's probably still out there on the ground under the tree, and my car is in the parking lot! Too late to do anything about it tonight. I'll take care of them tomorrow.*

~∾~

By the time Dr. Mason came in the next morning, Tank was sitting partway up in bed, and the nurse was helping him drink juice through a straw.

Treva sat quietly while the doctor examined Tank's eyes, praying for a good report. She could tell by the way Tank's leg and feet muscles tightened and relaxed each time the doctor pried open his eyes that he was in terrible pain. She had to turn her head away to keep from bawling out loud.

"Tank," the doctor said, finally backing away, "God must have been protecting you. I can't believe, with all the burns you sustained, your eyes weren't damaged. Oh, they'll be red and watery for a few days, but that will soon go away. My main concern now is your eyelids. They took the brunt of your burns, but they should heal pretty quickly. Just make sure you don't rub them, even in your sleep. We'll let Dr. Smithson tend to those. As far as I'm concerned, there's no need for me to see you again. Time and rest are the best prescriptions I can recommend for you." He gave Treva a knowing smile. "That, and the company of this pretty young lady sitting in the chair by your bed."

Treva thanked him on behalf of both of them then bent and kissed the top of Tank's head. "This young lady loves you, Mr. LaFrenz."

"Love you, too."

"You'd better love me, too, 'cause you're going to have a hard time getting rid of me. I'm here for the duration."

She excused herself when his mother arrived, saying she wanted to go freshen up and have breakfast, but breakfast wasn't what was on her mind. She wanted to locate the hospital chapel where she could be alone with God.

She stayed at the hospital all day and, despite his protests, stayed with Tank again that night, sleeping cramped up in the chair.

When she awoke the next morning, she let out a loud gasp. Some of the swelling seemed to be gone, and Tank was staring at her through two tiny slits!

"You can see me?" she asked him, joyfulness knotting itself in her throat.

"You're beautiful."

"You're a flatterer." She wanted so much to hug him but knew it would hurt him, so she settled for squeezing his ankle. Then, propping her hands on the bed, she leaned in close to his face and peered through the tiny slits. "I can actually see your eyes! Your beautiful brown eyes!" She reared back slightly with a laugh. "Of course they're more red than brown right now."

"Must look funny."

"Yes, I'm afraid you do. Did you know there's an article in today's paper about your accident?"

"Not accident."

"No, according to Captain Dillon, it wasn't." The thought made her heart beat wildly against her chest. "You really think someone intended to hurt you?"

"Yes."

"Well, good morning." Dr. Smithson came into the room, followed by a nurse. "Let's have a look at those burns."

Treva backed away from the bed and stood silently watching as the doctor checked out each area on Tank's upper body. When he finished, he made a few notes on the chart then handed it back to the nurse. "I spoke with Dr. Mason. He gave you a good report. Apparently there was very little damage done to your eyes. You can thank your eyelids for that. I know your lips are quite painful, but the swelling seems to be going down some. You'll need to keep salve on them at all times since that surface skin will begin peeling soon." He released a small chuckle. "I understand you're a handsome man, but for the next week or two I'm afraid you're going to look like an escapee from a horror movie. Until that skin replenishes itself, you may not want to venture far from home."

He lifted Tank's hand carefully. "This hand may take a little longer to heal. We'll need to keep a watch on it, to make sure no infection sets in. You must have used it to protect your face. It seems to have gotten the worst of it. I hope you're right-handed."

"He is," Treva said quietly.

"That's good. He'll have difficulty using his left hand for a few weeks." He nodded toward the nurse. "I think we can release Officer LaFrenz today, if he wants to go home."

"Yes, go home."

The doctor went over a few procedures with them, reminded Tank he needed to see him in his office in two days, then signed his release. He'd barely left the room when another of Tank's police officer friends came bolting through the door.

"Hey, buddy, I'd tell you you're lookin' good, but you look awful!"

Tank lifted his right hand and gave the man a slight wave.

"The doctor said he could go home today." Treva smiled and extended her hand. "I'm Treva Jordan. You must be Reece Donavan."

"How'd you know?"

"Tank said you had red hair."

"Tank told me about you, too. Said the reason he changed shifts was so he could spend the nights at your house. I heard you've had some trouble out there. Tank told me someone sent that old drunk out there with some kind of note he was supposed to leave on your bed."

A chill ran down Treva's spine at the mention of that awful night. "Yes, I'm afraid so. Tank refused to let me stay in the house alone at night, so I've been staying at his apartment while he stays at my place. He thought he could defend himself better than I could."

"How are you going to handle it now, old buddy? You can't defend yourself, and you sure can't protect Treva." Reece studied Tank's face thoughtfully then turned to Treva. "But I have an idea. Since I'm on the day shift, too, why don't you continue to stay at Tank's apartment as you've been doing, and I'll go out to the house and bunk in with him at night. I can keep an eye on him." He gave her a wink. "I don't have anyone to go home to anyway, bachelor that I am. Besides, I owe this guy. He's done a bunch of neat stuff for me."

"Oh, that's very nice of you, but—"

Tank raised his hand slightly. "Let him."

"Good." Reece gave his fingers a snap. "I'll be out there by nine o'clock tonight."

Treva grabbed onto Reece's arm. "That's asking too—"

"Hey, that's what buds are for. We help each other. That reminds me. How were you and Tank going to get home? Didn't someone bring you here the other night?"

"His truck and my car are still at the fairgrounds. I was going to call for a taxi."

"No way! If you two don't mind riding home in the squad car, I'll take you. I'm sure the captain won't mind. One of the guys and I can go get your vehicles later."

"Oh, thank you. That would be great. And I'd really appreciate it if you looked around the grounds for the quilt I'd taken for us to sit on. I left in such a hurry that I forgot all about it."

∽✑✑

Groucho greeted Treva as she opened the door. She gave his head a pat then stood back out of the way while Reece helped Tank across the porch.

"Look at the walls!" Tank called out through tender lips.

Chapter 10

Treva and Reece spun around to see what Tank was talking about. There, sprawled across their newly sanded and finished living room walls, painted in big, bold, sloppy letters, were the words: GO HOME. NO ONE WANTS YOU HERE.

"Who would do something like that?" Reece asked as he assisted Tank to the sofa. "And why? Look—it's on the hall wall, too, and paint is spattered all over the floor."

"I have no idea." Treva sank down on the sofa beside Tank, her head in her hands, her body shaking with grief. "Will this ever end? Why is someone doing this to me?"

"Someone crazy," Tank added.

Reece ran his hand over the wall and gave his head a shake. "Looks like whoever it is really wants to get rid of you. You sure you don't have any idea who it could be? Maybe someone from your past?"

She lifted her face and dabbed at her eyes with her sleeve. "Reece, I know this sounds crazy, but I haven't a clue."

"You want me to help you clean this up?"

"No, you need to get back to work. I'll handle it. Thank you for bringing us home."

"Okay, if you say so, but call me if you change your mind." He shrugged then headed for the door. "See you about nine."

"Thanks." Tank peered through the narrow slits and tried to force his eyelids wider, flinching with pain. He felt helpless and totally useless—less than half a man.

Groucho meandered into the room and sat down in front of him, his head cocked to one side, his eyes trained on his face.

"Don't recognize me, fella?" he asked the dog through cracked and drying lips.

"Of course he recognizes you. He's your number one fan—next to me!" Treva leaned forward and stroked Groucho's head. "Who did this to the house, boy? You must have seen them. If only you could tell us. Did you growl at them? Try to scare them off? Did they try to hurt you?"

Tank reached out his good hand and ruffled Groucho's fur. "Good dog."

She gazed up at Tank with misty eyes, her face contorted with concern. "I'm so sorry, Tank, so sorry. It's my fault this has happened to you. If whoever is doing this wanted to hurt somebody, they should have hurt me, not you."

"In this together." How he loved her. He'd wanted so much to spare her from this trouble and turmoil. Perhaps things would have been better if he'd kept out of her business. But, no, he had encouraged her to stay and remodel the old house. Hadn't Benson Cordell told her he could find a buyer and get her a fair price? But because he hadn't wanted to see her move back to Warren, he had gone out of his way to talk her into staying.

"I've made up my mind, Tank. When you're feeling better, I'm going to put this house on the market, unfinished." She gently cupped her fingers around his bandaged hand. "I don't care whether I make a dime on it or lose money. I must have been terribly greedy to think I could sell this old place for a huge profit."

If only he could take her in his arms and kiss her worries away. "If you want to sell—I want, too." He leaned back against the sofa's soft cushions, his forehead furrowed in a scowl. "Think these lips will ever heal?"

Treva scooted closer and stroked his hand. "Of course they will. You just have to give them time."

"Benson wants you to sell."

A slight frown creased her forehead. "I may not list with him. He's okay, I guess, and I know he's sold a lot of homes. But his breath smells like stale cigar smoke, and I don't like his pushy ways. I might list with someone else. Maybe with that woman who advertises in the Sunday paper."

"Good idea." Ignoring the pain, he slipped his bandaged hand around her shoulder, drawing her close, pleased when she smiled up at him.

"No telling what might have happened to me if you hadn't been watching over me."

He closed his eyes and released a pent-up sigh. "Can't even protect myself."

"Patience, my love." She rose and gave him a smile. "Try to take a short nap while I fix us some lunch."

Treva stayed by Tank's side the rest of the day, laughing and chatting as if everything were fine. He knew it was all for his benefit that she was trying to cheer him up, but inwardly he knew she was as frightened as he was. *How can we fight her enemies when we don't even know who they are?*

～❧～

"Wow! You look beautiful!" Tank told her the following Sunday morning when she arrived at the house.

"I thought if you felt like staying by yourself for a couple of hours, I'd go to church with your mom."

He forced a slight grin, hoping she wouldn't realize how lousy he really felt. "Wish I could go with you."

She sat down on the sofa beside him and lovingly touched his cheek with her fingertips. "How did you and Reece get along last night?"

"Went to bed early. Was on the phone with girlfriend when I dozed off."

"Were you able to sleep?"

"Had hard time getting comfortable. Finally took a pain pill."

"No problems though? No noises? Fires? Ghosts? Anything like that?"

"Just Reece's snoring."

"Well, I'd better hurry and get you some breakfast if I'm going to make it to church on time." She started to stand, but he shook his head.

"Reece fixed oatmeal."

"Okay. Anything you need before I leave?"

"If lips didn't hurt, I'd ask for kiss."

"You think a little thing like that is going to stop me?" She gave him a teasing smile then playfully eased her face toward his until her lips met his softly. "I'll miss you."

As he drank in her sweet, powdery fragrance, it was all he could do to keep from pulling her to him, but just the least little movement reminded him he still had some healing to do. "Hurry home."

Mrs. LaFrenz was already seated when Treva entered the sanctuary. It seemed as though the pastor had prepared his message with her in mind as he spoke of unforeseen troubles in our lives and how we should lean on the Lord, trusting Him and His care.

Mrs. LaFrenz latched onto Treva's arm when the service ended. "Come with me, Treva. I want you to meet some of my friends." Two ladies approached as she ushered her out into the Welcome Center.

"This has to be Treva," a petite, gray-haired lady said, hurrying toward them. "You're as pretty as I expected you'd be. By the way I'm Norma Bush."

Treva felt her cheeks grow warm. "Hello, Mrs. Bush."

"And I'm Helen Philson." The second lady, a few years younger than the first, gave her a friendly smile. "I heard about the fires at your house. Aren't you afraid to stay out there by yourself? I'd be terrified."

"I stayed there the first few nights, but since then I've been staying at Tank's apartment while he stays at my place. But I do worry about him being there. Because of all the trouble, I've decided to stop the remodeling and sell my house as is." It hurt her to say the words.

"Well, I can't say I blame you. Does this mean you'll be moving back to Varren?"

"I don't think Treva has had a chance to think that through yet," Mrs. LaFrenz said, giving Treva a wink. "We'd like to see her stay in Bristol."

"It was nice to meet you ladies, but I'd better be going. I told Tank I'd be back as soon as possible." She turned to Mrs. LaFrenz. "Are you coming out to the house for lunch?"

The woman shook her head as she gestured toward her friends. "I promised I'd have lunch with them, but I'll be out later."

Tank was still on the sofa when Treva got back home, looking forlorn and dejected. "You've been gone too long."

She kicked off her shoes then bent and kissed the top of his head. "The service ran long. Your mom is having lunch with her friends. She said to tell you she'd be over later."

"Doesn't have to come. I'm doing okay."

Treva touched the tip of his nose. "She's your mother, Tank. Mothers worry about their children—no matter what their ages. Are you hungry?"

The doorbell rang before he could answer. Treva hurried to see who was there.

"Hello, Miss Jordan. I brought the papers." Benson Cordell stood grinning at her, his beady eyes crinkling at the corners.

She narrowed her eyes and stared at him, not at all sure what he meant. "You have me at a loss, Mr. Cordell. I don't know what you're talking about."

"The listing papers. We'll need them filled out before I can show your house."

Tank struggled to his feet and joined her at the door. "Treva didn't call you."

She protectively slipped an arm about his waist. "Tank, you shouldn't be up."

Mr. Cordell leaned closer to the screen door. "It's nice to see you, Tank. I heard you had quite an accident."

Tank ignored the man's statement. "Why you here, Benson?"

"Like I said, to get these papers filled out."

"How did you know I'd decided to sell?"

"My secretary goes to your church. She overheard you talking about it this morning and called me."

Treva rolled her eyes. "I'm sorry, Mr. Cordell. It's true. I have decided to sell my home, but I'm not going to list it with you. I'm going to list it with someone else."

He grabbed the screen door handle and gave it a sharp tug, but the lock held. "You can't sign with someone else! I told you when you first got here I wanted to sell your house. I have buyers who are interested in it! You can't do this to me!"

"Not doing anything to you!" Tank said angrily. "Treva's house. Can do any thing she wants."

"I have to have this listing. I'm the best real estate salesman in Rhode Island."

Treva stepped in front of Tank. He didn't need to be involved in this. Not after what he had just gone through. "This is my house and my decision, Mr. Cordell. Look—I'm sorry. I know you had your heart set on selling my house, but I've made my decision. Now, if you'll excuse me, we were about to have lunch."

"But, I—"

"I'm sorry, Mr. Cordell." Treva forced a smile and closed the door.

"What's with him?" Tank took hold of her arm as they walked slowly back to the sofa. "Face was so red—thought he was going to explode."

"I kind of feel sorry for him. I guess he does have a reputation to maintain. Maybe I should have listed it with him. If he does have a list of qualified buyers, he might have been able to sell it for top dollar."

"Up to you, but if you don't like him, why list with him?"

"You're right. It is my decision." She watched as he carefully lowered himself onto the sofa then struggled to get comfortable. "Speaking of decisions—have you decided if you'd prefer to eat in the kitchen or would you like me to fix us trays?"

He gave her a boyish smile. "Trays."

"Good. That was my choice. You sit right there, and I'll—"

They both turned as someone pounded on the door.

Treva gave her head a disgusted shake. "Surely not." She moved quickly to the door and peered through the lace curtain. "Yep, it's him. Can you believe the gall of that man?"

"Don't have to open the door."

"I know, but I'm a softie. At least the screen door is locked. He can't come bolting in." She twisted the knob and threw open the door.

"I've been thinking about what you said," Mr. Cordell began without even saying hello. "I know you're anxious to get out of here, and whether I list your house or someone else does, you'll have to have an appraisal, and we'll still have to bring our buyers out here to look at the place. Then there is the negotiating of the contract and setting up the financing and doing the closing."

Treva gave him a questioning frown. "Isn't that the way property sales are usually handled?"

His reddened face took on a sly smile. "Not if you do business with me. I'm prepared to make you an offer right now. A cash offer!" He grabbed the door handle. "Let me in so we can discuss it."

Treva turned quickly toward Tank, hoping for direction, but all he did was shrug his shoulders.

"I'm prepared to make you an offer you won't be able to refuse," Mr. Cordell went on without missing a beat. "You'll be sorry if you don't hear me out." He tugged on the handle.

"You'll have to make it quick, Mr. Cordell. We were about to have lunch." She unlocked the screen and pushed it open.

He rushed past her and, placing his briefcase on the end of the sofa, pulled out a contract, nearly shoving it in her face. "Look right here. This isn't a listing form. It's a bona fide contract. I've decided to buy your place myself. I'm making you a very generous offer, and I'll take the property as is. All you have to do is take the money and go. You'll never get a better offer than this—and for cash."

Treva stared at the figure. Though it wasn't as much as she had expected to get out of it if they'd had a chance to finish the remodeling and add the carpet and new appliances, it was—as he'd said—a very generous offer. It, by far, compensated them for the work and expense they'd already put in, plus a healthy profit.

"Just sign your name there." He pointed to the place. "I'll have my bank draw up a cashier's check first thing in the morning."

"I—I don't know, Mr. Cordell. Your offer has come as a complete surprise. Why don't you leave the contract with me? I'll read it over and get back to you."

He pulled the cap off his pen and thrust it at her. "If you're as smart as I think you are, you'll sign this contract now. I don't make an offer like this often."

Treva stared at the paper. It would be weeks before Tank could help her again. There was no way she could finish the remodeling by herself, and she certainly didn't have the money to pay someone else to come in and do it. Maybe she should go ahead and sign. Selling the place for the amount Benson Cordell was offering would be the simplest way out. "If I sign, you'll have the cashier's check made out tomorrow for the entire amount?"

"Absolutely—it's written right there in the contract. Cash amount due within twenty-four hours of your signature."

Treva scanned the simply written contract then poised her pen over it thoughtfully. *Lord, am I doing the right thing? Should I sign?*

"I'll even give you two weeks to vacate the premises," he added, as if putting a little frosting on the cake.

She sent a quick glance toward Tank.

He gave her a subtle frown. "Better wait a day or two, think this over, before signing."

Mr. Cordell grabbed her arm, his eyes narrowed. "You'd better sign now, or

I might withdraw my offer."

Tank gave a snort. "Doubt it, but decision's Treva's, not mine."

She handed back his pen. "Tank is right. I do need some time to think th over. If you decide to withdraw your offer, I'll simply go with my original pla and list it with the other company."

He held up his palm between them and refused to take back his pen. "A you've said, Miss Jordan, this is your property, not Tank's. You'd be foolish refuse my offer. I suggest you go ahead and sign this contract right now and g rid of this albatross."

Tank struggled to his feet and pointed toward the door. "I suggest yo leave."

Frustration clearly showing on his face, Benson Cordell moved closer t Treva. "Are you going to let that man ruin the best offer you'll get on thi place?"

Treva forced herself around him and opened the door. "Thank you for com ing, Mr. Cordell. I will give your offer my consideration and get back to you."

He moved across the room with a huff. "I think you—"

"No more discussion." She pushed open the screen door. "Good-bye, M Cordell."

He stepped out the door then, his face redder than ever, spun around, an reached for the door handle, but he was too late. Treva had already pulled th screen door shut and flipped the lock. "You will call me when—"

"Yes, if I decide to accept your offer, I'll call you." She closed the door quickl cutting him off before he could respond.

"*That,*" Tank said, emphasizing the word, "is one pushy salesman."

Her hand on her hip, Treva rubbed at her temple with the other. "Is he alway this pushy?"

Tank nodded. " 'Fraid so. He has a reputation around town, but his pushines pays off. Sells more property than anyone."

"Tell me about it! I feel as if I have the scars to prove it."

He gave her a shy grin. "Let's eat."

~❧~

Tank sat on the sofa the next morning, going through the mail that had ac cumulated since his accident. Though his face was still red and swollen and hi skin was a mass of peeling flakes, basically he felt decent. Never one to sit aroun doing nothing, he enjoyed doing whatever he could with his good hand. "Oh, no Here's a reminder about my driver's license renewal. I forgot all about it."

Hearing his comment, Treva came in from the kitchen, a dish towel in he hand. "Maybe you can ask for an extension."

He gave her a puzzled look. "Why? I can drive with one hand. I think I'll take care of it today. Might look funny in the picture, but at least I'll have a current driver's license."

"Oh, Tank. Are you sure you're up to it?"

He stood and stretched. "Getting out of the house might be good for me. Should be back by lunchtime. I'll bring Chinese."

"Great."

As he moved to the door, the phone rang. "Let the machine pick up. Probably Benson."

They stood and listened. As soon as the beep sounded, Benson Cordell's voice came on, once again extolling the virtues of selling her property to him.

Treva let out a sigh when the message ended. "I don't want to talk to him, Tank. I still need time to think."

"Don't answer the phone, and don't answer the door if he comes back. You don't owe him a thing." He took her hand in his. "Be back in an hour."

Tank arrived at the courthouse with no trouble at all, except for some discomfort in his left hand. He renewed his license, visited some with an acquaintance who was also renewing his license, then headed toward the door, trying to decide which items he would order off the Chinese take-out menu.

"Hey, Tank! Wait up!"

He turned to find Reginald Sanders, a deacon from his church who worked in the city zoning department, coming up the stairs.

"I've been meaning to call you," the man said, panting for breath after his hasty climb. "That was a tragic accident. How you getting along?"

Tank smiled as he carefully stuck out his right hand. He liked Reginald. The man spent nearly all his free time helping the elderly of the church with their home repairs and anything else he could do for them. "Doin' pretty good."

"Glad to hear that. Hey, I was surprised to hear Treva had sold her aunt's place."

Tank frowned, not sure what the man meant. "What makes you think she sold it?"

Reginald scratched his head and pursed his lips. "Two men from New York came into my office asking about the zoning on the Gunther place. They said they had an option on the land and wanted to make sure they could get the zoning they needed for their building project."

"Building project? What building project?"

"You mean you don't know? They're planning on building a huge resort hotel on the place. It's a big project. They plan to break ground within the next few months."

Tank bristled. "Sure you have the right place?"

The man raised a brow. "Come on, Tank. Of course I'm sure. It's my bus
ness to know those things. It's the Gunther place, all right. Is Treva sure her au
didn't sell it before she died?"

Confused by everything Reginald was saying, Tank sucked in a breath
air to clear his head. "You have the men's names and phone numbers? Treva w
want to give them a call."

"Got them in my office. I'm on my way to a meeting right now, but I'll g
them and give her a call this afternoon."

Tank thanked the man then hurried to his truck as fast as he could, eager
tell Treva what he'd found out. His heart raced when he turned the pickup in
her driveway and found Benson's fancy car parked near her porch.

He rushed into the house and found Treva sitting at the desk with Benson
pen in her hand, ready to sign the paper.

Chapter 11

Don't!" he shouted out, hurrying to her side, his good hand grabbing the pen from her.

His eyes blazing, Cordell ripped the pen from Tank's hand and shoved it back into Treva's. "Leave her alone. You don't have any say in this! It's her property. Not yours," the man said rudely, his face contorted with anger.

"It's okay. I know what I'm doing." The look Treva gave him told Tank she was upset by his bizarre reaction. "Mr. Cordell has offered me another twenty thousand dollars if I sign the contract today. Oh, Tank, that's almost as much as I'd hoped to sell it for after we finished the remodeling."

"She'll never get another offer this good," Benson said in his haughty manner. "If you had her best interests at heart, you'd be encouraging her to sign instead of raving like a madman."

Tank bit back the words he'd like to say to the arrogant man. *I don't want to mess up a possible sale for her. If his offer is a legitimate offer, what right do I have to tell her what to do? Should I tell her what I know or wait until I hear from Reginald? She has to have a chance to hear those two men's side of the story before signing anything.* "Treva, please. At least wait until tomorrow."

Treva stared at him, as if she couldn't understand why he would want her to delay the best thing that had happened to her in weeks. "You really want me to wait? What if Mr. Cordell decides to withdraw his offer? I may never get this kind of offer again."

"If he wants it today, he'll want it tomorrow," Tank told her, meeting the man's glare with one of his own.

Treva let out a long, low sigh. "I'm sorry, Mr. Cordell, but I'm going to have to give you my answer tomorrow. I respect Tank's advice; and if he thinks I should wait, then I must wait. I hope you understand."

"What if I withdraw the extra twenty thousand? That was a bonus only if you signed today," the man snarled, his brows knitting together.

"Then I guess I'll be out twenty thousand dollars," Treva said, the disappointment in her voice gouging into Tank's heart.

Benson Cordell shook an accusing finger in Tank's face as he passed by him on the way to the door. "It's your fault. I hope you remember that if I decide to withdraw my offer."

A dozen words crept into Tank's mind, but he kept his silence. Lashing out at the man would serve no purpose and would add friction to an already inflammatory situation. Though he'd known Benson for a number of years and had always thought of him as an aggressive but decent man, now he had his doubts.

Treva reached for the phone when it rang, but Tank pulled it from her hand, excusing himself and carrying it into the kitchen.

"Here are the names and phone numbers," Reginald told him when he answered. "I sure hope you can get this thing figured out."

Tank wrote down the numbers then dialed the first one on the list and tried to speak distinctly, despite the pain in his lips. "Mr. Phillips? This is Tank LaFrenz, a close friend of Treva Jordan. Theodora Gunther was her aunt. I had a discussion with Reginald Sanders at the courthouse earlier today. He told me your company is planning on building a hotel–resort on the Gunther property. Is that right?"

"Yes, that's correct, Mr. LaFrenz. We purchased the property several months ago. The only thing that is holding up the actual closing is some minor detail with the deed, but we expect to have that worked out by sometime next week. If all goes as planned, we hope to break ground no later than early spring. I suppose Mr. Sanders told you the zoning has been worked out and our plans have been approved. May I ask why you and Miss Jordan are inquiring about this?"

Tank shot a quick glance toward the living room then spoke softly into the phone. "Perhaps you don't know Theodora Gunther turned that property over to her niece just a few weeks before she passed away. Treva Jordan is that niece. I don't know who you thought you were buying that property from, but Treva has never put it on the market."

There was a pause at the other end. "Is this some kind of joke? Because, if it is, I'm not laughing. My partner and I have invested a small fortune in this project."

"No, Mr. Phillips, this is no joke. Treva owns that property. She has a clear and indisputable title. I don't know who you've been dealing with or why someone would misrepresent themselves as the owner, but—"

"We were under the impression we were dealing with the owner. Benson Cordell."

Tank stared into the receiver, too shocked to speak.

"Do you know Mr. Cordell, Mr. LaFrenz?"

"Oh, yes, I know him," Tank finally managed to say. "He's been hounding Treva to sign a listing with him ever since the day they buried her aunt." He could hear a gasp on the other end.

"You mean that man doesn't own that property? He showed us the deed!"

"No. He does not own the property. In fact, he's in the living room with Treva right now, trying to talk her into signing a contract. He's furious with me because I advised her to wait and think it over before accepting his latest offer."

"This is outrageous. When we get through with that man, he'll not only lose his broker's license, but he'll never sell real estate in this state again. No doubt there will be criminal action taken against him, too. I know our company will be filing charges."

Tank nodded. "Treva is going to be furious when I tell her how Benson has misrepresented himself. This may be confidential information, but I'm sure Treva would like to know what you offered for her aunt's property."

"Normally I wouldn't disclose such a figure, but under the circumstances I think you deserve to know."

Tank nearly dropped the phone when Mr. Phillips gave him the figure. "That much? He offered Treva less than ten percent of that!"

"I'm turning this over to the authorities!" the man said adamantly. "I've prided myself in being an honest businessman. I can't believe I've allowed myself to be deceived like this."

"He's not going to get away with it. I'm a police officer, Mr. Phillips. I'll take care of Benson Cordell."

"I'll make a trip up there tomorrow. I want to see this man punished. By the way, do you think Miss Jordan will be interested in selling the property to us? We'll make her the same offer."

Tank was glad the man couldn't see the huge grin that blanketed his face despite the strain it put on his dry lips. "I'm sure she will."

Tank's next call was to one of the local judges, asking for a warrant for Benson Cordell's arrest. After that he called Captain Dillon, told him about the situation and the warrant, and asked him to send someone to arrest Benson.

"Oh, I see you're still here," Tank told the man as he walked back into the living room, struggling to keep his voice level. "Never asked you, Benson, but what did you plan to do with Treva's property if you could talk her into selling?"

Seemingly caught off guard by Tank's question, the man cleared his throat a few times then stammered, "I wasn't exactly sure. I've always liked this house. Maybe I'll move in myself."

Treva shot Tank a questioning glance. He was sure she wondered why he hadn't come barreling back into the room, demanding Benson Cordell leave immediately. "Then you hadn't planned to sell it? Make yourself a quick buck? As I recall when you were trying to get the listing, you told Treva a number of qualified buyers were just waiting to see this property."

Benson fidgeted with his hat, spinning it nervously in his hands. "I— might sell it. Don't know yet."

The three of them turned quickly as a patrol car roared into the driveway and stopped just inches from Benson's car.

Benson Cordell froze, his face turning as white as his hair.

Treva opened the door then stood aside as Officer Jay Garfield rushed in the door, a paper in his hand. Surging past the two, he handed the paper to Benson, explained what it was, then grabbed onto his arm and ordered him to his car.

"I have no idea what you're talking about," Benson said, his voice trembling as he tried to pull away from the man. The look on his face was almost too much to bear. Although he had been extremely arrogant and deserved whatever he would get, there was something pitiful about the man. His greed and lofty ambitions were about to cost him everything.

"Tell it to the judge," Tank said, narrowing his eyes and giving the man a look of disgust. "No telling how many people you've swindled. When I think of what you've done to Treva, I'd like to—"

Jay tightened his grip on Benson's arm and shoved him forward. "Let's let the court handle it, Tank. With the evidence against him I have a feeling Mr. Cordell is going to pay for his crimes."

"I'm counting on it." Tank relaxed a bit and stepped out of the way.

Treva wrapped an arm around Tank and cuddled close as they stood in the doorway, watching until Benson Cordell was secured in the backseat and the patrol car disappeared. "This is like a bad dream. Although I didn't care for the man, I would never have believed he could do something like this. Oh, Tank, I'm so glad you kept me from signing that contract."

"Me, too, but it wasn't just me. I'm convinced God caused me to run into Reginald at the courthouse." He lowered his face to hers, reveling in the love he saw in her eyes.

"He actually told those men he had already purchased this property?" she asked when Tank relayed the conversation he'd had with Reginald. "How can that be? I've never even met those men, and I certainly haven't signed any papers."

Tank shrugged. "If I'd heard about it from anyone besides Reginald, I would have thought they were talking about the wrong property. But, Treva, Reginald would never make a mistake about something that important, especially when the proposed project would mean so much to Bristol's economy. Just imagine what that huge hotel–vacation complex would do to boost the area's economy."

She sank onto the sofa, cradling her head in her hands. "Now what? Where do we go from here?"

All smiles, he sat down beside her and began to massage her shoulders with his right hand. "They still want to buy your property. They'll give you the same amount they offered Benson."

⁓

Treva reeled when he named the figure. "What Benson Cordell had offered me was a mere pittance to what he would make from selling my property to Mr. Phillips's company! No wonder he's been so persistent!"

He pulled her close, wincing when he cupped her hand with his injured one. "Well, that money is all coming to you now, and you deserve every penny after what you've been through."

"I'd never have made it this far without you, Tank. I'd have given up long ago."

He kissed her forehead then pulled away from her. "I'm going to the station. I have a few questions of my own I want to ask that man." Tank rose and headed for the door.

"You're not going without me!" Treva hurried across the room and caught up with him, reaching for his arm.

"Okay, come on." He pushed open the door and stood waiting.

She grabbed her purse from the table then hurried past him. "You don't think he's behind everything that's happened, do you?"

"It's obvious someone was trying to scare you off. He had the motive and the opportunity. It had to be him. Think what he had to lose."

She stopped at the bottom of the steps and spun around, her eyes rounded. "But, Tank! It couldn't have been—he was with me when I saw the ghost!"

He locked the door and hurried down the steps. "He was with you then, wasn't he? I guess that makes that old farmer, Homer Jones, the most likely one to be responsible for scaring you."

She shrugged. "That might let Mr. Cordell off, but I have a hard time believing Homer Jones, at his age, would have the strength and stamina to do all those things."

Jay was in the hallway when they reached the station. "Captain Dillon has already read Cordell his Miranda rights and is questioning him. He advised him to call his lawyer," Jay told Tank as they headed toward the interrogation room, "but the dumb guy refused—said he didn't need a lawyer."

Tank huffed. "That may be a decision he'll live to regret."

"He keeps telling the captain your aunt promised him he could list her property for sale before she died," Jay explained, turning to Treva and motioning toward the little interrogation room. "He's trying to claim her verbal agreement was as good as a signed one."

"Wait here," Tank told Treva. "I'm going in there." He opened the door quietly, slipped inside, and leaned against the wall.

"You're facing some pretty serious charges, Cordell," Captain Dillon was telling the man as he bent over him, their faces close together. "That development company has spent a lot of money on their project, based on a signed contract with you, a binding contract to sell them a piece of property you didn't own and didn't even have a listing on. I have a feeling you'll be meeting their team of fancy, highly paid lawyers in court. I sure hope you haven't spent their earnest money."

"Plus," Tank added, stepping up beside them, "Treva may be taking you to court. Someone has been frightening her by setting her house on fire twice and in other ways, too. And look at me! Someone nearly cost me my sight, not to mention all the pain I've endured." He bent low over the table, bracing himself with his good hand and staring into the man's eyes. "If you had anything to do with those things—"

Benson Cordell's fist came down onto the table with a thud. "I'm not taking the full blame for this!"

Tank shot Captain Dillon a questioning glance. "Was someone else involved?"

Benson leaned back in the chair, crossed his arms, and stared straight ahead.

"How about it, Cordell?" the captain asked, moving to stand in front of him. "Who helped you?"

"I didn't say someone helped me. I didn't say I did it!"

Captain Dillon leaned into the man's face, his expression sober and threatening. "It might go a little easier on you, Cordell, if you told us now. We're going to find out anyway. You wouldn't want that person to tell us what happened before you do, would you?"

Benson turned his head away, avoiding the captain's eyes.

It took every ounce of strength Tank could muster to keep from choking the information out of the sleazy man, but being bound by professional protocol, he kept silent and restrained himself.

Finally Benson turned toward Captain Dillon. "Okay, you win. If I'm going down, they're going down, too."

Tank sucked in a breath. "They?" He'd never considered anyone except Benson was involved in the plot to take Treva's property.

Benson nodded. "Yeah, Robert Bacon and Homer Jones."

"Homer Jones? What did he have to gain?" Although Tank had suggested the man's name to Treva, he hadn't believed Homer would have done all those things by himself. It had never occurred to him the man had a partner.

"That development company was interested in purchasing his property, too, if they could get hold of the Gunther property. I promised him a percentage of my profits if he would help me scare the Jordan woman into selling."

"You had yourself a pretty sweet deal, didn't you?" Captain Dillon asked with a sad shake of his head.

Tank glared at the man. "You planned on being at the house when Treva saw that supposed ghost to keep suspicion off yourself, didn't you? You wanted an airtight alibi in case you needed one! One of your partners did it!"

"Yep, Homer did that one! Did a good job, too. Made it look convincing." The arrogant man seemed proud of his deception.

Tank pulled up a chair and sat down next to him. "Okay, I can understand why Homer Jones would participate in your scheme, but who is Robert Bacon? I've never heard of him."

"He left here several years ago. Robert Bacon is Theodora's stepbrother." Captain Dillon straightened and stretched his arms. "Theodora was a friend of mine. She told me she'd begged her stepbrother to come and live with her when she got sick, but he wanted no part of it. As I recall she offered to leave half of the property to him and half to Treva if he'd come, but he refused, telling her he had more important things to do with his life than spend it taking care of a sick old lady. That's when she changed her will, leaving everything to Treva. She said Treva had gone out of her way to come and visit her summers and weekends and do whatever was necessary to help her, and she wanted everything to go to her. As I understand it, in her will she left her stepbrother the sum of one dollar, stating he was to have no other claims on any land or personal items she might have."

"That stupid old woman wouldn't budge!" Benson said, his face distorting with disgust. "Robert went to see her in the care home, begging her to leave the property to him, but she wouldn't hear of it. When I told him how she wouldn't let me sell her property and I was going to lose out on the development deal, we decided to get it from her any way we could. We talked to Homer, and the three of us came up with the plan to scare Treva so bad she'd beg me either to list or buy her place."

Tank wanted to strangle him. "I know you broke in through the basement door when you set that fire, but how did you get into the house all those other times? Treva made sure all the doors and windows were locked."

"That part was easy. Homer Jones used to help old Theodora with odd jobs. She always kept a spare key hidden outside and had shown him where it was so he could get in to check on her furnace. The day I heard Theodora died, I went out there and got it and had a duplicate made."

"Which of you started the fire in the basement?"

"Oh, that was me," he said almost boastfully.

"That money clip we found had to be yours," Tank said, shaking his head. "It was you who paid that old bum to leave that 'Boo!' note on Treva's bed. Then you put the twenty-five dollars in his mailbox, right?"

With a sly grin Benson slapped his knee. "I thought that was pretty ingenious. All I had to do was promise that old drunk enough money so he could buy himself some more liquor, and he'd do just about anything."

Tank balled his fists, his anger about to get the best of him. "Why did you pay him the other half of what you owed him? He didn't know who you were or where to come to get his money."

"I didn't want him unhappy. I thought I might have another job for him to do."

"And Treva's cat in the mailbox? That was your dirty work?"

The man shook his head. "No, not me! I'd never hurt an animal. Robert did that one. He hates cats. Said it was all he could do to keep from wrapping that scarf tight enough around that cantankerous old cat's neck to strangle it. She scratched his arms pretty bad."

Captain Dillon leaned forward, his palms resting on the table. "Who took the bolts out of the observation platform?"

Cordell reared back, jutting out his chin. "Don't blame that one on me. Robert took care of that. He painted all that stuff on her walls, too."

"And stole the cutlery set?"

"No, that was Homer. He said he'd wanted that set ever since he first started helping that old lady with the chores."

"And the box of fireworks? Who did that one?" Tank asked, fingering a nearly healed scar on his cheek.

"I didn't do that either. Robert was a genius with that kind of stuff. He learned how to set up detonators in the army. He rigged that one up then gave it to the boy to take to you. Poor kid thought he was doing you a favor. I'm not exactly sure how he did it. He said something about a wire hooked up to some sort of gizmo so that when you opened the box the thing would set off all those fireworks." He sent Tank a look that seemed filled with guilt. "I had no idea you'd get burned that badly, or I wouldn't have gone along with it. I only wanted to scare you."

Tank slammed his eyelids together and gritted his teeth. *Lord, give me strength to resist pinning this guy to the floor and beating him to a pulp. Their greed nearly cost me my eyesight. I can only imagine all they put Treva through!*

Benson gave a snort as he nodded toward Tank. "You came along and messed things up! If you'd stayed out of it, I'd have had that property weeks ago, and none of this would have happened. It's all your fault."

Tank closed his eyes again. *Thank You, Lord, for sending me into Treva's life!*

"I think you had better change your mind about calling your attorney." Captain Dillon motioned toward the door. "Tank, would you tell Jay that Mr. Cordell needs to make a phone call?"

Relieved and pleased Benson Cordell had confessed to his part in trying to cheat Treva out of what was rightfully hers, Tank couldn't contain his smile. "Sure, Captain. I'll be glad to."

⌇

Treva sat in the lobby, waiting, staring at the door to the interrogation room. *What are they doing in there? Why is it taking so long?* Knowing what a stubborn and headstrong man Benson Cordell could be, she wondered if questioning him would do any good.

Finally the door opened. The minute she saw the look of satisfaction on Tank's face, she knew he had good news.

"Benson confessed, Treva," he told her as she ran into his open arms. "How he had planned to cheat you by getting your aunt's property and then selling it at an unbelievable profit. And," he added, smiling as he tilted her face up to his, "he and two others were responsible for all the things that happened to you and the incident that nearly cost me my sight. The mystery is solved."

Her eyes widened. "Two others? He had partners?"

"Yes. Homer Jones was involved."

She shook her head sadly. "Not that old man."

"Yep, Homer. It's amazing what greed will do to some people. The other was your aunt's stepbrother."

"Robert Bacon? Why?" Treva couldn't believe what she was hearing. "Aunt TeeDee hadn't heard from him since before she went to live at the care home. It broke her heart when she asked him to help her and he walked out on her, refusing to have anything to do with her because she wouldn't finance some weird scheme he came up with. I don't think he was worth much. She said after he got out of the army he could never keep a job and was always coming to her for a handout."

Tank slipped an arm about her waist and motioned toward the door. "Let's head back to the house. I'll tell you all about it on the way." As soon as they were out the door, he pulled her into his arms and kissed her. "I guess you'll want to sell to the development company now, right?"

She laughed as she gazed up into his face. "For that kind of money? Of course! I'd be crazy not to!"

"I have an idea. Something you may want to consider when they draw up the contract."

Chapter 12

Y ou're right on time," Tank told the two men standing on the porch three
days later as he opened the door. "Treva is waiting for you."

He led them into the living room. "Gentlemen, this is Treva Jordan,
Theodora Gunther's niece." Then, turning to Treva, he introduced their guests.
"This is Hank Phillips, the man who told me the real story about the sale of your
place, and this is Mark Blunt, his partner."

After greetings had been exchanged all around and Treva had poured each
man a cup of freshly brewed coffee, they gathered around the dining room table
to discuss the purchase of her property.

"I hope your attorney has had adequate time to look over the new contract
we had drawn—this one in *your* name," Hank Phillips said, his eyes smiling at
her over the half-glasses perched precariously on the tip of his nose.

Treva nodded. "Yes, he has, and he assured me everything is in order."

"Do you have any questions?" Mark Blunt asked, looking from Treva to
Tank.

Tank shook his head. "She asked me to read it over, and—not that I understood all the gobbledygook—it seemed fine to me. I was as pleased as Treva to
see you were willing to exclude that one small piece of land."

Mr. Phillips gestured toward Treva. "I'll admit I hated to let go of that par-
cel, but after all she's been through I had no choice but to oblige her request. I
think our planners will be able to readjust a few things and work around it. It
shouldn't be a problem."

Treva gave him a grateful smile. "I've always loved that spot. I'm glad Tank
came up with the idea of my keeping it."

"Well, then, I suggest we get on with it." Mr. Phillips took a pen from
his pocket, placed it on the contract, and shoved it across the table toward her.
"Mark and I have already signed it. We need your signature right there next to
the X mark, and you'll need to date it, as well."

Treva stared at the figure on the contract. She could not even fathom that
amount of money. In addition to building a house, she began to think of all the
other things she could do with it. Things for the Lord. There were so many
needs out there. Her home church in Warren was badly in need of expanding the

nctuary. The church she and Tank attended here in Bristol was planning to add
veral new classrooms as soon as the finances became available. Then there was
television ministry she longed to support. Other worthwhile projects flooded
r mind. With this money she would be able to do many of those things. She
uld even have a stained glass window made for the Bristol church sanctuary in
emory of Aunt TeeDee.

"Miss Jordan? Is there a problem?" Mark Blunt asked kindly.

Treva smiled up at him with misty eyes. "No, Mr. Blunt. I was just think-
g about God and how good He has been to me." She picked up the pen and
gned her name.

❦

ater that afternoon Tank drove Treva to the observation platform, saying now
at the pressures of the remodeling project were over, the two of them needed
spend some quality time together.

Her fingers caressed his face. "Oh, Tank, if you'd lost your sight because of
e, I don't—"

He quickly put his finger to her lips. "But I didn't. God intervened. My face
nearly back to normal. Most of my other burns are healed, and my hand is well
its way to regaining full use. We have much to be thankful for. Looking back,
's easy to see how God's protective hand was on both of us."

"I have to admit at times my faith wavered, but as He promised He was
ithful and answered prayer." She leaned into him, resting her head against his
est. "The best part of all was the way He led the two of us together."

Tank pushed away slightly and shoved his hand into his pants pocket. "I
ought this on the way to the courthouse, planning to give it to you as soon as
got back home. But then I ran into Reginald Sanders, and he told me about
e development company having a contract on your land, and—well, you know
hat happened after that." He gave her a shy smile. "Now I'm not even sure I
ould give it to you."

Her heart sang. Could it be a necklace? Earrings? Or maybe—dare she
ink it—an engagement ring? Though Tank had never officially asked her to
e his wife, she hoped and prayed he would. She gave him a coquettish smile.
What is it?"

He pulled out a small velvet box. "I thought this was beautiful when I bought
, but now"—he shrugged—"now it seems small and cheap."

"Quit teasing me. Let me see what it is." Grinning, she playfully tried to
ke the velvet box from his hand, but he lifted it high above her reach. "I'm sure
ll love it—whatever it is—because you gave it to me."

"I—I bought it because I was going to ask you to marry me."

She gasped for air. "Marry you? Oh, Tank, I thought you'd never ask. I' been waiting for this moment!" She threw her arms about his neck, smotherin his face with kisses. "I'd love to be your wife!"

"You're sure? You haven't changed your mind about loving me?"

She stopped kissing him and stared up into his face. "Why would I chan my mind?"

He gave her a timid grin. "You're a wealthy woman now. You don't need m

Shocked by his words, she cradled his face in her hands. "Is that what you thought? That I only wanted you around because I needed you? Needed a bod guard? And someone to do the dirty work on the house?"

"I hoped that wasn't the reason."

"I do need you, sweetheart, but not for those reasons. I need your love, yo warmth, your strength. I need your sweet smile, your tender ways. You're n soul mate, my partner in Christ, my encourager. I could go on and on. I wa to spend the rest of my life with you, Tank LaFrenz, and if God wills, I want bear your children."

"You're sure that's what you want?"

"Very sure."

His face took on a seriousness that almost frightened her.

"There's one other thing we should talk about. My job. Remember how told you the wives of some of the guys I work with have walked out on the because of the crazy hours and the daily dangers they face?"

She nodded. "Yes, I remember."

"I'm a career cop, Treva. My dad was a cop. My grandfather was a cop. Eve my two brothers are cops. That's what we LaFrenz men are about."

"I realize that."

"It's in my blood, sweetheart. I was born to be a cop. It's my calling from th Lord, but my concern is you. Very few women can handle their husbands bein on the police force, especially if they decide to have children. I think it's som thing we need to discuss." He paused and took both her hands in his. "I've do a lot of thinking about this. I've asked myself—if push came to shove and yo insisted I quit my job—could I do it? Work at another occupation to please yo And, if I did, would I be miserable all of my life and resent what I'd done?"

"What did you decide?" she asked cautiously, knowing she'd prayed abo that very thing and had already settled it in her heart.

"It was a tough decision, but after hours of seeking the Lord for an answe I decided my love for you was stronger and more important to me than anythin else in my life, including my job." He gazed into her eyes. "If you want me quit, I will."

Treva lovingly touched his face with her fingertips. "I've thought a lot about , too, and I've also prayed about it. Several weeks ago your mother and I discussed this very thing. She warned me then that when a woman marries a dedicated, career police officer she marries not only him but also his job. You and I have been through a lot these past weeks. Many of those times could have developed into life-threatening situations, but God protected us, Tank. Cannot that same God protect you in the line of duty, the man He has called to be a police officer? Each time I think of how close I came to losing you on the Fourth of ily, I realize God's hand of protection was upon you. His guardian angels must have surrounded you, Tank. I think that day—when Jay came for me and I had o idea what had happened or if you were dead or alive—was the day I knew I oved you more than life itself."

She swallowed around the lump in her throat. "I've made my peace with his, dearest, because that same God has called me to be a cop's wife. I'm not saying I'll never be afraid when you're working your shift or that I'll sleep soundly when you're not there next to me. But I promise I'll take my concerns and fears o the Lord and will be there for you when you come home, smiling, with a heart ill of love, waiting with open arms to welcome you. I want our home to be a aven for you. A place of refreshing."

Blinking, he opened the box and pulled out a ring. A simple gold band with a single diamond. Taking her hand in his, he asked, "Treva Jordan, will you iarry me? Will you commit your life to being my wife? Will you let me love you, are for you and, yes—protect you?"

She stared at him through a mist of tears and tried to speak, but her heart as so full of love for this man, all she could do was utter an almost incoherent yes.

Tank slipped the ring onto her finger then wrapped his arms about her, olding her close to him. "I love you, Treva. With God as my witness I'll try to e the husband you deserve."

She held out her hand, admiring the ring he'd placed on her finger. "Oh, ank, it's so beautiful. I love it!"

"You don't have to say that, Treva. I know it's small, but someday I'll replace with the kind of ring I'd like to buy for you."

She gazed up into his face. "I'll never want this ring replaced. The cost f a ring and the size of the diamond aren't what's important. What the ring tands for is what really matters. This ring symbolizes the love between us and ur desire to spend our lives together as husband and wife. To me—this ring is riceless. I'll never let it go."

"I was hoping you'd say that." Laughing out loud, he picked her up and spun her around. "And I'll never let you go!"

"I love you, Tank—and I love this place." Treva felt euphoric as they stood i the middle of the platform, their arms wrapped around each other. "I'm so gla you came up with the idea of my keeping this one acre when we sold my aunt place. It's my favorite spot on the entire property."

Gazing into her eyes lovingly, he brushed a lock of hair from her forehea "Think your aunt would be pleased if we built our dream home here?"

Treva clapped her hands with joy. "Oh, yes! I know she would. It's a wonde ful idea!"

Cradling her in his arms, he nestled his chin in her hair. "With my ow hands I'm going to build you a house, sweetheart, right here on this land. O children will grow up here." He gestured toward the bench he'd built on th observation platform. "And when we're old and gray, we'll sit right there, hol ing hands, gazing out onto the bay and praising God for the way He brought together."

Overcome with both love for this man and gratefulness to God, she leane into the strength of his arms. "Tank, do you remember the first time we me The day Mindy and Chuck renewed their vows?"

He smiled down at her and nodded. "I sure do. I thought you were about th prettiest little gal I'd ever seen. Why?"

With a heart overflowing with love, she lifted her head and gazed into h eyes—eyes that told her that his heart, too, was filled with love. And she kne she'd always be safe with Tank—that he would risk his life, if necessary, to sav hers. He'd proven his love for her, time and time again. "I told the Lord that day she continued, finding it difficult to put her feelings into words, "that—that wanted a love like theirs, a love that would be beautiful and last forever. I aske Him to bring the right man into my life. I turned, and there you were, smilin at me." Rising on tiptoes to kiss his cheek, she whispered, "God answered m prayers. You, my love, are that man!"

Tank tightened his hold on her. "So when can I make you my wife?"

She grinned up at him. "You wouldn't rush a girl would you?"

He grinned back. "I would if you'd let me, but I have a feeling you won't. Ju promise to make it soon."

She gave him a flirtatious smile. "How about six months from now?"

He frowned. "Too long."

"How about three months?"

"Still too long."

Though she knew from experience, from watching her friends plan the weddings, how many plans would have to be made and the monumental amour details that had to be taken care of, she too wanted to be married as soon as possible.

"How about—one month?"

His face brightened. "I'll be in misery waiting a whole thirty days, but I guess one month is better than six. We'll go with one month, but not a day longer, okay?"

Her heart soared. "One month it is, providing you help me with the planning and the work."

A huge smile exploded across his face. "You got it!"

"I want to be married here."

His brow furrowed in a quizzical way. "Here?"

"Yes, right here." She gestured around them. "We can fashion this observation platform into an outdoor chapel. You know, maybe cut some branches from the trees and form them into an arch. We could even cover the railings with vines and add pots of flowers for color."

"What about our guests? The platform isn't big enough for them."

"We can mow the field in front of the platform and set up chairs for them here."

"You're serious. You don't want a church wedding?"

"A church wedding would be nice, but this place has so much meaning for us. You not only proposed to me here, this is where you saved my life. I'd love to be married here, but only if you want to."

"I hadn't thought of it before but I like the idea. Sure, let's do it. With an outside wedding, even Groucho and Miss Priss can attend."

"We could rent a big tent for the reception."

His face took on a thoughtful expression. "A tent would be handy in case it rained."

She gave him a playful jab at his arm. "Pessimist."

"Just being cautious. Come to think of it, it might be a good idea to reserve the church as a backup. I doubt you'd want a soggy wedding."

All traces of playfulness left as she turned somber. "You sure you're okay with our wedding being here? We can have it at the church if you'd prefer."

Tank raised her left hand to his lips, singled out her ring finger and kissed it. "I love the idea of having our wedding here, just promise you'll wear one of those frilly white wedding gowns."

She gave him a demure smile. "I will if you'll promise to wear a tuxedo and frilly shirt."

He skewed up his face. "My policeman uniform won't cut it, huh?"

"Not unless you want your bride turning up in blue jeans and a tee shirt."

He mischievously chucked her chin. "Naw, let's do it up right. Let's stick the frilly stuff. Someday our kids and our grandkids might want to see our wedding pictures. I wouldn't want to be embarrassed."

Treva smiled then gazed up into his eyes. "You'd look handsome in anything, my darling, but I am anxious to see you in a tux."

He circled her with his arms and pulled her close. "And I'm anxious to se you in all white, with one of those crown things on your head."

"A tiara?"

He responded with a shrug. "Whatever you call it."

"We have a lot of work to do if we're going to pull this off in four weeks. A you sure you're up to it?"

Bending, he kissed the tip of her nose. "Absolutely."

❧

Though each of the next thirty days were filled to the brim with phone call visits to the bridal shop, the caterer, the florist, and many other essential place Treva enjoyed every minute. Especially since on Tank's day off he took an activ part in their planning.

Finally their day arrived. "You did double-check with the pastor to mak sure the church would be available?" Treva asked Tank as they visited on th phone that morning. "I sure don't like the look of those clouds."

"Now who is the pessimist?"

"Like you said, it's better to have a backup plan."

"All taken care of, babe, but don't worry about it. The sun will be out i plenty of time."

"You promise we won't have a soggy wedding?"

Tank laughed. "I wish I could, but I'm not the one in control of the weathe But I do know the person who is, and I'm talking to Him about it."

"Well, as large as the tent is that we rented for the reception, there'll b plenty of room to move inside if it begins to rain." Even to Treva her voic sounded a bit insecure.

"Unless the wind blows it down."

"Tank! Don't say such things!"

Again, he laughed. "Don't worry your pretty little head about it, honey. It not going to happen."

"So you're saying I don't need to bring a raincoat?"

"I just checked with the weather service. Not even a sprinkle is predicted fc our area, and the clouds should be out of here by ten or so. By the time for ou wedding, they said the sun would be out and the day would be perfect. Thin pleasant thoughts, my love. See you at three."

Tank and the weather service were right. By the time Treva was dressed and ready, the day that had started out gloomy had turned glorious. Shar Wingate, the friend from her Sunday school class she'd asked to be her bridesmaid, showed up right on time to drive her out to the observation platform. After going over her checklist one more time to make sure she had something old, something new, something borrowed, and something blue, as well as a penny in her shoe, Treva allowed Shar to assist her to her minivan and into the seat, being careful not to muss up her beautifully pressed gown.

"Ready?" Shar asked as she turned the key in the ignition.

Treva's voice wavered with excitement. "Ready."

"You stay right there," Shar told her once she had gotten Treva safely into the tent without Tank seeing her. "I'll tell Pastor Leman you're ready."

Mrs. LaFrenz hurried over to her, grabbing hold of her hands and oohing and aahing over her gown. "Oh, Treva, you are the most beautiful bride I have ever seen. I'm so happy you and my son and going to be married."

Treva felt herself beam. "So am I. I love your son, Mrs. LaFrenz, and I—"

"Mother LaFrenz, please, dear. I want us to be like mother and daughter, as well as friends."

"I want that, too."

As the sound of the recorded music from Tank's boom box filled the air, Treva was so happy she felt she could float all the way to the little makeshift altar she and Tank had set up the day before. Just the thought of Tank standing there in his tuxedo and frilly shirt, waiting to make her his wife, filled her heart to overflowing.

Shar rushed into the tent. "You'd better let the usher seat you, Mrs. LaFrenz." Mrs. LaFrenz nodded, smiled at Treva, gave her a thumbs up, then disappeared through the opening.

Shar grabbed hold of Treva's hand. "It's time. Since you decided not to have a flower girl, I guess it's my turn to go first. Wait until you hear "Here Comes The Bride," then walk"—she gave Treva a teasing smile—"don't run, to the altar. Take your time, girl. This is your day. Enjoy it." After planting an air kiss close to Treva's cheek, she moved out of the tent.

Treva sighed. *If only Aunt TeeDee could be here, this day would be perfect, but I know she's watching from heaven.*

As the music swelled and the strains of "Here Comes The Bride" wafted in through the tent's opening, Treva swallowed hard, squared her shoulders, and moved out into the bright afternoon sunlight, catching her first glimpse of her bridegroom as he stood on the platform in his black tuxedo, looking more handsome than ever before. And though Shar's words, "Walk, don't run," came to her, she found it impossible to walk and hurried toward him much more quickly than she knew was proper.

The smile on his face as she reached his side made her shiver with delight, and when he slipped his arm about her waist and pulled her close she thought she would die with ecstasy. "Hi," she said softly, grinning and wondering whatever possessed her to say such a thing.

"Hi, yourself," he whispered back, his face shining with happiness and expectation. "How about it? Will you do me the honor of becoming my wife?"

Treva leaned into the strength of his arm. "Yes, oh yes, my darling. This is the happiest moment of my life."

"Mine, too."

Pastor Leman smiled then cleared his throat loudly, as if to get their attention. "Friends and family, we have gathered here today, in this special place, to witness the uniting of two of our favorite young people: Tank LaFrenz and Treva Jordon. Like me, many of you have seen the budding of romance develop between these two children of God and blossom into a love that will last a lifetime, and I know, with me, you are happy to be here and will do everything in your power to help them make their marriage a success. Life is filled with many pressures. Some of our own making, but most with what it takes to make a living and care for our families."

Taking Tank's and Treva's hands in his, he smiled at them in a way that said he really cared about them. "I challenge you, Tank and Treva, to always make time for one another. Never let your courtship end or your marriage grow cold. Keep God first in your life, your partner second, your family—should God bless you with children—and everything and everyone else in last place, and always in that order. It was God who ordained marriage. He has much to say about it in His word. Take time to study it, for it is the best marriage manual you'll ever read."

Treva listened to his words with rapt attention and was pleased when she noted that Tank did, too. The kind of marriage the pastor described was exactly the kind of marriage she wanted, and so did Tank. They'd discussed it many times during the month they had prepared for this day.

When it came time for their vows, turning her toward him and taking hold of her hands, Tank went first. "Treva, my love, my dear one, God brought us together. I know He did. As your husband, I will strive to do what I know God wants me to do. In addition to seeing that our home is centered around God, I will be your provider, your protector, your friend, and—" He paused with a timid smile. "And your lover. Always know you can come to me with anything. My arms are open to you, to hold you, comfort you, encourage you, to make you feel secure. And, with God as my witness, I promise to love you until death us do part." He smiled again. "And maybe beyond."

After hearing his words Treva was so filled with emotion, she was afraid to try to speak for fear the words wouldn't come. She blinked at the tears that trickled down her cheek then gratefully accepted the handkerchief Tank pulled from his jacket pocket. "Tank, my love," she said, pausing long enough to dab at her eyes. "I—I have so much love in my heart for you that I'm finding it difficult to speak."

Pastor Leman leaned forward and said in a whisper, "Take your time. Just say what's in your heart."

She nodded then swallowed hard. Why wouldn't that lump in her throat disappear? "You've already said it all, my precious one. I—I want all the things out of our marriage that you mentioned in your vows. Those are my vows, too. I wish I could say them as beautifully as you. Tank, I promise you all those same things." She blinked hard again then let out a sigh. "Just know I want to be everything you want in a wife and will do my best to be the woman both you and God want me to be. I—I love you, Tank. I'll always love you."

Their pastor gave Treva a smile that touched her heart, making her feel everything was okay in spite of her bungling her vows.

"Vows spoken from a heart," he said, "that intends to keep them are far more important to God than those spoken by the most eloquent speaker who doesn't mean them."

Treva melded into Tank's arms as Gloria Grisham, one of the church soloists, began to sing, "You Light Up My Life."

"You do light up my life," Tank murmured into her hair as they listened to the words.

Treva lifted her eyes to his. "And you light up mine."

When the song ended, Pastor Leman placed one palm on Treva's head and the other on Tank's. "In as much as these two people have vowed before God and their friends this day to love each other, serve each other, keep each other only for the other, and love God with all their hearts, by the power vested in me by the State of Rhode Island, I now pronounce them husband and wife, Mr. and Mrs. Tank LaFrenz." Then giving them an exaggerated smile, he said, "Tank, you may kiss your bride."

For some reason, as Tank wrapped her in his arms, the sight of all the fireworks going off on the Fourth of July, the night Tank could have lost his sight, came to mind, and she thanked God for answering prayer. But as he kissed her, that vision disappeared, and all she could think about was the man who had just become her husband.

When their lips parted and he finally released his hold on her, she gazed up at him. "I love you, Tank LaFrenz."

"And I love you, Mrs. LaFrenz. Thank you for being my wife."

A Letter to Our Readers

Dear Readers:

In order that we might better contribute to your reading enjoyment, we would appreciate your taking a few minutes to respond to the following questions. When completed, please return to the following: Fiction Editor, Barbour Publishing, Inc., P.O. Box 719, Uhrichsville, OH 44683.

1. Did you enjoy reading *Rhode Island Weddings* by Joyce Livingston?
   □ Very much—I would like to see more books like this.
   □ Moderately—I would have enjoyed it more if _____
   _____
   _____

2. What influenced your decision to purchase this book?
   (Check those that apply.)
   □ Cover   □ Back cover copy   □ Title   □ Price
   □ Friends   □ Publicity   □ Other

3. Which story was your favorite?
   □ *Down from the Cross*   □ *The Fourth of July*
   □ *Mother's Day*

4. Please check your age range:
   □ Under 18   □ 18–24   □ 25–34
   □ 35–45   □ 46–55   □ Over 55

5. How many hours per week do you read? _____

Name _____

Occupation _____

Address _____

City_____ State_____ Zip_____

E-mail_____

If you enjoyed

RHODE ISLAND
Weddings

then read

Wisconsin WEDDINGS

by Andrea Boeshaar

*Three Brides Can Never Say Never
to Love Again*

Always a Bridesmaid
The Long Ride Home
The Summer Girl